SEIZE
the
Night

SEIZE
the
Night

Sherrilyn Kenyon

St. Martin's

For my fans and friends who have kept me going through thick and thin, and especially the RBL ladies and those of you who take the time to visit the Dark-Hunter.com bbs. Your support means more to me than any of you will ever know.

To Kim and Nancy for all the hard work you do on my behalf, thank you. I can honestly never say that enough.

To my husband and sons who put up with all my wild imaginings and most importantly to my mother who indulged me when I was young. I miss you, Mom, and I always will. Love and hugs to all of you.

SEIZE the Night

Prologue

"Happy birthday, Agrippina," Valerius said as he laid a single red rose at the feet of the marble statue that held a sacred place in his home.

It was nothing compared to the sacred place that the woman herself had held within his heart while she had lived. A place she still occupied—even after two thousand years.

Closing his eyes, he felt crippled by the pain of her loss. Crippled by the guilt that the last sounds he had heard as a mortal man had been her wrenching sobs as she called out for his help.

Unable to breathe, he reached up and touched her marble hand. The stone was hard. Cold. Unyielding. Things Agrippina had never been. In a life that was measured by brutal formality and harshness, she had been his only refuge.

And he loved her still for the quiet kindness she had given him.

He clasped her delicate hand in both of his, then laid his cheek against the cold stone palm.

If he could have one wish, it would be to remember the exact sound of her voice.

To feel the warmth of her fingers on his lips.

But time had robbed him of everything except the agony he had caused her. He would die ten thousand more deaths if only he could have saved her the pain of that one night.

Unfortunately, there was no way to turn back time. No

way to force the Fates to undo their actions and give her the happiness she should have known.

Just as there was nothing that could fill the aching void inside him left by Agrippina's death.

Grinding his teeth, Valerius pulled away and noted the eternal flame that burned by her side was sputtering.

"Don't worry," he said to her image. "I won't leave you in the dark. I promise."

It was a promise he had made to her during her lifetime, and even in death, he had never broken it. For more than two thousand years he had kept her in the light even while he was forced to live in the darkness that had terrified her.

Valerius crossed the sunroom to reach the large Roman-style buffet table that held the oil for her flame. He removed the oil from the center of the buffet and took it to her statue; then he stepped up onto the stone pedestal to pour the last of it into the lamp.

In this position, his head was even with hers. The sculptor he had commissioned centuries ago had captured every delicate curve and dimple of her precious face. Only Valerius's memory supplied the honey color of her hair. The vivid green of her eyes. Agrippina had been flawless in her beauty.

Sighing, Valerius touched her cheek before he stepped down. There was no use in dwelling on the past. What was done was done.

He was sworn now to protect the innocent. To keep watch over humanity and make sure that no other man had to lose so valuable a light in his soul as Valerius had lost.

Assured the flame would last until tomorrow night, Valerius inclined his head respectfully to her statue. *"Amo,"* he said to her, whispering Latin for "I love you."

It was something he wished to the gods that he'd had the courage to say aloud to her while she had lived.

Chapter 1

"I don't give a damn if they throw me down into the deepest, slimiest pit for eternity. I belong here and no one is going to make me leave. No one!"

Tabitha Devereaux took a deep breath and struggled not to argue as she tried to pick the lock on the handcuffs that her sister Selena had used to fasten herself to the wrought-iron gate that surrounded the famed Jackson Square. Selena had hidden the key in her bra and Tabitha had no desire to search there for it.

No doubt that would get them both arrested, even in New Orleans.

Luckily there wasn't a big crowd on the street in the middle of October, right at dusk, but what people were there all stared at them as they passed by. Not that Tabitha cared. She was more than used to people looking at her and thinking her strange. Even insane.

She prided herself on both. She also prided herself on being available to her friends and family in a crisis. And right now, her big sister was in an emotional turmoil second only to the time when Selena's husband Bill had been in a car wreck that had almost killed him.

Tabitha fumbled with the lock. The last thing she wanted was to have her sister arrested.

Again.

Selena tried to push her away, but Tabitha refused to budge, so Selena bit her.

Tabitha jumped back with a yelp as she shook her hand in an effort to relieve the pain. Completely unremorseful about it, Selena sprawled on the cobbled steps that led into the Square in a pair of ripped jeans and a large navy sweater that obviously belonged to Bill. Her long, curly brown hair was braided and oddly sedate. No one would recognize Madame Selene, as she was known to the tourists, except for the big sign she was holding that said, "Psychics have rights, too."

Ever since they had passed that stupid, asinine law that psychics couldn't read cards in the Square for tourists anymore, Selena had been fighting it. Earlier, the police had forced her out of the federal building for protesting—so Selena had headed over here to chain herself to the gate not far from where she had once set up her card table for reading other people's futures.

Too bad she couldn't see her own fate as clearly as Tabitha could. If Selena didn't unhook herself from this blessed fence, she was going to be spending the night in jail.

Overwrought and angry, Selena kept waving her sign. There was no reasoning with her. But then, Tabitha was used to that, too. High emotions, obstinacy, and insanity ran deep in their Cajun-Romanian family.

"C'mon, Selena," she said, trying yet again to soothe her. "It's already dark. You don't want to be Daimon bait out here, do you?"

"I don't care!" Selena sniffed and pouted. "The Daimons won't eat my soul anyway since I have no friggin' will to live. I just want my home back. This is my spot and I'm not leaving." She punctuated each of the last words with a pounding of her sign against the stones.

"Fine." Sighing in disgust, Tabitha sat down near her, but not so close that Selena could bite her again. She wasn't about to leave her older sister out here alone. Especially since Selena was so upset.

If the Daimons didn't get her, a mugger would.

And so here the two of them sat like two immovable bumps on a log: Tabitha dressed all in black with her dark auburn hair pulled back into a silver barrette and Selena waving her sign at anyone who came near them on the pedestrian mall, urging them to sign her petition to change the law.

"Hey, Tabby. What's up?"

It was a rhetorical question. Tabitha waved at Bradley Gambieri, one of the docents who led vampire tours around the Quarter, as he headed toward the tourist center to drop off more brochures. He didn't even pause as he passed by. But he did frown at Selena, who called him an imaginative name because he didn't sign her petition.

Good thing he knew them or he really might be offended.

Tabitha and her sister knew most of the locals who frequented the Quarter. They had grown up here and had haunted the area around the Square since they had been young teenagers.

Of course, things had changed over the years. A few of the shops had come and gone. The Quarter was a good deal safer these days than it had been in the late nineteen eighties and early nineties. However, some things were the same. The bakery, Café Pontalba, Café Du Monde, and Corner Café were in the same place. The tourists still gathered in the Square to ogle the cathedral and the colorful natives who passed by . . . and the vampires and muggers still stalked the streets looking for easy victims.

The hair on the back of her neck rose.

Tabitha moved her hand instinctively to the hidden sheath in her boot that concealed a three-inch stiletto as she scanned the thinning October crowd around her.

For the last thirteen years, Tabitha had been a self-styled vampire slayer. She was also one of the few humans in New Orleans who actually knew what went on in this town after dark. She was scarred inside and out from her battles with the damned. And she had sworn her life to making sure that none of them ever hurt anyone else on her watch.

It was an oath she took seriously; she would kill anyone or anything she had to.

But as her gaze found the tall, exotically erotic man sporting a black backpack coming around the corner of the Presbytere building, she relaxed.

It'd been a couple of months since he'd last been in town. In truth, she'd missed him a lot more than she should have.

Against her will and common sense, she'd let Acheron Parthenopaeus worm his way into her guarded heart. But then, Ash was a hard man not to adore.

His long, sensuous gait was impossible to ignore and every female in the Square, except for the distraught Selena, was held transfixed by his presence. They all paused to watch him walk by as if compelled by some unseen force. He was sexy in a way very few men were.

He held an aura that was dangerous and wild; and by his slow, languorous moves, it was obvious that he would be incredible in bed. It was something you just knew intrinsically when you saw him and it rippled through your body like hot, seductive chocolate.

At six feet eight, Ash always stood out in a crowd. Like her, he was dressed all in black.

His Godsmack T-shirt was untucked and a bit large, but even so it didn't detract from that fact that Ash was seriously ripped. And his custom-made leather pants cupped a butt so prime, it begged for a groping.

Not that she ever would. An undefinable air about him warned people to keep their hands to themselves if they wanted to keep breathing.

She smiled as she noted his boots. Ash had a thing for German Goth clothing. Tonight he had on a pair of black biker boots that had nine vampire-bat buckles going up the length of them.

He wore his long black hair loose and flowing around his shoulders. It was a perfect drape for a face that was eerily pretty and yet wholly masculine. Flawless. There was something about Ash that made every hormone in her body stand up and pant for more.

Yet for all his sexual attractiveness, there was also an aura so dark and deadly that it kept her from ever thinking of him as anything more than a friend.

And he'd been a friend ever since she had met him at her twin sister Amanda's wedding three years ago. Since then, they had crossed paths repeatedly as he visited New Orleans and helped her keep watch against the city's predators.

Now he was a regular part of her family, especially since he often stayed at her twin's house and was, in fact, the god-father for Amanda's daughter.

He stopped beside her and cocked his head. With his dark sunglasses on, Tabitha couldn't tell if he was looking at her or Selena. But it was obvious he was bemused by the two of them.

"Hey, gorgeous babe," Tabitha said. She smiled as she realized his T-shirt paid tribute to the Godsmack song "Vampires." How strangely apropos since Ash was an immortal who came equipped with his own set of fangs. "Nice shirt."

Ignoring her compliment, he pulled the black backpack off his shoulder and flipped his sunglasses up to show eerie, swirling silver eyes that seemed to flash in the darkness. "How long has Selena been handcuffed to the fence?"

"About half an hour. I figured I'd hang out with her and keep her from becoming a Daimon-kabob."

"I wish," Selena muttered. She raised her voice and slung her arms wide. "Here I am, vampires, come and end my misery!"

Tabitha and Ash exchanged a half-amused, half-irritated look at her dramatics.

Ash moved to sit down beside Selena. "Hi, Lanie," he said quietly as he kept the backpack at his feet.

"Go away, Ash. I'm not leaving here until they repeal their law. I belong in this Square. I was raised here."

Ash nodded in understanding. "Where's Bill?"

"He's a traitor!" Selena snarled.

Tabitha answered the question. "He's probably at the courthouse holding ice to a private area after Selena racked him and accused him of being 'the man who is holding her down.'"

Ash's face softened as if the thought amused him.

"He deserved it," Selena said defensively. "He told me that the law is the law and that I had to obey it. Screw that. I'm not going anywhere until they change it."

"Guess I'll be here for awhile," Tabitha said wistfully.

"You can make them repeal the law," Selena said, turning toward Ash. "Can't you?"

Ash leaned back against the fence without commenting.

"Don't get too close to her, Ash," Tabitha warned. "She's been known to bite."

"That makes two of us," he said with a hint of humor in his voice as his fangs flashed. "But I somehow think my bite might hurt a little more."

"You're not funny," Selena said sullenly.

Ash draped an arm over Selena's shoulder. "C'mon, Lane. You know it's not going to change anything for you to stay here. Sooner or later a cop will come by—" /

"And I'll assault him."

Ash tightened his hold on her. "You can't assault them for doing their job."

"Yes, I can!"

Still he managed to remain calm while dealing with the Queen of Hysteria. "Is that really what you want to do?"

"No. I want my stand back," Selena said, her voice breaking from her grief and pain.

Tabitha's own chest was tight in sympathetic agony for her.

"I wasn't hurting anyone by having a table here. This is my space. I've had my stand right here in this spot since 1986! It's so not fair for them to make me leave because those stupid artists are jealous. Who wants one of their crappy paintings of the Quarter, anyway? They're stupid. What's New Orleans without her psychics? Just another boring, run-down tourist town, that's what!"

Ash held her sympathetically. "Times change, Selena. Believe me, I know, and sometimes there's nothing you can do about it except to let it go. No matter how much you want to stop time, it has to go forward and move on to something else."

Tabitha heard the sadness in his voice as he spoke comfortingly to her sister. Ash had been alive for more than eleven thousand years. He remembered New Orleans back in the days when it had barely qualified as a town. For that matter, he probably remembered New Orleans before any kind of civilization had claimed it.

If anyone knew about change, it was Acheron Parthenopaeus.

Ash wiped the tears from Selena's face and angled her
chin so that she was staring at the building across the street
from them. "You know, that building is up for sale. 'Madame
Selene's Tarot Reading and Mystical Boutique.' Can you
imagine it?"

Selena snorted at that. "Yeah, right. Like I can afford it.
Have you any idea what the real estate here goes for?"

Ash shrugged. "Money's not a problem for me. Say the
word and it's yours."

Selena blinked at him as if she couldn't believe what he
was offering her. "Really?"

He nodded. "You could put a sign up right here that
points people to your brand-new store where you can read
cards to your heart's content."

Finally seeing a solution to her sister's temporary de-
mentia and grateful to Ash for it, Tabitha sat forward so that
she could look at Selena. "You've always said you'd like to
be someplace where it can't rain you out."

Selena cleared her throat as she considered it. "It would
be nice to look out from a building instead of into it."

"Yeah," Tabitha said. "You'd no longer freeze in the winter or blister in the summer. Climate control all year long. No
more wheeling your cart up here and setting up the table and
chairs. You could even have a La-Z-Boy in the back room
and carry all sorts of tarot card decks. Tia would be jealous
as all get-out since she's been wanting a shop closer to the
Square. Think about it."

"You want it?" Ash asked.

Selena nodded enthusiastically.

Ash pulled out his cell phone and dialed a number. "Hey,
Bob," he said after a brief pause. "This is Ash Parthenopaeus.
There's a building for sale on St. Anne's in Jackson Square . . .
yeah, that one. I want it." He offered a close-lipped smile to Selena. "No, I don't need to see it. Just have the keys out here in
the morning." He pulled the phone aside. "What time can you
meet him here, Selena?"

"Ten?"

He repeated it into the phone. "Yeah, and make the deed out to Selena Laurens. I'll swing by tomorrow afternoon and handle the payment. All right. Have a good one." Ash hung up the phone and returned it to his pocket.

Selena smiled up at him. "Thank you."

"No problem." The instant he stood up, the handcuff fell free of the gate and Selena's arm.

Jeez, that man had some fearsome powers. Tabitha just wasn't sure which was more impressive. The one that broke the handcuff off Selena without a scratch or the one that allowed him to drop a couple of million dollars without blinking.

He held his hand out to Selena and helped her to her feet. "Just make sure you carry a lot of bright, shiny things for Simi to buy whenever we're here."

Tabitha laughed at the mention of Ash's demon . . . something . . . Tabitha still didn't know if Simi was Ash's girlfriend or what. The two of them had a very odd relationship.

Simi demanded and Ash gave without hesitation.

Unless it involved Simi killing and eating someone. Those were the only times she'd ever seen Ash put his foot down with the demon he kept secret from most of his Dark-Hunters. The only reason Tabitha even knew about Simi was that the demon often joined them for movies.

For some reason, Ash really loved the cinema and Tabitha had been going to see movies with him for the last two years. His favorites were horror and action flicks. Meanwhile the Simi was a most unusual and discriminating being who made him sit through "girl" movies that often left Ash groaning.

"Where is the Simster tonight?" Tabitha asked.

Ash brushed his hand over the dragon tattoo on his forearm. "She's hanging around. But it's too early for her. She doesn't like to be out and about until at least nine." He slung the backpack over his shoulder.

Selena stood on her tiptoes and pulled Ash down so that she could hug him. "I'll carry an entire line of Kirk's Folly just for Simi."

Smiling, he patted her on the back. "No more handcuffs, right?"

Selena pulled away. "Well, Bill did say that I could

protest with him later in the bedroom and I do owe him for that kick I gave him, so . . ."

Ash laughed as Selena scooped up the cuffs from the street.

"And you wonder why I'm nuts," Tabitha said as Selena tucked them into her back pocket.

Ash pulled his glasses back down to cover his eerie, swirling silver eyes. "At least she's entertaining."

"And you're way too charitable." But that was what Tabitha loved most about Ash. He always saw the good in everyone. "So what are you up to tonight?" she asked Ash while Selena folded up her handmade sign.

Before he could answer, a large black Harley came roaring down St. Anne. When it reached the turn that would have taken the rider down Royal Street, the bike stopped and was shut off.

Tabitha watched as the tall, lithe rider, who was decked out all in black biker leathers, held the bike upright between his thighs with ease and pulled the helmet off.

To her surprise, it was an African-American woman, and not a man, who set the helmet down before her on the bike's gas tank and unzipped her jacket. Extremely gorgeous, she was slender but muscular, with medium brown skin and a flawless complexion. She wore her jet-black hair in braids that were pulled back into a ponytail.

"Acheron," she said in a singsong Caribbean accent. "Where should I park me ride?"

Ash indicated Decatur Street behind him. "There's a public lot on the other side of the Brewery. I'll wait here until you get back."

The woman's gaze went to Tabitha, then Selena.

"They're friends," Ash said. "Tabitha Devereaux and Selena Laurens."

"Sisters-in-law to Kyrian?"

Ash nodded.

"I am Janice Smith," she said to them. "Nice to meet friends of the Hunters."

Tabitha was sure that was a play on words that stemmed not so much from Kyrian's last name as from his former occupation of being a Dark-Hunter—one of the immortal warriors like Janice and Ash who guarded the night against vampires, demons, and rogue gods.

Janice started her motorcycle and roared off.

"New Dark-Hunter?" Selena asked before Tabitha had a chance.

He nodded. "Artemis transferred her here from the Florida Keys to help Valerius and Jean-Luc. Tonight's her first night so I thought I'd give her a tour of the city."

"Need any help?" Tabitha asked.

"Nah. I got it. Just try not to stake Jean-Luc again if you meet up with him."

Tabitha laughed at his reference to the night she had inadvertently met the pirate Dark-Hunter. It had been dark and Jean-Luc had grabbed her from behind in an alley while she was stalking after a group of Daimons. All she had seen were fangs and tallness, so she had struck.

Jean-Luc had yet to forgive her.

"I can't help it. All you fanged people look alike in the dark."

Ash grinned. "Yeah. I know what you mean. All you soul-full people look alike to us, too."

Tabitha shook her head at him as she continued laughing. She wrapped her arm around Selena and started toward Decatur, where Selena had left her Jeep across the street.

It didn't take long to get her sister home and situated with a very hesitant Bill, who wasn't sure if Selena would rack him again or not. Once Tabitha was satisfied that Selena would be okay . . . and Bill, too . . . she headed back to the Quarter to patrol for Daimons.

It was a relatively quiet night out. She followed her usual habit of stopping in at the Café Pontalba and getting four plates of red beans and rice with Cokes to go, then taking the meals down to an alley off of Royal Street where many of the homeless were known to congregate. Since the city had decided to crack down on vagrants and the homeless, they weren't nearly as prevalent as before. Now they, like the vampires she sought, kept to the shadows where they were forgotten.

But Tabitha knew they were there and she never let herself forget about them.

Tabitha left the food on an old rusted barrel and turned to leave.

As soon as she reached the edge of the sidewalk, she heard people scurrying for the food.

"Hey, if you want a job—"

But they were gone before she could get anything more than that out.

Sighing, Tabitha headed down Royal. She couldn't save the world, she knew that. But at least she could see to it that some of the hungry were fed.

With no real destination in mind, she wandered down the lonely streets and browsed in the jewelry shop windows.

"Hey, Tabby, killed any vampires lately?"

She looked up to see Richard Crenshaw coming toward her. A waiter at Mike Anderson's Seafood, which was just a couple of doors down from her own store, had a bad habit of coming in whenever he got off work and hitting on the strippers who ordered custom-made costumes from her.

As usual, he was laughing at her. That was fine. Most people did. In fact, most people thought she was insane. Even her own family had laughed at her for years . . . until her twin had ended up married to a Dark-Hunter and had faced a vampire who had almost killed her.

Suddenly her family realized that her preternatural stories over the years weren't total hallucinations or fabrications.

"Yeah," she said to Richard, "I dusted one last night."

He rolled his eyes and laughed at her as he walked on past.

"You're welcome, Dick," she said under her breath as he kept going. The Daimon she'd killed had been hovering around the back door of Mike Anderson's, where Richard was known to take out the trash right before he got off work. If Tabitha hadn't killed the Daimon, Richard would most likely be dead now.

Whatever. She didn't really want thanks for what she did and she certainly didn't expect it.

She kept walking down the street, feeling extremely lonely tonight. How she wished she could live her life blindly, never knowing what was out here.

But she wasn't blind. She knew, and with that knowledge came the choice of either helping people or walking away. Never in her life had Tabitha been the kind of person who turned her back on someone in need. Her powers as an empath were too much for her sometimes. She felt the pain of others even more deeply than she felt her own.

It was what had drawn Ash to her in the beginning. Over the last three years, he had taught her several tricks to dampen down others' emotions and to focus on her own. He'd been a godsend to her and had done more for her sanity than anyone else. Still, his tricks didn't silence them totally.

At times it was all completely overwhelming. She was so bombarded by intense emotions that it set off hers and sometimes caused her to lash out verbally just from the stress of it.

So here she was, by herself, spending another lonely night walking the streets as she risked her life for people who mocked her.

Patrolling was certainly much more fun when she'd done it with a group of friends.

Tabitha forced herself not to remember Trish and Alex, who'd both died in the line of duty. But it was useless. Tears filled her eyes as she touched the jagged scar on her face that the Daimon Desiderius had given her. The worst sort of psycho, Desiderius had been out to kill her twin sister and brother-in-law. Luckily, Amanda and Kyrian had survived. Tabitha just wished she'd been killed that night instead of her friends. It wasn't right for them to pay such a high price when Tabitha had been the one to talk them into helping her in the first place.

God, why couldn't she have kept her mouth shut and just left them alone to live out their lives in ignorance and peace?

It was why she fought alone now. She would never again ask anyone to risk their life to do what she did.

They had a choice about this.

She didn't.

Tabitha slowed down as she got the familiar tickle down the center of her spine.

Daimons . . .

They were behind her.

Turning around, she knelt down and pretended to tie the

laces on her boot. Meanwhile she was well aware of the six shadows that were closing in on her . . .

Valerius pulled at the edge of his right leather Coach glove to straighten it as he walked down the virtually abandoned street. As always, he was impeccably dressed in a long black cashmere coat, a black turtleneck, and black slacks. Unlike most Dark-Hunters, he wasn't a leather-wearing barbarian. He was the epitome of sophistication. Breeding. Nobility. His family had been descended from one of the oldest and most respected noble families of Rome. As a former Roman general whose father had been a well-respected senator, Valerius would have gladly followed in the man's footsteps had the Parcae, or Fates, not intervened.

But that was the past and Valerius refused to remember it. Agrippina was the only exception to that rule. She was the only thing he ever remembered from his human life.

She was the only thing *worth* remembering from his human life.

Valerius winced and focused his thoughts on other, much less painful things. There was a crispness in the air that announced winter would be here soon. Not that New Orleans *had* a winter, compared to what he'd been used to in D.C.

Still, the longer he was here the more his blood was thinning, and the cool night air was a bit chilly to him.

Valerius paused as his Dark-Hunter senses detected the presence of a Daimon. Tilting his head, he listened with his heightened hearing.

He heard a group of men laughing at their victim.

And then he heard the strangest thing of all . . .

"Laugh it up, asshole. But she who laughs last, laughs longest and I intend to belly roll tonight."

A fight broke out.

Valerius whirled on his heel and headed back the direction he'd come from.

He drifted through the darkness until he found an ajar gate that led to a courtyard.

There in the back were six Daimons fighting a tall human woman.

Valerius was mesmerized by the macabre beauty of the battle. One Daimon came at the woman's back. She flipped him over her shoulder and in one graceful motion stabbed him in the chest with a long, black dagger. The Daimon burst into a golden dust.

She twirled as she rose up to face another one. She tossed the dagger from one hand to the other and held it like a woman well used to defending herself from the undead.

Two Daimons rushed her. She actually did a cartwheel away from them, but the other Daimon had anticipated her action. He grabbed her.

Without panicking, the woman surrendered her weight by picking both of her legs up to her chest. It brought the Daimon to his knees. The woman sprang to her feet and whirled to stab the Daimon in his back.

He evaporated.

Normally the remaining Daimons would flee. The last four didn't. Instead they spoke to each other in a language he hadn't heard in a long time: ancient Greek.

"Little chickie la la, isn't dumb enough to fall for that, guys," the woman answered back in flawless Greek.

Valerius was so stunned he couldn't move. In over two thousand years, he'd never seen or heard of anything like this. Not even the Amazons had ever produced a better fighter than the woman who now confronted the Daimons.

Suddenly a light appeared behind the woman. It flashed bright and swirling. A chill, cold wind swept through the courtyard before six more Daimons stepped out.

Valerius went rigid at something even rarer than the warrior-woman fighting the Daimons.

Tabitha turned slowly to see the group of new Daimons. Holy shit. She'd only seen this one other time.

The new batch of Daimons looked at her and laughed. "Pitiful human."

"Pitiful this," she said as tossed her dagger at his chest.

He moved his hand and deflected the dagger before it reached him. Then he slung his arm toward her. Something invisible and painful slashed through her chest as she went flying head over heels.

Dazed and scared, Tabitha lay on the ground.

Horrible memories ripped through her of the night when her friends had died. The way the warrior Spathi Daimons had torn through them . . .

No, no, no.

They were dead. Kyrian had killed them all.

Her panic tripled as she struggled to right herself.

She was dizzy, her vision blurry as she pushed herself to her feet.

Valerius was across the alley in microseconds as he saw the woman fall.

The tallest Daimon, who stood even in height to Valerius, laughed. "How nice of Acheron to send us a playmate."

Valerius pulled his two retractable swords from his coat and extended the blades. "Play is for children and dogs. Now that you have identified which category you fall into, I'll show you what Romans do to rabid dogs."

One of the Daimons smiled. "Romans? My father always told me that all Romans die squealing like pigs."

The Daimon attacked.

Valerius sidestepped and brought his sword down. The Daimon pulled a sword out of nothing and parried his attack with a skill that bespoke a man with years of training.

The other Daimons struck at once.

Valerius dropped his swords and swung out with his arms, releasing the grappling hooks and cords that were attached to his wrists. The hooks went straight into the chest of the tallest Daimon and the one he was fighting.

Unlike most Daimons, they didn't disintegrate instantly. They stared at him with hollow eyes before they burst apart.

But while he was distracted by them, another Daimon retrieved his sword and cut him across his back. Valerius hissed in pain before he turned and elbowed the Daimon in the face.

The woman was back on her feet. She killed two more Daimons while he killed the one who had wounded him.

Valerius wasn't sure what had happened to the others; in truth, he was having a bit of trouble moving because of the vicious pain of his back.

"Die, Daimon snot!" the woman snarled at him an instant before she, too, stabbed him straight in the chest.

She pulled the dagger out instantly.

Valerius hissed and staggered back as pain ripped through his heart. He clutched at his chest, unable to think past the agony of it.

Tabitha bit her lip in terror as she saw the man recoil and not explode into dust.

"Oh, shit," she breathed, rushing to his side. "Please tell me you're some screwed-up Dark-Hunter and that I didn't just kill an accountant or lawyer."

The man hit the street hard.

Tabitha rolled him over onto his back and checked his breathing. His eyes were partially opened, but he wasn't speaking. He held his jaw clamped firmly shut as he groaned deep in his throat.

Terrified, she still wasn't sure who she had mistakenly stabbed. Her heart hammering, she pulled up his turtleneck to see the nasty-looking stab wound in the center of his chest.

And then she saw what she had hoped for . . .

He had a bow and arrow brand above his right hipbone.

"Oh, thank God," she breathed as relief poured through her. He was in fact a Dark-Hunter and not some unfortunate human.

She grabbed her phone and called Acheron to let him know one of his men had been hurt, but he didn't answer.

So she started dialing her sister Amanda until her common sense returned. There were only four Dark-Hunters in this city. Ash who led them. Janice whom she had met earlier. The former pirate captain, Jean-Luc. And . . .

Valerius Magnus.

He was the only Dark-Hunter in New Orleans she didn't know personally. And he was the mortal enemy of her brother-in-law.

She hit the cancel button on her phone. Kyrian would kill this man in a heartbeat and bring the wrath of Artemis down fully upon his head. In return, the goddess would kill Kyrian for it and that was the last thing Tabitha wanted. Her sister would die if anything happened to her husband.

Come to think of it, if half of what Kyrian said about this man and his family was true, she should just leave him here and let him die.

But then Ash would never forgive her if she did that to one of his men. Besides she couldn't leave him here, not even she was that heartless. Like it or not, he had saved her life and she was honor-bound to return the favor.

Wincing, she realized she was going to have to get him to safety. And he was just a little too large for her to handle on her own. She dialed her phone again and waited for an answer that came in a slick, Cajun drawl.

"Hey, Nick, it's Tabitha Devereaux. I'm in the old court-yard off Royal Street with a man down and I need help. Any chance you want to be my knight in shining armor tonight and lend a hand to a damsel in distress?"

Nick Gautier's smooth laugh rippled in her ear. "Why, *chèr*, you know I live for such moments. I'll be right there."

"Thanks," she said before she gave him precise directions and hung up.

A New Orleans native like herself, Nick had been an acquaintance of hers for years since the two of them frequented many of the same restaurants and clubs. Not to mention, Nick had brought a few of his girlfriends in to browse some of the racier outfits that Tabitha sold in her adult boutique, Pandora's Box.

A charming rogue, Nick was about as handsome as any man she'd ever seen. He had dark brown hair that tended to stay in a pair of eyes that were so blue and seductive they really should be illegal.

And when it came to his smile . . .

Not even she was entirely immune to it.

She'd been stunned to learn at her sister's wedding three years ago that Nick actually worked for the undead. Rumors on the street had always abounded on what Nick did for a living. Every native who haunted the Quarter knew the man had a ton of cash and no real job that anyone could discern. When he'd shown up as best man for Kyrian, she'd been completely shocked.

But since that night, she and Nick had forged an odd alliance as drinking buddies and partners-in-crime who lived to rankle the Dark-Hunters. It was really nice to have someone she could talk to who knew that the vampires were real and who understood the dangers she faced every night.

Tabitha sat down on the cobblestoned walk to wait on Nick. Valerius still wasn't moving. She cocked her head to study Kyrian's great Satan. According to her brother-in-law, Valerius and his Roman family had been the worst sort of bastards.

They had killed and raped any- and everything that came into their paths as they led bloody campaigns across the ancient world. She would have taken Kyrian's aspersions with more grains of salt if it wasn't for the fact that other Dark-Hunters concurred.

To her knowledge, no one liked Valerius.

No one.

But as she watched him breathing lightly, he didn't look so ominous.

Probably because he's practically dead.

Actually, he was all dead. But still breathing. The moonlight cast shadows over the handsome planes of his face and showed the tears in his clothing where he was bleeding. If he could bleed to death, she'd hold a compress to his chest wound, but since he couldn't she stayed put.

"How did you die?" she whispered. Kyrian didn't know, and in all her readings about ancient Rome and Greece, Valerius's name had seldom been mentioned. For all the brutality that Kyrian accused him of, Valerius Magnus wasn't much more than a footnote in history.

"Hey, Tab, you in here?"

She breathed a sigh of relief at the sound of Nick's deep Cajun drawl. Thank goodness he only lived three blocks away and knew how to hustle in a jam. "I'm over here."

Dressed in a pair of faded jeans and a short-sleeved blue shirt, Nick quickly joined her, then cursed the instant he saw who was lying on the ground.

"You've got to be kidding me," he snarled after she asked him to help her get Valerius up. "I wouldn't throw piss on that man if he were on fire."

"Nick!" Tabitha said, shocked at his rancor. Normally Nick was the most laid-back of men. "That was uncalled-for."

"Oh, yeah, right. I notice you didn't call Kyrian for this. Why is that, Tabitha? 'Cause he'd kill you both?"

She stamped down her own temper, which would only set his off more if she started telling him how juvenile he was behaving. "C'mon, Nick. Don't be like that. I don't want to help him, either, but Ash won't answer the phone and no one else seems to like him."

"Damn straight. Everyone, but you, has a brain. Let him rot on the street."

She stood up and faced him with her hands on her hips. "Fine. You explain to Ash why one of his Hunters was killed, then. You deal with his anger. I'm out of it."

Nick narrowed his eyes on her. "You really suck, Tabby. Why didn't you call Eric for this?"

"Because it's awkward to ask your ex—who is happily married to someone else—for favors, okay? I somehow thought my friend *Nick* wouldn't hassle me over this, but I can see now that I was wrong."

He gave an exaggerated wince at that. "I really hate this man, Tabitha. I've known Kyrian too long and owe him too much to render aid to the man whose grandfather crucified him."

"And we are not responsible for the actions of our family members, are we, Nick?"

His jaw ticced at that.

Nick's father had been a convicted murderer who had died in a prison riot. It was well known by everyone that the man was a repeat felon who had spent the whole of Nick's youth in and out of jail for all sorts of unsavory crimes. Nick himself had been well on his way to repeating his father's fate when Kyrian had stepped in and saved him.

"That's low, Tab, *real* low."

"But it's true. Now, please, forget that he's a dickhead and help me get him home, okay?"

Nick growled at her before he came near them. "Do you know where he lives?"

"No, do you?"

"Somewhere over in the Garden District." Nick pulled out his phone and dialed a number. After a minute, he cursed. "Otto, answer the phone." He cursed again, then hung up and glared at her. "You know it's bad when the guy's own Squire won't answer to save him."

"Maybe Otto's busy."

"Maybe Otto's psychic."

"Nick . . ."

Nick put his phone in his pocket, then bent over, tossed Valerius over his shoulder, and headed out of the courtyard to where his Jaguar was parked on the street. He dumped Valerius unceremoniously into the passenger seat.

"Watch his head, Nick!" she snapped as Nick banged it against the car.

"Not like I could kill him or anything. What happened to him, anyway?"

"I stabbed him."

Nick blinked, then burst out laughing. "I knew I liked you for a reason. Oh man, I can't wait to tell Kyrian. He'll laugh his ass off."

"Yeah, well, in the meantime, take Valerius back to my place and give me Otto's number so that I can keep trying to call him."

"And you want to tell me how I'm going to get him to your place since Bourbon Street is closed off to traffic after dark?"

She gave him a droll stare.

He growled at her. "Fine, but you owe me big-time."

"Yeah, yeah. Get cracking, Squire."

He mumbled something under his breath that she was sure was less than complimentary before he walked to the other side of his car and got in.

Since his car was a two-seater, Tabitha headed out on foot to rendezvous with him at her store. As she walked into the crowd on Bourbon Street, she felt something evil brush up against her psychically.

Spinning around, she scanned the crowd, but didn't see anything.

Still, she felt it deep inside.

"Something wicked this way comes . . ." She breathed the title of her favorite Ray Bradbury book.

And something inside told her it was far more evil than anything she had faced before.

Chapter 2

Valerius came awake slowly to the sound of someone humming nearby.

Humming?

He blinked open his eyes expecting to find himself in his own bed in his own house. Instead, he was on a queen-size antique tester bed with an ornate wooden canopy that was padded in burgundy velvet.

The voice he heard was coming from a rocking chair on his left. He turned his head and was floored by what he found.

It was . . .

Well, at first glance it looked like a very large woman. She had long blond hair and was wearing a short-sleeved, pink furry sweater and a pair of khaki pants. Only the "woman" had shoulders every bit as broad as Valerius did and a pronounced Adam's apple.

She sat in the chair, flipping through the fall issue of *Vogue* with glossy, blood-red fingernails that could double for claws. She looked up and paused in her humming.

"Oh! You're awake!" she said excitedly, getting up immediately and fluttering around his bed. She awkwardly grabbed what appeared to be a walkie-talkie from the nightstand and pressed the button while making sure she didn't break a nail. "Tabby, Mr. Sexy is awake."

"Okay, Marla, thanks."

Valerius had a faint memory of that voice, but it wasn't clear as he tried to remember what had happened to him. "Where am I?" he asked.

"Hell" seemed the most apropos answer. But the pain in his body and the dimmed room that was a peculiar mixture of modern and antique said that not even hell would be this bad or tacky.

"Don't move, sweetie," the unknown woman said as she continued to gesture and hover around the bed. "Tabby will be right here. She said that I wasn't to let you go anywhere at all. So don't."

Before he could ask who Tabby was, another woman burst into the room.

She too was tall. But unlike the first one, she was slender, almost waif-like, except that her body was well defined, as if she lifted weights. Her long auburn hair was pulled back into a ponytail and she had a vicious scar over her left cheekbone.

Valerius froze at the sight of the warrior he'd seen the night before. Memories flooded him. Including the one where she had stabbed him straight in the chest—which was helped by the fact that she still held a large butcher knife in her right hand.

"You!" he accused, pushing himself to the furthest edge of the bed.

The woman visibly cringed before she turned to the first one and urged her toward the door. "Thanks, Marla, I appreciate your watching over him."

"Oh, anytime, hon. You just ring-a-ding if you need anything."

"I will." She pushed the larger woman out the door and slammed it shut. "Hi," she said to Valerius.

He stared at the knife in her hand, then looked down at the healing wound on his chest. "What? Are you back to finish me off?"

She frowned at him. "Wha . . . ?" Then her gaze went to the knife in her hand. "Oh, this. No, last night was a complete accident."

Tabitha placed the knife on the dresser, then turned to face him. She had to admit that Valerius looked extremely handsome in her bed. His long black hair was down, and draped around his face. His features were perfectly chiseled as if by some master artist. And that body of his . . .

Really, no man should look *that* yummy.

It was why she'd spent the night in her downstairs office and why she'd sent Marla up to watch after him first thing this morning.

Asleep he'd been more of a temptation than she wanted. He'd looked relaxed and gentle.

Inviting.

Awake he looked dangerous.

And still inviting.

She would give the goddess credit, Artemis had exquisite taste in men; and to Tabitha's knowledge, and according to Amanda's words, there was no such thing as an ugly Dark-Hunter.

She couldn't really fault the goddess for that. If you had to pick men for your own personal army, what woman wouldn't pick the tallest and best-looking of the bunch?

It also explained why Acheron was their leader.

Yes, it was good to be a goddess. Tabitha couldn't imagine how great it would be to command all that delectable testosterone.

And Valerius was prime DH material as he sat with one divinely carved arm braced on her mattress while the rest of him was all but bare to her sight. He looked like some coiled, wild beast ready to strike.

But he was confused. She felt his emotions reaching out to her. He was also angry but she wasn't sure why.

"You're safe here," she said, stepping near the bed. "I know what you are and I made sure all the windows are covered."

"Who are you?" he asked in a suspicious tone.

"Tabitha Devereaux," she said.

"Are you a Squire?"

"No."

"Then how do you know—"

"I'm a friend of Acheron's."

His anger snapped at that. "You're lying." He stood up suddenly, then hissed as he realized he was completely naked.

Tabitha bit her lip to keep from moaning at the sight of all that luscious skin bared. She had to give the Dark-Hunters credit, they were all incredibly well built.

Valerius grabbed the sheet from her bed and covered himself. "Where are my clothes?" he asked in the most disdainful voice she'd ever heard.

No wonder Nick and the others had a hard time with him. Arrogance and supreme superiority bled from every molecule of that masculine body. It was obvious Valerius was a man used to giving orders, which made sense since she knew he had once been a Roman general.

Unfortunately, Tabitha wasn't used to following anyone's orders, especially not a man's.

"Keep your shirt on," she said with a laugh at her bad joke. "Your clothes are at the laundry. They'll deliver them as soon as they're ready."

"And in the meantime?"

"Looks like you're naked."

His jaw worked as if he couldn't believe what he was hearing. "I beg your pardon?"

"Beg all you want, you're still going to be naked." Tabitha paused at the wicked image in her mind. "Come to think of it, a gorgeous, begging, naked man . . . that's the stuff of fantasies. Begging won't get you your clothes, but it could get you something else." She wiggled her eyebrows at him.

His fist tightened on the sheet he held around his waist. She could sense that he was both offended and yet oddly amused by her.

She cocked her head at him. "You know, you are Roman. You could just make a toga out of the bedsheet."

Valerius stood there feeling a strange urge to sputter. Had he been lowborn, he might actually have done that.

This had to be the strangest woman ever born.

"How do you know I'm Roman?"

"I told you, I know Ash and all the rest of you night dwellers." She gave him a playful look. "C'mon, make a toga for me. I tried to make one in college and ended up with it falling off in the middle of the party. Thank God my roommate was still sober enough to scoop it up and wrap it around me before the frat boys pounced."

Behind him, he heard a cuckoo clock chime. Valerius turned to see the time, then scowled as he realized the "bird" had a red mohawk.

It also had an eyepatch.

"Ain't it a hoot?" Tabitha asked. "I picked it up in Switzerland when I spent a year there studying."

"Fascinating," he said coldly. "Now if you'll leave me, I shall—"

"Whoa, wait a sec, bud. I ain't your servant and you don't take that tone with me. Capisce?"

"Saeva scaeva," Valerius muttered under his breath.

"Saeve puer," she shot back.

Valerius actually gaped at her. "Did you just insult me in Latin?"

"You insulted me first. Not that I'm particularly insulted by being called a rampant she-devil. It's kind of flattering, but still, I'm not the kind of person to take an insult in silence."

In spite of himself, he was impressed. It had been a long time indeed since he'd met a female who knew his native tongue. Of course, he didn't like being called an oafish boy, but there was something to be said for a woman who possessed such intelligence.

And it had been an eternity since he was around someone who didn't openly disdain him. She wasn't biting in her retorts. Rather she was sparring with him like a champion debater who took none of this to heart.

How unusual . . .

How frighteningly refreshing.

Suddenly, the theme song to *The Twilight Zone* chimed through the house.

"What is that?" he asked trepidatiously. Maybe he had actually walked into Rod Serling's domain.

"Doorbell. It's probably your clothes being delivered."

"Tabby!" Marla shouted from somewhere outside the bedroom. "It's Ben with your stuff."

Valerius stiffened at the crass behavior. "Does he always scream like that?"

"Hey, now," Tabitha said sternly. "Marla is one of my dearest friends on this earth and if you insult her or keep calling her a he, I'll stake your butt somewhere where it'll hurt a lot more than your chest." She dropped her gaze mean-ingfully to his groin.

Valerius widened his eyes at her threat. What kind of woman said such a thing to a man?

Before he could speak, she left the room.

Stunned, he wasn't sure what to do. What to think. He went to the dresser where she'd left her knife. Next to it was his wallet, keys, and phone.

He grabbed the phone and called Acheron, who immediately answered.

"I need help," Valerius said to him for the first time in two thousand years.

Acheron groaned slightly. "Help with what?" he asked. His heavily accented voice was groggy, as if Valerius had awakened him from a deep sleep.

"I'm in the home of a madwoman who claims she knows you. You have to get me out of here right now, Acheron. I don't care what it takes."

"It's noon, Valerius. We both should be asleep." Acheron paused. "Where are you anyway?"

Valerius was looking around the room. There were Mardi Gras beads draped all over the three-sided antique dresser mirror. Instead of a Persian rug, it was . . . a giant toy-car road map. There were parts of the room that showed impeccable taste and breeding and parts that were just plain scary.

He hesitated in front of what appeared to be a voodoo altar.

"I don't know," Valerius said. "I hear some godawful kind of music from outside, horns blaring, and I'm in a house with a mohawk cuckoo bird, a transvestite, and a knife-wielding lunatic."

"Why are you at Tabitha's?" Acheron asked.

Valerius was floored by the question. Acheron really did know her?

Granted, Acheron *was* a bit eccentric, but up until now, Valerius had assumed the Atlantean had more sense than to associate with such low-class humans. "Excuse me?"

"Relax," Acheron said with a yawn. "You're in good hands. Tabby won't hurt you."

"She stabbed me!"

"Damn," Ash said. "I told her not to stab any more Hunters. I hate it when she does that."

"*You* hate it? I'm the one with the festering wound."

"Really?" Acheron asked. "I've never known a Dark-Hunter to have a festering wound before. At least not externally."

Valerius clenched his teeth at the Atlantean's misplaced humor. "I do not find you amusing, Acheron."

"Yeah, I know. But look on the bright side: You're the third Dark-Hunter she's nailed so far. She kind of gets a little carried away sometimes."

"A little carried away? The woman is a menace."

"Nah, she's a good egg. Unless you're a Daimon—then she can give Xanthippe a run for her money."

Valerius doubted that. Even the infamous ancient Greek shrew had to be more composed than Tabitha.

The door opened to show Tabitha entering the room with his clothes wrapped in plastic.

"Who are you talking to?" she asked.

"Tell her I said hi," Acheron said a second later.

This time, Valerius did sputter. He just couldn't believe what was happening here. That these two knew each other so well.

He stared at Tabitha as she hung his clothes on the closet doorknob. "Acheron says hi."

She moved to stand in front of him, leaned forward, and raised her voice so that Acheron could hear her over the phone. "Hey, gorgeous babe. Shouldn't you be asleep?"

"Yes, I should," Acheron said to Valerius.

"You don't call Acheron 'babe,'" Valerius said sternly to Tabitha.

She actually snorted at him. Like a horse. "*You* don't call Acheron 'babe' because . . . well, that's just sick. But I call him 'babe' all the time."

Valerius was shocked.

Was she . . .

"No, she's not my girlfriend," Acheron said from the other end as if he could hear Valerius's thoughts. "I'm leaving that for some other poor sap."

"You have to help me, Acheron," Valerius said, tightening his grip on the sheet as he moved away from Tabitha, who continued to pursue him across the room.

"Okay, listen. Here's some help. You know your prized cashmere coat?"

Valerius couldn't imagine how that might help him, but at this point he was willing to try anything. "Yes?"

"Guard it well. Marla is about your size and she'll definitely try to steal it if she sees it. She has this strange coat and jacket fetish, especially if they've been worn by men. Last time I was in town, she ended up with my favorite motorcycle jacket."

Valerius gaped. "And how is it that you associate with drag queens, Acheron?"

"I have many interesting friends, Valerius, and some of them are even complete and utter assholes."

He stiffened. "Was that directed at me?"

"No. I just think you're way too uptight for your own good. Now if you're through wigging out on me, I'd like to go back to sleep."

Ash actually hung up the phone.

Valerius stood there, holding the cell phone. He felt like someone had just cut the line on his life preserver, and was leaving him to drift out into shark-infested waters.

Jaws herself was there, waiting to devour him.

Jupiter help him.

Tabitha picked the pillow up off the floor and returned it to the bed. She paused as she caught sight of Valerius's backside. Damn, he had the nicest posterior she'd ever seen on any man. Someone should stamp Grade A Prime on it. It was all she could do not to walk over to him and cop a feel, but his rigid, frigid stance kept her well at bay.

That and the multitude of scars that marred his back. It looked as if someone had beaten him repeatedly.

But who would have dared do such a thing?

"You okay?" she asked as he walked to the dresser and set his phone down.

He raked his hand through his long hair and sighed. "How many hours to sundown?"

"A little over five." She sensed he was still angry and confused. "You want to go back to bed and sleep?"

He gave her a harsh, menacing glare. "I want to go home."

"Yeah, well, I would have taken you home had Otto answered his phone last night."

"I gave Guido time off for bad behavior," Valerius said under his breath. Then his face went suddenly pale.

Tabitha sensed dread, followed sharply by a pain so deep that it actually made her wince.

"What's wrong?" she asked.

"I need to go home immediately."

"Well, unless you have some special relationship to Apollo that I need to know about, that's about as likely as me winning the lottery, which would be highly likely if Ash would ever share those damn numbers with me. Vicious cur that he is. He won't share squat."

She felt a wave of hopeless despair consume Valerius. Instinctively, she walked over to him and gently touched his arm. "It's okay, really. I'll take you back as soon as the sun goes down."

Valerius looked down at her hand on his biceps. No woman had laid a bare hand to him like that in centuries. It wasn't sexual. It was soothing. The hand of someone who offered him comfort.

He lifted his gaze to hers. She had searingly blue eyes. They were sharp and intelligent. Most of all, they were kind, and kindness wasn't something Valerius was used to.

Most people took one look at him and instantly had a strong disliking for him. As a human, he'd attributed it to his regal status and his family's well-earned reputation for brutality.

As a Dark-Hunter, it had stemmed from the fact that he was a Roman and since Rome and Greece had spent centuries warring against each other until Rome had finally brought Greece to her knees, it was only to be expected that the Greeks would hate him. Unfortunately, the Greeks and Amazons were a vocal group who had quickly turned all the other Dark-Hunters and Squires against their Roman-born brethren.

Over the centuries, Valerius had convinced himself that he didn't need any brothers-in-arms and had even started getting a morbid kind of enjoyment from reminding them of his regal Roman status.

From the first year of his rebirth, he'd learned to strike out at them before they struck him.

He'd finally embraced the rigid formality and sense of propriety that his father had beaten into him as a child.

But that formality fled before the kindness of this woman's soothing touch.

Tabitha swallowed as something passed between them. His dark, intense stare went through her and for the first time it wasn't condemning or judgmental. It was almost tender, and tenderness was not something she expected from a man of Valerius's reputation.

He laid his fingers against the scar on her cheek. She didn't see the sneer on his face that most men got when they saw it. Instead, he gently traced its line. "What happened?" he asked.

"Car wreck" almost came out. She'd told that lie for so long that it was practically automatic now. Honestly, it was a lot easier to say the lie than it was to live the truth.

She knew just how hideous her face was. Her family had no idea how many times she had overheard them make comments about her scar. How many times Kyrian had told Amanda that he would gladly pay for her to have plastic surgery.

But Tabitha had been terrified of hospitals ever since her aunt had died of a simple tonsillectomy gone bad. She would never elect to have something done just because she wasn't pretty anymore. If the rest of the world couldn't deal with her, it was their problem, not hers.

"A Daimon," she said quietly. "He said he wanted to give me a special memento so that I would always remember him."

A tic started in his jaw at her words and she sensed his anger on her behalf.

"I'll give him credit," she said past the lump in her throat. "He was right. I think of him every time I look in the mirror."

Valerius dropped his hand down to the scar on her neck where one of the Daimons had actually gotten a bite on her. If not for Kyrian coming to her rescue, she would most likely have died that night.

"I'm sorry," he whispered.

Those were words she was certain never crossed this man's lips. "It's okay. We all have scars. I'm just lucky that most of mine are on the outside."

Valerius was stunned by her wisdom. He'd never expected such depth of thought from a woman like her. She gave a light squeeze to his hand before she removed it from her neck and stepped back.

"Are you hungry?"

"Famished," he answered honestly. Like most Dark-Hunters he usually ate three meals a night. One not long after he awoke at sunset, another around ten or eleven at night, and the third one around three or four in the morning. Since he'd been wounded fairly early, he'd only eaten one meal last night.

"Okay, I have a well-stocked kitchen. What would you like?"

"Something Italian."

She nodded. "Sounds good. Go ahead and get dressed and I'll meet you downstairs. The kitchen is the door on the left. Don't open the one on the right that has a Biohazard sticker on it. That one leads to my shop and it's nothing but daylight in there."

She started to pull the door closed behind her, then stopped. "By the way, you might want to put your coat in my closet until you leave. Marla—"

"Acheron already warned me."

"Ah, good. See you in a few."

Valerius waited until she was gone before he went to dress. As he hung his coat in her closet, he was struck by the fact that she owned as much black as he did. The only color in her closet was a bright pink satin dress that stood out harshly amidst the sea of darkness. That and a red plaid miniskirt.

It was the miniskirt that held his attention as an unwanted image of Tabitha in it went through him and he wondered if she had nice legs.

He'd always appreciated a pair of shapely, soft feminine legs. Especially when they were wrapped around him.

His body hardened instantly with that thought. Valerius

grimaced as he felt suddenly like a pervert standing in her closet, daydreaming about her.

He shut the closet door instantly and left the room. The hallway was painted a bright yellow shade that was a bit harsh on his sensitive Dark-Hunter eyes. There was a room across the hall that had the door opened to display a well-kept, tastefully decorated bedroom. He saw a silver sequined dress lying across the antique bed and an ornate brunette wig resting on a foam head beside it.

"Oh, hi, cutie," Marla said as she left what must have been a bathroom. She was wearing a turban on her apparently bald head and a pink bathrobe. "Tabby's downstairs."

"Thank you," he said, inclining his head to her.

"Ooo, manners. What a nice change for Tabby. Most of the men she drags home are all crude ruffians. Except for that Ash Parthenopaeus who is remarkably well-mannered. But he's odd, too. Have you ever met him?"

"I am acquainted with him, yes."

She visibly shivered. "Ooo, I like the way you say 'acquainted,' shug. That's some accent you have there. Now you better go on before I take up any more of your time. God knows, I'll talk your ears off if you let me."

Smiling at her flamboyant gestures as she shooed him away, Valerius bid her adieu, then closed her door. There was something oddly charming about Marla.

He made his way down the beautiful cherry staircase that led to a small landing. He frowned at the Biohazard sticker that was right where Tabitha had said. He turned to the left where two French doors that could use a bit of repair led to a small dining room. Inside were an old brown-and-white farmer's table and ladder-back chairs that had seen better days.

The walls were painted a harsh white and held framed black-and-white posters of European landmarks such as the Eiffel Tower, Stonehenge, and the Coliseum. Black plantation shutters had been pulled closed over the windows to block out the daylight for him. And a black buffet was set against the far wall. The top of it was littered with pictures and collectible plates, including ones of Elvis and Elvira. Two large, antique silver candelabrums stood at each end of it.

But what amazed him was an 8 × 10 picture in the center of the buffet of what appeared to be Tabitha in a wedding dress standing beside a man whose face was covered by a small cut-out picture of Russell Crowe's head.

He reached out to remove the picture.

"There you are," Tabitha said from behind him.

Valerius straightened instantly. "You're married?" he asked.

She frowned until she saw the picture. "Oh, good grief, no. That's my sister Amanda at her wedding. The baby girl in the picture next to it is her daughter, Marissa."

Valerius studied the wedding picture. There was really no difference between the women except for the scar. "You have a twin sister?"

"Yes."

"And why is your sister married to Russell Crowe?"

Tabitha laughed. "Ah, it's a goof on my brother-in-law, the self-righteous, proselytizing schlemiel."

He gave her an arch look. "I take it you don't care for the man."

"Actually, I love him to death. He's really good to my sister and niece, and is a real sweetheart in his own way. But, much like you, he takes himself entirely too seriously. You guys need to lighten up and enjoy yourselves more. Life's too short . . . well, maybe not for you, but for the rest of us mortals it is."

Valerius was fascinated by this woman who should repulse him. She was tacky and uncouth and yet she was amusing and charming in a most unexpected way.

She plunked a small red can on the table that had a plastic spoon sticking out of what appeared to be some sort of elbow macaroni and marinara.

Valerius frowned. "What is that?"

"Ravioli."

He arched a brow at that. "*That* is not ravioli."

She looked down at it. "Well, okay. It's Beefaroni. My niece calls anything that comes in these small microwavable cans ravioli." She pulled a chair out for him. "Eat up."

Valerius was aghast at what she was offering him. "I beg your pardon? You don't actually expect me to eat that, do you?"

"Well, yeah. You said you wanted Italian. It's Italian." She picked the can up and indicated the label. "See. Chef Boyardee. He makes only the best stuff."

Valerius had never been more appalled in his life. Surely she was joking. "I don't eat out of paper cups with plastic cutlery."

"Well, la-di-da, Mr. Fancy Pants. Sorry if I offended you, but here on Planet Earth the rest of us plebeians tend to eat whatever's handy, and when something is given to us, we don't question it."

Tabitha crossed her arms over her chest as he went ramrod stiff. If looks could kill, her poor cup of Beefaroni would be splintered.

"I shall withdraw until nightfall." He gave her an imperious nod of his head before he headed back toward the stairs.

Tabitha gaped as he left her. He really was offended and deep inside, hurt. The latter made no sense whatsoever to her. She was the one who should be insulted. Picking up the Beefaroni, she sighed, took a bite, and headed back into the kitchen with it.

Valerius carefully closed the door to her room when what he really wanted to do was slam it. But then, nobility didn't slam through the house. That was for commoners.

Nobility held their emotions under careful restraint. Nor were they wounded by the opinion of crass women with no couth who insulted them.

He'd been foolish to think for even a moment that she . . .

"I don't need anyone to like me," he muttered under his breath. He'd lived all his life without anyone giving a damn about him. Why should it change now?

And yet he couldn't squelch that tiny part of him that yearned for someone to pass along a note of kindness to him. A simple, "Tell Valerius I said hi."

Just *once* in his life . . .

"You're being foolish," he growled at himself.

Better to be feared than liked. His father's words rang in his ears. *People will always betray someone they like, but never someone they truly fear.*

It was true. Fear kept people in line. He more than anyone knew that.

Had his brothers feared him . . .

Valerius winced at the memory and moved to sit in the director's chair in the corner of the room.

It was set next to a bookcase that held a wide assortment of novels. He frowned as he scanned the titles, which went from *The Last Days of Pompeii* and *The Life and Times of Alexander the Great* to Jim Butcher's Dresden novels.

What a peculiar woman Tabitha was.

As Valerius reached for a book about ancient Rome, his gaze fell to the trash can beside the chair. It was large like the kind that most people kept in the kitchen, but what caught his attention was the piece of black sleeve that peeped out from the closed top. Opening it, he found his shirt and coat.

His frown deepened as he pulled them out. They were still covered in blood and torn. He fingered the slash in the back of them from where the Daimon had cut him with a sword.

But he was wearing his . . .

Valerius stood up and pulled his silk turtleneck off. It was Ralph Lauren, identical to the one he'd worn last night. There was only one explanation.

Tabitha had bought him new clothes.

He went to the closet and examined the coat. It wasn't until then that he realized the buttons were a slightly different color of brass. Other than that, it was an exact copy.

He couldn't believe it. His coat alone had cost fifteen hundred dollars. Why would she do such a thing?

Wanting an answer, he headed back downstairs where he found her alone in the kitchen, cooking.

Valerius hesitated in the doorway. She stood sideways from him, a perfectly serene profile. She was truly a beautiful woman.

Her faded black jeans hugged long legs and an extremely attractive rear. She wore a short-sleeved, buttoned-up black sweater that rode high, leaving a large amount of tanned flesh exposed between the low-riding jeans and her navel, which, if he wasn't mistaken, was pierced.

Her long auburn hair was pulled back and she looked

strangely tranquil standing over the stove in her bare feet; a silver toe ring twinkled on her right foot. The radio was turned on, low, playing Martin Briley's "Salt in My Tears." Tabitha's hips moved in time to the music in an erotic rhythm that was far more alluring than he wanted to admit.

Indeed, it was all he could do to not move toward her so that he could dip his head down and sample some of the succulent skin that beckoned him.

She was a spitfire who would surely ride him well.

He took a step forward and she jumped, then kicked her foot out. Valerius cursed as said foot made contact with his groin and he doubled over with the pain of it.

"Oh my God!" Tabitha gasped as she realized she'd just racked her houseguest. "I'm so sorry! Are you okay?"

He gave her a menacing glare. "No," he growled, limping away from her.

Tabitha helped him toward the step stool chair that she kept in the small kitchen. "I'm really, really sorry," she repeated as he sat down and held the heel of his hand against himself. "I should have warned you not to sneak up behind me."

"I wasn't sneaking," he said from between clenched teeth. "I was walking."

"Here, let me get you some ice."

"I don't need ice. I just need a minute to breathe and not talk."

She held her hands up in surrender. "Take your time."

After he turned several interesting shades, he finally recovered himself. "Thank Jupiter you didn't have another knife in your hands," he muttered, then said louder, "Do you kick every man who comes into the house like this?"

"Oh, Lord, not another one!" Marla said as she entered the room. "Tabby, I swear it's a wonder you have a personal life at all the way you treat men."

"Oh, hush, Marla. I didn't do it on purpose . . . this time."

Marla rolled her eyes as she grabbed two Diet Cokes from the fridge. She handed one to Valerius. "Hold that to your wound, sweetie. It'll help. Just be grateful you're not Phil. I heard they had to perform a testicle retrieval operation after Tabby caught him two-timing on her." Then she popped the top on her drink and went back upstairs.

"He deserved it," Tabitha called after Marla. "He's lucky I didn't cut it off."

Valerius really didn't want to pursue that conversation. He stood up and set the Coke on the countertop. "Why are you cooking?"

Tabitha shrugged. "You said you didn't want something out of a can so I'm making you pasta."

"But you said—"

"I say a lot of things I don't mean."

He watched her as she turned the stove off, then took the pot of boiling pasta toward the sink. A bell sounded.

"Wanna get that for me?"

"Get what?" he asked.

"The microwave."

Valerius looked around the kitchen. In all his life, he'd seldom seen a kitchen and knew very little about the appliances that one cooked with. He had servants for such things.

The bell chimed again.

Assuming that was the microwave, he went to it and pulled the handle. Inside was a bowl of marinara. He took the fish-shaped potholder that was lying in front of the microwave and pulled the bowl out. "Where should I put this?"

"The stove, please."

He did as she said.

She brought a small bowl over to where he stood, then covered the pasta with sauce.

"Better?" she asked, handing it to him.

Valerius nodded, until his gaze dropped to the noodles. He blinked in disbelief as the shape of the pasta hit him.

No. Surely he was seeing things.

Was that a . . . ?

His jaw went slack as he realized that it was what it appeared. Little tiny pasta penises were swimming in the red marinara.

"Oh, come on," Tabitha said in an irritable voice. "Don't tell me a Roman general is having trouble with penironi."

"You don't honestly expect me to eat this?" he asked, aghast.

She huffed at him. "Don't you dare cop that superior attitude with me, buddy. I happen to know exactly how you Romans lived. How you decorated your houses. You come from the land of the phallus, so don't act so shocked that I gave you a bowl of them to eat. It's not like I have the flying phallus wind chime hanging in my house to ward off evil or something, but I'll bet you did when you were human."

It was true, but it had been centuries since . . . come to think of it, he'd never seen anything like *this*.

She handed him a fork. "It's not silver, but it is stainless steel. I'm sure you can make do."

He was still mesmerized by the pasta. "Where did you get this?"

"I sell it and boobaroni in my shop."

"Boobaroni?"

"I think you can figure that one out."

Valerius didn't know what to say to that. He'd never eaten obscene food before—and just what kind of shop did she own that she sold such commodities inside it?

"House of Vetti," Tabitha said, arms akimbo. "Need I say more?"

Valerius was well-versed about the Roman house she spoke of, as well as its risqué murals. True, his people had been rather overt with their sexuality, but he most certainly hadn't expected to come face to face with it in this modern age.

"Non sana est puella," Valerius said under his breath, which was Latin for *This girl is insane.*

"Quin tu istanc orationem hinc veterem antque antiquam amoves, vervex?" Tabitha shot back.

Would you stop using that obsolete language, you sheep-head?

Never before had Valerius been both insulted and amused at the same time. "How is it you speak Latin so perfectly?"

She pulled a piece of toast from her oven. "I have a master's degree in Ancient Civ. My sister, Selena, has her Ph.D. in it. We thought it was a goof in college to insult each other in Latin."

"Selena Laurens? The lunatic with a tarot-card table in the Square?"

She gave him a fierce glare. "That loon happens to be

my beloved big sister and if you insult her again, you'll be limping . . . more."

Valerius bit his tongue as he made his way to her table in the dining room. He'd met Selena several times over the last three years, and none of those encounters had gone well. When Acheron had first mentioned her, Valerius had been delighted at the prospect of having someone to talk to who knew his culture and language.

But as soon as Acheron had introduced them, Selena had tossed her drink into Valerius's face. She had called him every insult known to mankind and had even made up quite a few new ones.

He didn't know why Selena hated him so much. All she would say is that it was a shame he hadn't died under a barbarian stampede, ripped into pieces.

And that was one of her kinder wishes for his death.

It would most likely please her a great deal to know his real death had been far more humiliating and painful than any of her rants.

Every time he ventured into the Square to patrol for Daimons, she hurled curses at him, as well as anything else she had handy to throw in his direction.

No doubt she would be thrilled to find out her sister had stabbed him. Her only regret would be that he was still living and not lying dead in some gutter.

Tabitha paused in the doorway and watched as Valerius actually ate his pasta in silence. He held himself rigidly upright and his manners were impeccable. He appeared calm and composed.

But then he also looked so incredibly uncomfortable in her house. Not to mention out of place.

"Here," she said, moving forward to hand him the bread.

"Thank you," he said as he took it. He frowned as if looking for a bread plate. Finally, he set the bread down on the table and returned to his offbeat pasta.

There was an awkward silence between them. She didn't know what to say to him. It was weird to have this man in her presence when she'd heard so much about him.

None of which was good.

Her brother-in-law and his best friend Julian spent hours

at family parties, ranting about Valerius and his family and the fact that Artemis had transferred Valerius to New Orleans for pure spite because she hadn't wanted to let Kyrian go. Maybe that was true. Or maybe the goddess had only wanted Kyrian to face his past and put it firmly to rest.

Either way, the person who seemed to be punished most by Artemis's decision was Valerius, who was constantly reminded of Kyrian and Julian's hatred.

Funny how he didn't seem so bad to her.

True, he was arrogant and formal, but . . .

There was something more to him. She could feel it.

She went to the kitchen to get him something to drink. Her first thought was to give him water, but then, she'd already been vicious in giving him the penironi. It had been a childish impulse that she now felt extremely guilty over.

So she decided to break open her wine cabinet and get him something he would no doubt appreciate.

Valerius looked up as Tabitha handed him a glass of red wine. He half-expected it to be a harsh, cheap Ripple and was pleasantly surprised at the rich, full-bodied taste of it.

"Thank you," he said.

"You're welcome."

As she started away, he captured her hand and pulled her to a stop. "Why did you buy me new clothes?"

"How did you—"

"I found mine in the garbage."

She cringed as if it bothered her that he had learned what she'd done. "I should have emptied the can. Damn."

"Why didn't you want me to know?"

"I thought you might not take them. It was the least I could do since I was part of the reason they were ruined."

He offered her a smile that warmed her heart. "Thank you, Tabitha."

It was the first time he'd said her name. His rich, deep accent sent a shiver over her.

Before she could stop herself, she placed her hand against his cheek. She half-expected him to pull away.

He didn't. He merely stared up at her with those curious black eyes.

She was struck by his handsomeness. By his inner pain, which made her own heart ache for him. And before she could think better of it, she dipped her head down so that she could capture his lips with her own.

Valerius was completely unprepared for her action. Never had a woman initiated a kiss with him. Never. Tabitha was bold with her exploration, demanding, and it sizzled through his body like lava.

Cupping her face in his hands, he kissed her back.

Tabitha moaned at the decadent taste of her general. Her tongue brushed against his fangs, giving her a chill. He was lethal and deadly.

Forbidden.

And for a woman who prided herself on following no one's rules but her own, it made him even more appealing.

She straddled him in the chair and sat down in his lap.

He didn't protest. Instead, he dropped his hands from her face and trailed them over her back while she pulled the tie from his hair and loosened the thick, black strands that slid like silk against her fingers.

She could feel his erection as it pressed against the center of her body, igniting her desire even more.

It'd been so long since she'd been with a man. So long since she had felt a desire this potent to wrap herself around one. But she wanted Valerius badly, even though he should be completely off her menu.

Valerius's head swam as Tabitha trailed her lips along the length of his jaw, then under his chin, to his neck. Her hot breath blistered him. It had been centuries since he'd taken a woman who knew what he was.

A woman he didn't have to kiss carefully for fear of her discovering his fangs.

Not once had he ever been with a woman this exciting. One who met him so openly. So wildly. There was no fear whatsoever in this woman. No holding back.

She was fierce and passionate and completely feminine.

Tabitha knew she shouldn't be doing this. Dark-Hunters weren't allowed to get involved with women. They weren't allowed any emotional attachments at all except for maybe a Squire.

She could sleep with Valerius just once and then she would have to let him go.

But more than that, her entire family hated this man and she should, too. She should be repulsed by him. Only she wasn't. There was something about him that was irresistible.

Against all sanity and reason, she wanted him.

You're just horny, Tabby, let him go.

Maybe it was just that simple. It'd been almost three years since she'd broken up with Eric and in that time she hadn't been with anyone else. No one had even appealed to her as anything more than a passing curiosity.

Well, except for Ash, but she knew better than to make a move on him.

And even he didn't make her sizzle like this. But then, he didn't have the pain inside him that Valerius carried—or if he did, he was better at hiding it around her.

She felt as if Valerius needed her somehow.

Just as she reached for the zipper of his pants, the phone rang.

Tabitha ignored it until Marla used her walkie-talkie to say, "It's Amanda, Tabby. She says for you to pick up the phone. Now."

She groaned in frustration. She gave Valerius a hot, quick kiss before she got up. "Please don't say a word while I'm on the phone," she warned him.

Since Amanda had married Kyrian, she had become incredibly psychic, and if she heard Valerius's voice, she would know instantly who he was. Tabitha was sure of it. It was the last thing she wanted to deal with.

She picked up the wall phone in the kitchen. "Hey, Mandy, whatcha need?"

Tabitha turned to watch Valerius as he put himself back together. He pulled his hair back and replaced the small black tie she had removed.

He returned to being regal and rigid as he picked up his fork and began eating again.

Her sister was babbling on about a bad dream, but it wasn't until the term "Spathi Daimon" came up that Tabitha pulled her attention away from Valerius.

"I'm sorry, what?" she asked Amanda.

"I said that I had a bad dream about you, Tabby, that you were seriously hurt in a fight. I just wanted to make sure that you were okay."

"Yeah, I'm fine."

"Are you sure? You sound kind of strange to me."

"You interrupted me from work."

"Oh," Amanda said, accepting the lie, which made Tabitha feel a little guilty. Tabitha wasn't used to keeping anything from her twin. "Okay. In that case, I won't keep you. But you be careful for me. I have a really bad feeling that won't go away."

Tabitha felt it, too. It was something undefinable and at the same time persistent. "Don't worry. Ash is in town and there's an extra Dark-Hunter he moved in. Everything's fine."

"Okay. I'm trusting you to watch your back. . . . But, Tabby?"

"Yeah?"

"Stop lying to me. I don't like."

Chapter 3

Tabitha hung up the phone, feeling a little odd about her conversation. And she felt even odder about Amanda's prediction for her health. It concerned her a lot, especially when combined with her own uneasy feeling.

She'd almost died twice three years ago when Desiderius had been out to kill Amanda and Kyrian. Since then, no Daimon had gotten near her. Mostly because she had honed her skills and become much more observant.

But the ones last night . . .

They'd been tough kills and a group of them had gotten away. Surely they wouldn't be back. Most Daimons vacated the area very quickly after they ran into her or one of the Dark-Hunters. Courage wasn't exactly something they were known for: Since they were young and the idea was to stay alive, very few Daimons wanted to run head-to-head with Artemis's army, which was comprised of warriors with hundreds, if not thousands, of years of combat experience on them.

Only Desiderius—who had been a half-god—had possessed the strength and stupidity to fight the Dark-Hunters.

No, the Daimons from last night were gone and she would be fine. Amanda must have had bad chicken or something.

She returned to Valerius, who was finishing up his food. "What are your powers?" she asked.

He looked a bit taken aback by the question. "Excuse me?"

"Your Dark-Hunter powers. Do they include premonitions or precog?"

"No," he said before taking a drink of wine. "Like most Roman Dark-Hunters, I got rather, and please excuse the crassness of this, 'shafted' in that department."

Tabitha frowned. "How do you mean?"

He took a deep breath before he answered. "Artemis didn't care for the fact that in Rome, she wasn't a major deity. Rather, she was mostly revered by our lower classes, slaves and women. So she carried her grudge over to us when we were created. I'm stronger than a human and faster, but I don't have the elevated psychic powers that the rest of the Dark-Hunters do."

"Then how do you manage to fight the Daimons?"

He shrugged. "The same way you do. I battle more skillfully than they."

Yeah, maybe, but she often found herself bloody from her battles. She wondered how often he did, too. It was hard to fight a Daimon as a human.

"That's not right," Tabitha said, angry on his behalf that Artemis would create such a disparity among her Dark-Hunters. How could the goddess turn them loose, knowing what they were up against?

Man, Simi was right. Artemis *was* a bitch-goddess.

Valerius frowned at the anger he heard in Tabitha's voice. He wasn't used to anyone taking his side in any matter. Neither as a man nor as a Dark-Hunter. It had always seemed his ill fate to end up on the losing end of any matter regardless of whether he was right or wrong. "Few things ever are fair."

He drained the last of his wine and rose to his feet, then inclined his head to her. "I thank you for the food."

"Any time, Val."

He stiffened at her use of a nickname he despised. The only people to ever use it had been his brother Markus and his father, and then only to mock or belittle him. "My name is Valerius."

She looked at him dryly. "I can't call you Valerius. Jeez. It sounds like some broken-down Italian car. And every time

I hear that name I feel the deep need to break out into Vo-lar-ray, Oh, oh, oh—and then I start thinking of the movie *The Hollywood Knights* and believe me you don't want me to go there. So to save my sanity from that crappy song echoing in my head and images of a lunatic running around a high school gym doing unspeakable things, you can be known as Val or Babycakes."

His gaze darkened. "My name is Valerius and I will not answer to Val."

She shrugged. "Fine then, Babycakes, have it your way."

He opened his mouth to protest, but already he knew better than to argue. Tabitha had a way of doing just as she pleased, all arguments be damned. "Very well," he said grudgingly, "I shall endure Val. But only from you."

She smiled. "See how painless that is? Why would you hate the name, anyway?"

"It's coarse."

She rolled her eyes at him. "You must really be fun in bed," she said sarcastically.

Valerius was stunned by her words. "Excuse me?"

"I'm just wondering what it would be like to make love to a man who is so concerned about being rigid—then again . . . Nah. I can't imagine someone so regal getting down and dirty with it."

"I assure you, I've never had any complaints in that regard."

"Really? Then you must be sleeping with women who are so cold you could freeze ice cubes on them."

He turned to leave the room. "We are not having this discussion."

But she gave him no reprieve as she followed him toward the stairs. "Were you like this in Rome? I mean, from everything I've read, you guys were raw with sexuality."

"I can just imagine the lies they tell."

"So were you always this uptight?"

"What do you care?"

Her response stunned him as she pulled him to a stop. "Because I'm trying to figure out what made you like you are now. You are so closed off, you're barely human."

"I am not human, Ms. Devereaux. In case you haven't noticed, I'm one of the damned."

"Baby, open your eyes and look around. We're all damned in one way or another. But damned is a far cry from dead. And you live like you're dead."

"I'm that, too."

She ran a hot look over his scrumptious body. "For a dead man you look remarkably fit."

His face hardened. "You don't even know me."

"No, I don't. But the question is, do *you* know you?"

"I'm the only one who does."

And that simple sentence told her everything she needed to know about him.

He was alone.

Tabitha wanted to reach out to him, but could sense that she needed to give him some space. He wasn't used to interacting with people like her . . . then again, few were.

As Grandma Flora, the gypsy seer of their family, always said, Tabitha tended to come on to people like a freight train and mow them down where they stood.

Tabitha sighed as he took another step away from her. "How old are you, anyway?"

"Two thousand, one hundred—"

"No," she interrupted. "Not Dark-Hunter years. How old were you when you died?"

She felt a profound wave of pain go through him at the thought. "Thirty."

"Thirty? Jeez, you act like an old, wrinkled-up prune. Did no one laugh where you came from?"

"No," he said simply. "Laughter was not tolerated or indulged."

Tabitha couldn't breathe as his words sank in and she remembered the sight of the scars on his back. "Never?"

He didn't respond. Instead, he continued up her stairs. "I should retire now."

"Wait," she said, rushing up the stairs to sneak around him so that she could keep him still. She turned to face him.

She could feel turmoil inside him. Pain. Confusion. She knew just how hated this man was. Maybe he deserved it, but deep inside she wasn't so sure.

People didn't close themselves off from the world without reason. No one was happily this stoic.

And in that moment, she realized something. It was his defense mechanism. She got brash and wild whenever she was out of sorts or uncomfortable.

He turned cold. Formal.

That was his façade.

"I'm sorry if I said anything that offended you. My sisters often tell me that I've made offending people an art form."

A smile tugged at the edges of his lips and, if she didn't miss her guess, his eyes softened ever so slightly. "I wasn't offended."

"Good."

Valerius was tempted to stay here and talk to her, but he felt uncomfortable with the thought of it. He'd never been the kind of person other people chatted with. Even as a man, his conversations had revolved around battle tactics, philosophy, and politics. Never chit-chat.

His conversations with women had been even fewer than his conversations with men. Not even Agrippina had ever truly spoken to him. They had passed comments, but she had never shared her opinions with him. Merely agreed with him and did as he asked.

He had a feeling Tabitha would never agree with anyone, even if she knew they were right. It seemed a matter of principle that she had to disagree with everything.

"Are you always so outspoken?" he asked.

She smiled widely. "I know no other way."

Suddenly Lynyrd Skynyrd's "Gimme Three Steps" started playing on the radio.

Tabitha let out a small squeak of happiness and dashed down the stairs. Valerius barely had time to blink before she cranked the volume up, then ran back toward him.

"I love this song," she said as she danced to it.

Valerius found it hard to focus on much of anything except the sway of her hips as she danced and sang to the song.

"C'mon, dance with me!" she said at the first guitar solo. She ran up the stairs to take his hand.

"This isn't really dancing music."

"Sure it is," she said before she broke into the chorus.

In spite of himself, he was greatly amused by her. In all his lifetime, he'd never known anyone who enjoyed life so much, who took such pleasure from something so simple.

"C'mon," she tried again when the singing paused. "It's a great song. You have to admire anyone who can rhyme 'feller' with 'the head color yeller.'" She winked at him.

Valerius laughed.

Tabitha paused. "Oh, my God, he does know how to laugh."

"I know how to laugh," he said lightly.

She pulled him from the stairs and two-stepped around him before she used him as a maypole and continued dancing.

She let go, snapped her fingers and twisted down, then rose back up. "One day, I think you're going to bust out of those hand-polished loafers and actually cut loose."

Valerius cleared his throat and tried to imagine such a thing. It wasn't possible. There had been a time once, back when he'd been human, when he might have attempted it.

But those days were long gone.

Anytime he'd ever tried to be anything other than what he was, someone else had paid a terrible price for it. So he'd learned to stay as he was and to leave everyone else alone.

It was for the best.

Tabitha watched as his face turned to stone once again. She sighed. What would it take to reach this guy? For someone who was immortal, he certainly didn't seem to enjoy life very much.

In spite of all of Kyrian's faults, she had to give him credit. The former Greek general did enjoy every breath he took. He lived his life to its fullest.

Meanwhile, Valerius just seemed to exist.

"What do you do for fun?" she asked.

"I read."

"Literature?"

"Science fiction."

"Really?" she asked, surprised. "Heinlein?"

"Yes. Harry Harrison is one of my favorites, as are Jim Butcher, Gordon Dickson, and C. J. Cherryh."

"Wow," she said, amazed. "I'm impressed. Go, Dorsai."

"Actually, I rather like Dickson's *The Right to Arm Bears* and *Wolfling* novels better."

Now that she found surprising. "I don't know, *Soldier, Ask Not* seems more your style to me."

"It is a classic, but the other two spoke to me more."

Hmmm . . . *Wolfling* was about a man alone in an alien world with no friends or allies. That further confirmed her suspicions about his life. "Have you ever read *Hammer's Slammers*?"

"David Drake. Another favorite."

"Yeah, you have to love the military stuff. Burt Cole wrote a book years ago called *The Quick*."

"Shaman. He was quite the complex hero."

"Yeah, strangely amoral and yet moral at the same time. Never sure what side of the fence he's on. Kind of reminds me of a few friends I've had over the years."

Valerius couldn't keep from smiling. It was so nice to have someone who was familiar with his guilty secret. The only other person he knew who read science fiction was Acheron, but the two of them seldom ever talked about it.

"You're a remarkable woman, Tabitha."

She smiled up at him. "Thanks. Now, I'll let you go on to bed," she said gently. "I'm sure you could use the rest."

She ached to give him a tender, friendly kiss on the cheek, but thought better of it. Instead, she watched as he headed out of the room, up the stairs.

Valerius made his way silently back to Tabitha's room. She had such a powerful presence that he literally felt drained just from having been around her.

He removed his clothes and hung them back up so that he wouldn't wrinkle them, then returned to bed to sleep.

But sleep was something that didn't come to him. For the first time, he smelled the perfume on her sheets.

It was Tabitha's scent. Warm, vivacious. Seductive.

And it made him instantly hard for her. He covered his eyes with his hand and ground his teeth. What was he doing? The last thing he could do as a Dark-Hunter was have a relationship with a woman. Even if he could, Tabitha Devereaux was the last woman on the planet he could have.

As a friend to Acheron, she was so far off limits to him that he should call Acheron again and demand he find some way for Valerius to leave.

But Acheron had left them together.

Rolling over, he did his best not to breathe in deeply or to imagine what Tabitha might look like in this bed. Her bare limbs entwined . . .

He cursed, then pulled a second pillow over toward him. As he did so, he saw a small black silk gown. An image of Tabitha in it seared him.

He couldn't breathe. Before he could think better of it, he pulled it close and let the cool silk caress his skin. He held it to his nose and inhaled her scent.

She is not for you.

It was true. He'd already killed one woman because he'd been foolish. He had no desire to retread that path.

He tucked the gown back beneath his pillow and forced himself to close his eyes.

But even then, he was haunted by images of a woman who should, by all reason, repel him and yet completely captivated and beguiled him.

Tabitha spent the rest of the day between her store and walking to the foot of the stairs where she forced herself to reverse direction and go back to business.

But she felt a horrible pull toward the Dark-Hunter who slept in her bed. It was stupid. He was an ancient warrior who didn't seem to even like her.

Yet his kiss had said something else. There for a few minutes, he had been as eager for her as she had been for him. He wasn't completely repulsed by her.

She waited until four, then went to wake him.

Opening the door slowly, she paused as she caught sight of him asleep. He lay with his back to her, but what made her stop was the fierce scars that crisscrossed his flesh. Those weren't battle scars. They were the kind of marks you would find on someone who had been beaten with a whip. Many times.

She couldn't take her eyes off it. Without thinking, she crossed the room and placed her hand on his arm.

He rolled over with a hiss and seized her.

Before she even realized what he was going to do, he had her on the bed beneath him, with his hand at her throat.

"Let go of me, Valerius, or I'm going to hurt you bad."

He blinked as if he were coming out of a dream. His grip loosened immediately. "Forgive me," he said as he lightly stroked her neck. "I should have warned you not to wake me by touch."

"You always assault people when you wake up?"

Valerius couldn't speak as he felt the softness of her skin beneath his fingertips. In truth, he'd been dreaming of her. Only she had been in his world. Dressed in nothing but a pearl necklace and covered by rose petals.

She was incredibly beautiful. Her eyes were so blue. Her nose pert and her lips . . . they were the stuff of legends. Full and lush, they begged for his attention.

Before he could stop himself, he lowered his mouth to hers.

Tabitha moaned at the taste of Roman warrior. His kiss was tender and soft, a total antithesis to the steely feel of his body. It melted her as she wrapped her arms around his bare back and traced the scars she found there.

And she was all too aware of the fact that he was completely naked.

Valerius growled at the feel of her tongue lightly stroking his. Of her scent and soft curves wrapped around him. The denim of her jeans scraped against his flesh as she opened her legs and cradled him with those long, lush legs. She raked one hand through his hair, brushing it back from his face before she sank her hand deep and held him to her.

He lifted the hem of her sweater so that he could gently cup her breast through the satin of her bra. She moaned deep in her throat, a husky raw sound that sizzled through him.

As Tabitha had pointed out earlier to him, he'd spent far too many nights with women who had never reacted so openly to his touch. She ran her hands over his shoulders, then down to the small of his back.

All he could think of was taking her. Of sliding himself deep inside until they were both sated and weak.

As he fingered the front catch of her bra, a tiny shred of sanity reared its ugly head. She was not for him.

He pulled his hand away.

Tabitha cupped his head in her hands and pulled back. "I know what you are, Val. It's okay."

She took his hand into hers and led it back to her breast. She pushed the satin aside until he felt her hard, swollen nipple teasing his palm. He couldn't breathe as he cupped her soft breast. She was so warm, so welcoming that he found it hard to believe he was anything special to her.

"Do you sleep with all the Dark-Hunters?"

She stiffened. "What?"

"I was just wondering if you'd been with Acheron . . . Talon."

She bucked him off of her at that. "What kind of question is that?"

"I just met you and twice now you've offered yourself to me."

"Oh, you arrogant jerk!" She grabbed her pillow off the bed and assaulted him with it.

Valerius held his hand up to shield himself, but she didn't stop.

"You are so stupid! I can't believe you'd ask me such a thing. I swear, I will never again be in the same room with you!"

Finally the pillow bashing stopped.

He lowered his arm.

She nailed him with a final blow upside his head, then released the pillow. "For your information, buddy, I am not the town bike. I don't sleep with every guy I get near. I thought you were . . . Oh never mind. To hell with you!"

She turned and stormed out of the room. She slammed the door so hard that it actually rattled the windows and shook the beads on her mirror and altar.

Valerius lay on the bed completely stunned by what had just happened. She had beaten him with a pillow?

He knew from his encounter with her last night that she could have assaulted him with something much more painful, yet she had refrained.

In all honesty, he was relieved by her untoward reaction. Her indignation had been too great to be feigned.

And that brought a strange warmth to his chest. Could it be that she might actually like him?

No. It wasn't possible. No one liked him. They never had.

"You are worthless. I weep for the day Mother bore you into this world. I'm only glad that she died before she could see what an embarrassment you are to the family." He flinched at the harsh words that his brother Markus had repeatedly hurled at him.

His own father had despised him. *"You are weak. Pathetic. I should have seen you dead rather than waste the water and food it has taken to rear you."*

Their words were kind compared to what his Dark-Hunter brethren had uttered.

No, there was no way Tabitha "liked" him. She didn't even know him.

He didn't know why she was so receptive to his touch.

Maybe she was merely a woman of strong passion. He was a handsome man. Not that he was vain about it. It was a simple statement of fact. Countless women had offered themselves to him over the centuries.

But for some reason that didn't bear thinking on, he wanted something more than a one-night stand with Tabitha.

He wanted . . .

Valerius forced his thoughts away from that. He didn't need anyone, not even a friend. His life was best spent alone, far away from other people.

Getting up, he dressed and left her room to go downstairs. He met Marla in the dining room.

"Ooo, shug, I don't know what you did to Tabby, but you have her panties in a tight wad. She said to tell you to eat before she poisoned your food or did something worse to it."

Valerius was surprised to see veal marsala and an Italian salad with garlic bread waiting for him.

"Where did that come from?" he asked Marla.

"Tony's from down the street. Tabitha sent me over there to get it. She and Tony aren't on speaking terms at the moment. God love her, she tends to make everyone irritated with her. But he'll get over it. He always does."

Valerius took a seat and then bit into heaven. He'd never

tasted anything better. Why would Tabitha have gone to such trouble for him?

He was halfway through the meal before Tabitha came out of the door that led to her shop.

"I hope you choke on it," she snarled as she headed toward the kitchen.

Valerius swallowed his bite of food, wiped his mouth, then slid out of his chair to go after her.

"Tabitha?" He pulled her to a stop. "I'm sorry for what I said. It's just . . ."

"Just what?"

"People are never nice for no reason." And they were never nice to him.

Tabitha paused at that. Was he serious? "Was dinner okay?"

"It was delicious. Thank you."

"No problem." She pulled her hand away. "You probably know that it's already dark. I can get you home whenever you're ready."

"I just need to stop and pick up some lamp oil."

"Lamp oil? Don't you have electricity?"

"I do, but it's imperative that I get some tonight and get home."

"Okay. The chariot awaits four blocks over at my sister Tia's. We can grab the oil at her shop."

"She has lamp oil?"

"Yeah. She's a voodoo priestess. You probably saw the altar upstairs that she made for me. She's a bit offbeat, but we love her anyway."

Valerius inclined his head respectfully to her, then returned upstairs for his coat.

Tabitha was about to pick up his dishes when Marla shooed her away.

"I'll take care of that for you."

"Thanks, sweetie."

Marla wrinkled her nose. "Anytime. You two go and have a wild time for me. I want all the details."

Tabitha laughed as she tried to imagine what a "wild" time with Valerius might entail. It would probably be nothing more miraculous than getting him to wear a pair of tennis shoes and drink out of a paper cup.

Valerius rejoined her. She quickly ushered him out the shop door before Marla saw his coat and confiscated it.

He stopped so short inside her store that she actually ran into him. His jaw slack, he scanned the shop with a look of complete horror on his face. "Where are we?"

"My store," Tabitha said. "Pandora's Box on Bourbon. I cater to the strippers and drag queens."

"This is . . . it's a . . ."

"Adult store, yes, I know. I inherited it from my aunt when she retired. Now close your mouth and stop gulping. I make a lot of money and friends in this place."

Valerius couldn't believe what he was seeing. Tabitha owned a den of iniquity? Why was he even surprised?

"And this is exactly what has caused the Western world to decline," he said as she led him past a glass case of pasties and thongs.

"Oh, yeah, right," Tabitha said. "Like you wouldn't give your right arm to have a woman dressed in my stuff strip for you. Good night, Franny," she called to the woman behind the register. "Make sure you give Marla the receipts and deposit when you close up tonight, okay?"

"You got it, boss. Have a good night."

Tabitha led the way to the street. The city was already placing the barricades at the intersections that would turn Bourbon into an after-hours pedestrian mall. She hung a left onto Bienville Street toward her sister's house; all the while, she scanned for any suspicious activity.

Valerius remained remarkably silent.

As they neared the next intersection, she heard Valerius curse.

Two seconds later a lightning bolt struck him.

Chapter 4

Tabitha gasped as Valerius was thrown against a building from the lightning strike. Before she could take a step toward him, it literally started pounding rain on him and no one else. In fact, the *only* place it was raining was where Valerius lay on the ground.

"What on earth?" she asked.

Valerius took a deep breath as he slowly pushed himself to his feet. His lip was split, and he had a cut on his cheek from where he'd hit the building. Without a word, he wiped the blood off with the back of his hand, then felt the wound on his cheek.

He was soaking wet while the rain continued to fall on him in a pounding staccato beat. "It'll stop in a minute."

And it did.

Valerius wiped the water from his face and then wrung out his ponytail.

Tabitha was aghast. "What just happened?"

"My brother, Zarek," he said wearily as he shook his arms and sent water flying. "He was made a god a couple of years ago and has since turned me into his full-time occupation. It's why I no longer drive anywhere. I grew rather tired of my engine just falling out of my car for no apparent reason whenever I stopped for a light. The only safe mode of transportation I have is my feet and as you have just witnessed, not even it is completely safe." There was no missing the anger in his tone.

"Is my car safe?"

He nodded. "He only comes after me."

She started to approach him.

"Don't," he said, his breath suddenly forming a small cloud as he spoke. "It's freezing here."

Tabitha reached out her hand and felt the arctic air that surrounded Valerius. It was colder than a freezer where he stood. "Why does he do this to you?"

"He hates me."

"Why?" She felt a wave of shame come over him. "What did you do to him?"

He didn't answer. Instead, he breathed into his hands and headed down the street again.

"Valerius," she said, stopping him even though she wasn't sure she didn't get frostbite to her hand for the effort. "Talk to me."

"And say what, Tabitha?" he asked quietly. "I felt sorry for Zarek when we were children and every time I tried to help him, I only ended up hurting him more. He's right to hate me and everyone else in our family. I should have just left him alone and ignored him. It would have been better for all of us if I had."

"It's not wrong to help someone."

He gave her a dry stare. "My father always said, *'Nullus factum bonus incedo sine poena'*—No good deed goes unpunished. In Zarek's case, he made a point of proving it."

She was dismayed at what he was telling her. "I thought my family was odd. You guys sound like you really were the dysfunctional crew."

"You've no idea." He started back down the street.

Tabitha followed, but to be honest, she felt really sorry for him. She couldn't imagine having one of her siblings hate her. It was true they didn't all get along all the time. With eight sisters and a wide assortment of fruits and nuts in the family, there was always someone who wasn't talking to someone over something, but in the end, family was family and anyone who threatened them quickly got a dose of Devereaux solidarity.

Even if they weren't technically speaking to each other, they could always count on the family in a pinch. Even as kids. In high school, Tabitha had sworn she would never talk to her older sister Trina again because Trina had gone out with a guy she knew Tabitha had a crush on.

When the jerk had broken Trina's heart by two-timing her with a cheerleader, Tabitha had let loose Aunt Cora's prized boa constrictor in the guy's car. He'd been so scared, he'd wet his jeans before Tabitha had pulled the snake out.

It'd still taken two more days before she and her sister had reconciled. But they had reconciled. No one carried a grudge in their family for more than a few weeks. And no matter how angry they were, they would never, ever really hurt one another.

Goodness, what kind of family did Valerius have that two thousand years later his brother was still hurling lightning bolts at him?

By the time they reached her sister's shop, Val's eyebrows and lashes were frozen white. His skin had a terrible grayish tint to it.

"Are you okay?"

"It won't kill me," he said quietly. "Don't worry. He'll get bored in a few minutes and leave me alone for awhile."

"How long?"

"Usually a few months, sometimes longer. I never really know when he's going to strike. He likes to surprise me."

Tabitha was aghast at what she was witnessing. "Does Ash know he does this to you?"

"Zarek is a god now. What can Acheron do to stop it? Much like you with your brother-in-law, Zarek thinks it's fun to 'goof' on me."

"I'm never deliberately cruel to him. Well, maybe just the one time I sent him a box of Rogaine on his birthday, but that was just a gag gift until he opened the real one." She touched his ice-cold hands and realized he was shivering unmercifully.

Her heart ached for him. She blew into her hands and rubbed them together before she placed them to his face, which was so cold that it instantly took the heat from her skin.

He gave her a grateful look before he pulled back.

Suddenly a cloud of sulphuric something engulfed them.

Tabitha coughed at the rank smell before she held her nose and turned to see her sister Tia mumbling something she couldn't understand.

"What are you doing?" she asked.

"He got the evil funk of death on him. You weren't really going to bring him into my store like that, were you?"

"Yeah." She snatched the small wooden bowl out of Tia's hand. "Would you please lay off the nasty voodoo crap? It's stinks."

Tia reached for it. "Give me that."

"Quit grabbing or I'll dump it in the street."

Tia stood back instantly.

Tabitha looked at the reddish-gold powder and curled her lip at the rancid smell of it. "You know I really could have done without the Shower to Shower in poop. And here I was telling Val that my family wasn't so bad." She handed it back to Tia.

"You need protection," Tia said defensively. "There's something here. I can feel it."

"That might be your sanity. You might actually want to invite it in."

Tia gave her a peeved glare.

Tabitha smiled. "I'm just kidding. I know what you mean. I can feel it, too."

Tia looked up at Valerius, who was still shivering. "Why is he frozen and wet?"

"Long story," Tabitha said. She had a feeling Valerius wouldn't appreciate her telling her sister about his psycho brother. "This is my sister Tiyana. Tia for short."

"Hi," Tia said before she grabbed Valerius's arm and pulled him toward the entrance to her store.

He gave Tabitha a panicked look.

"It's okay. She's mostly nuts, but doesn't have a mean bone in her body."

"I don't want to hear about my insanity from the loon who stalks vampires in her spare time. You should see her," Tia said to Valerius as she hauled him through the narrow shop that was lined with shelves of all manner of gris-gris, charms, voodoo dolls, candles, and tourist items. "She thinks any guy in black is a vampire. Have you any idea how many men in New Orleans wear black? She's frightening. Really."

Tia turned toward her clerk. "Chelle, watch the store for a minute," she said to her employee, who was stickering a new batch of alligator-tooth key rings.

Tia led them through the back door to the storeroom. She sat Valerius down on a barstool and then pulled out a large box of Mexican ponchos, before she grabbed several of them and wrapped Valerius in them.

She went to the bathroom and came out with a towel. "Dry his hair while I make him something warm to drink."

"Thanks, sis," Tabitha said as she took the towel from her.

Valerius was taken aback by the untoward kindness. No one had ever treated him this way . . . like he mattered. Like they cared. "I can dry my own hair."

"Stay under the ponchos and get warmed up," Tabitha said as she pulled the tie from his ponytail.

Her tenderness amazed him as she carefully towel-dried his hair, then combed it with her fingers.

Tia came back with a large, steaming skeleton mug that had a warm, odd smell to it. "Don't worry. It's not a potion. Just a homemade cinnamon-chocolate blend that I sell at Christmas that's supposed to ward off melancholy." She handed it to him.

"Does it work?" he asked.

"On most people. The chocolate stimulates endorphins to perk you up and the cinnamon makes most people think of home and mother's love." Tia smiled. "You'd be amazed how much science there is in magic."

Valerius took a hesitant drink. It was surprisingly good and did in fact warm him. "Thank you," he said.

Tia nodded. "You guys here for your car?" she asked Tabitha.

"Yeah. I didn't mean for us to disturb you."

"It's okay. I was waiting for Amanda to show up. I called her earlier and told her I made a talisman for her and Marissa."

Tabitha went cold. It wouldn't do for Amanda to find Valerius here. She was sure her sister wouldn't understand how she could be helping him. Not that Tabitha was ashamed for what she was doing, but it was still a complication she wanted to avoid for all their sakes. "Cool, but we need to get going. We have some things to do. Give Mandy a kiss for me."

"Will do."

Tabitha motioned for Valerius to follow her out the back door that led to the courtyard where Tia's Mitsubishi was parked beside her Mini Cooper.

She unlocked the car for him. "Get in, I'll be right back."

Valerius did as she asked and was surprised that the car had more leg room inside than what it appeared to have from the outside. Even so, he felt a bit cramped in it.

She ran back into the store and came out a few minutes later with a plastic sack. She got into the car and handed it to him.

"Your lamp oil," she said.

He was stunned that she had remembered it, especially since it had slipped his own mind. "Thank you."

She didn't say anything as she started the car and backed them out of the driveway. As soon as they were on the street, she popped the gear into drive and squealed off.

He sat quietly while she weaved them in and out of traffic at a rate that would have left him terrified had he not been immortal.

The interior of the car was so tiny compared to what he was used to that it was hard not to notice her. She drove like she lived: fast and on the edge.

"Why are you so intense?" he asked as she took a corner he swore left the car with only two wheels on the ground.

"My mother says I was born that way. She thinks Amanda must have gotten both shares of restraint while I took all the courage."

She turned serious as she shifted gears and whipped around a slow-moving car. "Actually, that's not true. The fact is that I'm what some call a magnet. My psychic powers don't lie in special abilities like my sister Amanda's do. Mine are more quiet. Intuition, psychometry. Things that are virtually useless to a human, but are highly prized by the Daimons."

She paused at a light on Canal Street and looked at him.

"I was only thirteen when the first group of Daimons attacked me. I would be dead now if Talon hadn't saved me."

Valerius frowned at her words. She was right. Magnets gave off a powerful lure to Daimons. With her fierce nature and zest for living, she would be all the more alluring to them.

"Unlike most humans, I wasn't allowed to live in ignorance of your world. It was either learn to defend myself or end up dead. No offense, dead doesn't appeal to me."

"No offense taken. Having been dead for more than two thousand years, I can't exactly recommend it myself."

She laughed at that. "I don't know. Dead and in Armani. I think most people would be hurling themselves off buildings if they could come back loaded like you."

"I had just as much money as a mortal man and a lot more . . ." He let his voice trail off as he realized he'd almost said *friends*. That wasn't really true, but at least back then people who openly disdained him, with the exception of his family, generally kept it to themselves.

It wasn't something he liked to think or talk about.

"Lot more what?" she asked when he didn't finish his sentence.

"Nothing."

Valerius directed her to his house on Third Street down in the Garden District.

Tabitha let out a low whistle as they neared it. She pulled into the drive, which was shielded by a variety of greenery and stopped before the large, wrought-iron gate. She lowered her window and pressed the button on the security box.

"Yes?"

He leaned forward and spoke loudly. "It's Valerius, Gilbert. Open the gate."

The gates opened a few seconds later.

"Nice," Tabitha said as she drove down his circular drive and parked before the front door, right behind what appeared to be a run-down primer and red Chevy IROC that must belong to one of Valerius's employees. She couldn't imagine Val being caught dead in it and since he *was* dead . . .

"I take it that isn't yours, or did your brother just get really pissed off one day and nail it?"

Valerius didn't comment.

Tabitha paused to stare at the fountain in the bend of the drive that had blue lights at night. It was a tribute to the goddess Minerva and had been one of the reasons Valerius had chosen this as his home.

"Does Artemis know about that statue?"

"Since I'm still breathing, I rather doubt it," he said quietly.

He led her up the old stone steps. As soon as they reached the door, Gilbert opened it.

"Good evening, my lord." His butler didn't comment on the fact that Valerius was coming home wet. There was something about the rigid, older Englishman that reminded Tabitha of Alfred from *Batman*.

"Evening, Gilbert." He stood aside to let the older man see Tabitha. "This is Ms. Devereaux."

"Very good, sir." Gilbert inclined his head stiffly to Tabitha. "Charmed, madam." Then he looked back at Valerius. "Would your lordship and madame care for something to drink or eat?"

Valerius looked at her.

"I'm fine."

"No, thank you, Gilbert."

The butler inclined his head to them, then headed toward the back of the house.

Valerius led her toward the left. "If you would, please wait in the library and I'll be back in a few minutes."

"Where are you going?" she asked, wondering at his suddenly somber mood.

"I need to change into something dry."

She nodded. "Okay."

He headed up the stairs.

Tabitha wandered through the arched doorway into a dark room that was covered from floor to ceiling with books. She was in a corner skimming titles when she felt someone come into the room behind her.

She turned to find a handsome man around her own age staring at her.

"Amanda? What the hell brought you here?"

"I'm not Amanda," she said, crossing the room so that he could see her scarred face. "I'm her sister Tabitha. And you are?"

"Otto Carvalletti."

"Ah," she said in understanding. "Val's Squire."

"Yeah, don't remind me."

She didn't need her empathy to feel his rancor. "Why do you serve someone you hate?"

"Like I have a choice. The council sent me here, so here I am, locked in hell."

"Bud, I don't know where you hail from, but I take exception to people who hate my town."

He scoffed at that. "I got no problem with New Orleans. I love this town. It's Count Penicula that I take issue with. Have you met him?"

"Count who?"

"The dick who lives here. Valerius. You know, old 'Don't breathe in my presence, you prole.' "

This had to be the strangest man Tabitha had ever met— and given the odd crew of friends she had, that said a lot. "Prole as in proletariat?"

He looked relieved that she got it. "Oh, thank God you have a brain."

She wasn't sure if she should feel complimented or not. "I'm still confused. Why did the Squire's Council send you here? Don't they know how you feel about him?"

"Since my father happens to be one of the board members, yes, they know. Unfortunately, no one else will take this post. And since Lord Valerius demanded someone who could speak Italian *and* Latin there weren't that many of us to choose from. Pompous windbag."

"What's so pompous about wanting someone who speaks your native tongue? I noticed Talon has taught Sunshine Gaelic; and every time Julian and Kyrian get around Selena, they immediately break into ancient Greek."

"Yeah, but they don't demand that their Squires know it. Notice Nick ain't real swift in Greek."

Tabitha snorted. "Nick's not real swift in English most of the time."

"Hey now, don't insult my friend."

"Nick happens to be one of my friends too and I love him like a brother, but that doesn't make it open season on Valerius."

"Yeah, right. Hon, you should invest in a textbook and read up on what Valerius Magnus did in his lifetime."

She folded her arms over her chest and cocked her head. "Excuse me, Mr. Carvalletti, I'll have you know I hold a master's in Ancient Civ. Do you?"

"No, I hold a doctorate from Princeton."

She was impressed in spite of herself. Princeton didn't let in stupid people. "In Ancient Civ?"

"No. Film Studies," he said in a low tone.

"Pardon?" she asked, her eyes wide. "Did you say film?" She was aghast at that. "You majored in movies? Oh, and I was almost impressed."

"Hey," he said defensively, "I'll have you know I worked my ass off for that degree, thank you very much."

"Oh, yeah, right. I was a Fulbright Scholar. Did you ever attend a school where Daddy didn't put up a building?"

"My father didn't put up a building there . . ." He paused before adding, "My great-grandfather did."

Tabitha snorted. "I'm sorry, but I had to learn four languages to get my degree. What about you?"

"None. I grew up speaking twelve."

"Well aren't you Mr. Fancy Pants? Ooo, and you have the nerve to crack on Val? At least he doesn't walk around flaunting his superior intellect."

"No, he just flaunts his superior breeding. Bow down before me, all you plebeian scum."

"Maybe he wouldn't act that way if all of you weren't damned nasty to him all the time."

"*I'm* nasty to *him*? Lady, you don't even know me."

Tabitha backed off, especially since she felt his hurt. "You're right, Otto, I don't know you and I'm probably doing the same thing to you that you did to Val when you met him. I took one look at you, listened to three seconds of your conversation, and made some really harsh judgments that could be wrong just as easily as they could be right."

She approached him with her hands clasped behind her back. "Case in point. Your hair, while attractive, is shaggy, but it's that kind of shabby-chic that only comes from a really expensive beautician. You haven't shaved in what? Two days?"

"Three."

She ignored him. "You're wearing a loud, obnoxiously bright red Hawaiian shirt that I know belongs to Nick because he only wears it whenever he wants to jerk Kyrian's chain. He had to special-order it online for the mere tackiness of it alone. You're barefoot and I saw the beater IROC outside, which, I assume now, is yours."

He stiffened noticeably, which confirmed her suspicion.

She continued her summation. "At first glance, you look like one of those out-of-work party guys who come into my shop browsing the video closet that we keep in back because no self-respecting woman will go out with you. The kind of guy who buys all the naked boob and fornicating Mardi Gras beads to hang around his neck and then spends the entire week drunk and puking, screaming at women to show him their cans."

He folded his arms and gave her a sullen glare.

"Now let's contrast that with a few other facts I've noticed. You're a Squire and from your own admission you're a Blue Blood, which means you come from entire generations of Squires. Your family has had more money than God for a long time. You actually went to Princeton, and even with a laughable major, you went through the trouble of getting a doctorate. That tells me that status does mean something to you. Let me guess: That really cool, metallic black Jag that literally glistens in darkness that Nick has parked at his house and yet never drives is actually yours."

She paused beside him and looked him up and down. "Not to mention you carry yourself like a man used to being respected, even while trying to pretend to be a tasteless slob. Anyone with even an ounce of perception isn't fooled by the tough way you stand."

She lifted his hand, where a spiderweb was tattooed. "Nice watch," she said dryly. "Patek Philippe Grand Complications Chronographs. Let me guess: it's the 5004P which sells for one hundred fifty thousand dollars."

"How do you know that?"

"I come from a long line of store owners and my Aunt Zelda has a jewelry store." She held her arm up to him.

"Look, see my coffin watch? It retails for thirty-two dollars at Hot Topic and it has the same time yours does. It takes a Daimon licking and keeps on ticking."

He rolled his eyes at her.

Tabitha continued her rant. "And you're not just a regular Squire." She tapped the spiderweb tattoo on the back of his hand that all Squires of his ilk were marked with. "You're a Blood Rite. Why, Dr. Carvalletti, I do believe that in real life, you're not too far away from being just like Val yourself. Tough, arrogant, and willing to do whatever is necessary to get your job done."

She tilted her head. "I think what bothers you most is that if you were a Dark-Hunter, you'd be just like him. I think it kills you to know exactly how similar the two of you are. Where is your black Armani suit hanging? Nick's house?"

"What are you? Friggin' Sherlock Holmes?"

She smiled. "Pretty much, except it usually doesn't take me as long to get to the truth."

He looked at her stonily. "I don't need you to teach me a moral lesson, babe. I know how the world works."

"I've no doubt about that. But you have a lot to learn about people. What they say and what they feel are seldom the same. I know right now that you hate my guts. You would like nothing better than to toss my ass out of here and slam the door shut. But notice you haven't done either one of those to me."

"So what's your point?"

"My point is this. Blood Rite Squires are the ones charged with keeping the dictates of the Council and keeping the lid on the Dark-Hunter world. That means they are willing to take whatever steps are necessary, including murder, to protect their secrets. I am sure somewhere in your past, you have had to do something distasteful to you in order to uphold your Squire's oath and perform your duties. When you were reading that textbook about Valerius did you ever wonder how much of it he enjoyed? Or did he simply do what he did because it was his job?"

Otto cocked his head at her. "Anyone ever tell you you should be an attorney?"

"Only Bill when we argue. Besides, I like killing bloodsuckers too much to ever be one of them." She held her hand out to him. "Tabitha Devereaux. Pleased to meet you."

His confusion engulfed her. He hesitated before he shook her proffered hand.

"Don't worry, Otto," she said with a smile. "I'm an acquired taste. Most of my best friends had to know me for years before they could even stand my presence. I'm like mold, I usually grow on you very slowly."

"You said it, not me."

She patted his arm. "Do me a favor, be nice to Penicula. I think there's a lot more to him than what we see."

"You're the only person I know who feels that way."

"Yeah, well, I guess I feel like all of us misfits need to hang together. At least that way we don't swing alone."

He gave her a confused scowl, but before he could comment, his cell phone rang.

Tabitha stepped away from him to give him privacy with his call. She wandered toward the foyer to ogle the really impressive tile work on the floor.

It wasn't until she stood in the doorway that she saw Valerius standing on the bottom stair. At first glance, he might pass for one of the statues that flanked the stairs, but unlike them he was flesh and blood.

Valerius stared at Tabitha as her words rang in his head. To his knowledge, no one had ever defended him. Not once in all of his two thousand years of life and death.

Even if they had, he doubted they would have done so so eloquently. She was in the shadow of his doorway, her long auburn hair framing a face that was open and honest.

The face of a woman who wasn't afraid to stand up to anyone or anything. He'd never known anyone more courageous.

"Thank you," he said quietly.

"You heard?"

He gave a subtle nod.

"How much did you hear?"

"A lot."

She appeared uncomfortable with that. "You could have let us know you were here. It's not nice to eavesdrop."

"I know."

She moved to stand before him.

Valerius descended his step. He wanted to pull her into his arms and kiss her so badly, but he couldn't.

She was human while he wasn't. The last time he had deigned to feel compassion for a woman who wasn't meant for him, he had caused her the pain no woman should ever have to bear and himself death.

It still didn't stop his body from craving Tabitha. His heart from feeling a strange pang over the fact that she had stood up for him.

Before he could stop himself, he reached out and cupped her scarred cheek with his hand.

He'd been alone for so long. Isolated. Hated.

And this woman . . .

She filled some inner emptiness that he had forgotten was even there.

Tabitha's heart pounded at the warmth of his hand on her face. The gentleness she saw in his dark eyes and the gratitude she sensed inside him. No, he wasn't what Otto thought.

He wasn't cold and unfeeling. Brutal or vicious. If he were, she'd know it. She'd feel it.

None of that was there. She sensed only loneliness and pain from him.

She covered his hand with hers and offered him a smile.

To her surprise, he returned it with one of his own. It was the first time she'd seen a real smile from him. The gesture softened his features and tugged at her heart.

He dipped his head toward hers.

Tabitha opened her lips, wanting to taste him.

"Hey, Valerius?"

He jerked upright as she fought back a curse at Otto's timing.

Valerius stepped away from her two seconds before Otto came into the foyer. "Yes?"

"I'm heading out for the night. I'm going to meet up with Tad and Kyl from the Dark-Hunter Web site. I'll have my phone on if you need anything." Otto's gaze slid to hers and she felt his disdain.

Tabitha smiled at him. "Night, Otto. Don't let Tad get you into trouble."

"You know Tad, too?"

"Babe, I know almost everyone in this town."

"Great," Otto muttered under his breath as he headed for the door.

As soon as the door closed behind him, Valerius started past Tabitha.

For some reason she couldn't fathom, she reached out and caught his head in her hand.

Startled, he opened his mouth.

Unable to resist the temptation, she stood on her tiptoes and kissed him.

Chapter 5

Tabitha was completely unprepared for his reaction to her kiss. In one swift, tender motion, he pulled her to him, lifted her off her feet, spun about, and then laid her down on the polished stairs. It wasn't the most comfortable of positions, but it was strangely erotic.

Still, it was no match for his hot, demanding kiss that left her weak and breathless. His long, masculine body lay between her legs as he kept all of his weight on one knee. She could feel his erection pressing against the center of her body as her own body burned to feel him like this naked.

The rich, delicious scent of him tore through her, exciting her even more.

There was nothing civilized or proper about the way he kissed her. Nothing civilized about the way he held her. It was raw and earthy. Promising.

Tabitha wrapped her legs around his lean waist as she returned his kiss full force.

Valerius couldn't think as he tasted her. Felt her. She cocooned him with her warmth and passion.

And it was all he could do not to take her on the stairs like some barbarian warlord.

"You have to stop kissing me, Tabitha," he breathed raggedly.

"Why?"

He hissed as she gently nipped his chin. "Because if you don't, I'm going to make love to you and that is the last thing either one of us needs."

Tabitha traced the outline of his lips with her tongue as he spoke. All she wanted was to strip off his clothes and explore every inch of his lush, male body with her mouth. To lick and tease him until he begged her for mercy.

But he was right. It was the last thing either of them needed. He was a Dark-Hunter forbidden to have a girlfriend and even worse, he wasn't the kind of guy she could ever introduce to her family.

They would all turn on her for befriending her brother-in-law's most hated enemy. Kyrian had been more than accepted into her large family. Everyone loved him.

Even Tabitha did. How could she hurt him this way?

No, it wasn't fair to any of them.

"All right," she said quietly. "But you'll have to get off me first."

That was the hardest thing Valerius had ever done. All his heart wanted was to stay right where he was. But he couldn't and he knew it.

Taking a deep breath, he forced himself to get up and help her to her feet.

His body was still hard, his breathing a struggle. He couldn't stand to be close to her without touching her. But then, he was used to restraint.

He had been bred to it.

What he had never expected was the almost animal-like need he had to take her. It was primitive and demanding. Fierce. And the only thing it craved was a taste of Tabitha.

"I suppose this is where we part company," he said, his voice catching.

Tabitha nodded. He passed so close to her that she could smell his raw, innately masculine scent. It made her heart pound and fueled her desire even more.

It was all she could do not to reach out for him. Aching, she watched him open the front door to his house.

"Thank you, Tabitha," he said quietly.

She felt his sadness and it made her hurt all the more. "Stay out of trouble, Val. Try not to get stabbed again."

He nodded and kept himself rigid and formal. But he refused to look at her.

Sighing wistfully over something that couldn't be helped, Tabitha forced herself to leave.

It was over.

Impulsively, she looked back as the door closed. There was no sign of Valerius. None.

Except for a sixth sense that told her he was still watching her.

Valerius couldn't take his eyes off Tabitha as she got into her car. He had no comprehension of why he felt the compulsion to run out of the door and stop her.

She wasn't like Agrippina. Tabitha wasn't soothing or comforting, and yet . . .

His heart ached as she whipped her car out of his driveway and herself out of his life.

He was alone again.

But then, he'd always been alone. Even when Agrippina had lived within his household, he had kept to himself. He'd watched her from afar. Lusted for her every night and yet he'd never touched her.

It wasn't his place. He'd been a nobleman and she nothing more than a low-born slave who served in his household. Had he been one of his brothers, he would have taken her without question. But it hadn't been in him to take advantage of her. To force her to his bed.

She wouldn't have dared deny him. Slaves had no control whatsoever over their lives, especially not when it involved their masters.

Every time he had seen her, it had been on the tip of his tongue to ask her to sleep with him.

And every time he had opened his mouth, he had quickly clamped it shut and refused to ask her something she had no say about. So, he had brought her into his household to save her from what the other members of his family would have done to her.

Valerius winced as he remembered the night his brothers had come for him. The night they had found her statue and realized who it was.

Cursing, he turned away from the window and forced all those thoughts out of his mind.

It had never been his destiny to help anyone.

He had been born to be alone. To know no friends or confidants. To never laugh or play.

There was no fighting destiny. No hope for anything more. He was born to this life just as he had been born to his previous one.

Tabitha was gone.

And it was for the best.

His chest tight, he made his way up the mahogany stairs toward his room. He would shower, re-dress, and then do the job he had sworn himself to.

Tabitha drove her car back to Tia's, where she saw Amanda's Toyota on the street. She pulled in and was getting out as Amanda and Tia came out the back door.

"Hey, Mandy," Tabitha said, closing the distance so she could hug her twin.

"So who was the gorgeous man you were with? Tia said you didn't tell her his name."

Tabitha forced herself not to send any unconscious thought or emotion out to her twin sister. "He's just a friend."

Amanda shook her head. "Tabby," she chided. "You need to stop hanging out with your gay friends and find a boyfriend."

"He didn't seem gay to me," Tia said. "But he was well dressed."

"So where's baby M?" Tabitha asked, trying to get both of them off the topic.

"At the house. You know how Ash is. He refuses to let her leave the premises once the sun goes down."

Tabitha nodded. "Yeah, I agree with him. She's a very special little girl in need of protection."

"I agree too, but I hate leaving my baby behind. I feel like I'm missing a vital organ." Amanda held up her silver talisman. "Tia made me promise to hang it in Marissa's room."

"Good advice."

Amanda frowned at her. "Are you sure you're okay? There's something very odd about you tonight."

"There's always something odd about me."

Amanda and Tia laughed. "True," Amanda agreed. "All right, I'll quit worrying then."

"Please. One mother is quite enough."

Amanda kissed her on the cheek. "I'll see you guys later."

Neither Tabitha nor Tia spoke until after Amanda had gotten into her car and left. Tabitha put her hands in her pockets and turned to face her sister's scowl.

"What?"

"Who was he, really?"

"What is it with you guys? He was nobody for you to worry about."

"Was he a Dark-Hunter?"

"Stop it, Gladys," Tabitha said, referring to the nosy neighbor from *Bewitched*, the show that had given Tabitha her name. "There's no bonus round here for Twenty Questions and I've got stuff I need to do. See ya."

"Tabitha!" Tia followed her toward the street. "It's not like you to be secretive about anything. It makes me nervous."

Tabitha took a deep breath and faced her older sister. "Look, he was just someone who needed some help and I gave it. Now he's back to his life and I'm back to mine. We don't need a family powwow over it."

Tia made a noise of disapproval at her. "You are so aggravating. Why can't you just answer my one question?"

"Good night, Tia. Love you." Tabitha kept walking and was grateful her sister stopped and went back toward her shop.

Relieved, she headed for Bourbon Street with no real destination. She'd pick up some food for the homeless and then do her rounds.

"Oh, it's Tabitha!"

She turned at the distinctive singsongy voice she knew extremely well. Rushing up behind her was Ash's demon, Simi, who externally appeared to be a nineteen- or twenty-year-old woman. Tonight Simi had on a black miniskirt, purple leggings, and a risqué corset top. She wore a pair of black thigh-high stiletto boots and carried a PVC coffin purse. Her long black hair was loose about her shoulders.

"Hey, Simi," Tabitha said, scanning the street behind the demon. "Where's Ash?"

She rolled her eyes and let out a disgusted noise. "He got waylaid by that old heifer-goddess who said she had to speak to him and so I said I was hungry and that I wanted to eat something. So he said, 'Simi, don't eat no people. Go to Sanctuary and wait for me while I talk to Artemis.' So here the Simi is going to Sanctuary all alone to wait for *akri* to come and get her. You going to Sanctuary, Tabitha?"

It always amused Tabitha that the demon referred to herself in the third person. "Not really. But if you want me to walk with you that way, I can."

A man whistled as he walked past them while he eyeballed Simi.

The demon gave him a sultry glance and a small smile.

He headed back toward them. "Hey, baby," he said. "You looking for company?"

Simi huffed. "Are you blind, human?" she asked. She gestured dramatically toward Tabitha. "Can't you see the Simi has company?" She shook her head.

He laughed at that. "You got a number I can call and talk to you sometime?"

"Well, I do have a number, but if you call it, *akri* will answer and he will get all angry at you and then your head gonna explode into fire." She tapped her chin. "Hmmm, come to think of it, barbecue . . . It's 555—"

"Simi . . ." Tabitha said in a warning tone.

"Oh, poo," Simi said as she let out another disgusted breath. "You are right, Tabitha. *Akri* just get all mad at me if the Simi makes him make this man barbecue. He can be so particular sometimes. I swear."

"*Akri?*" the man asked. "Is he your boyfriend?"

"Oh no, that's just sick. *Akri* my daddy and he get all upset whenever a man looks at the Simi."

"Well, what Daddy doesn't know won't hurt him."

"Yeah," Tabitha said, stepping between them. "Trust me, her 'Daddy' isn't someone you want to mess with." She took Simi's arm and led her away.

The man followed. "C'mon, I just want her number."

"It's 1-800-get-a-clue," Tabitha called over her shoulder.

"Fine, bitch, have it your way."

Before Tabitha could blink, Simi broke her hold and lunged at the man. She grabbed him by his neck and threw him up against the side of a building where she held him effortlessly while his feet were about a foot off the ground. "You don't talk to the Simi's friends like that. You hear me?"

He couldn't respond. His face was already turning purple, his eyes bulging.

"Simi," Tabitha said, trying to pull the demon's hand away from the man's throat. "You'll kill him. Let go."

The demon's brown eyes flashed red a second before Simi released him. Bending double, he coughed and wheezed as he struggled to breathe again.

"You better never insult another lady, you stupid human," she said. "The Simi means that, too."

Without another word or thought about the matter, Simi swung her purse over her shoulder and sashayed down the street as if she hadn't almost killed someone.

Tabitha's heart was still pounding. What would have happened had she not been there to stop Simi?

"So, Tabitha, do you have any more of them yummy mints that you gave to the Simi when we went to the movies?"

"Sorry, Simi," she said, trying to regain some composure as she watched the poor guy stumble down the street. No doubt it would be quite awhile before he tried to pick up another woman he didn't know. "I didn't bring them with me."

"Oh poo, I really liked them. I especially liked that green tin. It was very nice. The Simi needs to make *akri* buy her some."

Yeah, and Tabitha needed to make sure Ash didn't let his demon loose unattended anymore. Simi wasn't evil, she just didn't understand right or wrong. In the demon's world, there wasn't such a concept.

Simi only understood Ash's orders and she carried them out to the letter.

But at least they were headed somewhere where most of the people knew and understood Simi. Sanctuary was a biker bar at 688 Ursulines Avenue that was owned by a family of Were-Hunters. Unlike the Dark-Hunters, the Were-Hunters were cousins of the cursed Apollites and Daimons with one profound difference: They were also half-animal.

Aeons ago, the Were-Hunters had originally been half-Apollite, half-human. In an effort to save his sons from dying at twenty-seven as the Apollites did, their creator had magically spliced animal essence with his sons' bodies.

The result had created two sons who possessed human hearts and two who held animal hearts. Those who were human were called Arcadians and those who were animals were called Katagaria. The Arcadians spent most of their lives as humans who could take animal form, whereas the Katagaria were animals who could take human form.

Even though they were related, the two groups warred against each other because the Arcadians thought their animal cousins were lesser beings and the animals fought because that was their nature.

It was a Katagaria bear pack who owned the bar. Inside the walls of Sanctuary, anyone was welcomed. Human, Apollite, Daimon, god, Arcadian, or Katagaria. There was only one rule: You don't bite me and I won't bite you.

Sanctuary was one of the few sacred areas on this planet where no paranormal being could attack another. And the bears would gladly keep Simi occupied until Ash was able to rejoin her.

Simi chattered endlessly until they reached the saloon-style doors of the bar.

"Are you coming inside?" she asked Tabitha.

Before she could answer, Tabitha saw Nick Gautier headed toward them. Since Nick's mother worked at the bar, he was an almost constant visitor there.

"Ladies," he said with a charming smile as he joined them.

"Nick," Tabitha said in greeting.

Simi smiled warmly. "Hi, Nick," she said, twisting a strand of hair around her finger. "You going into Sanctuary, too?"

"I was planning on it. What about you two?"

Tabitha's phone rang. "Hang on," she said to Nick and Simi before she answered it.

It was Marla in hysterics.

"What?" Tabitha asked, trying to understand Marla's words that came out in staccato between her sobs.

She glanced at Nick, who was watching her with a frown. "How about Nick Gautier—"

The question was cut off by Marla's scream of terror.

"Okay, okay," Tabitha said, realizing immediately why Marla was upset. Nick was wearing one of his heinous Hawaiian shirts along with ragged blue jeans and a pair of tennis shoes that looked as if they'd been fed to a garbage disposal. "Stop crying and get dressed. I'll get someone, I promise."

Marla sniffed. "You swear?"

"Cross my heart."

"Thank you, Tabby. You're a goddess!"

Tabitha had serious doubts about that as she hung up. "Nick, can you entertain Simi for a little while? I have to go prevent a disaster."

Nick grinned. "Sure, *chèr*. I'll be more than happy to keep Simi company if she doesn't mind."

Simi shook her head. "You know, I really like them blue-eyed people," she said to Tabitha. "They's all quality."

"You two have a good time," Tabitha said as she left them and rushed for Chartres Street.

Valerius was blow-drying his hair when he heard a commotion in his bedroom. It sounded like Gilbert and . . .

Turning off the dryer, he left the bathroom to find Gilbert trying to pull Tabitha out of his bedroom.

"Forgive me, my lord," Gilbert said as he released Tabitha. "I was coming to let you know you had a visitor when she followed me into your rooms."

Valerius couldn't breathe as he saw the impossible. Tabitha back in his home.

An unexpected happiness consumed him, but he refused to even smile.

"It's all right, Gilbert," he said, amazed at how even his tone was when all he really wanted to do was grin like an imbecile at her. "You may leave us."

Gilbert inclined his head before he obeyed.

Tabitha swallowed at the amazing sight of Valerius wearing nothing but a damp burgundy towel wrapped around his lean hips. It seemed completely incongruous to find him like that. With his imperious air, she would have thought him to have a collection of silk bathrobes or something.

His dark hair was damp and loose, framing a face that was chiseled to perfection.

Wow, he looked good like that. He'd probably look even better naked like he'd been when he jumped out of her bed . . .

She squelched that thought before it got her into trouble.

"To what do I owe this honor?" he asked.

She smiled. Oh yeah, he was perfect for what she needed . . . and she didn't even want to contemplate that double entendre.

"I need you dressed." Tabitha paused at the thought. Yeah, right, there was something seriously wrong with a woman who said that to a man this finely made.

"Excuse me?"

"Hurry and dress, then meet me downstairs." She shooed him toward the bed where he had a suit laid out. *"Fretta! Fretta!"*

Valerius wasn't sure what stunned him more, her wanting him dressed or her speaking Italian.

"Tabitha—"

"Dress!" Without another word, she left his room.

Before he could move, she opened the door and stuck her head back in. "You know, you could have dropped that towel, slowpoke . . . oh, never mind that thought. Keep your hair down and make sure you wear something really elegant and expensive. Preferably Versace if you have it, but Armani will do, too. And make sure you wear a tie and bring your coat."

Completely baffled and yet oddly curious about her request, he exchanged the suit on his bed for a black Versace silk and wool blend with a black silk shirt and matching silk tie, then opened the door.

Tabitha turned as the door swung open and she felt her mouth go dry. Her jaw dropped.

It wasn't as if she hadn't known he was gorgeous, but . . . *Oh . . . my!*

It was all she could do to breathe. She'd never seen a man wear a totally black suit before but it was haute couture of the first right. He looked debonair and regal.

Marla was going to die!

That is, if Tabitha didn't die first of hormonal overload poisoning.

"You know, I've always heard people say it should be illegal to look that good, but in your case, it really is true."

He frowned at her.

Tabitha grabbed his hand and pulled him toward the stairs. "C'mon, there's no time to waste."

"Where are you taking me?"

"I need a favor from you."

Valerius was oddly flattered by her request. It was extremely rare that anyone ever asked him for a favor. Those were things most people reserved for people they considered friends.

"What do you need?"

"Marla needs an escort for the Ms. Red Light pageant."

Valerius stopped immediately. "She what?"

Tabitha turned to face him. "Oh come on, please don't be a prude here. You're Roman, for heaven's sake."

"Yes, but that doesn't mean I have some innate qualification to be an escort for a transvestite. Tabitha, please."

She looked so disappointed that it actually made him feel guilty.

"Marla has been practicing for this for months now and her guy cancelled on her tonight. Her number-one competitor bribed him to escort her instead. If Marla loses, this will kill her."

"I have no desire to be paraded around a group of gay men."

"It's not a parade . . . exactly. All you need to do is walk her out in the very beginning when they introduce her. It'll only take a few minutes and that's it. C'mon, Val. She spent a year's salary on this gorgeous Versace gown."

Tabitha looked up at him with the most pathetically heartfelt gaze he'd ever seen. It absolutely melted him.

"There's no one else to call on such a short notice. She

needs a really elegant man. Someone who's first class and I don't know anyone else who fits the bill. Please? For me? I swear I'll make it up to you."

Personally, he'd rather be beaten and killed . . . again. And yet he couldn't find it within himself to disappoint her.

"What if one of them gropes me—"

"They won't. I promise, I'll protect all your . . ." She arched a brow as she looked at his derriere. "Assets."

"And if anyone *ever* learns of this—"

"They won't. I'll take it to my grave."

Valerius let out a long breath. "You know, Tabitha, anytime in my life I have ever sought to help anyone, I've only made it worse for them. I have a bad feeling about this. Something will go wrong. Watch and see. Marla will fall off the stage and break her neck, or worse, her big wig will catch on fire."

She waved her hand dismissively. "You're being paranoid."

No, he wasn't. And as she led him toward the front door, every horrible memory of his life played through his mind . . . The time when he'd felt sorry for Zarek and had tried to soothe him after a beating. His father had then forced him to beat Zarek more. He'd pulled back the strokes, hoping they wouldn't be as painful as the ones his father had given Zarek. Instead, he'd ended up blinding the poor slave.

Then when he'd tried to keep Zarek from being caught outside the confines of their villa, he'd caused his father to pay a slaver to take Zarek away from everything the boy had known.

As a first-time general, he'd had a young soldier under his command who was the last surviving son of his family. Hoping to keep the youth away from the battlefield, he had sent him as a messenger to another Roman camp.

The boy had died two days out from an attack by rogue Celts who had stumbled across him.

And Agrippina . . .

"I can't do this, Tabitha."

Tabitha paused on the front steps to look at him. There was a catch in his voice that told her this wasn't him being ridiculous.

She actually felt a wave of fear go through him.

"It'll be okay. Five minutes. That's it."

"And if I cause Marla to be hurt?"

"I'll be right there. Nothing bad is going to happen. Trust me."

He nodded, but she felt his reluctance as she tugged him toward the taxi she'd left waiting for them. Getting in, she gave directions to the driver to the Cha Cha Club on Canal Street.

It barely took them fifteen minutes to get there. Tabitha paid for the cab while Valerius stood on the sidewalk looking like he was ready to bolt, especially since some of the club's clientele had already taken notice of him.

"Don't worry," Tabitha said as she joined him. "They really won't bother you."

Valerius couldn't believe he was doing this. He must have lost his mind.

Tabitha took his hand and led him through the bright pink double doors.

"Hey, Tabby," a bouncer at the door called. He was large and muscular, wearing a sleeveless T-shirt. His dark brown hair was cut short and he had a Celtic band tattooed around his exposed biceps. At first glance he appeared intimidating, but his open, honest smile stole the ferocity from him.

Tabitha pulled out her wallet to pay their cover charge. "Hi, Sam. We're here to help out Marla. Is she in the back?"

"Put that away," Sam said, pushing her wallet back toward her. "You know your money's no good here. Yes, Marla's in back and please go help her. My boyfriend's about to lose his mind because she won't stop crying."

Tabitha winked at him. "Don't worry. The cavalry's here."

Valerius took a deep breath as he followed Tabitha into what had to be the scariest place he'd ever been. Personally, he'd rather walk straight into a nest of Daimons who were armed with chainsaws and guillotines.

But by the time they reached the bright yellow door beside the stage, he felt a little better. Though many of the men in the club stopped to gawk at him, none of them made a move toward him.

"Don't worry," Tabitha said as he walked past her. "I've got your flank covered."

Valerius jumped as she pinched his butt playfully. "Please don't give them ideas."

She laughed at that.

They walked through a crowd of people who were in the process of applying makeup, wigs, and elaborate dresses. Marla sat in a back corner, wailing while another man flitted around her, complaining. Her bald head was covered by a pink net turban and her makeup was completely wrecked.

"You're ruining all my hard work, honey. You have to stop crying or I'll never get it fixed in time."

"What does it matter? I'm going to lose. Damn you, Anthony! All men are pigs. Pigs! I can't believe he'd sell me out."

Valerius felt bad for Marla. It was obvious this pageant meant a lot to her.

"Hey, babe," Tabitha said. "Buck up. We got something a lot better than old Tone. In fact, both he and Mink will die when you step out with this by your side." She pushed Valerius forward.

"Hi, Marla," he said simply, feeling like a complete and utter jackass.

Marla's jaw dropped. "You're going to do this for me?"

He glanced over his shoulder to see Tabitha watching him closely. There was actually fear in her eyes that he might back out.

God knows, he truly wanted to.

He really, really didn't want to go through with this. But Valerius Magnus was tougher than this. He had never run in his life and he would do this favor for Tabitha no matter how distasteful it might be to him.

Straightening himself, he turned back to Marla. "I would be honored to be your escort."

Marla let out an ear-piercing scream as she jumped up and grabbed him in a hug so hard that he feared his ribs might crack. She screamed even louder as she left him and grabbed Tabitha up into a hug that brought Tabitha's feet off the floor.

"Oh, girlfriend, you are the best friend anyone ever had!

Imagine Marla Divine going out there on the arm of the only straight man in the house. Girl, they will die of envy." She let go of Tabitha. "Carey, get over here and redo my makeup, pronto. I need to be fabulous! Fabulous!"

Carey was smiling at Marla's dramatics. "Sit down, darling, and you will be."

While Carey worked on Marla, Valerius and Tabitha stood off to the side, out of the way.

"Thank you," Tabitha said. "Really."

"It's okay."

Tabitha watched Valerius. Before she could stop herself, she wrapped her arms around him and smiled up at him and laid her head against his chest.

Valerius couldn't breathe at the sensation of her hold. His heart thudded at the sight of her head lying against him, at the warmth of her body pressed against his. An unexpected tenderness swelled inside him.

He reached up and lightly stroked her hair while he hoped nothing went wrong with Marla because he was helping her.

The last time he had tried to help someone had been over a year ago when Acheron had asked him to help fight Daimons off a Katagaria wolf pack. He'd gone willingly but during the fight, Vane and Fang, the two wolves they'd been helping, had lost their sister to an ill-placed Daimon strike. She'd died in her brothers' arms.

The sight haunted him to this day.

Valerius had told Vane that anytime he needed him, he'd gladly lend his sword arm to the wolf. Luckily, Vane had never needed him.

You're being ridiculous.

Perhaps, but it wouldn't bother him so much if he was the one who bore the brunt of it. The disaster always seemed to fall onto the ones he tried to help.

He put that thought away and focused on the woman with him. A woman unlike any other he'd ever met before.

She was truly special. Unique.

Time seemed to hold still as he stood there, just letting the warmth of Tabitha seep into him.

He was actually startled when Marla stood up and gestured for him to follow her.

"Dum-da-dum-dum . . . dum . . ." Tabitha hummed the theme song to *Dragnet* as if to portend his doom as they followed Marla back through the dressing room into a hallway that was crowded with drag queens.

Tabitha kissed Valerius's cheek, then left him so that she could make room for others.

She headed out into the club and found Marla's best friend, Yves, sitting at a table in front of the runway with a group of his pals.

"Hey, vampire slayer," Yves said as she pulled a chair up to the table. "Are you here to cheer Marla on?"

"Of course. Where else would I be?"

A cheer went up from the table while they bantered around and laid bets on who would win until the show finally started.

Tabitha was a nervous wreck until Marla and Valerius appeared. The crowd went wild the minute they saw Valerius, who walked as if he was completely comfortable in his role as escort. Only Tabitha could sense his discomfort and she had a feeling it stemmed more from his fear of causing Marla to be hurt than anything else.

When they reached the stairs that would lead them off the runway to where the rest of the earlier contestants were gathered, Valerius descended first and, like a true gentleman, reached up to help Marla down.

Tabitha wanted to weep at what a kind thing he was doing for someone he didn't even know.

She couldn't think of any other straight man who would do something this ridiculous to help out a woman he'd just met. A woman who had stabbed him no less.

As soon as the escorts were dismissed, she pushed through the crowd to find him. The instant she reached him, she threw herself into his arms and held him close.

Valerius was completely stunned by Tabitha's exuberant reaction. She felt so good in his arms that it was all he could do not to crush her to him and kiss her until they both made a spectacle of themselves.

She squeezed him tight, then laid a gentle kiss on his lips. "You are the best!"

Shocked, he didn't know what to say to that.

"If you want, we can leave now."

Valerius looked about. "No," he said honestly. "I've come this far and I didn't kill Marla, so I think we should stay and see how she does."

The look on her face made his entire body burn. "Does Ash have any idea just what a sweetheart you are?"

"I shudder at the mere prospect."

She laughed, then took his hand and led him to a table near the stage.

A large group of men greeted them.

"You were great!" the one closest to them said.

Valerius inclined his head as Tabitha introduced all of them. They sat there for a little over an hour while the contestants held a talent and bathing suit competition. The latter of which made Valerius even more uncomfortable than being on stage.

"You okay?" Tabitha asked, leaning toward him. "You look a little green."

"I'm fine," he said, even though he was cringing at the thought of how a man could restrict himself so much in a bathing suit as to leave no trace of his gender.

Some things just didn't bear thinking on.

After an hour, the judges had finally narrowed it down to three contestants.

Tabitha sat forward. She wrapped her arm around Valerius and perched her chin on his shoulder as she held her breath and prayed for Marla.

Valerius didn't move, but the sensation of his hand on hers made her warm considerably. No matter the outcome, she was so grateful to him for bailing her out.

Neither Kyrian nor Ash would be caught dead here.

Tabitha caught Marla's nervous gaze as they came down to the winner's name.

She couldn't breathe. Not until they announced . . .

"Marla Divine!"

Marla screamed and grabbed the contestant closest to her. They jumped up and down and cried as more contestants moved in for hugs and congrats.

Tabitha shot to her feet, screaming and whistling her support. "Go, Marla, go!"

She looked down to see Valerius staring at her in horror.

Huffing at him, she pulled him to his feet. "Let's hear it, General," she said. "Shout out."

"I only shout when calling orders to troops and that was a long time ago."

Well, there was only so much loosening up a person could do in one night.

She blew him a raspberry, then continued yelling for her roommate.

The emcee placed the crown on Marla, and the sash, then handed her a dozen roses and directed her toward the runway.

Marla walked down it, crying and laughing as she blew kisses to the audience.

When it was all over, Tabitha and Valerius fought the crowd to her side. Marla hugged Tabitha first, then grabbed Valerius. "Thank you!"

Valerius nodded. "My pleasure. Congratulations on winning, Marla."

Marla smiled. "I owe the two of you. Don't think I'm going to forget, now. Y'all go on and I'll catch up to you later."

"All right," Tabitha said. "I'll see you at home."

They made their way out of the club, to the busy Canal Street that bordered the French Quarter.

Tabitha checked her watch. It was almost ten. "I don't know about you, but I'm famished. Want to go grab a bite?"

Valerius gave her an amused stare. "You have to be the only woman alive who would ask a man with fangs that question."

She laughed. "You're probably right. So would you like to join me?"

"We don't have reservations anywhere."

She rolled her eyes at him. "Hon, where I'm going we don't need no stinking reservations."

"Where are we going?"

She headed down Royal Street, which connected Canal to Iberville. "The Antoine's of seafood. Acme Oyster House."

"Acme? I've never eaten there."

And as soon as Tabitha reached the door of the place,

Valerius knew why. It actually had plastic black-and-white checked tablecloths.

He hesitated in the doorway as he scanned the small restaurant. The place was tiny and the crowd thinning. It had a bar to his right that stretched along the wall, and tables set up to his left. The walls were a tawdry mixture of mirrors, pictures, and neon signs. It was loud and obnoxious.

Not to mention, Valerius had to quickly catch himself and mentally force his image into the mirrors before someone realized he didn't cast a reflection.

Tabitha turned to look at him. She put her hands on her hips. "Would you stop looking like someone just scuffed your brand-new shoes? They have the best oysters on earth here."

"It's so . . . neon."

"So put on your sunglasses."

"It doesn't look sanitary," he said in a low tone.

"Oh please, you're about to eat something that is the vacuum cleaner of the ocean. You do know how pearls are formed, right? All an oyster does is ingest trash. Besides, you're immortal, what do you care?"

"Valerius?"

He looked past Tabitha to see Vane and Bride Kattalakis seated at the oyster bar, where two men behind the counter were shucking oysters for the handful of people who sat there. Valerius let out a relieved breath. Finally, someone he could relate to. A little, anyway since Vane was an Arcadian wolf and Bride his human mate.

Dressed in jeans and a long-sleeved T-shirt, Vane was Valerius's height and had long dark brown hair that he wore loose around his shoulders. Bride was a plump, beautiful woman whose long auburn hair was worn up in a messy bun. She had on a tan sweater over a brown dress with little white flowers.

Valerius crossed the floor to shake Vane's hand. "Wolf," he said in greeting . . . it was always polite to refer to the Arcadians and Katagaria by their animal selves. "Nice seeing you again." He looked to Bride. "And you, my lady, always an honor."

Bride smiled at him, then looked at Tabitha. "What are the two of you doing here? Together?"

"Val was doing a favor for me," Tabitha said as she came up behind him. She turned to one of the men behind the counter, who was wiping his hands after shucking a plate of oysters. "Hey, Luther, two beers and a fork."

The tall African-American laughed at her. "Tabby, this is what, the fourth time this week you've been here? Don't you have a home?"

"Yeah, but we don't have oysters in it. At least not good ones. And I have to come here just to harass you. Imagine a whole day without Tabitha in it . . . What would you do?"

Luther laughed.

Valerius didn't miss the strange look that passed between Vane and Bride before Luther handed Bride the plate of shucked oysters and went to get Tabitha the beers.

"Is there something I should know?" Valerius asked them.

The instant Vane opened his mouth to speak, Tabitha kicked his shin. Hard.

Vane yelped, then frowned at her.

"What was that?" Valerius asked. "Why did you kick him?"

"No reason," Tabitha said, reaching over the bar to pluck an oyster from the pile.

She looked angelic, which meant something truly evil was going on.

Valerius looked back at Vane. "What were you going to say?"

"Absolutely nothing," Vane said before he took a drink from his longneck.

Valerius had a bad feeling about this.

Luther returned with two bottles of beer and handed them to Tabitha, who in turn held one out for Valerius.

He stared at it blankly.

"Aren't you thirsty?" Tabitha asked.

"Don't we get glasses?"

"It's beer, Val, not champagne. Take it. Really, it doesn't bite."

"Tabby, be nice," Bride chided. "Valerius probably isn't used to beer."

"I do drink it," Valerius said, taking the bottle reluctantly, "just not like this."

"You want oysters?" Tabitha asked him.

"I'm not sure after your rather blunt reminder of what they are."

Tabitha laughed at him. "Set us up, Luther, and keep them coming until I pop."

Luther grinned at her. "I don't think you have a limit, Tabby. It's a wonder we have any left to serve after you leave."

Tabitha sat on the stool beside Bride and indicated for Valerius to assume the one on the opposite side of her. Valerius set his beer on the counter before he complied.

"You look so uncomfortable here, Valerius," Bride said sweetly. "How on earth did Tabitha talk you into this?"

"I'm still not quite sure."

"You two been dating long?" Vane asked.

"We're not dating, Vane," Tabitha answered quickly. "I told you, Val is only doing me a favor."

"Whatever you say, Tab. I just hope your sis—"

His words were cut short by Bride clearing her throat. "Tabitha knows what she's doing, Vane. Don't you, Tabby?"

"Usually not, but this is okay. Really."

Valerius would sell his soul again for a chance to read Vane's mind. "Vane, may I have a word with you privately?"

Bride poured Tabasco sauce over an oyster. "You leave that barstool, Mr. Kattalakis, and you really will be 'in the doghouse' literally for the rest of the week. In fact, I'll sic your brother Fury on you and change the locks."

Vane actually cringed. "As much as I would like to help you out, Valerius, you have to remember that her father neuters dogs for a living, and he trained his daughter well. I think I'll have to pass."

Valerius looked at Tabitha, who was busy taking an oyster from Luther. She refused to meet his gaze.

What did Vane know that he didn't?

They sat at the bar, with Tabitha and Bride chatting about

clothes, old friends, and nothing important while both men were ill at ease. The restaurant closed at ten, but Luther served them oysters for another fifteen minutes.

"Thank you, Luther," Tabitha said. "I really appreciate you not running me off."

"It's always a pleasure, Tabby. I like the way you appreciate my service and food, and I have to say this one is easier to feed than your friend Simi. That little girl eats like a demon."

"Oh, you have *no* idea."

Valerius went to pay while Vane stayed with the women. Once the bill was settled, Vane and Bride headed off toward Royal while he and Tabitha headed toward Bourbon.

"Ready to patrol?" Tabitha asked.

"I'll drop you at your—"

"I'm not going home," she said, interrupting him.

"Where are you going?"

"Stalking Daimons. Just like you."

"That's not safe."

She stopped and glared at him. "I know what I'm doing."

"I know," he said quietly. "You have the spirit and strength of an Amazon. But I would really rather you not kill yourself for something best left to those of us who have already died. Unlike you, we have no one to mourn us if we perish."

Tabitha was taken aback at his unexpected words. More than that, she was taken aback by the concern she felt from him. The pain. "Who mourned for you when you died?" she asked, not sure why she wanted to know.

He paused, then looked away. "No one."

"No one? Didn't you have any family?"

He laughed bitterly at that. "My family was a Shakespearean tragedy. Trust me when I say they were gleefully rid of me."

"How can you say that? I'm sure they cared. Surely—"

"My brothers are the ones who killed me."

Tabitha felt the vengeful agony that surged through him as he growled those heartfelt words at her. Her chest ached for him. Was he telling her the truth?

"Your brothers?"

Valerius couldn't breathe as the past tore through him.

But in truth, he felt a wave of relief at finally, after two thousand years, telling someone the truth about what had made him a Dark-Hunter.

He nodded as he forced the twisted images of that night out of his mind. When he spoke, his voice was surprisingly level. "I was an embarrassment to my family so they executed me."

"Executed you how?"

His eyes were blank. "You're an ancient scholar. I'm sure you know what Rome did to her enemies."

Tabitha covered her mouth as a wave of nausea consumed her. Before she could stop herself, she took his arm and pulled back his sleeve so that she could see the scar on his wrist. There was all the proof she needed.

Like Kyrian, he had been crucified.

"I'm so sorry."

Stiff and formal, he withdrew his arm and straightened out his sleeve. "Don't be. I find it oddly fitting given my family history. He who lives by the sword . . ."

"How many people did you crucify?"

She felt his shame before he turned and headed away from her. Unwilling to let him go, she rushed after him and pulled him to a stop. "Tell me, Valerius. I want to know."

The agony on his face tore through her. His jaw ticced. "None," he said after a long pause. "I refused to ever kill a man like that."

Tears pricked her eyes as she stared up at him.

He wasn't what Kyrian and the others thought. He wasn't.

The man they described wouldn't have hesitated to humiliate or kill someone. And yet Valerius had.

He cleared his throat and looked as if the words pained him. "When I was a young boy, I saw a man executed. He was one of the greatest generals of his time."

Tabitha's heart paused its beating as she realized he was talking about Kyrian.

"My grandfather tricked him and then spent weeks interrogating him." His breathing was labored, his entire body tense. "My father and grandfather insisted my brothers and I be brought in to witness it. They wanted us to learn how to break a man. How to strip the dignity from him until there's nothing left. And all I saw was blood and horror. No one should suffer like that. I looked into that man's eyes and I saw his soul. His strength. His pain. I tried to run and they beat for me for it, then brought me back in and forced me to watch."

He gave her a fierce, tormented stare. "I hated them for that. Two thousand years later and I can still hear his screams as they raised his broken body up and carried the once-proud prince out to the square to die like a common criminal."

Tabitha covered her own ears as she imagined what it must have been like for Kyrian to die that way. She knew from her sister that his death still haunted him, too. Though Kyrian's nightmares were much fewer now than they had been when he and Amanda had first married, he still had them. He still woke up in the middle of the night to make sure his wife and child were safe.

Some nights, he didn't sleep at all for fear that someone would come and take it all away from him again.

And he hated Valerius with an unreasoning vengeance.

Valerius took a deep breath as he saw the way Tabitha cringed. He cringed too, just not openly.

His heart had carried the guilt and horrors of his child-hood throughout time. If he could go back in time, he never would have sold his soul to Artemis. Better to die and silence the resonance of his father's cruelty than to live interminably with all of their voices echoing in his mind.

He was sure Tabitha hated him now, just like the others. She had every right to. What his family had done was inexcus-able. It was why he made a point to avoid Kyrian and Julian.

There was no need in reminding either one of them of their past lives in ancient Greece. It would be even crueler now that both of them had happiness in the modern world.

He'd never understood why Artemis had moved him into New Orleans. It was something his father would have done to ensure that the two Greeks had no peace whatsoever.

But that was something he would never speak of. And should he ever cross paths with Kyrian and Julian, he knew better than to apologize. He'd tried that once centuries past with Zoe, who had been killed by his brother Marius. The Amazon had run him through, trying her best to kill him.

Valerius had been forced to overpower her.

She had spat on him. *"Roman filth! I'll never understand why Artemis allows you to live when you should be gutted like a squealing pig."*

Over the centuries, he'd learned to just hold his head high and carry on regardless of what the other Dark-Hunters thought. He couldn't give them peace from their pasts any more than he could have peace from his own.

Some ghosts refused to be exorcized.

Now Tabitha knew the truth and she would hate him as well. So be it.

Valerius turned to leave.

"Val?"

He paused.

Tabitha wasn't sure what to say to him. So she didn't speak with words. She reached up and pulled his head down to hers, then kissed him soundly.

Valerius was stunned by her actions. He crushed her to him as he tasted the warmth of her mouth. The warmth of her embrace.

He pulled back. "You know what I am, Tabitha . . . why are you still here?"

She looked up at him, her blue eyes searing with tenderness. "Because I know what you are, Valerius Magnus. Believe me, I know. And I want to take you home with me, right now, and make love to you."

Chapter 6

Valerius would never understand this woman or her strangeness. In the back of his mind was an image of Tabitha in the slinky black negligee he'd found under her pillow.

The image haunted him.

"I would love to go home with you, Tabitha," he said. "But I can't right now. I have to do my job."

She smiled, then kissed him again so passionately that it made his entire body sizzle.

Pulling back, she breathed in his ear. "And that makes me want you even more." He shivered as she delivered one long, sensuous lick to his lobe. "When the dawn comes, I'm going to make you scream in pleasure."

His groin jerked in eager anticipation.

"Promise?" The word was out before he could stop it.

She took a step back and let her hand fall from his face to his chest where she traced a path to his belt. He burned in the wake of her touch.

"Oh yeah, baby," she said teasingly. "I intend to squeeze you until you pop."

That thought alone was enough to turn his blood into lava. He couldn't suppress the fantasy of Tabitha's long legs wrapped around his hips, her body warm and wet as she welcomed him in.

He pulled her close to him so that he could kiss her even

though they stood in the middle of the street. He'd never done anything so lowborn. Nor had he ever enjoyed anything more than the taste of her lips.

Her spicy-sweet scent invaded his senses and made his entire body burn for her.

This was going to be the longest night of his life.

Taking a deep breath, he reluctantly stepped away from her. "So where should we start patrolling?"

"You're not going to try and force me home?"

"Could I?"

"Not bloody likely."

"Then where should we start patrolling?"

Tabitha laughed. "Aren't you a little overdressed for stalking the undead?"

"Not really. It's rather fitting, don't you think, that I should look like I'm going to a funeral?"

She laughed at his morbid sense of humor. "I suppose. Do you always wear a suit?"

"I'm most comfortable in one. I'm not really a jeans and T-shirt sort of man."

"Yeah, I imagine you look like I do whenever I have to wear a suit. Itchy." Tabitha indicated the street with a tilt of her head. "Shall we?"

"Do we have to do Bourbon? Can't we go down Chartres or Royal?"

"Bourbon's where the crowd is."

"But the Daimons like to kill over by the Cathedral." He was suddenly very uncomfortable.

"What's wrong with Bourbon Street?"

"There are lots of unsavory people there."

Now that offended her. "Excuse me, I live on Bourbon. So you're calling me unsavory?"

"No. Not exactly. But you do own a sex shop."

That set off her hackles even more. "Oh! That's it. Nothing for you tonight, Count Penicula. You can go roast your own—"

"Tabitha, please. I don't like Bourbon Street."

"Fine," she said sharply as she stalked away from him. "You go that way. I'm headed this way."

Valerius clenched his teeth as she left him standing there. He truly hated to step one foot into this area. It was bright, loud, and filled with people who hated his guts.

Just go. Forget her.

He should. He *really* should, but he couldn't.

Before he could stop himself, he headed off after Tabitha. By the time he caught up to her, she was already on Bourbon Street.

"What are you doing here?" she asked as he came up beside her. "I would hate to sully you."

"Tabitha, please stay with me. I didn't mean to offend you."

She turned on him with a curled lip.

The instant Tabitha opened her mouth to let him have it, someone tossed a bucket of foul-smelling water from over a balcony and doused Valerius.

He went ramrod stiff while she frowned, then looked up to see Charlie, one of the doormen for the Belle Queen strip club, laughing. He set the bucket up and high-fived another man standing beside him.

"Charlie Laroux, what the hell are you doing?" Tabitha yelled up at them.

"Me?" he asked indignantly. "Since when are you hanging out with enemies? Nick done told us all about that asswipe and I promised Nick that if I ever caught Dick on our street again, I'd make him regret it."

Tabitha couldn't have been more stunned had Charlie slapped her. She looked at Valerius, who'd taken a handkerchief out of his pocket to wipe his face while that angry tic worked in his jaw.

"I swear, Charlie, if you were down here, I'd wring your neck."

"Why? You know our code, Tabby. Why you violating it?"

"Because there's nothing wrong with Val other than the fact that Nick needs to get a life. Just you wait, Charlie. I'm going to have a nice long talk with Brandy and when I finish with her, you'll be lucky if she lets you park your car in her driveway to sleep in it."

Brandy was Charlie's girlfriend, a regular customer in Tabitha's shop.

Charlie went pale while she reached to take Valerius's arm. She pulled him across the street, toward her store.

"I can't believe them!" she snarled.

"It's why I hate this street," he said in an emotionless voice. "Every time I come here, I end up walking the gauntlet through Nick's friends."

"That asshole!"

Tabitha had never been more furious in her life. She led him into her store and didn't even stop to chitchat with her employee. She took him upstairs to her bathroom and grabbed a towel and washcloth from the closet.

"Go ahead and take a bath. I'll borrow some clothes from my roomie."

He went pale. "No offense, but silver sequins and pastels are not my style."

She smiled in spite of herself. "I won't borrow from Marla, I'll borrow from Marlon."

"Marlon?"

"Her alter ego. He doesn't visit here much, but she keeps a few of his things for whenever he feels the need to come out."

"I don't think I quite understand."

"Go bathe," she said, urging him into the room.

Valerius didn't argue. The fetid stench of the water was truly unbearable. He was just grateful that Tabitha was willing to tolerate him long enough to allow him to clean up.

He'd barely stripped his clothes off and entered the shower before the door opened.

Valerius froze.

"It's just me," Tabitha said from the other side of the shower curtain. "I found a pair of black slacks and sedate black shirt for you. The pants are probably a little too big in the waist, but they should be long enough. I'm not sure about the shirt. You might end up wearing one of my tees."

"Thank you," he said.

Before he realized what she was doing, the curtain opened to show her standing outside with a hungry look on her face. "You're welcome."

Valerius didn't move as he stood facing her with the hot

water sliding down his spine. Her bold, intense stare made his body harden against his will.

She didn't seem to mind at all. Indeed, a small smile spread across her face.

"Do you always spy on your guests?" he asked quietly.

"Never, but I couldn't resist getting a peek at what I intend to savor later."

"Are you always this brazen?"

"Honestly?"

He nodded.

"No, I'm not normally quite this obnoxious and you're the last man on the planet I should be considering. But I can't seem to help myself."

Valerius reached out to touch her. She really was too good to be true. "I've never known anyone like you."

She covered his hand with hers, then turned her face to kiss his palm. "Hurry and shower. We have work to do."

She pulled away and he felt her absence immediately. What was it about her?

Unwilling to think about it, he quickly bathed, then dressed. He found Tabitha in her bedroom, sitting in the chair and flipping through one of her books.

Tabitha looked up as she felt Valerius's presence. He stood silently in the doorway. He appeared to be completely in his element, except for the clothes that didn't quite fit.

Getting up, she offered him a kind smile. Once she reached him, she unbuttoned the cuffs of the sleeves that were a little too short for his arms and rolled them back on his forearms.

Then she untucked his shirt.

"I know it's not your style, but it looks much better this way."

"Are you certain?"

He looked delectable. "Oh yeah."

He held a long, retractable sword in his hand. "The only problem is if I don't have long sleeves, I can't wear this."

Tabitha sucked her breath in at the quality of his weapon. "Very nice piece of work. Is it Kell's?" she asked. Kell was a

Dark-Hunter stationed out in Dallas who made a lot of the heavy weapons the Dark-Hunters used.

"No," he said with a deep breath. "Kell doesn't deal with anyone from Rome."

"Excuse me?"

He took the weapon from her. "He's from Dacia and his people waged war against mine. He and his brothers were captured and taken to Rome to be gladiators. Two thousand years later, he's still rather upset at all of us."

"Okay, I've had it with this. Why doesn't Ash stop them from treating all of you like dirt?"

"How can he stop it?"

"Beat some sense into them?"

"It wouldn't work. My brethren and I have learned to just leave the rest of them alone. We're few in number and there's no need in even arguing."

Tabitha growled. "Fine, let them all rot then."

Valerius placed his sword on her dresser and left it there before the two of them went back outside.

Tabitha quickly led him away from the sidewalks so that no one else could toss a bucket at them and kept her arm wrapped around his. "You know, I don't see how you can do your duties with Zarek taking potshots at you from Olympus and the rest of the losers on the street gunning for you."

"I learned quickly to avoid Bourbon Street and leave it for Talon or now Jean-Luc to patrol while I take the areas where no one knows Nick."

"And Zarek?"

He didn't comment.

They turned down Dumaine Street. Neither spoke. They hadn't gone far when Tabitha felt a weird sensation whip through her. "Daimons," she whispered, unaware she had spoken until Valerius let go of her.

He pulled a dagger from his pocket as he turned around in the street as if trying to catch a scent.

There was nothing.

Tabitha could feel the evil presence, but she couldn't pinpoint it either.

Something whistled before an unexpected wind danced down the street. It carried the sound of faint, maniacal laughter.

"Tabitha . . ."

Her blood ran cold at the sound of her name whispered out of darkness.

"We're coming for you, little girl." The laughter echoed loudly, then faded into nothing.

Terrified, Tabitha couldn't breathe.

"Where are you?" Valerius called.

No one answered.

Valerius wrapped Tabitha in his arms as he reached out with every sense he possessed, but could find no trace of who or what had spoken.

"Tabitha?"

Valerius turned sharply at the sound of a voice directly behind him.

It wasn't human. Nor was it Daimon. It was a spirit. A ghost.

It opened its mouth as if to scream, then evaporated into an eerie mist that ran over and through her, leaving her body completely cold.

It was as if something had actually brushed her soul.

Valerius could feel Tabitha shaking, but to her credit, she didn't scream or lose control of herself.

"Is it gone?" she asked.

"I think so." At least he no longer felt it.

"What was that thing?" she asked with a tiny trace of hysteria in her voice.

"I'm not sure. Did you recognize it or the voice?"

She shook her head.

A human scream rang out.

Valerius let go of her so that he could run toward the sound. He knew Tabitha was right behind him and he made sure he kept her there. The last thing he wanted was to leave her behind for that thing to attack.

It didn't take long to reach the small, dark alcove where the scream had originated.

Unfortunately, they were too late. A body lay on the street in a heap.

"Stay back," he told Tabitha as he inched closer to it.

Tabitha started to argue, but didn't really want to see what was obvious. To be honest, she'd seen more than her share of dead bodies.

Valerius knelt down and felt for a pulse. "He's dead," he said.

Tabitha crossed herself, then glanced away. As her gaze touched on the building, she frowned. There on the old faded brick was bloody Greek writing. Tabitha could speak the language, but couldn't read the Greek words. "Do you know what that says?"

Valerius looked up. His face turned to stone. "It says, 'Death to those who meddle.'"

As soon as he read it, the words vanished. She swallowed as a new wave of panic swept through her. "What is going on here, Val?"

"I don't know," he said before he pulled out his phone and called Tate, the parish coroner who was a long-time friend of the Dark-Hunters.

"I'm surprised Tate will talk to you," she said after Valerius hung up.

"He doesn't like me, but after Ash had a talk with him, he's learned to tolerate me." Valerius rejoined her. "We better go before Tate arrives with the police."

"Yeah," she said, feeling sick to her stomach. "Do you think we should call Ash and tell him what happened?"

"We don't really know what happened. There wasn't enough time for a Daimon to kill him and steal his soul."

"So what does that mean?"

"Have you or your sister conjured up anything?"

"No!" she said indignantly. "We know better."

"Well, something seems to have your number, Tabitha, and until we find out what it is, I don't think I should let you out of my sight."

Tabitha couldn't agree more. In all honesty, she didn't want to be out of his sight. Not if that . . . thing was going to come back.

"Tell me something, Val. Are Dark-Hunters any good against ghosts?"

"Honestly?"

She nodded.

"Not a damn bit. In fact, if we're not careful, we can become possessed by them."

She went cold at his words. "Are you telling me that if that spook comes back, he could take you over?"

Valerius nodded. "And God help you and the rest of this city if it does."

Chapter 7

Tabitha felt uneasy for the rest of the night. She couldn't shake the notion that even the air around her was evil. Tainted. Something was out there and it was gunning for her.

She only wished she knew who or what.

Why?

Valerius didn't speak much as they patrolled and yet found no sign of any Daimon. It was less than an hour before dawn when they returned to her place on Bourbon Street.

Valerius stood back while she unlocked her door. Tabitha paused as she noticed that he didn't make any move to enter.

"You had a bad fright tonight," he said quietly as he kept his hands in his pockets. "You should get a good sleep and you'll feel better."

Tabitha watched the way the moonlight cut across his handsome features. The sincerity she saw in those tormented black eyes haunted her. "Honestly, I don't want to be alone. I would really like for you to come in."

"Tabitha—"

She placed her fingers over his warm lips to stifle his protest. "It's okay, Val. If you're not interested in sex with me, I won't take it personally. But—"

He broke her words off with a hot kiss. Tabitha moaned at the taste of Roman as he placed one hand on the back of her head and buried his fingers in her hair.

Wrapping her arms around him, she pulled him inside

and pinned him to the wall so that she could kiss him wildly.
She pulled at his clothes, practically ripping his shirt off before she realized she hadn't even closed the door.

She slammed it shut, locked it, then returned to Valerius.

"Marla," he said huskily as she reached to undo his pants.

Tabitha cursed. Valerius was right. If Marla heard them,
she'd come and investigate.

"Follow me," she whispered, taking him by the hand to
lead him up the stairs to her room.

Luckily Marla's door was closed. Tabitha took him into
her bedroom, then shut and locked her own door.

She should be nervous about this and yet she wasn't. It
was like some part of her needed this intimacy with a man
who was a total anathema to her entire family.

It didn't make sense.

Yet here she was, breaking every taboo she knew. Amanda
would kill her for this. Kyrian would never forgive her.

But her heart wouldn't hear reason. Against all sanity, it
wanted her Roman general.

Tabitha kissed him fiercely, needing him to drive away
her fear.

Valerius growled at how good she tasted. He wasn't used
to a woman taking the lead in sex and he found her lack of
modesty refreshing. She broke from his lips long enough to
pull her own shirt off before she seized him again.

He couldn't think as she pressed her body against his.
Her lace-covered breasts were small and inviting as they
brushed against his chest. She unzipped his pants, then slid
her hand down to gently caress his cock.

He hissed in pleasure as she moved her hands around his
hips to his butt. Slowly, seductively, she slid his pants down,
baring him to her. He'd never experienced anything more
erotic.

Kneeling down before him, she removed his shoes, and
socks, then pulled his pants free.

He didn't understand this woman. He found it impossible to believe that she was here with him like this. It'd been
so long since he'd been with a woman. As Tabitha had
pointed out, most of the ones he'd met had been frigid and
formal in bed.

Never passionate. Not like this.

Not like her.

She was priceless and special, a rare treat he wanted to savor. It was that fire in her that warmed him. That fire that drew him in even against his will.

Tabitha paused as she felt an odd sensation from him. "What's wrong, Valerius?" she whispered, rising to stand before him.

"I'm just trying to understand why you're with me."

"Because I like you."

"Why?"

She bit her lip seductively before she shrugged. "You're strangely amusing and you're kind."

He shook his head. "I'm not kind. I only know how to be cold."

She buried her hands in his unbound hair and let the silken strands caress her fingers. "You don't feel cold to me, General."

Tabitha ran her tongue along the edge of his bottom lip before she kissed him.

Valerius's head spun at her actions and her words. Starving for her, he reached behind her back and unhooked her bra. Without breaking her kiss, she lowered her arms to let it fall to the floor.

He pulled her up against him so that her bare breasts were flush to the heat of his chest. Her silver moon-shaped belly button ring brushed against his hip, bringing a foreign thrill to him. His groin burned in need of her.

As did his heart.

He'd never made love to a woman who really liked him. As a man, his lovers had been political alliances. Women who only sought to claim him as a well-connected, wealthy husband or lover.

As a Dark-Hunter, his liaisons had been with women who didn't even know him.

But Tabitha . . .

Growling low in his throat, he finished undressing her as quickly as possible. The glow from streetlights drifted in from her shades, cutting across her bare body. She was beautiful. Lean, muscled. He'd never wanted anyone more.

Valerius lifted her from the floor and pinned her against her door.

Tabitha laughed at the strength of him. At his raw, earthy passion. No, her general wasn't frigid. He was hot and exciting. Delectable.

Holding her with nothing more than the strength of his arms, he slid himself deep inside her.

Tabitha moaned deep in her throat as he filled her to capacity. "That's it, baby," she groaned. "Give me all you've got."

Valerius buried his head against her neck and inhaled her warm sweetness as he thrust against her. She had one leg wrapped around his waist. He'd never made love to a woman like this. It was animalistic and fierce.

And he loved it.

She arched her back, drawing him in even deeper as she met him stroke for stroke. She had one leg on the floor that she used for leverage against him as she raised and lowered her body on his, heightening the depth of his penetration. It was all he could do to wait on her as she took from him the same pleasure he felt with her.

Valerius cupped her breast in his hand while he savored the sleek wetness of her body welcoming his.

He watched her bite her lip as she wrapped her other leg around his waist and squeezed him tight between her thighs. She was incredible.

She licked and teased his neck as he continued to thrust for both of them.

Tabitha couldn't think past the sensation of his hard thickness inside her. Her body burned and ached for him. She could feel herself clutching him, needing him.

And when she came, she had to stifle her cry.

Valerius growled as she scoured his back with her nails and moaned in his ear. Yet it wasn't painful.

He smiled at the sight she made coming in his arms. She actually laughed and purred, then cupped his face in her hands before she kissed him blind.

That kiss drove him over the edge. He could swear he saw stars as his body released itself inside hers.

He held her tight until the last tremor shook him. His

head spinning, he leaned his forehead against the door while she slid her legs slowly down his body.

"You are the wild one, aren't you?" she asked playfully, nipping at his bare shoulder.

Valerius grinned at that, taking an odd sense of satisfaction from it.

Tabitha slid out from between him and the door to head for the stereo she kept under a pile of clothes in the far corner.

"What are you doing?" he asked.

Suddenly Elvis filled the air with "Can't Help Falling in Love." She turned the volume low before she came back to him and pulled him into her arms.

"Tabitha?"

"Dance with me, Val. Everyone should have at least one night of naked dancing in their lives."

"I don't dance."

"Everyone dances to Elvis."

Before he could protest further, she wrapped her arms around his neck and leaned her head against his chest, then started slow dancing with him.

Valerius had never been more uncertain. Yet as she led him through the song, he felt the most surreal calmness of his life. It was magical. Special.

His heart light, he brushed his hand through her hair while he silently held her and they swayed to the music.

Tabitha's soft, melodic voice sang quietly along with Elvis.

"You have a beautiful voice," he whispered.

She kissed the center of his chest. "Thank you. I was the lead singer in an all-girl heavy metal band in college."

He smiled at the thought as her breath tickled across his chest. He could just see her on stage, singing to a wild crowd. "Really?"

"Mmmm." She looked up at him with the sweetest expression he'd ever seen on a woman's face. "We thought we'd be the next Vixen. We weren't. Shelly got pregnant and Jessie decided she wanted to go out to Las Vegas and be a hotel manager."

"And you became a vampire slayer."

She twirled out of his arms, then came back flush with his chest. "Yes, and I'm damned good at it."

He looked down at the tiny scar on his chest where she'd stabbed him. "I would concur."

The song stopped, but was followed by Aerosmith's "Sweet Emotion."

Tabitha let go of him to sway seductively to the music. Valerius couldn't breathe as he watched her, especially when the beat picked up and she kicked one leg over her head.

And when she used the poster of her bed like a stripper's pole, he came dangerously close to moaning.

There was nothing on the planet more erotic than watching this woman dance. She came closer, then turned her back to him and lifted her hair up to let it trail all over her as she gently ground her hips against his groin.

Valerius couldn't take any more of it. Dipping his head, he teased her shoulder with his lips as he wrapped his arms around her. He trailed his hands over her breasts, then down her stomach, over her belly ring, until he could touch the triangle of auburn curls between her legs. She was still wet from their lovemaking.

The instant he touched her, she hissed, then rubbed herself against his hand. To his amazement, she trailed her hand down his forearm and covered his hand with hers as she urged him on.

She was completely shameless in letting him know exactly what she needed and he loved every minute of it. There was no guessing if she liked his touch. She reacted to every stroke and when he sank two fingers inside her she cried out.

She turned in his arms and seized him. Before he realized what she was doing, she literally flipped him onto the bed and was on top of him, straddling his hips.

Valerius laughed. "You know, a lesser man might actually be afraid of you."

Laughing, she slung her hair over her shoulders to trail down her back. "Are you afraid of me, Val?"

"No," he said honestly. "I like that you know what you want and aren't afraid to take it."

The smile she gave him melted his heart.

She trailed one finger over the bridge of his nose, letting the nail lightly scrape his skin as she traced a path over his lips and down his throat.

Tabitha dipped her head down and suckled him. She growled at the taste of his hard nipple under her tongue. He tasted even better than she had thought he would. There was nothing better than the feel of all his lush, tawny skin underneath her.

What she liked most of all was that he didn't feel threatened by her. He had no problem with her voracious appetite for his succulent body.

It was a nice change of pace.

She trailed her lips from his chest, down that lean, hard abdomen, to his hipbone. She felt the chills spread over his body. Laughing, she raked her fingers through the crisp hairs at the center of his body. He was already hard again.

Pulling back, she examined him in the dim light of the room. He was gorgeous. She teased the tip of his cock with her fingers, letting his moisture coat her.

He watched her without comment while she explored the length of him, down to his soft sac. He arched his back.

Delighting in her power over him, Tabitha bent her head down and took the tip of him into her mouth. His entire body jerked in response, urging her on to please him more.

She took great pride in his deep moans.

Valerius lay there, cradling her head in his hands as she gently tongued him from tip to hilt. In all eternity, he'd never known this feeling that was deep down inside him. What was it about Tabitha that she was able to see past his facade?

I figure all of us misfits should hang together, that way we don't swing alone. Her words to Otto drifted through his mind.

But she wasn't a misfit. She was vivacious and wonderful.

Tabitha inhaled the rich, masculine scent of him as she took her time tasting his body. She looked up to find him watching her, his eyes glazed by desire.

Smiling, she slowly licked her way up his body until she could claim that decadent mouth that begged for her kisses. He growled and held her tight as she ran her hand over his shoulders. Tabitha broke away so that she could nip his chin. His whiskers prickled her tongue and lips, his breath caressed her cheek.

She pulled back, then slowly slid herself onto him, inch by long, luscious inch.

Valerius cupped her face as she rode him with a gentle, easy rhythm that left him even more breathless than their earlier rowdy session.

She was like a whisper as she made love to him. And it was making love. It was soft, tender. She covered his hand with hers and opened her lips to taste his fingers.

Valerius hissed as her tongue worked its magic on the pads of his fingertips. Smiling even more, she nipped his fingers playfully.

He pulled her down to capture her lips as he lifted his hips, driving himself even deeper into her.

This time when they came, it was together.

She collapsed on his chest as they both lay sweaty and panting.

Valerius cradled her gently. He never wanted to let her go. If he could, he would spend the rest of his immortality lost in this one perfect moment of them nestled together, his body spent and sated.

Closing his eyes, he felt himself drifting off to the first undisturbed sleep he'd had in over two thousand years.

After making sure no daylight would threaten Valerius, Tabitha lay quietly in Valerius's arms as she listened to him sleeping.

She still felt uneasy about the ghost they had seen. About the feeling inside her that wouldn't relent. Part of her wanted to call Acheron, but she didn't want to disturb him with something stupid. He needed to rest.

Whenever they awoke in the afternoon, she'd ask him about it.

For now, she had Valerius and he brought her a strange sense of peace.

She shouldn't feel this way, not for a man her twin would never accept into her house. Part of her felt like she was a traitor to Amanda and Kyrian and the other part of her couldn't resist the tormented gleam in Valerius's eyes.

He was a calm anchor to her chaotic life and truthfully, she liked his dry sense of humor. His ability to take things in stride without blowing a gasket. It was rare in her world to meet such a man.

He's not a man.

No, he wasn't. She knew that, just as she knew there was no hope of any kind of future for a relationship. Dark-Hunters didn't have significant others of any sort. They could never be together. Never.

Once she and Valerius left this bed, they'd have to part company. He would just be another passing friend.

And yet she didn't want to let go of him.

"Stop," she whispered to herself. She needed her rest.

Closing her eyes, she forced herself to sleep. But her dreams were far from comforting. All morning long, they haunted her with vivid, horrific images of her sister and Kyrian. Of baby Marissa crying for someone to help her.

Most of all, they haunted her with the faces of her friends who had died and with scenes of Valerius being tortured. She could see him stretched out and hear mocking laughter as he struggled not to die.

She could feel his pain, his betrayal.

Hear his scream of vengeance as it echoed throughout time.

Tabitha came awake just after noon with her entire body shaking from her dreams. She'd only been sleeping a few hours, but she was so upset that she couldn't go back to sleep.

"Tabitha?"

She looked at Valerius, who squinted at her.

"Are you all right?" he asked hoarsely.

She kissed his bare shoulder and offered him a smile. "I can't sleep. You go ahead and rest."

"But—"

She placed her finger on his lips. "Sleep, baby. I'm fine. Really."

He nibbled her finger before he rolled over, gave her a tight hug, then returned to sleep.

Tabitha lay in the shelter of his arms with her thoughts racing. She honestly didn't want to get up. But after a few minutes, when she heard Marla and Debbie chatting somewhere downstairs about inventory, she finally decided to rise.

She quickly showered and dressed, taking care not to wake the delicious guy in her bed. As soon as she went downstairs, she called Otto and asked him to bring clothes over for Valerius.

"Why didn't he come home last night?" Otto asked.

"It was too close to dawn."

"Uh-huh," Otto said as if he didn't buy it. "I'll be over in about an hour with something for him."

"Otto," she said with a warning note in her voice. "It better be something he wants to wear and not some Nick-I-want-to-piss-off-Kyrian knockoff."

"You take all the fun out of this."

Tabitha shook her head as she hung up the phone. With nothing better to do, she headed into her store, where Debbie was ringing up a customer.

Otto came about an hour later and dropped off the clothes without so much as a grimace. But Tabitha noted that he was wearing a stylish black sweater and a pair of nice jeans instead of his regular wear. He probably looked like this whenever Valerius wasn't around.

After Otto left, she took the clothes upstairs and laid them out for Valerius to see when he awoke, then crept back to her shop, where she cleaned and reworked a pasties display.

She'd just finished matching the pasties to thongs when Nick Gautier came into the store with a bright smile on his face as he whipped his sunglasses off. "Afternoon, *chèr*," he said, walking up to her.

He kissed her lightly on the cheek.

Tabitha frowned. It'd been a long time since Nick had done something like that. "What has you in such a good mood?" she asked.

He flashed that devilish, charming grin at her. "What do you think? Man, I owe you dinner out, big-time."

She was even more confused than before. "For what?"

"That friend of yours . . . Simi. She was something else."

Tabitha went cold at the sound of reverence in his voice.

"I can't wait to see her again," Nick continued, increasing her sense of dread. "You wouldn't happen to have her number handy, would you? I was supposed to meet her at six tonight, but I'm going to run a little late and didn't want to leave her waiting for me."

Tabitha struggled to breathe as panic and fear consumed her. This couldn't be happening. Nick didn't do what she thought he'd done—had he?

Surely not even Nick Gautier was that stupid.

"Simi? You want *Simi's* number?"

"Yeah. She cut out so fast last night that I didn't have a chance to get it."

"Why did she cut out fast?"

"She said she was supposed to meet someone." He frowned at her. "What's up? Is there something I need to know? She's not married, is she?"

Tabitha felt the color drain from her face. "Tell me you didn't do anything with Simi last night, did you? You just took her into Sanctuary and—"

"I took her out for barbecue. She said it was her favorite and those bears don't know shit about mesquite."

Tabitha rubbed her head to help alleviate some of the bitter ache that was starting right between her eyes. This was so bad . . . "And after you two ate, you what?"

His grin turned wicked. "You know a gentleman never kisses and tells."

Tabitha covered her mouth as she felt an urge to be really sick.

Nick sobered instantly. "What?"

"You didn't happen to ask her who she was going to meet, did you?"

"No, I assumed it was a friend."

"Oh, Nick," she said, wanting to cry for him and his ignorance, "it was more than a friend. Let me put it to you this way: Her phone number is 555-562-1919."

He scowled. "That's Ash's number."

"Yes, it is."

His pallor now matched her own as the true horror of his situation dawned on him. "Not our Ash as in Parthenopaeus Ash?"

She nodded glumly.

He turned a multitude of colors as that registered. "Oh, God, Tabitha, why didn't you tell me?"

"I thought you knew her. She knows you."

"No, I never met her before last night." Nick raked a hand over his face as he set off cursing.

Tabitha shook her head. "Ash is going to kill you."

"Don't you dare tell him!" Nick snarled.

"I'm not about to. But what if Simi—"

"I'll call him and tell him I need to talk to him. I'll confess . . ."

"Nick, he *will* kill you. He loves Simi and I mean *loves* Simi. He'll never forgive you for this. You'll be lucky to come away with all parts attached."

Nick couldn't believe what he was hearing. There had been several times over the last few years that Ash had intimated that he had a girlfriend and Nick had taken to goofing on him for it.

The last thing he'd ever expected was to meet Ash's girlfriend in the Quarter without him.

Oh God, this couldn't be happening. How could he have slept with his best friend's girl? Why hadn't Simi told him? If, as Tabitha said, Simi knew who he was, why would she do such a thing?

"Is she fighting with Ash?" he asked, hoping, praying it was a possibility.

"No, Nick. You're not that lucky."

He cursed again. "I have to tell him," he said to Tabitha. "I'm not going to be a coward. I owe him that much."

"Then you better make sure you go over to the St. Louis Cathedral and confess before you do."

Nick crossed himself, unable to believe what he'd just gotten himself into. He should have known Simi was too good to be real. She'd been a lot of fun, and in truth, he'd been looking forward to seeing her again.

Tabitha was right. He was a dead man.

"Hey, Tabby," Marla said as she stuck her head into the shop. "Valerius is up and showering in the bathroom."

Nick gaped, then glared. "Valerius?"

"Sh," Tabitha snapped at Nick.

He didn't take the hint. "Valerius as in Valerius, dickhead Valerius? What the hell is he still doing here, Tabitha?"

"It's none of your business."

His anger snapped at that. "Oh, yeah, right. Excuse me, but between the two of us . . ." He paused as he thought over what he was about to say, then reconsidered it. "Okay, I'm still more screwed than you are, but you are seriously screwed blue. Amanda will tear your heart out if she finds out."

Tabitha turned on him with her eyes flashing anger. "So help me, Nick, you breathe a word of this and I'll press the speed dial on my phone straight for Ash."

He held his hands up in surrender. "Deal. But you better get that Roman prick out of here."

She pointed toward the door. "Good-bye, Mr. Gautier."

He put his sunglasses back on. "Later, Ms. Devereaux."

Tabitha rubbed her hands over her face as she contemplated what a horror this day was and that it wasn't even close to over yet.

Aggravated, she headed toward the door that led to her apartment. Upstairs, she heard Valerius in the shower.

Tabitha went ahead and called to have a pizza delivered in case he was hungry.

By the time he was finished and dressed, the pizza arrived. Tabitha paid for it and set it on the table as she waited for Valerius to come down.

She still had the sickest feeling her stomach. "There really needs to be a do-over button for days that suck this much," she muttered as she set out two paper plates.

Valerius was buttoning the last button on his shirt as he came down the stairs, looking for Tabitha. She was standing with her back to him.

He paused on the stairs to admire her there. She was leaning over the table to give him one nice view of her derriere. A small smile played at the edges of his lips as he remembered what that rear had looked like last night naked against him as she danced in her room.

He hardened instantly.

Getting a little hold on his treacherous body, he walked into the room and frowned as he saw a large white box on Tabitha's kitchen table. It smelled good, but . . .

"What is that?" he asked.

"Pizza," she said, turning to face him.

He scowled in revulsion.

"Oh, c'mon," she said irritably. "It's Italian."

"It's pizza."

"Have you ever had pizza?"

"No."

"Then sit down and hush while I get us some wine. You'll

like it, I promise. It was handmade by an Italian named Bubba."

Valerius arched a doubtful brow at her words. "There are no Italians named Bubba."

"Sure there are," she said saucily. "It's more Italian than Valerius is. At least Bubba's name actually ends with a vowel."

Valerius opened his mouth to contradict her, then stopped. There was no reasoning with Tabitha when she was in this saucy mood. "Are you testy because you didn't get enough sleep or do you wish for me to leave?"

"I didn't get enough sleep and if you know what's good for you, you'll sit down and eat." She headed to the kitchen.

Valerius didn't listen. He went into the kitchen, picked her up, and tossed her over his shoulder.

"What are you doing?" she asked, her tone angry.

He sat her down in a chair and braced his hands on its arms so that she was pinned there. "Good evening, Tabitha. I'm fine tonight. How are you?"

"Irritated at you."

"I'm sorry to hear that," he said, lifting one hand up to caress her cheek. "I woke up to the smell of you on my skin and I have to say that it put me in a rather good mood that I don't want you to destroy."

Tabitha melted at those words and the tender look on his face. Not to mention that the fresh, clean scent of his skin could undo even the worst mood imaginable. His lips were so close to hers that she could already taste them.

And those dark eyes . . .

They were beguiling.

"You really know how to be aggravating, don't you?" she asked him. She forced her ire aside and offered him a smile. "Okay, I'll play nice." She pulled his head to hers so that she could kiss him.

She was just getting into that kiss when her phone rang. Cursing at the ill timing, she got up to answer it.

It was Amanda. Again.

Tabitha wasn't really paying attention to her as her sister rambled on about Marissa and Kyrian and another dream she'd had.

At least not until she mentioned Desiderius and her.

"What?" she said, forcing herself not to watch Valerius who was poking at the pizza as if it were a UFO.

"I said I'm scared, Tabby. Really scared. I dreamed during my nap that Kyrian and I were killed by Desiderius."

Chapter 8

Tabitha hung up the phone, terrified. She'd never heard so much fear in Amanda's voice. Worse, she knew her sister's powers—if Amanda had foreseen her own death. . . .

Without hesitation, Tabitha called Acheron.

"Hey, Ash," she said, noting the way Valerius's attention turned from his pizza to her. "I have a problem. Amanda just called and said that she had dreamed her own death and last night I ran across something really spooky. It—"

Ash appeared before her. "What?" he asked.

Tabitha froze for a second as she realized what Ash had just done. He really was scary at times.

She hung up the phone again and repeated everything, including details about the ghost they'd seen the night before.

Ash got a faraway look in his eyes, tilting his head as if listening to someone.

"Can you see her death?" she asked him.

Ash stood there, his heart thumping wildly as he tried to clear the mist that surrounded Amanda and Kyrian's future.

He saw nothing.

He heard nothing.

Dammit. It was why he did his best never to let anyone too close to him. Anytime he allowed himself to care about someone or they were a part of his own future, he was blind to their destinies.

There was nothing but blackness where Kyrian and Amanda were concerned and he hated that most of all.

"Talk to me, Ash."

He looked back at Tabitha and heard and felt the fear and panic in her mind. Her thoughts that rambled as she sought a comfort he couldn't give.

Even her future was forbidden to him now.

"Her destiny was to be happy," he said quietly. But the key word to that statement was *was*. Free will could, and often did, alter fate.

What had changed?

Something must have and Amanda had glimpsed it in her sleep.

He held enough belief in Amanda's powers not to doubt her in the least. If she foresaw their deaths, then it was a likely outcome unless he could find the cause and change it before it was too late.

Ash closed his eyes as he let himself feel the minds of the humans. He searched for what could possibly change Amanda's fate, but he found nothing.

Nothing.

Dammit!

Valerius was behind him now. Ash stepped aside so that his back wasn't exposed to the Roman.

"Tell me exactly what happened last night," Ash said to Tabitha.

Tabitha related the whole scene with the ghost while Valerius filled in a few details.

"Urian!" Ash called, summoning his Spathi contact.

Tabitha frowned. Ash was acting very strange and she could sense his worry. "Who's Urian?"

Before she finished the question another tall, insanely handsome man appeared in her kitchen. Dressed in black leather pants and a black shirt, he had white-blond hair and blue eyes.

He looked less than pleased as he narrowed those baby blues on Ash. "Don't take that tone of voice with me, Ash. I don't care who you are, I don't like it."

"Like it or not, I need to know what the Spathis are up to.

More precisely, I need to know if Desiderius is back on the playing field."

Horror filled her.

Urian curled his lip. "Why are you worried about him? Des is a punk."

"Desiderius is dead," Tabitha said emphatically. "Kyrian killed him."

Urian scoffed. "Yeah, and I'm the Easter Bunny—see my fluffy tail? You don't just kill a Spathi, little girl. All you do is take him out of commission for awhile."

"Bullshit!" Tabitha snarled.

"No, Tabitha," Ash said, gentling his voice. "Desiderius's essence was released. But if one of his brethren or children wanted to bring him back, they could. It's not easy to do, but it is possible."

She was aghast that Ash had kept something this important from them. "Why didn't you ever tell us this?"

"Because I was hoping it wouldn't happen."

"Hoping?" Tabitha shrieked. "Please tell me you weren't pinning my sister's life and Kyrian's on a hope."

Ash didn't answer.

Meanwhile the true significance of the last few days settled fully on her shoulders. "So those really were Spathis I fought the night I met Valerius."

Urian snorted. "Trust me, little girl, you must have faced the neophytes. Had those been true Spathis, you'd both be dead now."

His arrogance was seriously starting to piss her off. Just who was this jerk anyway? "How do you know so much about them, Dr. Intellect?"

"I used to be one."

Her fury breaking, Tabitha rushed him.

Ash caught her and pulled her back. He lifted her up off the floor. Tabitha kicked and cursed as she struggled to reach Urian, who watched her with a smirk.

"Stop it, Tabby," Ash breathed in her ear. "Urian is on our side now. Believe me, he has paid for his allegiance to the other side more than you will ever know."

Yeah, right.

"How could you bring a Daimon into my house after what they did to me? To my family?" she demanded.

"Oh, I'm not a Daimon anymore, little girl," Urian said, his eyes flashing dangerously. "If I were—"

"You'd be dead," Valerius said, cutting him off with a sinister tone. "By *my* hand."

Urian laughed. "Yeah, right." He looked at Ash. "The arrogance of your Hunters truly knows no bounds. You should spend more time educating them about us, Ash."

Ash released Tabitha, then spoke to Urian. "I need you to go in and find out what's going on. Are there any left who might still be loyal to you?"

The Daimon shrugged. "I can probably dredge up a flunky or two. But . . ." Urian's gaze went to Tabitha. "If Des really is back, he'll want to finish what he started. May the gods help you all if he has been reincarnated. It's going to get bloody in New Orleans."

"Who would want to bring that monster back?" Tabitha asked.

"His children," Urian and Ash said simultaneously.

Tabitha still couldn't believe what she was hearing. But as she seethed, Urian's face finally looked compassionate.

Haunted.

When he spoke, the arrogance was gone from his voice. "Trust me, it's hard to let go of the loyalty you feel to a father who saved you from dying a horrible death at twenty-seven." Something in his tone said he spoke from experience.

"Is your loyalty to your father?" she asked.

Urian's face turned to stone. "I would have done *anything* for my father until the day he killed me and took from me the only thing that meant more to me than my life. Any bonds I felt for that man were shattered instantly." He looked at Ash. "I'll see what I can find out."

A bright orange engulfed Urian an instant before he flashed out of her kitchen. Even so, his malevolence still clung to the air around them.

"Damn," Ash muttered. "Urian and his dramatics. I have got to remind him to lay off the pyrotechnics when he comes and goes."

"That is one angry man," Tabitha said.

"You've no idea, Tab," Ash said. "And he has every right to his hatred." He shook his head as if to clear it, then spoke to them quietly. "While Urian is busy, I need for the two of you to stay together and watch each other's backs. Desiderius is the son of Dionysus, and Dionysus is still upset at me over what happened at Mardi Gras three years ago. I don't think he's stupid enough to help Desiderius, but I wouldn't put anything past either one of them."

He looked meaningfully at Tabitha. "Even if Daddy doesn't help him, Desiderius still has a lot of god powers that can be deadly, as you no doubt remember."

"Yeah," she said sarcastically as she recalled the way he and his Daimons had cut through her and her friends as if they were straw. "I remember."

He looked at Valerius. "Desiderius can manipulate people. Possess them, if you will. Tabitha is stubborn enough that the only thing that can possess her is the spirit of chocolate. We're lucky there. But Marla could be swayed. Otto *should* be safe. But the rest of your staff . . . you might want to think about giving them some time off."

By the look on Valerius's face, Tabitha could tell he'd rather be dead. "I can handle them."

"You have to sleep sometime. One of the servants could easily break into your bedroom and kill you. I don't think any of them love you so much that they will hesitate over Desiderius's orders the way Kyrian's cook did."

Valerius's nostrils flared.

Ash ignored the pain that Tabitha felt from Valerius. "I need you two together on this. I have to go warn Janice and Jean-Luc about what's up." He turned to face her. "Tabitha, pack a bag and move in with Valerius for awhile."

"What about my store?"

"Have Marla watch over it for a couple of weeks."

"Yeah, but—"

Ash's features hardened. "Don't argue with me, Tabitha. Desiderius is a major power with one hell of a grudge against you, your sister, and Kyrian. He's not going to be playing with the three of you this time. He's going to kill you."

Normally, she would argue with him just for spite. But she knew that tone of voice. No one argued with Ash for long. "Fine."

"You have your orders, General," Ash said sternly to Valerius.

Valerius gave him a rather sarcastic Roman salute.

Rolling his eyes, Ash flashed out of the room.

Now that they were alone, Valerius stared at her without speaking. Fury was burning so raw inside him that it actually hurt her.

"What?" she asked.

Without a word, he went to the picture on her buffet of Amanda's wedding and pulled the Russell Crowe picture off Kyrian's face.

He cursed. "I should have known when you told me her name was Amanda."

The look of repugnance on his face set her off. "Yeah, and my name is Tabitha, not Amanda. What has that got to do with anything?"

But he didn't hear her. She knew it.

He stalked quietly from the room and went back upstairs. She jumped at the sound of her bedroom door slamming.

"Fine," she said out loud. "Be a baby. I don't care."

Valerius sat motionless on the edge of the bed as his mind ranted over who Tabitha really was.

The twin of Kyrian's wife had saved him. This was priceless, truly priceless. Here he'd spent the last two thousand years avoiding the Greek so as not to hurt him by reminding him what Valerius's family had done to him, and now this . . .

He clenched his teeth as he felt for Kyrian's betrayal. Valerius's grandfather, an exact look-alike for Valerius, had seduced Kyrian's beloved wife Theone centuries ago and used her to betray her husband. Kyrian hadn't been captured on the battlefield as befitted a man of his stature. He'd been drugged by the hand of his wife in his own home as he tried to save her, and then handed over to his mortal enemy.

Valerius's stomach churned as he remembered the weeks where his father and grandfather had tortured the Greek general for information and for fun. Remembered Kyrian's screams.

The sight of the man lying bloody and defeated haunted him to this day. Kyrian had lain there with his eyes pain-filled and empty. Only once during those weeks had their gazes met and the look in Kyrian's eyes was still seared into Valerius's soul.

Worse, Valerius remembered his grandfather laughing at dinner the night Kyrian had been crucified after Kyrian's father had tried to save him.

"You should have seen his face as his wife came in my arms right in front of him. I had his whore moaning and begging for my cock as he watched me fuck her. Too bad he died before he could see her face when I threw her out."

Valerius had never understood that cruelty. It was enough to defeat an enemy, but to use his woman in front of him . . .'

And now he was sleeping with the identical twin of Kyrian's wife.

History did, in fact, repeat itself.

And Acheron had known and not told him. Why would the Atlantean insist on the two of them being together when he had to know what this would do to Kyrian? It didn't make sense. Any more than Tabitha saving him when she herself knew Kyrian hated him.

Jupiter knew the man had every right to wish him dead. No wonder Selena had hated him so passionately. As Kyrian's sister-in-law, it was a wonder she hadn't been even more violent toward him.

The door opened.

Valerius tensed as he saw Tabitha come inside. She didn't speak to him as she set about packing a small suitcase . . . of weapons.

"What are you doing?" he asked.

"What Ash said to do. I'm going to move in with you."

"Why not go and stay with Kyrian and Amanda?"

"Because I trust Ash. If he says I should be with you, then I'm going."

"Will you be spitting on me as well?" The question was out before he could stop it.

Tabitha paused at his untoward question. "Pardon?"

A tic started in Valerius's jaw. "It's what your sister Selena does every time she sees me. I was wondering if I should make sure to keep a good lougie distance from you, too."

Tabitha would have laughed had he not been deadly serious. "*Lougie*. Interesting word for you. I wouldn't have thought you knew that one."

"Yes, well, your sister and my latest Squire have tutored me well on the mighty lougie." He stood up and moved toward the door. "I shall wait outside until you're through."

Tabitha kicked the door closed before he reached it. He turned with a supreme look of arrogance.

"What has crawled up your butt and died?"

"Excuse me?" he asked, his voice every bit as icy as his look.

"Look, there are a few things you need to know about me. One, I don't take crap from anyone. Two, I don't hold anything back. Whatever I feel about something or someone, I let it be known."

"I noticed."

She ignored his interruption. "And three, I am an empath. You can stand there and act all nonchalant as you want to, but at the end of the day, I feel what you do. So don't act all secretive and cold when I know better. It just pisses me off."

His jaw slackened ever so slightly. "You're an empath?"

"Yes. I know that Ash's presence in the kitchen hurt you, but I don't know why, and I felt your fury flare the minute you uncovered Kyrian's face." She reached up and placed her hand to his cheek. "My mother always said that still waters run deep. The only time your actions have matched your emotions was last night when we were making love and when you came up here and slammed the bedroom door."

He tried to move away, but she refused to let him. "Deal with me, Val, don't walk away."

"I don't understand you," he said, his heart pounding. "I'm not used to anyone liking me, especially not people who have every right to hate me."

"Why should I hate you?"

"My family ruined your brother-in-law."

"And my Uncle Sally was a loan shark who died when one of his shakedowns shot him dead in the street. Every family tree has an asshole in it. That's not your fault. You're not the one who killed Kyrian, are you?"

"No, I was just a child when he died."

"Then what's your problem?"

For an unreasonable person, she had moments of strange lucidity. "Every person I have met in this town who knows Kyrian has hated me from the moment they saw me. I assumed you would be like them."

"Well, you know what they say about assume . . . it makes an ass out of u and me. Jeez. I love Kyrian, but the man really needs to learn how to let go of the past."

He couldn't believe her. That she would be so accepting of him was . . .

She pulled him into a tight, oddly invigorating hug. "I know I can't keep you, Valerius. Believe me, I understand fully the life you have and the calling. But we are friends and we are allies."

He held her close as those words resonated deep inside him.

She let go and stepped back. "And we have things to do tonight. Right?"

"Right."

"Very good then, let's rocket."

He frowned. "Rocket?"

She gave him a silly grin. "My nephew Ian is addicted to the Power Rangers. I think I've been watching the videos way too long with him."

"Ah," he said, reaching for her suitcase. "Let's get you settled at my place and then we can head out tonight and see what Daimons we find."

Fearful of running into Tia and risking more questions, Tabitha called a cab to take them over to Valerius's house. Otto was already gone by the time they reached his mansion.

As expected, Gilbert met them at the door. He seemed stodgy as ever as he greeted them formally.

"Nice seeing you again, Gil," Tabitha said as Valerius handed him her suitcase. "Nice rigid stance."

Gilbert frowned before he looked down, then gave her a quizzical stare.

Valerius almost smiled. "Ms. Devereaux will be staying with us for awhile, Gilbert. Would you please have Margaret ready a room for the lady?"

"Yes, my lord."

Valerius started for the stairs, then paused. "After Margaret is finished, I would like for the entire staff to take a few weeks off."

Gilbert looked shocked. "My lord?"

"Don't worry. It's with full pay. Consider it an early Christmas present. Just leave a number on my desk where I can contact everyone to have them return."

"As you wish, my lord."

Tabitha felt Valerius's sadness. In spite of what Acheron said, Valerius did like Gilbert and seemed to hate the thought of the man leaving.

"Where are you off to?" Tabitha asked as Valerius took another step up the regal mahogany staircase.

"I was going to get new weapons. Would you care to join me?"

"Ooo," she said suggestively. "I've always been a sucker for a man with lots of weapons. Show me what you got, baby."

She wasn't quite sure if he was amused or not as he waited for her to join him. Tabitha followed him up the stairs, then turned down the long hallway on the right. He led her halfway down before he paused in front of a door and opened it.

Tabitha whistled low as she caught sight of his training room. It was huge, and held a variety of punching bags, mats, and dummies. One in particular looked like it had been seriously abused.

It also wore a bright Hawaiian shirt.

"Is this supposed to be someone we know?" she asked as she noted the stab wounds to the dummy's head.

"I plead the Fifth."

"I take it Otto doesn't participate in your training sessions."

He glanced at the dummy. "I guess you could say that in a way he does."

She shook her head as Valerius headed over to the closet. Inside was an arsenal she was sure the ATF would have some issues with.

"Grenade launcher?"

"EBay," Valerius said. "You can find anything on there."

"Apparently so. Who needs Kell when you have all this?"

He gave her a wicked grin as he strapped a long, lethal blade to his forearm. "What's my lady's choice?"

Tabitha pulled a small crossbow off a hanger on the door. "I've watched one too many *Buffy* reruns. I'm a crossbow girl all the way."

Valerius stood back while Tabitha picked her weapons. He had to admit that he enjoyed seeing a woman who knew how to take care of herself. She weighed and examined each one carefully with the precision of a pro.

He would never have believed such a thing could be a turn-on and yet his body was already hard for her. It was all he could do not to take her right now in the closet.

Tabitha looked over her shoulder as she caught the sizzling wave from Valerius. His black eyes blazed at her.

He was close to breaking, she could sense it. The fire of his desire reached out to her, igniting her own until she struggled to breathe.

"Here," she said, handing him one of the polished steel stakes.

He stepped back and slid it into his pocket.

Before he could comment, the door from the hallway opened to admit Gilbert.

"Ms. Devereaux?"

She turned to find the butler nearing her. "Yes?"

"Your room is prepared."

Valerius cleared his throat. "Please make sure it's to your liking before the servants leave."

"Okay," she said, knowing he needed some breathing room. In truth, she did, too. If she didn't get out of this room for a few minutes, they were both going to be naked and sprawling.

Tabitha left the closet to follow Gilbert back down the hall to the other wing. He led her to a room at the end of the hallway, then opened the door.

Tabitha gaped at the palatial room. It was, after all, the very best. She wouldn't expect anything less from Valerius and still the room was awe-inspiring.

It was decorated in dark navy blue and gold. The lush navy duvet was already turned down for her.

Gilbert headed for an intercom, then stopped himself. "I don't suppose there will be anyone here to answer if you call," he said under his breath.

"You don't want to leave?"

He looked a bit startled by that. "I've been with Lord Valerius a long time."

By the note in his voice, she could tell "long" had a meaning all itself.

"Are you another Squire?"

He shook his head. "They don't even know I exist. It's why Lord Valerius changes Squires out so often. He took me in when I was fifteen and he was stationed in London. No one else would have me."

She frowned at his words. "Why didn't they make you a Squire?"

"The Squire's Council refused to grant Lord Valerius that request."

"Why?" she asked, not understanding it. The Council had let Nick Gautier in when Kyrian had asked and heaven knew that boy had an extremely shady past.

"They don't think much of the general or his requests, I'm afraid."

Tabitha growled low in her throat. She'd never been the kind of person who could stand those who sat in judgment of others. As her Aunt Zelda so often said, but for the grace of God, there go I.

"Don't worry, Gilbert. I'll make damn sure no one messes with Valerius while you're gone. Deal?"

He smiled at her. "Deal." He bowed to her, then took his leave.

Tabitha crossed the room only to discover that her clothes had already been unpacked and everything placed neatly in drawers, the armoire and in the bathroom.

Wow. A woman could get used to this kind of treatment.

She sorted through her weapons, which had been placed

in a drawer by themselves. Her favorites were the retractable knives that fastened to her wrists with Velcro. A high-pressure release shot them from her arm into her hands, but you had to be careful or they would cut a nasty wound into the palm.

She lifted her pants leg and slid another stiletto into her boot and tucked a butterfly knife in her back pocket. Most of her weapons were illegal, but she had enough friends in the police department that they didn't harass her for them.

She was pulling on a long-sleeved sweater to cover up her arms when someone knocked on her bedroom door.

Opening the door, she found Valerius on the other side. He had to be the most handsome man she'd ever seen. His hair was still damp, pulled back into his almost requisite ponytail, though to be honest, she preferred it loose and wild.

His chiseled features betrayed nothing, but she could sense delight in him.

"I'm on my way out to patrol."

"I'm ready."

The amusement she sensed doubled. The lines in his face also softened and it was all she could do not to pull him back into her arms.

Really, no one should be so tempting.

He widened the opening for the door. "Come, my Lady Dangerous, your Daimons await."

Tabitha led the way down the stairs where Otto was waiting for them.

He must have come back while they'd been upstairs.

"There's an alert going out to New Orleans," he said to them. "All the Squires except the Blood Rites are being evacuated. Ash is also bringing in a couple more Hunters from upstate and Mississippi. Did you know about this?"

"No," Valerius said. "I didn't realize an alert had been issued."

"Are the Addamses leaving?" Tabitha asked.

Otto nodded. "Even Tad. They're transferring the control of the Dark-Hunter site up to Milwaukee until the alert breaks."

Amanda's words of warning went through Tabitha's

head. She pulled her phone out of her back pocket and called to check in on them as Valerius and Otto spoke to each other.

She was relieved the minute she heard Amanda's voice. "Hey, sis," she said, trying to sound normal. "What are you guys up to?"

"Not much. And yes I know about the alert. Ash has already moved in here along with some Dark-Hunter named Kassim."

"Why aren't you being evacuated?"

"It'll just follow us, Ash said. He thought it better that we fight on our own ground than to be someplace unfamiliar. Don't worry, Tab. I really do feel better with Kassim and Ash here."

"Yeah. I know Ash would never let anything happen to any of you. You guys take care and I'll talk to you later. Love you."

"You, too. 'Bye."

Tabitha sighed as Amanda hung up and her stomach contracted even more with unfounded fear.

Why was she so nervous?

"I'll make sure all the help is out of here by tonight," Otto said before taking his leave.

Valerius gave an imperious nod.

As soon as they were alone, Tabitha struggled to get rid of her somber mood. "Do you know a Dark-Hunter named Kassim?"

"I know of him."

"What do you know?"

Valerius adjusted his coat sleeve around his wrist. "He was an African prince in the Middle Ages. He was stationed in Jackson, Mississippi, until Ash moved him to Alexandria a few years ago. Why?"

"He was moved into Amanda's house, so I was just curious about him." She indicated the front door with her thumb. "Shall we?"

He took her hand as she started away from him. "Whatever this is after all of you, we'll get them, Tabitha. Don't worry."

The sincerity of his voice cut through her. "You would protect your mortal enemy?"

He glanced away. When his gaze came back to hers, it seared her. "I *will* protect your loved ones. Yes."

There was no reason for him to do such a thing. None. She had no doubt that in his place, Kyrian would go back upstairs, lock his door, and do nothing.

But Valerius . . .

Before she could stop herself, she pulled his lips down to hers and kissed him fiercely. The taste of him permeated her head. How she wished she had nothing more to do tonight than to pull him upstairs and make love to him.

If only she could . . .

Sighing regretfully, she nipped his lips and pulled back. She felt his reluctance as he released her. Forcing herself to let go of him, she stepped away, opened the door, and walked outside.

Otto was heading up the driveway from where his car was parked on the street as they left and it dawned on her that he still wore his black jeans and sweater from that afternoon . . . he hadn't morphed into tacky Otto tonight. He actually looked like a grown-up.

"I forgot something," he said. He handed Valerius a device that looked like a small transmitter. "Just in case. The Council wants everyone tagged so that if something happens we can pull you out."

To her amazement, he handed her one as well.

"Thanks, Otto."

He inclined his head to her. "You two be careful. Talon will be out around the Square tonight along with Kyrian and Julian. They'll also be scoping on Ursulines around Sanctuary and Chartres, and the French Market. You guys might want to patrol somewhere else."

"We'll hang around the northwest side of the Quarter. Bourbon, Toulouse, St. Louis, Bienville, and Dauphine."

Valerius cringed as soon as Bourbon came out, but didn't say anything.

"Ash is taking the cemeteries," Otto continued, "Janice will be down along Canal, Harrod's, and the Warehouse District while Jean-Luc takes the Garden District. Ulric is in the Business District and Zoe is at Tulane. Which leaves Kassim, who has been told by Ash that if he, Amanda, or Marissa leave Kyrian's house before dawn, he'll be toast."

"Who's Ulric?" Tabitha asked.

Otto gave her a droll stare. "He's the Dark-Hunter from Biloxi who arrived about half an hour ago. He's blond, so try not to stab this one should you meet him in an alley."

Tabitha was offended. "What? It's not my fault I stab all the fanged people. They shouldn't look like Daimons."

"I didn't look like a Daimon, but you stabbed me."

Otto laughed.

"Yeah, well, you looked like a lawyer so I had to kill you. It was a moral imperative."

Valerius shook his head at her.

Sobering, she looked back at Otto. "How many Squires are left in town?"

"Just me, Kyl, and Nick. The last ones out were Tad and your ex Eric and his wife, who hopped a chartered flight about an hour ago. Everyone else from Liza on down is out of here until Ash gives the thumbs-up to return."

"What about the Weres?" Valerius asked.

"They're all hanging close to Sanctuary to protect their young and women. Even Vane and Bride are bunking over there for the time being."

"Will the Weres help us at all?" Tabitha asked.

Otto shook his head. "They view this as a human problem and don't want to get involved."

Tabitha huffed at that. "I can't believe them."

"You don't know much about animals, then," Otto said. "It's why Talon wants to keep an eye on the club. The Apollites and Daimons know that once they're inside Sanctuary, no one, not even Ash, can touch them."

Tabitha laughed at that. "Ash doesn't have to touch them to kill them."

"Excuse me?" Valerius and Otto asked simultaneously.

"What?" she asked them. "You didn't know that? Ash is seriously impressive in a fight. He'll take your ass out permanently before you even know he's there. He moves so fast you can't see him half the time."

"Sounds like Corbin," Otto said. "She's a teleporter. She'll poof in, stab a Daimon, and poof out before it disintegrates."

"Corbin?" Tabitha asked.

"A former Greek queen turned Dark-Huntress," Valerius said.

Tabitha rolled her eyes. "Let me guess, not friendly to you?"

"Do I really need to answer that?"

No, he didn't.

"Yeah," Otto said, "but she's a walk in the park compared to Zoe and Samia. You say 'Roman' around them and you better cup yourself fast." He looked at Tabitha. "Well, not you, but those of us with things to protect down there have to."

"Okay," Tabitha said, stepping away from him. "And on that most interesting note, I think it's time we headed off." She gestured toward the beat-up red IROC that was parked on the other side of Valerius's gate. "Mind if we borrow your car, Otto?"

Valerius looked horrified.

Otto laughed evilly as he pulled out the keys. "Be my guest."

Valerius spoke up instantly. "I have my—"

"This'll work," Tabitha said as she winked at Otto and took the keys.

Valerius was rigid. "Really, Tabitha, I think—"

"Get in the car, Val. I promise you it won't bite."

He looked less than convinced.

Laughing, she started down the driveway toward the IROC.

To her surprise, Otto called out after them, "You guys be careful. I may not appreciate either one of you, but I don't want the bad guys to win."

"Don't worry," Tabitha said as she kept walking. "This time, I know what to expect."

"Don't be cocky," Valerius said, giving her a gimlet stare. "It was a far better man than I who said, 'Pride cometh before the fall.' "

She took his words to heart. "Good advice." She looked over his shoulder. "Night, Otto."

"Night, Tabitha. Take care of my car."

Valerius actually cringed.

She stifled her laughter at his reaction. "Mmm," she said, taking a deep breath of air that was all New Orleans as she opened the small gate next to the drive to let them outside the grounds. "Smell the beauty."

Valerius frowned at her. "All I smell is the stench of decay."

She gave him a menacing glare as he joined her on the sidewalk next to Otto's car. "Close your eyes."

"I'd rather not. I might step in something and then I might bring it home and smell it all night."

She gave him a disgusted look that he took in stride.

"You're the only woman I know who can smell this rancid air and think it pleasant."

She shut the gate. "Close your eyes, Valerius, or your nose might be the only part of you that is in working order tomorrow."

Valerius wasn't sure if he should obey her or not, but he found himself reluctantly doing so as he drew up short.

"Now take a deep breath," she said, her sultry voice in his ear. It sent a shiver over him as he did it.

"Do you smell the dampness of the river with a hint of Cajun gumbo scenting it? Not to mention the Spanish moss?"

He opened his eyes. "All I smell is urine, rotten seafood, and river slime."

She gaped at him. "How can you say that?"

"Because it's what I smell."

She growled at him as she got into the car. "You're a tough sell, you know that?"

"I've been called worse."

Her gaze turned serious and sad. "I know you have. But new times are upon you. I'm taking that stick up your butt out and tonight we're going to cut loose, kick Daimon ass, and—"

"I beg your pardon?" he asked in an offended tone. "The what up my where?"

"You heard me," she said with a wicked smile. "You know, half the problem people have with you is that you don't laugh much and you take yourself and everything else way too seriously."

"Life *is* serious."

"No," she said, her passion glowing in her blue gaze. "Life is an adventure. It's thrilling and scary. Sometimes it's even a bit boring, but it should never be serious."

Tabitha saw the hesitancy in his eyes. He was so unused to trusting people and for some reason, she wanted him to trust her. "Come with me, General Valerius, and let me show you just what life can really be and why it's so damned important that we save the world."

She watched as he opened the door handle like a man who was touching a baby's dirty diaper. She'd never seen anyone sneer more. It was quite impressive.

But he didn't say anything more as he got into the car and she dropped it into gear and squealed away from the curb.

Valerius wasn't expecting much to come of this night; but he had to admit that he did like the vibrancy of this woman. The zeal with which she lived. She was fascinating to watch. No wonder Ash had befriended her.

When one was an immortal, the freshness of life had a way of dying even more quickly than one's body had. As the centuries blended together, it was easy to forget the human side of oneself. To remember why humanity needed saving.

It was hard to remember how to laugh. Then again, laughter and Valerius were virtual strangers. Until Tabitha, he'd never really shared a laugh with anyone.

Tabitha had the enthusiasm of a child. Somehow she had managed to hold on to her youthful ideals even in the face of a world that didn't entirely accept her. She truly didn't care what he, or anyone else, thought of her. She went through her life doing what she needed to do and handling everything on her own terms.

How he envied her that.

She was a powerful force to be reckoned with.

Valerius laughed in spite of himself.

"What?" she asked as she whipped the car around a corner so fast that she practically threw him into her seat.

He righted himself. "I was just thinking someone should name you Hurricane Tabitha."

She snorted. "You're too late. My mother already did. Actually, she named me that the first time she visited my dorm room and saw the chaos of me without my sister Amanda around to pick up after me. You should be grateful that after twelve years of living on my own, I finally learned to pick up for myself."

He shuddered at the thought. "Truly, I am grateful."

She cut the car sharply into the Jackson Brewery parking lot and whipped it into a parking space that wasn't really supposed to be a parking space.

"The police will tow the car."

"Nah," she said as she shut it off and placed a small silver medallion on the dashboard that had her name engraved on it. "This is Ed's route and he knows better. I'll get my sister to hex him and his brother if he tries."

"Ed?"

"One of the cops assigned here. He keeps an eye out for me. We used to go to high school together and he dated my older sister, Karma, for years."

"You have a sister named Karma?" Valerius asked.

"Yes and it's very apt. She has a nasty tendency to come back and hurt anyone who does her wrong whenever they least expect it. She's like the big, black spider, lying in wait." The words weren't nearly as amusing as the gesture Tabitha made where she held her hands up and nibbled like a rabid mouse. "Just when you think you're safe from her wrath . . . bam!" She slapped her hands together. "She knocks your feet out from under you and leaves you lying on the floor, bleeding profusely."

"I do hope you're joking."

"Not at all. She's a scary woman, but I love her."

Valerius got out of the car, then paused as a thought occurred to him. Every time he turned around, she pulled out another relative. "Just how many sisters do you have?"

"Eight."

"Eight?" he asked, stunned at the number. No wonder he couldn't keep them all straight. He wondered how she did.

Tabitha nodded. "Tiyana who goes by Tia. Selena and Amanda you know. Then there's Esmerelda, or Essie, as we call her. Yasmina or Mina. Petra, Ekaterina who goes by Trina mostly, and Karma who refuses to have a nickname."

Valerius gave a low whistle at her roll call.

"What?" Tabitha asked.

"I'm just pitying whatever poor males lived in that house with all of you. It must have been truly frightening at least one week out of every month."

She gaped, then laughed out loud. "Was that a joke from you?"

"Merely a frightening statement of fact."

"Yeah, right. Well, truth be told, my father did spend a lot of time at work during that time of the month and he did make sure that all our pets were males so that he wouldn't feel too terribly outnumbered. What about you? Did you have any sisters?"

He shook his head as she joined him over on the passenger side of the car and they headed toward Decatur Street. "I only had brothers."

"Whoa, just imagine if your father had married my mother, we'd have had the Brady Bunch."

He scoffed at her. "Hardly. Believe me, my family made the Borgias look like Ozzie and Harriet."

She cocked her head at him. "For a man who prides himself on being prim and proper, you certainly know a lot of pop icons."

He didn't comment.

"So how many brothers did you have?" she asked, surprising him with her quick return to their previous topic.

He started not to answer and yet it came out before he could stop himself. "Until a couple of years ago, I thought I only had four."

"What happened then?"

"I found out that Zarek was one of them, too."

Tabitha frowned at his disclosure. "You didn't know while you were alive?"

Guilt and anger tore through Valerius at her innocent question. He really should have known. Had he ever bothered to look at Zarek when they were human . . .

But then, he was his father's son.

"No," he said sadly, "I didn't."

"Yet you knew him?"

"He was a slave in our house."

She looked aghast. "But he was your brother?"

He nodded.

Tabitha was as confused as he'd been the night he learned the truth. "How could you not know?"

"You don't understand the world I lived in. You didn't

question certain things. When my father spoke, it was truth. You didn't look at servants, and Zarek . . . he wasn't recognizable in those days."

Tabitha felt a wave of grief so profound that it made her ache with him. She wrapped her arm around his and gave a light squeeze.

"What are you doing?" he asked.

"I'm standing beside you so that Zarek won't whack you again with another lightning bolt. You said he wouldn't hurt innocent people, right?"

"Yes."

She smiled at him. "Call me Shield."

Valerius smiled in spite of himself as he placed a hand on her forearm. "You're such a strange woman."

"Yeah, but I'm growing on you, aren't I?"

"Yes, you are."

Her smile widened. "Fungus are us. Next thing you know, you'll actually like me."

The problem was, he already did like her. A lot more than he should.

"Where are we going?" he asked as she scooted him down Decatur toward Iberville and away from where they might run into one of the crew who begrudged him every breath he took.

"Well, it's early still, so I figured an early perimeter check followed by an intense search of the Abyss, which is a club I am sure you have never stepped foot into. A lot of Apollites like to hang there and I've dusted quite a few Daimons in and about the area."

"Isn't that one of the clubs Acheron frequents?"

"Yes, but since he's in the cemeteries, I have a feeling the Daimons will be congregating where they think it's safe."

He couldn't argue that.

Tabitha led him over to the Magnolia Café.

"Are you hungry again?" he asked in disbelief as she entered the restaurant.

"No."

"Then why are we in here?"

"Don't worry about it." She went to the counter and ordered five meals to go.

Valerius was completely baffled as he glanced around what most people would call a "homey" place. It had red-and-white checked plastic tablecloths and small tables and chairs that someone might find in a normal home.

It most definitely wasn't the kind of place Valerius ate at, but it did look like Tabitha's cup of tea.

When the orders were ready, Tabitha grabbed them up and led the way back to the street.

Valerius followed behind her, curious about what she was going to do with them.

His curiosity ended in a dark alley. She left the bags of food, then pulled him out by the arm. He heard people scurrying in the darkness.

"You're feeding the homeless," he said quietly.

She nodded.

"Do you do this a lot?"

"Every night about this time."

He pulled her to a stop and stared at her. "Why?"

"Someone has to." When he opened his mouth to speak, she placed her hand over his lips. "I know all the arguments, Val. Why should they work when people like me are willing to feed them for free? You can't save the world. Let someone else take care of them, etc. But I can't do it. Every night when I come out here, I know they're there and I know they're in pain. One of the men, Martin, was at one time a prominent business owner who got sued and lost everything. His wife divorced him and took the kids. And since he had dropped out of high school and was fifty-six when he had to go bankrupt, no one would hire him. He worked for me in my store, but it wasn't enough to support him and he didn't want to take charity, so he slept in alleys. I wanted to give him a raise so badly, but if I did that, I'd have to give one to everyone and I can't afford to pay every part-time employee in my store thirty thousand dollars a year."

"I wasn't going to say anything about that, Tabitha," he said quietly. "I only wanted to tell you that your compassion for other people overwhelms me."

"Oh." She offered him a tenuous smile. "I'm just used to people condemning everything I do."

He lifted her hand to his lips and kissed her knuckles. "I don't condemn you, my lady. I only admire you."

Her smile turned full fledged and floored him. She squeezed his hand with hers, then did the most unexpected thing of all. She put her arm around his waist and started walking down the street with him.

Valerius felt so strange. He'd seen lovers do this for centuries, but had never had anyone do it with him. Hesitantly, he draped his arm over her shoulders and just let the warmth of her body and touch seep into him.

There were no words for what he felt right now. It was a very common thing they were doing. People shouldn't touch so intimately in public. And yet he'd never known a better feeling than to have this odd woman by his side.

The breeze brushed strands of her hair over his hand. It was soft and light and brought images to his mind that he shouldn't have of her wild in his bed. Untamed.

And it played havoc with his body.

They didn't speak much as they walked through the dark city where the humans went about their business oblivious to the danger that was hanging over them. It was eerily peaceful.

It was a little after midnight when they made their way over to Toulouse Street. The Abyss wasn't the typical New Orleans club scene. It was dark and far from inviting like most of the more touristy places that beckoned the mainstream inside.

Tabitha led him down a long alleyway that was narrow and a bit spooky in feel.

"Hey, Tabby," a tall, African-American man greeted her as he was checking the IDs of the couple in front of them. He was bald with tattoos marking every inch of exposed flesh . . . even his hands.

"Hi, Ty," Tabitha said. "How's it going tonight?"

"Not bad," he said with a wink as he waved the couple in. "Who's your friend?" he asked, raking Valerius with a frown.

"Val. He's a friend of Ash and Simi's, too."

"No shit?" Ty said before he extended his hand to Valerius. "Ty Gagne. Nice to meet you."

Valerius shook his hand. "You, too."

"You two have fun, and Tabby, no weapons tonight, deal?"

"Yeah, yeah, Ty. No bloodshed. Gotcha."

Once inside the club, Valerius was taken aback by the sea of black-garbed humans. It looked like a Dark-Hunter convention. It was extremely easy to pick out the tourists who had stumbled inadvertently into the club or maybe had been dared into it. There were more body piercings and tattoos than he'd ever seen in one room in his entire two thousand years of living.

Many of the regulars knew Tabitha on sight.

"Hi, Vlad," Tabitha said to one emaciated, tall man with skin so pale it was translucent. He wore a white ruffled shirt, blood-red velvet tuxedo jacket, and black slacks. His long, black hair hung around his gaunt face, and his eyes were covered by a pair of round, black sunglasses.

"Good evening, Tabitha," the man said, before he smiled to show Valerius a set of fangs. He saluted them with a brandy snifter that looked like it held blood. Valerius's Dark-Hunter sense could tell it was red vodka. Vlad's long, skinny fingers were covered with silver claws.

Valerius felt an urge to laugh and show the man his own set of real fangs, but refrained.

"Vlad is a fifteenth-century vampire," she told Valerius.

"Son to Vlad Tepes and named for my esteemed father," Vlad explained in a faked Transylvanian accent.

"Really?" Valerius said. "I find that fascinating since Vlad's only son, Radu, was slain by the Turks when he was eighteen. Vlad's only surviving child was a daughter, Esperetta, who now lives in Miami."

"Vlad" rolled his eyes. "Really, Tabitha, where do you find these people?"

Valerius did laugh as the fake vampire drifted off.

Tabitha joined him. "Seriously," she said, sobering. "Is there any truth to that bull you just spieled?"

He nodded. "Ask Ash. Retta's husband was made into a Dark-Hunter around 1480, I believe, and she followed him over. Her husband is one of the few Dark-Hunters who will actually speak to me in a civil tone."

"Kewl!" Tabitha stepped back as another Goth princess walked between them.

She indicated a stairway with the tilt of her head. "There are three bars here and an area called the Library. Daimons are usually found lurking in the Library or the Sound bar. The other two are the Main bar and the Aphrodite bar. Oh, and I should probably warn you that Eros and Psyche tend to haunt the Aphrodite bar as well, so you might want to leave that to me in case they show up."

"Hey, Tabby!" a plump blonde said as she grabbed Tabitha in an overbearing hug. "You seen any vampires tonight?"

"Hi, Carly," she said, casting an amused look at Valerius. "Not tonight. Why?"

"Well, if you find one, send him my way. I'm ready to be bitten and made immortal."

Tabitha rolled her eyes. "I told you they can't do that. It's a Hollywood myth."

"Yeah, well, I wanna be mythitized. So if you find one, tell him I'm in the Library, waiting."

"Okay," she said with a nod. "I'll do it."

"Thanks, doll."

Valerius rubbed his eyebrow as the blonde woman left them. "You know a lot of interesting people."

She laughed at him. "This from someone who takes orders from a man who's been walking around for almost twelve thousand years, not to mention that you actually do know the daughter of Count Dracula. I don't want to hear it from you, buddy."

She had a point with that.

"Could you relax?" She tugged his coat collar up before she untied and then started mussing his hair.

"What are you doing?"

"Trying to make you blend in. It would certainly help if you didn't look like you were constipated right now."

"I beg your pardon?"

"C'mon," she said, brushing her hand against his lips as she tried to smooth them. "Stop curling your lip and looking like you're afraid you're going to catch something. It's not like you can die or anything."

"You're the one who should be worried."

She made a rude noise at him. "This from a man whose culture actually invented bulimia. Tell me, how many times did you visit the old vomitorium anyway?"

"We didn't all do that, thank you."

"Yeah, right." She drifted off.

Valerius hastened his steps to catch up to her. The last thing he wanted was to be left alone with the strangeness of the people gathered in this place. Granted, they couldn't hurt him, but they were disturbing nonetheless. He couldn't imagine why Acheron preferred to "hang" at a place such as this. It was so loud that he couldn't hear himself think. The lights played havoc with his eyesight, and the skeleton and bat decor . . .

It just wasn't where he would spend his spare time if he had any choice in the matter.

But Tabitha blended in with an eerie kind of conformity. This was her environment. Her people and culture.

There was nothing stodgy about anyone here.

She led him toward the dance floor, where she was hailed by a woman with an extremely tall, electric blue mohawk.

Valerius watched in horror as Tabitha dashed across the floor to dance with the woman and what appeared to be a man dressed in shiny plastic that was held to his body by large silver buckles. The man's eyes and lips were painted black and his hair looked as though it had never been brushed.

Tabitha didn't seem to notice as she swayed to the loud, thrashing music. She was lovely.

She didn't care who watched her. There was no such thing as decorum or rules that held her back.

She merely was.

And he loved her for that.

Laughing at something the man said, she swooped low to the floor, then came up with a limber rhythm that ignited more fantasies than he would have thought possible. Every masculine part of him was aware of her. Aware of the softness of her face, the way the lights made her skin luminescent.

The way her body moved like liquid to the pounding beat.

She looked at him then. The minute her blue eyes met his, his groin jerked with needful anticipation.

Smiling, she crooked a finger for him to join her.

Valerius actually took a step forward before he caught himself. Dancing wasn't something he did in public. As a Roman, his father had thought it crass and lowly, and had forbidden all of them to partake of it. As a Dark-Hunter, he'd never thought to learn.

Unwilling to embarrass her before her friends, he stepped back.

Tabitha paused, then said something to the man and woman. She kissed the man on his cheek and hugged the woman, then joined him.

"Let me guess, Romans have no rhythm?"

"Not any that I wish to share."

She smiled even wider. "I would put that to the test, but having seen you dance, I . . ." Her voice trailed off as her gaze went past his shoulder.

Valerius turned his head to see what had her transfixed. He spied the Daimons instantly.

There were five of them.

And they were headed toward the exit with a small group of women.

Chapter 9

Tabitha headed for the Daimons without thought until Valerius pulled her to a stop. "What are you doing?" she asked him indignantly.

"It's a trap."

She frowned up at him. "What?"

There was a strange look on his face as he tightened his grip on her arm. "Can't you feel it? Even without powers I sense this one."

"No and if we don't go out there, they're going to kill those people." She tried to twist her arm out of his grasp, but he held tight.

"Tabitha, listen to me. This isn't right. Daimons are never that bold and they had to know I was in here."

He was right. It was too obvious. In this crowd Valerius stood out like sunshine in darkness. "What do you suggest we do, then? Just let the innocent die?"

"No. You stay here and I'll go."

"Bull—"

"Tabitha," he snapped at her, his black eyes burning into her. "I'm immortal. You're not. Unless one of them is wielding an ax, they can't hurt me much. Whatever they do to me, I will survive. *You* might not."

She wanted to argue with him, but she knew he was right. Not to mention she could feel inside that he was sincere. This wasn't some macho move to prove himself superior to her.

He was concerned for her safety, and if he was worried about her, he wouldn't be able to fight clear headedly.

"Okay," she said. "You go and I'll try not to follow."

A tic worked in his jaw. "For my sake, please do more than try. Succeed." He released her and before she could blink, he was out of sight.

Valerius hurried through the crowd, after the Daimons. He paused at the entrance long enough to ask Ty to keep Tabitha in the bar for her own safety. He wasn't sure if the man would help him with that or not, but if Ty could slow her down some, maybe it would give him enough time to kill the Daimons before she got there and endangered herself.

Leaving the bar, he hesitated on the street. The loud music still rang in his ears. But even so, he could sense the Daimons . . .

At the end of the block, he turned down Royal and headed in the direction that he was certain they had vanished. The Daimons were moving fast, drawing him into the darkness.

Unless he was mistaken, which was unlikely, there was a large group of them.

He slowed a bit as he approached St. Louis Street and turned onto it. He hadn't gone far before he came upon a gate slightly ajar.

They were inside. Quiet and still.

Waiting.

Had they killed the humans already?

Pulling out a dagger and holding it so that the blade was in line with his forearm while the hilt rested lethally in his palm, he pushed the gate wider, taking care not to make a sound as he slipped inside the pitch-black courtyard.

It was a moonless night, and unlike most of New Orleans, there were no lights back here. He moved around the side of the building, knowing exactly what to expect.

The Daimons were lying in wait for him.

He could hear someone clucking his tongue.

"It's been a long time since I faced a truly intelligent Dark-Hunter. This one already knows we're here."

Valerius came around the shrubbery to find a group of

nine Daimons waiting in the courtyard. The women he had thought were human weren't.

They were fanged.

Damn.

Valerius drew himself up to his entire, imperious height and arched a brow at the group. "Well, when one puts out a cosmic calling card, I assume one wants it answered."

A slow smile spread over the Daimon's lips who'd spoken as he moved slowly through the group so that he could stand before Valerius. An inch shorter, the Daimon had a lean build and, like all of his kind, was perfect in his male form.

"The call wasn't for you." The Daimon sighed wearily. Obviously disgusted, he looked at the group behind him. "I thought I told you to draw the woman out, not the Dark-Hunter."

"We tried, Desiderius," one of the women said. "She stayed behind."

Valerius saw red at the name of the Daimon who had scarred Tabitha's face. He wanted to tear the Daimon to shreds, but knew better than to betray himself or Tabitha by acting as if she were special to him.

Had he maintained his composure the night his brothers had killed him, they would have left Agrippina alone. He wasn't about to sacrifice Tabitha needlessly.

Desiderius frowned. "Tabitha Devereaux stayed behind?"

"The Dark-Hunter told her to," another Daimon supplied. "I heard them."

"Interesting." Desiderius turned to face him. "I find it hard to imagine Tabitha would listen to anyone. You must be *special* indeed."

"She didn't think of you as a threat," Valerius said nonchalantly. "You weren't worth her time." He yawned at them. "No more than you're worth mine."

The Daimon moved to blast him.

Valerius caught his arm, whirled, and elbowed him in the throat. Desiderius staggered back, cursing.

"I know all about Greeks and their tricks," he snarled as he seized Desiderius's neck in his fist and flipped the Daimon onto the street. "Most of all, I know to kill them."

Before he could move his dagger and kill Desiderius, the

others swarmed him. One grabbed him from behind while one of the females moved in to stab him with a long, vicious-looking dagger.

Valerius kicked her back, then twisted to confront the ones behind him. One of the Daimons slugged him across the face. He ground his teeth as pain exploded along his cheek to his nose, and he tasted blood.

But then, pain was nothing new to him. As a mortal, he'd been well acquainted with beatings and pain.

Valerius returned the blow with one of his own that sent the Daimon to his knees.

Out of nowhere, a god-bolt struck him hard in the center of his chest. It knocked him off his feet and sent him slamming into the brick wall behind him. Valerius couldn't breathe. He tried to stay standing, but the sheer agony of it overrode his desire and he crumpled to the ground.

"Hurts, doesn't it?" Desiderius said. "It was a gift inherited from my father." Desiderius bent down and seized Valerius's right hand and studied his Roman seal ring. "Now there's something I find interesting, too. A Roman in New Orleans. Kyrian of Thrace must truly love you."

Valerius glared at him as he forced himself to roll.

He'd barely moved before Desiderius hit him with another shocking bolt.

"What are we going to do with him?" one of the women asked.

Desiderius laughed once again, then seized him.

But it was Valerius who laughed hardest as he kicked the Daimon back and shrugged off his pain.

He caught Desiderius and slung him against the wall where he rebounded with a thud. "The question isn't what are you going to do with me. It's what I'm going to do to you."

Tabitha couldn't stand waiting any longer. But she wasn't completely stupid, either. Pulling out her cell phone, she called Acheron, who answered on the first ring.

"Hey, Tabby," he said with a laugh, "Valerius's cell is 204-555-6239."

"I really hate it when you do that, Ash."

"You know what you're going to hate even more?"

"I can't imagine."

"Turn around."

She did and found him standing on the other side of the bar. At six feet eight and wearing a pair of tall Goth boots that added a good three inches to his height, he was impossible to miss.

In spite of what he said, she felt a wave of relief at seeing him there. Hanging up her phone, she crossed the room to meet him. "What are you doing here?"

"I knew you were going to head off after Valerius and I'm here to go with you."

"Then you think he's in trouble, too."

"I know he is. Let's go."

Tabitha didn't ask him to elaborate. She knew him better than that. Acheron Parthenopaeus seldom ever answered anything. He lived life on his own terms and was eerily secretive about everything.

Ash led the way out of the club and into the street. Tabitha didn't know where they were headed, but he seemed to know instinctively.

"I have a really bad feeling," she said to Ash as they practically ran down the street.

"So do I," he said, ducking into an open gate.

Tabitha followed him inside, then skidded to a halt as she caught sight of the most incredible thing she'd ever seen in her life.

Valerius fighting. He held a sword in each hand as he fought off four Daimons who lunged and parried with consummate skill of their own. It was fluid, violent, and morbidly beautiful.

Spinning about, Valerius caught one of the blond Daimons with an uppercut that tore through his chest, piercing the dark spot over their hearts where the human souls gathered. It caused the Daimon to explode into a golden powder.

Ash joined the fight by catching two of the Daimons with a staff. He drove them away from Valerius, allowing the Roman to concentrate on the other Daimon.

Tabitha took a step forward only to feel something cold and evil brush up against her.

"Predictable," came that sinister, haunting voice again.

A flash of something sizzled past her, heading toward Acheron.

One moment Ash was piercing a Daimon with his staff and in the next, he was on his knees as Valerius killed his own Daimon.

The second Daimon Ash had been fighting moved to stab Ash, only to have his blow intercepted by Valerius, who kicked the Daimon back, then killed him.

Tabitha ran to Ash, who was on the ground, hissing as he held his arm as if it were broken.

"Simi," he panted. "Human form. Now!"

The large dragon tattoo on Ash's forearm peeled itself off his skin into a dark red shadow that quickly transformed into the demon Tabitha knew so well.

"*Akri?*" Simi asked as she caught Ash's head. "*Akri*, what hurts?"

Tabitha knelt down beside them and tried to see Ash's arm. It was literally turning into stone, only it wasn't growing hard. His skin was turning a grayish-white color and it was spreading up his arm, toward his shoulder.

His face battered from his fight, Valerius fell to his knees on the other side of Ash. "What is that?"

Ash writhed as if he were on fire. "*Simi . . . Akra . . . Thea Kalosis. Biazomai, biazomai.*"

Tabitha saw the terrified look on Simi's face before the demon vanished.

"Ash?" she asked, panicking. "What's going on?"

"Nothing," he gasped. He grabbed Valerius's shirt. "Get Tabitha home. Now!"

"We can't leave you," they said in unison.

"Go!" Ash snapped an instant before the grayish stone- . like skin crawled over more of his body.

They didn't.

Ash fought and screamed as the grayish color spread all over his body. Tabitha laid him out flat on the ground. Ash panted as if trying to fight off whatever had him.

It was a losing battle.

His swirling silver eyes bulged before they too turned gray and he was as still as a corpse. Ash wasn't breathing. He wasn't moving. It was as if something held him completely paralyzed.

"What do we do?" she asked Valerius.

"You die."

Tabitha spun at the malevolent voice behind her to face the ghost again. It was surrounded by more Daimons.

"Good Lord, who spread the Daimon fertilizer around? They're cropping up like a bad horror flick," Tabitha said.

Valerius rose to his feet.

Before she could move, Valerius engaged them.

Tabitha rushed to join the fight.

"Don't kill the woman!" the ghost snarled to the Daimons. "I need her alive."

Another blond Daimon laughed. "Yeah, but feel free to rough her up all you want."

Tabitha turned to find yet another Daimon behind her. She struck out with her arm only to have him dodge her blow, then straighten up to deliver a staggering strike to her ribs.

The pain drove her straight to her knees.

Valerius cursed and started for her. Two Daimons cut him off.

With nothing more than sheer strength of will, Tabitha regained her feet.

The Daimon looked impressed.

Tabitha went to hit him, only to have him move away, lightning fast. This time when he tried to strike her, he was slammed into the building beside her.

"Leave her alone," Valerius snarled. He put himself between her and the rest of the Daimons.

Tabitha pulled her sleeve back and shot a crossbow bolt into the nearest Daimon. He disintegrated.

Suddenly, something ricocheted through the Daimons, killing two instantly before it vanished.

Tabitha looked past the Daimon horde to see a cavalry. Julian, Talon, and Kyrian were coming in, weapons drawn.

She'd never been happier to see any of them.

Alone each one of the blond men was dangerous. Together, they were invincible.

Side by side with Valerius, she fought the Daimons while Kyrian, Julian, and Talon joined the fight. With the five of them, it didn't take any time at all to finish the Daimons off. In truth, it was a colorful display as one by one the Daimons disintegrated.

Except for the one who had struck her. The ghost wrapped itself around that particular Daimon and the two of them appeared to evaporate into nothing.

Tabitha frowned at the peculiar sight.

Until she heard Kyrian's resonant curse.

One moment Valerius was beside her, the next he was being slammed face-first into the wall.

"You bastard!" Kyrian snarled as he pummeled him.

Valerius ducked the blows and whirled to the side. He slammed Kyrian into the wall and would have pinned him had Julian not grabbed him from behind.

The next thing she knew, Julian was hitting Valerius, too.

Without thinking, Tabitha rushed Julian, knocking him back. She put herself between the Roman and the two Greeks.

"Get out of my way, Tabitha," Kyrian said as he glared his hatred at Valerius. "I don't want Amanda pissed at me because I hurt you for being stupid."

"And I don't want Amanda pissed at me because I permanently maimed you for being an idiot."

"This isn't a game, Tabitha," Julian said sternly.

In his human life, Julian had been the Greek general who had commanded Kyrian. Unfortunately, he'd run afoul of the gods, who had cursed him into a book to be a sex slave to whatever woman summoned him out.

Selena's best friend Grace Alexander had set the half-god free.

Since then, Julian had often joined ranks with the Dark-Hunters to fight the Daimons, and now he was joining ranks with Kyrian to kill Valerius.

It was something she would never allow.

She held her arms out to keep them back. "No, it isn't."

"It's all right, Tabitha," Valerius said from behind her. "This is a confrontation that's been a long time coming."

"Talon," Tabitha said, glancing over to the tall blond Celt who was standing behind his Greek friends. As always, Talon was dressed like a biker in a black motorcycle jacket,

T-shirt, and leather pants. His hair was cut short except for two thin braids that hung from his left temple. "Are you going to help me?"

Talon grimaced. "Unfortunately, yes." He moved to stand with her.

"Celt—" Kyrian snarled.

His face determined, Talon crossed his arms over his chest.

"Look," Tabitha said between clenched teeth. "We have bigger problems right now than you two hating Valerius and his family."

"Like what?" Kyrian asked.

Tabitha pointed to the ground where Ash still lay.

Kyrian's face went pale as his gaze focused on Ash's body. "What happened?"

"I don't know," Tabitha said. "One of the Daimons did that to him and we need to get him to safety."

Kyrian passed a grudging, angry look at Valerius. "We're not through."

Valerius said nothing as he moved toward Ash.

When he started to lift Ash up, Kyrian shoved him back. "Get your filthy hands off him, Roman. We don't need your help. We take care of our own."

"Valerius happens to be the only Dark-Hunter here," Tabitha snapped at her brother-in-law. "He has more right to help Ash—"

"Greeks don't want or need Roman help," Julian said as he brushed roughly past Valerius.

Tabitha felt Valerius's anger, his pain, but most of all, she felt shame from him.

Why?

"Val?"

As soon as it was out of her mouth, Tabitha realized she'd just made a strategic mistake. Kyrian let out a vulgar curse. "Oh, don't tell me you've taken up with *him*. Shit, Tabitha, I thought even you had more sense than that."

That was it! Tabitha went to stand in front of him. "Get off the cross, Kyrian. Literally." She gestured behind her to Valerius. "He didn't hurt you."

Kyrian curled his lip at her. "How do you know? Were you there?"

"Ooo, childish much? No, I wasn't there. But I can do math and I know how old he was when you were killed. What? You let a five-year-old nail you down?"

Someone grabbed her from behind. Tabitha started to attack until she realized it was Valerius pulling her back. "Don't, Tabitha. Just let it go."

"Why should I? I'm tired of the way they treat you. Aren't you?"

Valerius's face was completely stoic, but his heart wasn't. She felt his pain. "I honestly don't care what they think of me. I really don't. And you don't need to alienate your entire family. Just leave this alone."

"Why?"

Valerius looked past her to Kyrian, then he stared at her. Hard. "This will wait. Right now, Acheron and you need to be safe. Go with Kyrian."

Tabitha wanted to argue, but he was right and she wasn't so stubborn as to not recognize that basic fact. The longer they stood out here arguing, the more danger Ash was in, especially since Simi wasn't here to protect him.

Their first priority was to get Ash to safety. "You be careful."

Valerius gave her a strangely tender Roman salute, then spun on his heel and left them.

"You're unbelievable," Kyrian snarled as he and Julian lifted Acheron's body up from the ground. "I can't believe you screamed at Amanda about me and you'd cuddle up to that bastard."

"Shut up, Kyrian," Tabitha said. "Unlike Amanda, I don't mind staking you straight through the heart."

"Where are we taking T-Rex?" Talon asked as he grabbed Ash's feet and helped to carry him.

"Back to my house," Kyrian answered. "After the attack of that demon on Bride Kattalakis when she was visiting us, Ash put some kind of mojo on it to make it safe. I figure whatever did this to him can't come back and hurt him if he's there."

Talon nodded. "What exactly did this to him?"

Tabitha shrugged. "I don't know. He was hit with something and poof, down he went. It happened so fast, I didn't even see what they hit him with."

Talon let out a slow breath. "Man, I wouldn't have thought anything could bring down Ash. Not like this."

"Yeah," Tabitha agreed, "but at least he's still alive. Kind of . . . in a freaky sort of way."

She didn't want to admit to them just how frightened she was of the fact that the Daimons had brought the powerful Atlantean down without breaking a sweat. If they could do this, then there was no telling what they could do to the rest of them.

Which begged the question of why the Daimons had left them alone when they could have killed them, too.

It didn't make sense.

They wended their way down the darker, less traveled alleys, watching for Daimons and innocent passersby who might call the cops if they saw them carrying what appeared to be a dead body as they headed for Julian's Land Rover.

Tabitha got in the backseat with Ash while Talon stayed behind to continue patrolling for Daimons. Getting into the front passenger's seat, Kyrian remained sullenly silent while Julian drove them over to the Garden District where Kyrian's mansion stood less than two blocks away from Valerius's.

She wondered if either man realized just how close they lived to each other. They were practically neighbors and yet they were divided by infinite hatred.

Putting that out of her mind, she ran her hand over Ash's hair. It had an odd, spongy texture. His eyes were half-open and for once the silvery color didn't swirl. It was terrifying to think something could do this to him and none of them knew what it was or if they could restore him.

God, what would happen if they couldn't?

What would happen to the Dark-Hunters if they didn't have Ash to lead them anymore? It was a terrifying thought. He always knew what to do and to say. How to make things better for everyone.

Biting her lip, Tabitha fought her panic down. Simi would get help for Ash. There was no way she wouldn't.

The men got out and pulled Ash from the seat, then carried him into the house with Tabitha one step behind them.

Amanda came off the sofa the instant she saw Ash being carried into her foyer. "Oh my God, what happened?"

"We don't know," Kyrian said as he and Julian carried Ash toward the mahogany stairs.

"Tabby?" Amanda asked.

She shrugged as she followed after the men. Amanda joined the procession up the stairs. As they reached the top landing, a tall African-American man came out of one of the guest rooms.

"Acheron?" he said, his voice thickly accented.

"We don't know what happened," Kyrian said in answer to his unasked question as they brushed past him.

"Hi, I'm Tabitha," she said, extending her hand to the new Dark-Hunter who was guarding her family.

"Kassim," he said, shaking her hand before they both followed the men into Ash's room.

Once they had Ash safely tucked into the bed, Kyrian curled his lip at Tabitha. "Why don't you ask your sister about her new friend, Amanda?"

"Kyrian," Tabitha said in warning. "Lay off or you will limp."

"What friend?" Amanda asked.

"Valerius Magnus," Julian said. "They were rather friendly tonight when we found them."

"Yes, we were," Tabitha said. "And it's none of your business."

Amanda gave her a harsh stare. "Tabitha—"

"Shut up!" Tabitha snapped. "Look, I will gladly submit to the 'jump all over sister Tabitha' session *after* we help Ash. Right now, I'm going to start calling some people and see if anyone knows how to fix this. You guys can stand here with your thumbs up your butts and roast me all you want, but I'm not listening."

Pulling her phone off her belt, Tabitha headed for the stairs, then down to the living room and called Tia, who was completely useless for this.

"C'mon, T," Tabitha begged her sister. "There has to be an undo spell."

"Not if you don't know what caused it. Ash isn't exactly human, Tab. One wrong move and we could really do some damage to him."

Tabitha growled into the phone, then hung up. Amanda had just joined her in the living room when they heard something hit the front door so hard, it rattled the hinges.

Handing the phone to Amanda, Tabitha pulled her stiletto from her boot.

"Akri!" Simi's maniacal wail echoed through the house like vicious thunder. "Let the Simi in, *akri!*"

"What *is* that?" Amanda asked, her face ashen.

"It's Ash's demon."

"Simi is making that godawful sound?" Kyrian asked as he and Julian ran down the stairs.

"Looks like," Tabitha said as she headed toward the door. Kyrian beat her to it. "No!" he snarled. "It could be a trick."

"Trick my ass," she muttered. "Simi? Is it you outside?"

"Tabitha, let me in. I can't help *akri* if I can't see him. I gots to help my *akri*. Lemme in or the Simi will barbecue this door, so help me."

"You can't, Simi. The shield would hurt you if you tried to. They have to invite you in."

Tabitha froze as she heard the unfamiliar, gentle feminine voice on the other side of the door. It held just a faint hint of a foreign accent. "Who's with you, Sim?"

"One of the bitch-goddess's *koris*, they them people who serve her in her temple on Olympus. Katra good quality people who gonna help my *akri*. Now let the Simi in!"

"It's okay," Tabitha said to Kyrian. "I know Simi well enough to vouch that it's really her out there."

Kyrian gave her a menacing stare. "Yeah, and you know Valerius, too. That gives me so much faith in your judgment—not."

Tabitha went rigid. "Amanda, if your husband's balls have any meaning to you, I suggest you move him out of my way or he's going to be singing in soprano."

"Let her open the door, Kyrian."

"Like hell," he snarled. "My daughter is asleep upstairs."

"Her niece is asleep upstairs," Amanda reminded him. "Tabitha would never endanger Marissa. Now move."

Kyrian made a gesture as if he'd like to choke both of them, then stepped aside.

Tabitha swung open the door to see Simi outside with an extremely tall, robed woman.

Neither woman asked where Ash was, they seemed to know instinctively.

"Don't worry, Tabby," Simi said as the unbelievably tall woman headed toward the stairs. "Katra will never hurt my *akri*. She loves him like us."

Katra didn't listen to Simi as she made her way up the stairs of the unfamiliar house. Then again, there was no such thing as an unfamiliar house to her. She'd inherited great powers from both her father and mother, including the ability to feel the essence and layout of buildings.

This house echoed warmth, respect, and love. No wonder Acheron liked to stay here whenever he visited New Orleans. This was a wonderful home and Marissa was a lucky child to live here. How she wished she'd known such a place as a little girl.

She opened the last door on the hallway to find Acheron lying prone on a large, four-poster bed.

Kat paused at the sight of Acheron there. Never in all these centuries had she been so close to him. As a young woman, she'd often tried to catch glimpses of him as he came and went on Olympus to see Artemis. Like all of the goddess' servants, Kat was banished from the temple whenever he visited.

She more than any other was forbidden to ever be near him. And now . . .

She'd waited all her life for this one, single moment. For one chance to touch him. Know him.

To feel his arms around her, just once.

Her heart pounding, she crossed the room to stand beside the bed that didn't really accommodate his tall, lean frame. The pallor and odd color of his skin did nothing to detract from the fact that he was without a doubt the most handsome man who had ever been born.

But he was so much more than external beauty.

Even in stasis, he was commanding and frightening. She could feel his powers reaching out to her. Calling to her.

He was power incarnate.

More than that, he was invaluable to the order of the universe. If Acheron should ever die . . .

It didn't bear thinking on.

Using her own powers, which were second only to his, Kat shut and locked the bedroom door with her thoughts before she lowered her cowl and sat beside him. She wanted a few minutes alone with him where no one could observe them.

"You are so handsome," she breathed as she traced the line of his eyebrows.

Since the moment she had first glimpsed him when she was a young child, she'd yearned to touch his hand. Yearned to have him call her by name.

Or better yet, yearned just to have him know she existed at all.

But it wasn't meant to be.

Artemis would always stand between them. She had ordained centuries ago that no one, especially not Kat, could ever touch the sacred Acheron.

Yet here she sat, alone with him, far away from the goddess's watchful stare.

Deep-seated emotions engulfed her. Unable to stand the tide of them, Kat lay against him and hugged him close, wishing he were awake to know her. To feel her.

But he wasn't.

He would never know she'd been here. That she had been the one to help him. Simi was forbidden to tell him and as soon as she vanished, the others below would forget they had ever seen her, too.

"I love you," she whispered against his ear. "I always will." She placed a chaste kiss on his cheek before she pulled back and took his large hand into hers.

Tears streaked her face as she brushed his fingers against her cheek. "One day," she breathed, "we will know each other. I promise."

Kat unlocked the door with her powers, then pulled a small satchel out of her pocket. It held three leaves from the Tree of Life that only bloomed in the garden of the Destroyer, deep in the halls of her temple in Kalosis. It alone could break the *ypnsi,* the sacred sleep that Orasia had once dispensed from the sacred halls of Katoteros back in the days when the ancient Atlantean gods had ruled the earth.

This alone could restore Acheron to his full strength.

Kat wrung the leaves until they were moist. Holding them over Acheron's lips, she twisted more until they were able to drip nine drops into his mouth.

She watched as the color spread from his lips, slowly, over the rest of his body.

He took a deep breath, then opened his eyes.

She vanished instantly.

Ash felt the air stir around him. He sat up quickly, then wished he hadn't as pain swept through his body.

Wiping his lips, he grimaced at the bitter, nasty taste in his mouth.

"Akri?"

His heart stopped beating as he heard Simi's hesitant voice an instant before she burst into the room and leapt onto the bed beside him.

Suddenly, everything came back to him. The Daimons. The blow . . .

What the hell had hit him?

"Simi, what am I doing here?"

She tackled him with a hug that left him flat on his back with her wrapped around his upper torso. "You scared the Simi, *akri*. She didn't know what was wrong with you. You turned all gray and nasty like one of them statues or something. You not supposed to do that! You said so."

"I'm okay, Sim," he said, cradling her. "I think. Why am I in Kyrian's house . . . with you in human form?"

"We brought you here."

Ash tensed at the sound of Kyrian's voice. He sat up slowly with Simi still hugging him.

With his arms folded over his chest, Kyrian stood in the doorway with Julian and Amanda.

"You okay?" Kyrian asked.

Ash nodded. "I think so. Still a little fuzzy, but breathing." Or at least trying to given the fact Simi was latched onto him like a protective mother bear.

"Do you know what happened to you?" Tabitha asked from somewhere out in the hallway.

Unfortunately yes, but it wasn't something they needed to know about since Simi had gone for the antidote and restored him. Thank the gods she'd understood his order.

If the others ever learned who and what he was . . .

But that begged the question: Who among the Daimons knew the truth of him? How did they know to strike him with the one compound that could actually neutralize him?

Not that it would work again. As long as he knew to expect it, he knew to guard against it.

Pain to the next one dumb enough to attempt hurting him.

"Okay, Simi," Ash said, patting the demon on her back. "You can let go."

"No, I can't," she said as she tightened her hold. "You got all grisly, *akri*. Like one of them things at home. Ew! The Simi don't like that. You gots to stay nice and pink like you're supposed to. Or blue. I don't mind it when you're blue. In skin, that is. When you blue in spirit, it makes the Simi sad, too."

"Okay, Simi," Ash said, cutting her off before she told something she wasn't supposed to.

"Your skin turns blue?" Kyrian asked.

"Everyone's skin turns blue when they're cold," he answered evasively.

Ash slid off the bed in spite of Simi's hold, which had yet to lessen. He needed to get out of this room to distract them from the fact that he'd come about as close to dying as his kind could.

Simi moved to stand behind him and kept her arms locked tightly around his waist.

"I think someone's attached to you, T-Rex," Talon said with a laugh.

"Yeah, just a little." Ash made his way from the room.

"Can we have some ice cream?" Simi asked as she finally let go. She started for the stairs, then veered off to Marissa's nursery to peek inside the closed door. "Sh!" Simi said loudly as she straightened up. "The baby's sleeping."

"Yeah, and Tabitha's sneaking away," Kyrian said. "Are you running off to meet up with Valerius?"

Tabitha went rigid at his question. "Tell me something, Ash," she said in a low tone as she neared him on the stairs. "Would Artemis care if I killed an ex–Dark-Hunter?"

"No, but I think your sister would."

Tabitha looked over her shoulder to see Amanda. "Then she better up her insurance on him. 'Cause he's one step away from a nasty tumble down these stairs."

"Don't threaten me, Tabby," Kyrian said. "You were so foul to me when you found out I was with Amanda. You actually tried to kill me. Now you're hooking up with the worst sort of lowlife. Tell her, Ash. His kind killed without compassion."

Tabitha whirled at the top of the stairs to face him. "His kind? What, an ancient general? Seems like I know two other people who were *his* kind." She looked meaningfully from Kyrian to Julian.

"Tabitha," Amanda said. "Enough. You knew how Kyrian felt about Valerius. How could you do this to us?"

Ash rubbed his head as if he had a headache. "People, leave Tabitha alone. I'm the one who put her with Valerius."

"Why?" Kyrian, Julian, and Amanda asked in unison.

Ash paused on the top step to give Tabitha a dry stare. "Tabby, what's your ideal man like?"

"Honestly?"

Ash nodded.

"You," she said without hesitation. "Someone tall, gorgeous, hip, and Goth."

"And what do you think of Valerius?"

She glanced hesitantly at her sister. "He's a stick in the mud, but I really like him."

Kyrian and Julian cursed.

"Tabitha . . ." Amanda said in a warning tone.

"Don't 'Tabitha' me. Jeez, I'm tired of all of you jumping on me." Tabitha descended the stairs and headed for the door to leave.

As soon as she opened it, she met Nick on the steps, who grinned at her before he entered the foyer. He brushed by her before she thought to warn him Ash was in the house . . .

With Simi.

Gawking, Tabitha turned.

"Hey, Nicky!" Simi said, her face beaming as she danced away from Ash finally to wave at Nick.

Tabitha went cold with dread.

And she knew the instant Ash realized Simi "knew" Nick. His face mottled red with fury.

Nick froze, then gaped.

Simi appeared oblivious to the mayhem she caused. "Nicky," she said, putting her hands on her hips as she pouted at him. "Why didn't you meet me tonight like you said you would?"

Nick's mouth opened and closed as Ash let out a bellow of rage. He grabbed Nick by the throat and slung him against the wall. Nick hit it so hard, he actually went through the plaster.

Tabitha cringed in sympathetic pain as Nick struggled to rise through the powder of the plaster. "I didn't know she was your girlfriend, Ash," Nick panted. "I swear it."

Ash's silver eyes turned a glowing shade of red. "She's not my girlfriend, you asshole. She's my daughter."

Tabitha wouldn't have thought it possible, but Nick turned even paler. "But she's so . . . so young . . . you're so young . . ." Nick swallowed audibly. "I'm so screwed."

Ash's eyes appeared to boil red and yellow as he hit Nick so hard, Nick was knocked back twenty feet into Kyrian.

Marissa started crying from upstairs.

"Amanda, tend your baby," Ash snarled in a voice that wasn't human. It was deep and rumbling. Frightening.

While he was distracted, Tabitha ran at Ash, but he held his hand out and she stopped dead in her tracks and was held there by some invisible force.

"*Akri!*" Simi shrieked. "No!"

Ash moved toward Nick, but before he could take more than two steps Simi was between them.

Tabitha cringed as Ash let out an agonized cry.

"You were never to have carnal knowledge!" he said to his demon.

While the rest of them feared for their lives, Simi was completely unperturbed by his anger.

"Why not?" Simi asked. "Everyone else has it."

Ash raked his hands through his black hair. "Because, dammit, Simi, now you'll be like everyone else. I'll never have any peace from you."

Simi screwed her face up as if that was the most disgusting thing she'd ever heard. "Pah-lease, *akri*. You got a big opinion of yourself. That just sick. You been hanging out with that heifer too long. Bleh! I mean, you a good-looking person and all, but you ain't no Travis Fimmel. Now, he's fine. But honestly, the Simi didn't like all that heaving and sweating very much. It seems like an awful lot of work for such a short amount of pleasure. Personally, I'd rather go shopping. It much more fun and you don't have to shower afterward. Well, not unless you go someplace dirty, but most malls are really clean nowadays."

Nick opened his mouth as if to refute her words, but was cut off by Talon, who shook his head.

"Boy," Talon said sharply. "Be damned glad you suck in bed and take the out she's offering you before you lose your life."

"Yeah, Nick," Kyrian added. "Keep your damned mouth shut."

Ignoring the two of them, Ash pulled Simi to him and held her close as if afraid of letting her go.

Whatever invisible force held Tabitha released her. She took a deep breath as the very air around them seemed to settle down.

But when Ash looked back at Nick, his eyes were still blazing red. "You're dead to me, Gautier. If I were you I'd kill myself to save me from the trouble of doing it later."

"Hey!" Tabitha snapped as Ash headed for the door. "That was harsh."

"Back off, Tabitha," Ash snarled in warning. "Simi, return to me."

The demon turned into a fine, black mist before she laid herself over Ash's arm and became a dragon-shaped tattoo.

Ash immediately slammed out of Kyrian's house.

Without hesitation, Tabitha ran after him. "Ash!" she snapped, pulling him to a stop in the driveway. "What are you doing?"

"I'm leaving before I kill Nick."

"You can't blame this solely on him."

"Like hell I can't. He slept with my Simi."

"Well, if you want to hate someone, then hate me. I was the one who left them alone together."

His eyes snapped fire at her. Literally. "Leave me, Tabitha. Now."

"No," she said earnestly. "If you want to hurt someone for this, then hurt the one who is really responsible. You and Nick are best friends. Don't think I don't know it. He loves you like a brother and you just crushed him."

"He slept—"

"I heard you the first time. And I also know how ill Nick was when he found out Simi belonged to you. Tell me something, Ash. Why didn't Nick know about her?"

His jaw worked furiously. "I didn't want any man to know about her. I knew the day would come when she would . . ." He winced as if the thought cut through him. "You don't understand."

"You're right, I don't. I don't know what happened to you tonight. I don't know what's after me. I don't understand what the hell you turned into a few minutes ago or why your eyes are doing the freaky ˋfire dance now. What are you? 'Cause right now, I'm wondering if you were ever human."

His eyes flashed red to silver. "I was human, once," he breathed.

"And now?"

"Now it's time for you both to die."

The eerie, threatening words barely registered before something hot pierced Tabitha's stomach.

Chapter 10

Tabitha gasped as pain engulfed her. She'd never felt anything like this. It was as if something had invaded her body.

Ash cursed as he threw his hand out and blasted her.

Tabitha screamed from the agony of his blast. It was as if something was trying to rip her apart.

Unable to stand against it, she started to fall, only to realize someone was holding her against a strong chest.

"I've got you," Valerius said as he picked her up in his arms and held her close.

Tabitha's heart soared at his nearness. She didn't know how he'd gotten there to catch her, she was only grateful that he had.

"Careful," she said between the teeth she had clenched to keep from moaning out at the pain that overwhelmed her.

Her eyes blurred by tears, she feared the ghost was now trying to move into Ash or Valerius.

"Forget it," Ash said.

The spirit laughed, then vanished.

Ash was beside her in an instant. "Breathe easy," he whispered.

Tabitha couldn't speak anymore as she laid her head against Valerius's neck and inhaled the warm scent of his skin. She would have never thought to feel this way about anyone.

She felt strangely protected even though she couldn't fight for herself.

"We need to get her to safety," Valerius said sharply.

Ash nodded.

One second they were in the driveway outside of Kyrian's house and in the next they were in Valerius's room in his home.

Valerius looked relieved as he laid her gently down on his mattress. "Are you all right?"

"I think so," she whispered. The pain was starting to abate a bit.

He offered her a warm smile before his face hardened and he turned to look at Ash. "What are we facing?"

Ash took a deep breath and appeared to debate what to say for several minutes. "That ghost outside of Kyrian's house was Desiderius. The good news is he isn't corporeal . . . yet."

"But I fought him in corporeal form," Valerius said. "He attacked me earlier."

"When?" Tabitha asked as her terror returned tenfold. "I didn't see him."

"He was the one the ghost protected at the end of the fighting. Remember?"

Tabitha shook her head. "That wasn't Desiderius. Believe me, I remember that bastard's face." She touched the scar on her cheek.

"No," Ash said. "It was his eldest son. According to Urian, they share the same name."

Tabitha rolled her eyes. "What is it with you ancient people that you only had, what? Three names in the whole family lineage and everybody recycled them?"

"It was tradition," Valerius said. "One I'm glad to have seen broken. Believe me, I take no joy from a name that reminds you of a cheesy song and a man doing unspeakable things in a high school gym. But I suppose, all things considered, 'Valerius' is infinitely better than 'Newbomb Turk.'"

Tabitha laughed at his unexpected comment, amazed that he'd actually understood her earlier reference to the movie *The Hollywood Knights*.

"Knowing Tabitha, I'm not even going to ask about that one," Ash said, rubbing a hand over his eyebrow.

Ash went suddenly rigid. Tabitha could sense his dread. "Ash?"

"What happened?" Ash whispered without acknowledging her. It was as if he were talking to someone else.

"Ash?"

"You two stay here and do not leave this house again tonight." He vanished instantly.

She looked at Valerius, whose frown made a mockery of her own. "What was that about?" she asked.

"I don't know, but I have a feeling it's not good."

Ash entered his home in Katoteros with a whirlwind maelstrom flowing behind him. The fifteen-foot-tall, solid oak doors echoed menacingly as they slammed shut of their own accord in his wake. The minute he crossed the elegant threshold, his clothes changed from his modern-day Goth to ancient Atlantean. The seams of his jeans turned into tightly woven, crisscrossed laces that held the tight black leather pants perfectly sculpted to his lower body. His shirt and jacket dissolved away into a heavy black silk *foremasta*, a long duster-like robe that was left to flow regally around his lithe, muscular body. On the back of the *foremasta* was embroidered the emblem of a golden sun pierced by three silver bolts of lightning.

It was his personal symbol of power and it marked everything he owned.

Without stopping, he walked directly across the large black marbled foyer that held the same design in the center of the floor.

There was no furniture in the circular foyer, but the golden domed ceiling above him was supported by sixteen columns that had been carved into statues of the most prominent of the Atlantean gods.

Gods who had once made this realm their home. In those days, they had gathered affectionately here in this hall to share time with each other as they watched over the human world and protected it.

But those days were long gone.

The ancient gods themselves were long gone.

Ash headed for the throne room that faced the main doors. The doorway to it was flanked by the likenesses of Apollymi the Destroyer and her husband Archon Kosmetas, a surname that meant Order. At one time, the two of them had presided over the nether realms of Katoteros and Kalosis, and in one fit of anger, Apollymi had laid waste to all who dwelled here.

All of them.

Not a single Atlantean god had remained standing after she had swept through this temple in her violent fury. Ash had never understood what could possess her to do such a thing.

But as he entered the throne room of the ancient gods, he was beginning to have enlightenment.

"Urian!" he growled, summoning his servant to him.

Urian popped into the Atlantean throne room ready to take on the devil himself. He drew up short as he caught sight of Ash's true form while the Dark-Hunter stood before the gilded dais that contained two gold thrones that were carved into the shape of dragons.

Urian was still having trouble dealing with Ash when the man looked like this. The blood-red, flaming eyes were enough to make even a demigod like Urian cringe, and Ash's iridescent blue-streaked, marbled skin tone . . .

Errr . . .

But the most disturbing thing was the deep, vicious scar that ran from Ash's navel to his throat where someone's handprint had been branded. It looked as if someone had once held the man down by his throat as they sliced him open.

Urian had learned from Alexion on the day he had arrived at Katoteros that while the hand scar came and went, the vertical scar was only visible in this realm and that he should *never* react to it.

Not if he valued his life, anyway.

Ash's unbalanced temper was present in the lightning bolts and thunder that crackled and sparked outside the leaded windows of the temple.

There were very few things in life that frightened Urian. The extremely powerful man before him was one of them.

Not even Ash's pet *pterygsauri* would come out to be

with their master in this mood. Unlike Urian, the small winged dragon-like creatures had stayed wisely hidden.

"What have you to report?" Acheron asked him, his voice thick with his Atlantean accent.

"Basically that all hell is breaking loose in hell."

Acheron looked less than pleased by the news. More lightning shot across the sky outside the floor-to-ceiling windows behind the thrones. It gave an eerie glow to Acheron's body. Thunder clapped ominously as it shook the temple floor where Urian stood.

"What is happening?"

Urian bit back his sarcasm as he started to point out that the weather in Kalosis mirrored the weather here in Katoteros. That would most likely be suicidal.

"I don't know. Desiderius came back to the hall with his son in tow a little while ago. I was told that he said something to Stryker that caused him to reward Desiderius by giving him the ability to reincarnate. Apollymi the Destroyer is locked inside her temple and no one is allowed to see her. Apparently someone did something wrong and she has since sent her Charonte demons off on a blood hunt throughout Kalosis to find the perpetrator. There are Spathis dropping like flies all over the place and everyone is pretty much wetting their pants in fear of her wrath."

"And your father?"

Urian tensed at the reminder that Stryker, the leader of the Spathi Daimons who were controlled by the Destroyer, had fathered him. "I don't know. The minute Desiderius left, he flipped out in the main hall and has been tearing the place apart ever since." His face hardened. "He keeps screaming out my name and I don't know why. Maybe he learned that I'm alive."

Acheron looked away from him.

"What's up with all this, Ash? I know you know."

"No, I don't. The Destroyer is silent to me. I hear nothing from her and that's what concerns me most. She's never silent in our battles."

Urian cursed at what that signified. "What could have set them both off at once?"

The muscle in Acheron's jaw beat an impressive staccato

rhythm. "My guess is Stryker sent Desiderius out with a test for me. Once Desi saw that it was effective, he reported it back to Stryker, who had all the confirmation he needed."

"Confirmation of what?"

Acheron's gaze cut through him. "What he really is to Apollymi."

Urian gave a low whistle. "Yeah, that would freak him out. Maybe we'll get lucky and he and the Destroyer will kill each other."

Acheron shot him a look that made him take a step back.

"Sorry," he said quickly.

Acheron started pacing. With his robe flowing eerily out behind him and his silver-soled boots clicking against the black marble floor, he was a spooky sight.

"Why would Desiderius try to take over Tabitha's body?"

"What do you mean?" Urian asked.

"He tried to take over her while I was there. After I blasted him out of her, he came for me."

That didn't make sense. How stupid could . . . well, it was Desiderius, after all. "Why would he attempt that if he knew what you were?"

Ash gave a low, ominous laugh. "I don't think Stryker shared that information with Desiderius. He wouldn't dare. It would undercut his own authority in Kalosis if he did so."

Good point. "So I guess the real question is who will be the body donor."

Acheron cocked his head as if he just realized something. "He's after Kyrian and Amanda. Since he couldn't get either Tabitha's body or mine, he'll probably go after someone else they know and trust. And that's the next bit I need you to find out. Stryker has me blocked so that I sense nothing in regard to Desiderius."

"For the record, I'm beginning to feel like cannon fodder here. There are a lot of people in Kalosis who rejoiced the day Stryker cut my throat. If one of them finds out that I'm there spying on them, they'll send me back to you in pieces."

Acheron gave him a wry, wicked grin. "It's okay. I'll just put you back together again."

"Thanks, boss. And I find that thought even more disturbing. Humpty Dumpty here doesn't want to fall off the wall, okay?"

Acheron's face hardened once more. "Go, Urian."

Inclining his head, Urian stepped back and willed himself to Kalosis.

Acheron stood silently in his throne room, listening. Still, he heard nothing from the other side. More lightning clashed outside as the winds whistled against the glass panes.

"Talk to me, Apollymi. What are you doing?"

But for the first time in eleven thousand years, she was utterly silent.

The only sound he heard in the deafening silence of his mind was his sister's faint voice. "Be careful what you wish for, little brother. *You* will get it."

Tabitha hung up the phone from talking to Amanda. Kyrian and Julian had been in the process of taping up Nick's ribs while she'd warned her sister about Desiderius's attack just outside of their house.

"I'm scared, Val," she said as she put her phone down. "Really scared. I keep hearing Amanda's voice telling me about her dream where she and Kyrian die. I know you hate the man, but—"

"I don't hate Kyrian, Tabitha. He hates me."

She nodded as Valerius pulled her into a tight hug that she really needed. He held her carefully against his chest while one hand played in her hair.

She inhaled his rich, welcoming scent, which soothed her even more than his touch.

"Acheron won't let her die," he said comfortingly. "You know that."

"I hope so, but her vision . . ."

"Those can be altered. Acheron is always saying that fate is helpless against free will. What she saw was one *possible* outcome."

Tabitha choked on her tears as she thought about what life would be like without Amanda. It was more than she could stand. "I can't lose my sister, Valerius. I can't. We've always had each other."

"Shh," he breathed before placing a gentle kiss on the top

of her head. "I'm sure she feels the same way about you, and I swear on my life that neither one of you will ever have to fear losing the other. Not on my watch."

Tabitha was amazed by his tenderness when it was obvious he'd never been shown any himself.

She pulled back to look up at him. "How could your brothers have ever killed you?"

He released her instantly and took three steps back. By the look on his face, she could tell her question had hurt him deeply.

"I'm sorry, Val. That was insensitive of me."

"It's all right. Things were different in those days."

That seemed to be his answer for everything, and it seemed too easy for her to accept.

"I shall call Otto and have him bring us dinner. I don't know about you, but I'm hungry."

Tabitha nodded and gave him the reprieve she sensed he needed. Without looking back, he left her alone in his library.

"Whatever do you see in that bastard?"

She turned quickly at the sudden voice behind her to find a man of Val's height, staring angrily at her. Dressed in black jeans and a black T-shirt, he was incredibly handsome with a neatly trimmed goatee, short, jet-black hair, and electric blue eyes. "Who the hell are you?"

"Zarek."

The unexpected name caught her off guard. So this was the infamous whipping boy who had lived in Valerius's Roman home. Offhand, there wasn't much other than the dark hair and height that marked them as brothers.

Tabitha folded her arms over her chest as she faced him. "So you're the dirtbag with the lightning bolt."

He laughed evilly at her insult. "I'd be careful if I were you. There's no law that says I can't fry your ass, too."

She scoffed at that and refused to give in to his intimidation. "Sure there is. Ash would kill you if you hurt me."

"He might try, but I doubt he'd succeed."

She sucked her breath in between her teeth at his daring tone. "You are arrogant, aren't you?"

He shrugged nonchalantly.

"So, why are you here?" she asked him.

"I've been watching the two of you."

She was disgusted at his confession, and the thought of being his personal viewing choice. It made her shiver in revulsion. "You unbelievable perv!"

His gaze narrowed dangerously. "Hardly. I've made sure to look away when you two start the lovey-dovey shit. I've already been blind once in my life. I have no wish to go back to it."

"Then why were you watching us?"

"Curiosity mostly."

"And you're here now, why?"

"Because I'm curious as to why the sister-in-law of Kyrian would fuck someone like Valerius."

She sneered at him. "That's none of your damned bus . . ." Tabitha trailed off as the room spun around her.

Suddenly, Valerius's library was gone and she found herself in what appeared to be a mirrored hallway. She saw herself reflected in the mirrors with Zarek by her side.

"Where are we?"

"Olympus. I have something I wanted to show you."

The mirror before her shimmered and changed. It no longer reflected them.

Instead it showed her the past.

She saw an ancient canvas tent with a bloodied man tied to a wooden frame inside it, being tortured. His screams rang out as he begged for mercy in Latin while another man beat him with a barbed whip.

Cringing, Tabitha covered her ears until the beating stopped and another man dressed in Roman armor stepped forward.

It was a young Valerius. His dark face was in need of a shave and his armor was spotted with bloodstains. He looked tired and ill-kempt, as if he hadn't slept in days, but still he held that regal air of superiority.

He threw water into the man's face. "Tell me where they're marching to."

"No."

The Latin words echoed in her head along with the sight of Valerius ordering a soldier to beat the man more.

"It was your lover who blinded me," Zarek snarled in her

ear as the mirror clouded, then cleared to show her the image
of two small boys.

One lay on the ground, curled into a ball while the other
beat him with a whip. One of the lashes cut deep into the one
boy's eye, causing him to scream as he covered it with one
grimy hand.

"I'm the one on the ground," Zarek snarled in her ear. "Valerius is the one beating me mercilessly and you fucked him."

Unable to watch the cruelty, Tabitha turned and ran into
someone else.

She started to fight until she glanced up to see Ash looking less than pleased.

"What are you doing, Z?"

"I'm showing her the truth."

Ash shook his head at the former Dark-Hunter. "I can't
believe you married a justice nymph and have yet to learn anything from her. There are always three sides to every memory,
Z. Yours, theirs, and the truth, which lies somewhere in between the two. You're only showing her a single sound bite to
prove *your* point. Why don't you give her the whole clip?"

Ash turned her back toward the mirror. "I'm not going to
lie to you, Tabby, or try and sway your opinion. This isn't
Zarek's memory or Valerius's. It's just the untarnished, ob-
jective truth of what happened to them."

She saw the child Valerius again as a man in a toga who
looked remarkably similar to Zarek stepped forward. He had
to be their father.

Laughing, he patted Valerius on the shoulder. "That's it,
my son. Always strike where they're the most vulnerable.
You'll make a fine general one day."

The child Zarek glared at both of them as if he could kill
them where they stood. Their father jerked the whip from Valerius's hand and commenced to beating him again.

His face horrified, Valerius ran from the room, sobbing.
He looked as if he were going to be ill as he stumbled across
an old Roman courtyard until he fell down by a huge fountain in the center of the atrium. He braced his folded arms on
the edge of the fountain and lay his head down.

"I'm sorry, I'm sorry, I'm sorry," he repeated over and
over again as he cried.

His father came running out of the house, toward him.

"Valerius!" he snarled as he came up to the child. "What are you doing?"

Valerius didn't answer. His father pulled him up from the ground by his hair.

The horror on the boy's face seared her.

"You pathetic little worm," his father sneered. "I should have named you Valeria. You're more woman than man."

His father backhanded him so hard the sound echoed and sent several birds into flight. Unbalanced by the blow, Valerius fell back to the ground.

His nose and cheek bleeding, Valerius tried to push himself up, but before he could regain his feet, his father brought the whip down across his back. The boy dropped instantly.

Still, his father beat him.

Valerius covered his head as the blows rained down on his little body.

"Get up," his father snarled after he'd delivered twenty lashes.

Valerius was crying so hard he couldn't speak.

His father kicked him in the ribs. "Up, damn you, or I'll give you twenty more."

Tabitha had no idea how he managed it, but somehow Valerius pushed himself to his feet, where he shook and trembled. His clothes were tattered, his face covered in dirt and blood.

His father seized him by the throat and shoved him back against a rough wall so that his ravaged back was scraped by it.

She cringed in sympathetic pain, trying to imagine how a child so young could stand there and not collapse.

"You will stand here until nightfall and if you so much as bend your knees to rest them, I will see you beaten every day until you learn to stomach your pain. Do you understand me?"

The boy Valerius nodded.

"Markus?" his father shouted.

Another boy who closely resembled Valerius came running out of the house. It was obvious he was a few years older. "Yes, Father?"

"Watch your brother; if he sits down or moves, you come for me."

Markus smiled as if his father had just given him a present. "I will, sir."

Their father turned and left them. And as soon as he was out of sight, Markus turned to laugh at Valerius. "Poor little Val," he said tauntingly. "I wonder what Father will do to you if you fall down." Markus struck him in the stomach.

Valerius groaned at the pain, but didn't move from the wall.

That only made Markus angrier. Growling at Valerius, he began striking him. Valerius fought back, but it was no use. In no time, Markus had him on the ground again.

"Father!" Markus cried, running for the door where their father had vanished. "He fell down!"

Tabitha turned away, afraid of what additional punishment Valerius's father had heaped on him. She'd already seen his back firsthand. Had run her hands over those scars that he bore with grace and dignity.

He must truly hate his father, and yet he never spoke a word against any of them. Valerius merely went on with his life, quietly suffering and keeping all the painful memories to himself.

He was remarkable to her.

The screen went black.

"It changes nothing," Zarek said, curling his lip. "So he was beaten, too. I notice you didn't correct the fact that he was torturing—"

"A Greek soldier whose army had marched on a Roman village," Ash said, interrupting him. "Every woman and child there had been locked inside Minerva's temple before they burned it to the ground. Valerius was after the army to stop them before they killed any more innocents."

Zarek scoffed. "They weren't all innocent."

"No," Tabitha said, her throat tight. "But he was a general during a time when things were violent."

"Yes," Ash said quietly. "And he did what he had to do."

Zarek snorted. "Yeah, right. Valerius spent his entire human lifetime trying to please his father, trying to make that animal proud."

Ash refuted that as well. "And when you were children, he was so afraid of your father that he stuttered every time he was in his presence."

"He never hesitated to commit an act of cruelty to please his family."

"Never?"

Tabitha watched the mirror as it again showed her Valerius as a child. He was around the age of eight, lying in bed asleep. Her heart pounded at the peaceful, sweet sight he posed.

Until his bedroom door was slung open.

Valerius jerked upright as lamplight cut across him.

His father seized him from the bed and literally threw him to the ground. Valerius looked at his father and then to the one who held the lamp.

It was Markus.

"What is this?" his father asked as he threw a blanket at Valerius.

Valerius turned pale.

"What is that blanket, Zarek?" Ash asked.

Zarek's blue eyes turned cold. "It's the piece of shit old horse blanket that the little bastard gave to me one winter night and I was beaten for it."

"Valerius!" his father shouted as he slapped the boy. "Answer me."

"B-b-blanket."

"I saw him give it to the slave, Father," Markus said. "So did Marius. He didn't want the slave to be cold."

"Is this true?"

Valerius looked horrified.

"Is it true!"

Valerius swallowed. "He was c-c-c-cold."

"Was he now?" his father sneered, "Well, better a slave to suffer than you, is it not? Perhaps it's time you learn that lesson, boy."

Before Valerius could move, his father tore his clothes from him, then wrenched him up by his thin arm and hauled him from the room. Completely naked, Valerius was taken outside, where his father tied him to a hitching post. It was so cold that their breaths formed icy clouds around them.

"P-p-pl-"

Valerius's plea was cut short by another vicious backhand. "We're Roman, boy. We don't beg for mercy from anyone. For that you'll be beaten even more come morning. If you live through the night."

Shaking from the cold, Valerius bit his lip to keep his teeth from chattering.

Markus laughed at him. "I think you're being too kind, Father."

"Don't question me, Markus, unless you wish to join him."

Markus's laughter died instantly. Without another word or looking back, the two of them turned back toward the house and left Valerius outside alone.

The small boy sank to his knees while he tried to loosen his hands. It was no use. "I swear I'll be a good Roman," he whispered quietly. "I will."

The scene faded.

"You're not convincing me, Acheron," Zarek said coldly. "I still think he's a ruthless bastard who deserves nothing."

"Then how about this?"

This time when the mirror lightened, she saw what appeared to be a seriously disfigured version of Zarek chasing an older version of his father through the ancient Roman house she now knew was theirs.

The middle-aged man was bleeding, his face ravaged as if he'd been knocked around.

The man spilled into what appeared to be a dining hall where Valerius sat at a desk wearing his armor, writing a letter. Frowning, he rose to his feet as he saw his father's frantic run.

His father fell against him and grabbed the metal straps of Valerius's cuirass. "For Jupiter's sake, help me, boy. Save me!"

Zarek drew up short as he saw Valerius in full military regalia. Candlelight shone off the golden armor that was contrasted by his blood-red cape.

Valerius made a fearsome sight as he pushed his father aside and pulled his sword out slowly from its burgundy leather scabbard as if to engage Zarek.

"That's it, boy," his father said with an evil laugh. "Show the worthless slave what I taught you."

"Go ahead, you bastard," Zarek snarled defiantly. "I'm

here for my vengeance and you can't kill someone who's already dead."

"I wasn't planning on it," he said simply.

"Valerius," his father snarled. "What are you doing, boy? You have to help me."

His face completely stoic, Valerius looked at his father as if the man were a complete stranger. "We're Roman, Father, and I've long since ceased being a boy. I am the general you made me and you taught me well that we don't beg for mercy from anyone."

He handed his sword hilt-first to Zarek.

With those words spoken, Valerius saluted his brother, walked out of the room, and closed the door.

His father's screams echoed as he walked slowly down the corridor.

Tabitha couldn't breathe as she witnessed the tragedy that was both their lives. Part of her couldn't believe Valerius had left his father to die like that and another part of her understood it completely.

Poor Valerius. Poor Zarek. They both were victims of the same man. One son spat upon because he was a slave and another because he wasn't cold-blooded and unfeeling. At least not until that one moment.

She looked at Zarek, whose eyes still bore the hatred and pain of his past. "If you hate Valerius so much, why didn't you kill him, too, Zarek?"

"Pardon the bad pun, but the blind man was shortsighted at the time."

"No," she whispered. "You knew, didn't you? You knew who deserved your hatred and who didn't."

Zarek's sneer turned even colder as he shot a menacing glare from her to Acheron. "This changes nothing. Valerius still doesn't deserve peace. He doesn't deserve anything except contempt. He is his father's son."

"And what are you?" Tabitha asked. "It seems to me that you're the one carrying around the acidic hatred that won't let you live in peace. Valerius doesn't strike out at other people. Ever. To me that makes him twice the man you are."

Zarek's look pierced her. "Oh, you think you're so special. That he's worth defending. Tell you what, sweetie, if you want to know who Valerius really loves, go to the solarium in his house. Imagine how much Agrippina must have meant to him that he's been lugging her stone statue around for more than two thousand years."

"Zarek . . ." Ash growled in warning.

"What? It's true and you know it."

Zarek took a step back and then looked as if he were trying to disappear. "What the . . . ?"

Ash gave him a droll stare. "Just for the record, Zarek. If you ever do hurt Tabitha, I *will* kill you. Gods and goddesses be damned."

Zarek opened his mouth as if to argue, but vanished before any words could escape.

The next thing Tabitha knew, she was back in Valerius's library right where she'd been standing.

"Tabitha?" Valerius asked as he walked back into the room. "Did you not hear my question?"

Tabitha reached out to touch the shelf nearest her to confirm that she was here. Yeah, she was back. But she felt rather strange all of a sudden.

"No," she said to Valerius. "I missed your question, sorry."

"Otto wanted to know if you like mushrooms."

"I'm totally ambivalent to them."

Valerius cast an amused look at her before he relayed the information to Otto. After he finished ordering their dinner, he put the phone back in his pocket. "Are you all right?"

No, she wasn't. The images and words of Zarek and Ash tumbled through her mind.

And she wanted to know who to believe.

"Where's your solarium?"

There was no missing the wave of apprehension that went through Valerius. "My what?"

"Your solarium. You do have one here, right?"

"I . . . uh, yes, I have one."

At least he didn't lie about it. "Can I see it?"

He went rigid. "Why?"

"I like solariums. They're nice rooms." Tabitha headed out of the library toward the other side of the house. "Would it be this way?"

"No," Valerius said as he followed her. "I still don't see why you'd want—"

"Humor me. Just for a sec, okay?"

Valerius debated. Something wasn't right with Tabitha, he could sense it. And yet he couldn't hide from the past; and for some reason he didn't understand, he didn't want to hide anything from her.

Inclining his head to her regally, he took a backward step toward the stairs. "If you'll follow me."

He led her up the stairs to the room beside his bedroom where the door was sealed with a keypad.

Tabitha watched him key in the code. The lock clicked. Valerius took a deep breath before he swung it wide.

Tabitha's heart shrank as she saw the statue in the middle of the solarium of a beautiful young woman. There was an eternal flame burning beside it.

She looked up at Valerius, who refused to meet her eyes while he stared at the floor.

"So this is why you were freaking out about the lamp oil. You must really have loved her."

Chapter 11

Valerius looked up at the statue as Tabitha's words rang in his ears. As always Agrippina's face stared out into nothingness. Blank. Cold.

Unfeeling.

His chest ached from the harsh reality of the past and his own particular stupidity of trying to hang on to something good from his human life.

"Honestly, I didn't even know her," he said quietly. "I most likely never spoke more than a handful of words to her during her lifetime and yet if I could have had a woman to love me, I would have been grateful for it to have been her."

Tabitha was stunned by his confession. "I don't understand. Why do you take care of a statue of a woman you didn't know?"

"I'm pathetic." He gave a bitter laugh. "No, actually I'm too pathetic for even the average pathetic. I take care of her statue because I wasn't able to take care of her." His anger and pain reached out to her and seized her heart.

"What are you talking about?"

His entire body rigid, he stared off to the side of the room. "Do you want the truth of me, Tabitha? Really?"

"Yes, I do."

Folding his arms over his chest, he moved away from her so that he could stare out the dark windows of the room, into the elegant courtyard in back. "I was a genetic screw-up of titanic proportions and I've never understood why. I've spent my entire life trying to understand why I give a single shit about anyone when no one ever gave a damn about me."

His profanity shocked her. It wasn't like him to speak that way and that alone told her how volatile his mood was. "There's nothing wrong about caring for other people."

"Yes, there is. Why should I care? If I died right now, no one would miss me. Most of the people who know me would openly rejoice."

Her throat tightened at the truth of his statement and yet the thought of him dying . . .

It hurt to an unfathomable level. "I would care, Valerius."

He shook his head at her. "How could you? You barely know me. I'm not stupid. I've seen the people who are your friends. None of them look like me. None of them act or speak like me. All of you mock anyone you see who looks or acts like I do. Your kind hates us. You dismiss us. I'm rich and cultured, I come from a noble Roman family, therefore I must think myself above everyone else, so it's okay to be vicious and cold whenever I'm around. We have no feelings to hurt. How could a Roman nobleman give a single rat's ass for a slave? And yet two thousand years later, there she stands and here I am, a noble watchdog for a humble slave because she was afraid of the dark as a child, and I once made a promise to her that she wouldn't have to sleep in darkness."

His words touched her so deeply that it tightened her chest and almost succeeded in bringing tears to her eyes.

The mere fact that he'd kept his vow to a simple slave . . .

"Why was she afraid of the dark?"

A muscle worked in his jaw. "She'd been the daughter of a wealthy merchant in a town my father had destroyed. He'd brought her back to Rome intending to sell her at market when my grandmother saw her and thought she'd make a good companion. My father made her a gift to my grandmother, and Agrippina lived in terror all her life that someone else would come for her in the dark of night and destroy her world again."

His gaze turned haunted. "She found out the hard way that the light can never keep the real monsters away. They could care less who sees them."

Tabitha frowned. "I don't understand."

He turned to face her with a menacing glare. "Do you know what *asterosum* is?"

"No."

"It's an ancient drug that completely paralyzes your body, but leaves you completely able to see, hear, and feel. Roman physicians used it whenever they needed to amputate."

He winced as if something painful went through him. She felt the agony of it in her own chest.

Valerius wrapped his arms around himself as if that could protect him somehow from the horror of his past. "It was the drug my brothers gave me the night they came to my villa. I had just taken over the Celtic city of Angaracia. Instead of razing it to the ground and killing everyone as any other male in my family would have done, I negotiated a surrender with the Celts. I thought it would be better if their children didn't grow up to hate Rome and strive to avenge their people as so many had done before them." He laughed bitterly. "It was my fatal flaw."

"How could mercy be a flaw?" she asked, aghast.

And even as the words came out, she remembered the sight of his father. In Valerius's world, it would have been a crime.

Valerius cleared his throat. "Most of my assignments were in the outer provinces, fighting the Celts. I was the only Roman of my time who had ever been truly successful against them, mostly because I understood them. My brothers hated me for that. To them, the only way to conquer a people was to destroy them."

"So they thought to kill you?"

He nodded. "They came into my house and drugged me. I lay on the floor completely helpless as they destroyed everything around me. After they had ransacked my hall, they took me out into the back courtyard to kill me. It was there they discovered Agrippina's statue."

Tabitha looked up at the white marble face from his past. "Why did you have her statue there?"

"Like my grandmother, I thought she deserved to be saved. To be preserved. So, I commissioned the piece for my private garden not long after she came to live with me."

A vicious stab of unwarranted jealousy went through her. He might not have loved the woman, but he obviously felt deeply for her. Especially since he'd spent thousands of years keeping a promise to her.

"How did she end up with you?" she asked quietly.

He drew a deep, ragged breath. "My grandmother had summoned me home from the battlefield because she knew she was dying and she was afraid for Agrippina. She knew the temperament of her sons and grandsons, and Agrippina was a very beautiful and delicate woman who had grown to mean a lot to her. I was the only one who had ever come to call on her that she didn't have to keep from Agrippina's bed. So she asked me to take Agrippina into my house and to keep her safe from the others."

Tabitha's throat tightened at his kindness. "You fell in love with her?"

"I loved the idea of her, she was beauty incarnate. Soft and kind. Things that had never existed in my world before. Whenever I was home, I spent hours watching her from afar as she went about her duties. And I often wondered if someone so beautiful could ever love something as vile as me. Then I would castigate myself for wanting the love of a slave. I was a noble Roman general. What did I need with a slave's regard?"

Yet he had craved it. She knew that. She could feel it.

Valerius grew silent. If she didn't know better, she'd swear she saw tears in his eyes.

"They raped her in front of me and I couldn't help her."

"Oh, Val," she breathed.

He moved away from her as she sought to touch him. "I couldn't even close my eyes or turn my head. I lay there completely helpless as they took pleasure violating her. The more she screamed, the more they laughed, right up until the end when Markus ran her through with my sword." The words were torn from his throat as tears welled in his eyes.

"What good was I?" he asked between clenched teeth, his nostrils flared by impotent rage. "What good did I do her in the end? Had I never taken her into my home, they would have at least allowed her to live."

Tabitha choked on her own tears as he finally allowed her

to pull him into her arms. She tried to blot out what must have happened after they killed Agrippina.

She'd seen the scars on his wrist and knew from him that they had crucified him. The horror that must have been that night! No wonder he didn't want to remember the past.

And she would never again ask him anything about it.

He was rigid for several seconds before he relaxed. Then he wrapped his arms tightly around her and held her close.

"What kind of man am I that every act of kindness I ever attempt ends up hurting the very people I seek to help?"

"You didn't hurt me or Marla or Gilbert."

"Yet," he breathed. "Agrippina lived in my home almost ten years before the Parcae hurt her."

"No one's going to hurt me, Valerius, trust me."

He brushed his hand lovingly over her scarred cheek. "You have so much fire inside you. It warms me every time you near me."

"Warms you? Most people are consumed by it. My ex used to say that I was completely exhausting to be around. He'd tell me that I wore him out and that he needed at least two to three days to recoup for every hour he spent with me."

He offered her a small smile. "I don't find you exhausting."

"And I don't find you pathetic."

That succeeded in bringing out a laugh from him. "What is it about you, Tabitha? I've only known you a few days and I feel as if I could tell you anything."

"I don't know, but I feel the same way about you." She reached up and pulled his head down so that she could kiss him.

Valerius moaned at the taste of her. At the feel of her. In her arms, he didn't feel pathetic or rigid. She allowed him to laugh and to feel joy again.

No, she allowed him to feel joy for the first time in his life. No one but Tabitha had ever reached out and embraced him.

She knew he was stodgy and she accepted it. Instead of turning him away, she poked gentle fun at him and then worked around it.

She didn't write him off.

In all of history, she alone had befriended him. And that made her the most precious woman on earth.

Tabitha pulled back. "How much time do we have before Otto gets here with food?"

He checked his watch. "Probably twenty to thirty minutes. Why?"

She smiled. "That'll do."

Before he could ask her more, she pulled her shirt off and wrapped it around his neck, then crooked her finger for him to follow her.

"Come with me, General. I'm going to rock your world."

Little did she know, she'd done that the minute he'd first seen her fighting the Daimons, and she'd been doing it steadily ever since.

Stryker had finally managed to calm himself. At least on the outside.

Inside he was still seething.

Damn the Destroyer and her lies and damn Acheron Parthenopaeus for his honesty.

If it was the last thing he did, he would rid the world of both of them. But he had to move carefully.

Strategically.

If the Destroyer ever learned that he'd been the one to give *Aima* to Desiderius so that the Spathi could wound Acheron, his life would be meaningless. No, he'd have to move with great skill to defeat them both, and he would.

Eventually.

The air around him sizzled with a request from Desiderius for a bolt hole so that the Spathi could return from New Orleans to the realm of Kalosis, the Atlantean hell realm.

Here there was no light. It was perpetually dark and dismal. Up until the night he had slain his own son, that hadn't bothered him.

Now it did.

Stryker held his hand out and opened the portal.

Desiderius returned, still a bodiless mist.

Stryker curled his lip at the incompetent Daimon. There had been a time once when he'd held the Daimon in regard, but Desiderius's failure against a simple Dark-Hunter and his human paramour had left Stryker completely disgusted with the being.

If it wasn't for the fact that he didn't want to bring himself under the fire of the Destroyer, he wouldn't have even allowed Desiderius this one chance to return to corporeal form. But in exchange for Desiderius wounding Acheron, Stryker was willing to reincarnate the Daimon.

"I thought you were going to—"

"What am I up against?" Desiderius asked as his faceless, formless essence flickered in the dimly lit chamber.

"You know what you're up against."

"No," Desiderius said. "What was that substance you gave me that took down the Dark-Hunter leader?"

"It's of no concern to you. Your only concern is to bring me the child."

"I don't understand why."

Stryker laughed. "And you never will. Bring me the child or I will blast you into oblivion."

If he didn't know better, he'd swear the ghost actually sneered at him.

"I was blasted out of the bitch's body by Acheron. They are now guarded. I need another body."

Stryker paused as he heard Daimons shrieking from outside his hall. No doubt Apollymi's Charontes were still seeking the one who had stolen the *Aima* from her.

None of them would look to him for it. They wouldn't dare.

In truth, he was in no mood to play any longer. His mother, the Destroyer, had said to wait.

He was through waiting.

The day he had spilled his own son's blood to appease the Destroyer was the day he had started to notice some things.

And when his mother had bade him to bring her the little child of a former Dark-Hunter and a human sorceress, he had realized something. That child, known as Marissa Hunter, held in her hands the very balance of the universe.

Whoever possessed her, possessed the key to control the most primal, ancient power of all time.

She was the fate of the entire world.

The Destroyer sought to have the child for her own so that she would be in control.

Stryker bit back his bitter laughter. She would have

Marissa over his own dead body. In the end, it would be he who controlled the Final Fate. Not Apollymi.

"Arod, Tiber, Sirus, Allegra!" he called.

The four Spathi commanders appeared before him. Three men and one woman. Stryker took a minute to scan their perfect, beautiful bodies. All four Daimons appeared physically to be no older than twenty-seven . . . just like him. And just like him, they had been around since time immemorial. Allegra was the youngest of their group, but even she was a staggering nine thousand years old.

Trained to kill and to take and possess human souls to live, his army had no equal.

It was time mankind met them.

"You called us, *akri*?" Tiber asked.

Stryker nodded. "Desiderius is in need of a body to do my bidding."

The four Daimons looked at each other nervously.

"Relax," Stryker said. "I'm not asking any of you to volunteer yourselves. Oh, no. Far from it. The four of you are to be his bodyguards."

"But, *akri*," Allegra said quietly, "he has no body to guard."

Stryker laughed maniacally. "Yes, he does." He splayed his hand out and an image appeared in the center of the room. Dressed all in black, the Dark-Hunter was walking alone on the streets of New Orleans.

"There's your body, Desiderius," he said. "And there's your ticket into the Hunter household. Now you bring me that baby or all of you will die . . . permanently."

As they started to shimmer out of the room, Stryker stopped them with one last order. "Acheron took from me the only thing I have ever loved. In memory of my son he stole from me, I command you to make the humans Acheron loves pay. I want to see blood flowing in the streets of New Orleans. Do you understand?"

Desiderius smiled wickedly. "Understood, *akri*. Definitely understood."

Valerius growled at how good Tabitha felt against him. Completely naked in his arms, she kissed him fiercely as her hand gently stroked his hard cock from tip to hilt.

His black shirt hung open. Unlike her, he was still mostly dressed.

"Otto is on his way," he said raggedly as she dipped her head down to suckle his hard nipple.

It was difficult to think straight while her hand massaged him so expertly.

"Then we better get down to business," she said with a laugh as she climbed up on his bed.

Valerius couldn't breathe at the sight of her naked on his black duvet.

He watched as she spread her legs open in invitation. She hooked her ankles around his hips and pulled him forward.

He hissed as she reached between their bodies and lowered his pants enough so that she could slide herself onto him.

Arching her back, she drew him in deep as she moaned and writhed against him. Valerius leaned forward onto one arm as he stared down at her naked body moving underneath him. With both feet still on the floor, he thrust deep inside her warm, wet body.

"That's it, baby," she panted as she met him equally.

Valerius thrust harder as he let her touch soothe him. He cupped her breast with his hand, delighting in the soft, supple texture of it. His mouth watered for a taste of her.

Tabitha groaned as Valerius dipped his head down and took her breast into his mouth while he continued to thrust against her hips. She loved the way this man felt when he was inside her. The way he looked, primal and savage.

There was something seriously erotic about a man this controlled losing it all whenever he touched her. She liked the fact that he could drop his guard when they were alone.

That he didn't judge her.

Closing her eyes, she clutched his head to her as he moved even faster against her. There was nothing better than him pounding himself into her over and over again. Than his tongue working its magic on her breast.

Unable to stand it, she pulled his lips away from her breast so that she could kiss him. His eyes were dark with his passion, his face a bit flushed from their exertion.

She ground herself against him as she sank her hands into his long hair and nipped his lips with her teeth.

Valerius growled in his throat as Tabitha licked her way to his ear where her tongue swirled around his lobe and made chills spread all over his body.

It drove him past his control. He wanted to be even deeper inside her.

Pulling out of her, he rolled her over, onto her stomach and positioned her so that she was bent over the bed with her buttocks exposed.

"Val?"

He brushed the hair away from her neck as he drove himself back into her body. She cried out in pleasure as he buried himself all the way to the hilt.

Some inner, wild part of him roared to life. He cupped her breasts in his hands while the scent of their passion filled his head.

Tabitha couldn't breathe as Valerius took control. He left one hand cupping her breast while the other trailed down her body, past her belly ring to bury it between her legs.

"Oh, Val," she sobbed, aching from the pleasure of his touch. His fingers delved deep in her cleft as he stroked her in time to his thrusts.

Her head spun.

She'd never felt so strangely desirable. So needed.

"I love the way you smell, Tabitha," Valerius breathed in her ear.

She felt him brush his fangs against her throat. "Are you going to bite me, Val?"

She felt him hesitate as one fang hovered dangerously close to her jugular.

"I've never wanted to bite anyone before," he said raggedly.

"And now?"

He moved even faster against her. "I want to devour you."

Tabitha cried out as she came instantly.

Valerius clenched his teeth as he felt her shuddering. The foreign part of him still begged to taste her. It begged to possess her.

It was wild and frightening.

He nipped her throat, but forced himself not to break her skin. But it was hard.

It was damn near impossible.

And when he climaxed a minute later, he heard that alien part of himself roar in triumph.

He held her close until the last tremor shook him. Completely drained, he turned her around and then sank to his knees in front of her.

Tabitha was awed by the sight of the proud Roman warrior kneeling before her. He wrapped his arms around her waist and laid his head carefully against her stomach.

Gently, she ran her hands through his hair.

He pulled back to look up at her with a searching gaze that seared her. "I don't know why you're here, Tabitha, but I'm glad that you are."

She smiled down at him.

His gaze locked on hers, he nibbled the sensitive flesh of her stomach, just below her belly ring. Biting her lip, she moaned as he tongued the moon that dangled from her hoop, Then he licked in and around her navel, making her body burn even more.

And when he sank two fingers inside her, she thought she might actually collapse.

"You are beautiful, Tabitha," he said, spreading her open so that he could stare at the most intimate part of her body.

She couldn't breathe as he took her into his mouth and used that incredible tongue to taste her intimately. She spread her legs even wider, to give him more access as he slid his tongue through the tender folds.

Tabitha stared down at him. He seemed to enjoy tasting her as much as she enjoyed being tasted.

And he took his time exploring her.

"Hey, Valerius?"

He jerked away at the sound of Otto in the hallway. Still he left one finger inside her that continued to pleasure and probe her.

Rising slowly to his feet, he slid another finger into her body. "What have you done to me, Tabitha?" he breathed raggedly in her ear. "Otto's in the hallway and all I can think of is being inside you again. Of licking you until I can taste your climax."

His unexpected comment made her moan deep in her

throat at the thought of what he described. "Get rid of Otto and I'm yours for the night."

He kissed her passionately, then squeezed her butt in his hands. "Stay naked. I want to eat my dinner off you."

Tabitha bit her lip as a shudder went through her. "You got it."

Valerius pulled away and quickly buttoned his shirt and fastened his pants. He cast one hot, promising look at her before he slipped out of the bedroom and left her alone.

Tabitha pulled down his bedcovers and slid herself between the dark silk sheets that held his spicy masculine scent.

Wrapping her arms around his pillow, she inhaled deeply.

"What am I doing?" she asked herself. She was literally sleeping with the enemy and she was enjoying it way too much.

Worse, she didn't want to leave.

Ever.

"My gift in life," she said under her breath. She seemed to be forever drawn to the men she could never have.

She should leave here and go bunk with Amanda and Kyrian, but she couldn't bring herself to leave Valerius. What would he do without her?

More importantly, what would she do without him?

Chapter 12

Ash drew up short as he saw Kyrian in his upstairs office through the slightly ajar door. It was well after four a.m. and though Kyrian occasionally stayed up late with Amanda, it was unusual to find the former Dark-Hunter up alone.

Cocking his head, he watched through the crack as Kyrian bent over a stack of papers, pulling at his hair. Ash could sense the frustration.

He knocked lightly on the door so as not to startle him.

Kyrian looked up, then pulled the glasses off his face. "Oh, hey," he said in a low tone as Ash pushed the door open a bit. "I thought you might be Amanda, begging me to come to bed."

"Not for all the money in the universe," Ash said as he walked in. He moved to stand in front of the black, kidney-shaped, Chippendale desk where official papers and hand-written notes were scattered. "What are you doing up so late?"

"I couldn't sleep. I . . . ." Kyrian ground his teeth.

"What?" Ash asked, worried about his long-time friend.

Kyrian let out one long, tired breath. "You have no idea what this is like, Ash. How hard every day is. Do you even remember being human?"

Ash set his backpack down on the floor as he heard Kyrian's thoughts. They were disoriented and panicky.

Normally, Ash wouldn't answer any questions about his

past, but his friend needed comfort; in all honesty, given the crap that had gone on tonight between Nick, Simi, Zarek, Tabitha, the Destroyer, and Daimons, so did he. "Yeah, I remember being human, but I do my damnedest not to dwell there."

"Yeah, but no offense, you were young when you died. You have no idea of the responsibility I carry."

Ash had to bite back a bitter laugh at that. If Kyrian only knew . . .

He'd trade fates and responsibilities with the former Greek general in a heartbeat.

"Look at this," Kyrian said, pushing a sheet of paper at him. "Forget the damned Daimons, the scariest thing on this planet are lawyers and insurance brokers. My God, do you know the statistics for traffic accidents? I'm terrified to put my kid or wife in the car at all. My medicine cabinet that used to hold nothing but toothpaste and bandages now has Advil, Sudafed, Bengay, Lipitor, and Benicar. I have high blood pressure, high cholesterol—"

"Well, you did abuse your body for the last forty years with junk food."

"I was immortal!" Kyrian snapped, then his face went ashen. "I'm going to die again, Ash. Only this time, I doubt Artemis will be there to offer me a trade." He raked a hand through his hair. "My wife is going to die one day, and Marissa . . ."

"Don't think about it."

Kyrian's eyes snapped at him. "Don't think about it? That's easy for you to say. You're not going to die. And death is all I can think about, especially since Amanda keeps having her nightmares. I'm human now. I can't protect them like I could before."

"That's why Kassim and I are here."

Kyrian shook his head, then reached for his glasses. "And I hate these damned things that I have to wear so I can read all the fine print that's designed to steal my soul even more effectively than the goddess did. What happened to me, Acheron? Yesterday, I was the baddest thing stalking the night. The Daimons trembled in fear of me. Now what am I? I'm so pathetic that I have to bribe Nick to slip beignets into the house and hide in a closet to eat one so Amanda doesn't find out and ream me a new one. I have sinus problems. My back aches at night if I sleep wrong. My knees are shot to hell and yesterday when I bent over to pick up Marissa, I almost fell. Growing old really sucks."

Ash gave him an arch stare. "Are you telling me you want to go back?"

Kyrian looked away sheepishly. "At times I do, and then I look at my wife and I think what a selfish bastard I am. I love her so much that it hurts deep down in places I never knew existed. Whenever I think of her being hurt or Marissa . . . I can't breathe. I can't live. I hate feeling helpless. I hate knowing that I'm going to grow old and die on them."

"You're not going to die, Kyrian."

"How do you know?" he snapped.

"I won't let you."

Kyrian scoffed at him. "As if you could stop it. We both know I have no choice except to die as an old man . . . if I'm lucky and make it that long and don't drop dead of a heart attack, car accident, food poisoning, or a million other catastrophes." He hung his head in his hands.

Ash truly felt for his friend. It was hard to be human. Hell, it was hard to live at all.

Life was definitely not for the meek. Every time something seemed to go right, at least three or four things had to go wrong. It was just the law of nature.

"Amanda's pregnant again," Kyrian breathed after a small pause.

In spite of the dire tone, Ash sensed his happiness. And his terror. "Congratulations."

"Thanks." Kyrian looked at the stack of papers on his desk. "I'm trying to get my will in order, just in case."

Ash stifled an urge to laugh at his fatalistic friend. "You're not going to die, Kyrian," he reiterated.

He knew Kyrian wasn't listening to him. He was too busy fixating on all the things that could go wrong with not just Amanda and the baby, but himself.

"Will you be the baby's godfather again?" Kyrian asked quietly.

"Of course."

"Thank you. Now, if you don't mind, I have to have this in with the attorney and insurance company tomorrow."

"All right. Good night, General."

"Night, Acheron."

Ash pulled his backpack up from the floor and shut the door as he left. He paused in the hallway to find Amanda standing in her bedroom door, wrapped in a cream bathrobe. There were tears in her eyes.

Ash closed the distance between them. "You okay?"

She shrugged. "Is it like this for all of those who regain their souls?"

Sighing, he nodded. "It's hard to readjust. You spend hundreds to thousands of years thinking you literally have all the time in the world where nothing can touch you and your body never hurts for more than a few hours, only to become mortal and realize that you only have thirty or forty years left if you're lucky. You're now susceptible to death and disease just like everyone else. It's not an easy mindset. The first real paper cut damn near kills them."

A single tear went down her cheek. She wiped it away and sniffed daintily. "I wish I had left him as he was. I wish you had told me this would happen."

"Told you what, Amanda?" he asked. "That the two of you would spend the rest of your lives loving each other? Raising your kids? Neither one of you have any idea how miraculous your life is. How many people would gladly sell their souls for what you have. Forget Artemis and immortality. What you have is infinitely more precious and rare."

His heart clenched as his anger at both of them swelled over the fact that they were doubting their love and whether they had made the right decision. "Even I would trade all my immortality for one single day of what you two have."

He took her scarred hand into his and held it up so that she could see the place where Kyrian's soul had burned her hand when she returned it to his body. "I asked you once if he was worth it. Do you remember what you said to me?"

"I would walk through the fires of hell to die for him."

Ash nodded. "And I would walk through the fires of hell to keep you both safe."

"I know."

He tightened his grip on her hand. "Do you really wish you had left him to his Dark-Hunter life?"

She shook her head. "I would die without him."

"And he would die without you."

She wiped her eyes and smiled at him. "Oh, I'm just tired and pregnant. I hate this emotional hormonal state. I'm sorry to dump all over you when I'm sure it's the last thing you need." Standing on her tiptoes, she pulled him down so that she could hug him.

Ash clenched his hand into a fist against her back as he savored the kindness of her touch. It was rare for anyone to touch him as a friend and it meant everything to him.

"I love you, Ash," she breathed before she kissed his cheek. "You're the best friend anyone could ever ask for."

Except for Nick . . .

Ash winced as he recalled his earlier anger. He shouldn't have done what he did. It wasn't often he gave rein to his rage. Simi was one of the few triggers that was still left inside him. Up until Nick had sullied her, she had been the only pristine thing left in his life.

Part of him hated Nick for what he'd done.

But the sane, rational part of him understood. Even so, he couldn't forgive what they had done. He was afraid of how it would change Simi. Of what she might become . . .

"Is Nick okay?"

Amanda looked extremely uncomfortable. "He was busted up pretty badly. I tried to get him to go to the hospital, but he refused. He said he'd had enough broken ribs in his life to know how to tend them. So Kyrian and Talon taped him up and sent him home."

Ash nodded. "Keep an eye on him."

"What about you? Aren't you going to check on him?"

"I can't. At least not for awhile. I need time to get past this and I can't guarantee that I won't hurt him again. God knows, Nick has a true gift for saying the wrong thing in any given situation."

He saw the agreement on her face. "You know he loves you, right?"

"Yeah, but emotions don't have brains."

"No, I don't guess they do."

Ash gently pushed her toward her bedroom. "Go get some sleep."

Amanda took a step away, then paused and turned back to face him. "Ash?"

"Yeah?"

"Why did you put Tabitha with Valerius?"

"For the same reason I handed you Kyrian's soul on the day we first met."

"You have to know that there will never be peace between the two of them. Ever. Tabitha can't bring Valerius into our family. It's just not fair to Kyrian."

"Maybe, but the real question is this: Had you met Valerius before Kyrian, would you still feel the same way toward the Roman? And if Tabitha had married Valerius and then you found Kyrian, how would you feel if she told you that you had to let him go?"

Amanda looked away.

"Exactly, Amanda. In order to have a future, Kyrian needs to let go of the past."

Tabitha sucked her breath in sharply between her teeth as Valerius licked the salted garlic butter off her breast. He laughed playfully with her nipple between his teeth as he looked up at her.

He pulled back long enough to dip another piece of shrimp in butter before holding it up for her to bite into. Tabitha licked his fingers sensuously as she ate from his hand.

"I think we set a record for longest meal in history."

Valerius smiled at that as he placed another shrimp on her right nipple. The butter ran down the side of her breast. He licked it off her skin before he went after the shrimp and devoured it.

Tabitha smoothed his hair back from his face. "See, I knew you Romans were raw with this kind of stuff. I was right, wasn't I?"

"You were right," he said as he squeezed a lemon over her stomach.

Her toes actually curled as he lapped the juice off her.

His whiskers gently brushed her stomach, sending chills all over her. "You are so wonderful," she said quietly.

Valerius froze at her words. No one had ever said such a thing to him before.

No one.

And in that moment, he had a terrifying thought. He was going to have to let her go.

Some unknown force slammed into his chest at the thought. It stole the breath completely away from him.

Life without Tabitha.

How could such a thought slice through him when he'd only just met her? And yet as he tried to imagine going back to his cold, sterile world where people ignored, mocked, and disregarded him, he wanted to shout at the injustice.

He wanted to keep her.

The desire to bind her to him was feral and unreasoning. It was also selfish and wrong.

Tabitha had a family who loved her. Her family had always been a major part of her life. He'd seen it himself. The love. The care.

His family had been a nightmare of jealousy and cruelty. But hers . . .

He couldn't take her away from them. It wouldn't be right.

"Valerius? Is something wrong?"

He offered her a half-smile. "No."

"I don't believe you."

Valerius lay on top of her and just listened to her breathe. She cradled him with her body and he reveled at the feel of her skin against his. Of her arms and legs wrapped around his bare body.

But it wasn't just his skin that was naked. His spirit was stripped bare as well.

He would give anything to have this woman and she was the one person he could never keep.

It wasn't fair.

Tabitha stroked Valerius's back as she felt his emotions. He was filled with angry despair and she didn't know why.

"Baby," she whispered. "Talk to me."

"Why do you call me baby?" His breath tickled against her breast.

"Does it bother you?"

"No. I've just never had anyone else use an endearment when they talked to me. It's odd to hear it from you."

She ran her hand over the scars of his back as her heart clenched for him. "Were you ever in love?" she asked.

He shook his head. "I only had Agrippina."

"But you never touched her?"

"No. I slept with others who had a choice about being with me."

She frowned at that. "But you didn't love any of them?"

"No." He angled his head so that he could look up at her. "What about you? Have you ever been in love?"

She sighed as she remembered her past and the one person she had wanted to share the rest of her life with. "I loved Eric. I wanted to marry him so badly that when he broke up with me, I thought I would die from the pain of it."

She felt jealousy cut through Valerius. "Why did he break up with you?"

She traced the fine line of his left eyebrow, then buried her hand in his hair to toy with it while she explained herself. "He said I burned him out."

Tears filled her eyes as she remembered that summer day when Eric had come over and ended the only decent relationship she'd ever had. "He said that as hard as it was to keep up with me while he was in his mid-twenties, he was terrified of trying to keep up with me at forty. He told me that if I could give up the vampire hunting and my store that we might stand a chance. But how could I ever give up the things that mean so much to me? I live to hunt. I owe it to those who can't fight for themselves."

Valerius lifted himself up and gently kissed away her tears. "Eric was a fool."

She smiled at that as his lean, muscled body slid sensuously against hers. Oh, he was delectable. All that strength and power . . .

And she wondered who he'd gone after once he became a Dark-Hunter.

"Who did you take revenge on?" she asked quietly.

He went rigid as he pulled away. "Why do you want to know?"

"I was just curious. I slashed Eric's car tires when he broke up with me."

His face was aghast. "No, you didn't."

She nodded. "I would have done more, but decided that that was enough to get my anger out. He had really *nice* Pirelli tires," she confessed.

He shook his head at her and laughed. "It's a good thing I don't drive, then."

"And you're avoiding my question," she said, tapping the end of his nose with her finger. "Tell me, Valerius. I won't think any less of you, I swear."

Valerius lay down beside her as his buried memories surfaced. He normally did his best not to recall those last hours of his human life. To remember the first night of his immortality.

He propped himself up on his elbow as he traced circles around Tabitha's breast. He adored the fact that she wasn't body conscious. Their nudity didn't bother her in the least.

"Val?" she prompted.

She wasn't going to let him escape. Taking a deep breath, he paused his hand over her belly ring. "I killed my brothers."

Tabitha traced the line of his jaw as she felt his pain and guilt.

"They were drinking and wenching with their slaves when I arrived. I will never forget the look of terror on their faces when they saw me and realized what I was there for. I should have let them go, but I couldn't." He moved away from her with eyes that were filled with torment and pain. "What kind of man kills his own brothers?"

Tabitha sat up and caught his arm as he left the bed. "They killed you first."

"And as the old saying goes, two wrongs don't make a right. We were family and I cut them down like they were enemy strangers." He raked his hand through his hair. "I even killed my own father."

"No," she said earnestly, tightening the grip on his arm. "Zarek killed your father, not you."

He frowned at her. "How do you know that?"

"Ash told me."

His face turned to stone as he glared at her. "And did he

tell you how Zarek killed him? He ran my father through with *my* sword. A sword I handed to him after my father begged for me to save him."

She felt his ache and wanted to give him peace. "No offense, but your father was a bastard who deserved to be butchered."

"No," he said, shaking his head. "No one deserves what happened to him. He was my father and I betrayed him. What I did was wrong. So wrong. It was just like the night when . . ."

Tabitha couldn't breathe as a terrible wave of guilt sliced through her. She sat up on the bed. "What, baby? What night?"

Valerius clenched his fists as he tried to block out the memories of his childhood. It was impossible.

Over and over he saw the violence, heard the screams that echoed across the centuries even now.

He had never been able to block it out.

Before he realized what he was doing, he told her what he had never told another single soul. "I was five when Kyrian died and I was there the night he came for his vengeance against my grandfather. That was how I knew what Zarek was the night he came for my father. How I knew to call out Artemis when I died. I . . ."

He shook his head to clear it. But it was hard. The images of the past were still crystal clear and haunting. "My grandfather had kept me up late that night to tell me how glorious it was to triumph over a worthy adversary even if it's by treachery. I was in the hall with him when we heard the horses outside reacting to something. You could feel that something evil was there. It clung to the air. Then we heard the guards shouting and dying. My grandfather pushed me into a cabinet to hide while he grabbed his sword."

Valerius winced. "There was a crack in the wood and I could see straight into the hall. I saw Kyrian come in. He was completely wild as he and my grandfather fought. My grandfather was no match for his fury. But Kyrian wasn't content to just kill him. He butchered him. Piece by piece. Inch by inch, until there was nothing left that resembled a human being at all. I kept my ears covered and choked on my sobs. I wanted to be sick, but I was terrified that Kyrian would hear me and butcher me, too.

"So I sat there like a coward in the darkness until there was complete silence in the hall. I looked and saw nothing but the red-stained floor and walls."

He raked his hand over his eyes as if to blot out the images that still tormented him. "I crept from the cabinet and remember staring at the way my grandfather's blood coated my sandals. And then I screamed until I lost my voice from the terror of it. For years, I kept thinking that if I had run for help maybe I could have saved him. That if I'd left the cabinet, I could have done something."

"You were just a child."

He refused her comfort. He knew better. "I wasn't a child when I walked away and left my father to die."

Valerius cupped her cheek in his hand. She was so beautiful. Courageous.

Unlike him, she had morals and kindness.

He had no right to touch something so precious, so priceless. "I am not a decent man, Tabitha. I have destroyed everyone I've ever touched and you . . . you are goodness. You have to leave while you can. Please. You can't stay with me. I'll destroy you, too. I know I will."

"Valerius," she said, taking his hand into hers. She felt his aching need to touch her. Felt his desire to keep her safe and protect her.

Pulling him into her arms, she held him quietly in the darkness. "You are a good man, Valerius Magnus. You are honor and decency, and I'll hurt anyone who says otherwise . . . even you."

Valerius closed his eyes as he held her. He cupped her head in his hand and savored her warmth and kindness.

And in that moment, he realized something that terrified him more than anything else.

He was falling in love with Tabitha Devereaux. Brazen temptress, vampire slayer, complete uncouth lunatic woman that she was, he loved her.

And there was no way he could have her. None.

What was he going to do?

How could he give up the only thing he'd ever had that

was worth anything? Yet it was because he loved her that he understood why he had to do this.

She belonged with her family and he belonged to Artemis.

He'd sworn himself to the goddess's service centuries ago. The only way for a Dark-Hunter to be free of that oath was for someone to love them enough to survive Artemis's test.

Amanda had loved Kyrian enough. Sunshine had loved Talon, and Astrid had loved Zarek.

Tabitha was certainly strong enough to survive the test. But could a woman like her ever love someone like him enough to free him?

Even as the thought went through his head, he realized just how stupid he was.

Artemis wasn't about to let another Dark-Hunter go free, and even if she was, Tabitha would never be his. He refused to ever come between her and her family.

He might need her, but in the end, she needed them a lot more. He was used to surviving alone. She wasn't.

He wasn't cruel enough to ask her to choose the impossible when the impossible would cost her everything she held dear.

Chapter 13

The next two weeks were truly hell on earth after dark. It seemed as if the Daimons lived only to play with and torment them.

No one was safe. The city had even tried to implement a curfew at Acheron's behest, but since New Orleans was a twenty-four-hour party town, they hadn't been able to enforce it.

The body count was unlike anything Tabitha had ever heard of outside of a Hollywood Movie, and the Squire's Council and Acheron were having a hard time hiding all the deaths from the police and news agencies. But what scared her most was the fact that what few Daimons they caught were damn near impossible to kill.

Every night she came back to Valerius's house in pain from the abuse to her body. She knew he didn't want her to go out with him to patrol and yet he never said anything.

Valerius merely spent an hour or two after they returned home massaging Icy Hot into her pains and bandaging up her wounds.

It was unfair that he never had aches and pains, and what few scuffs his body suffered were always gone after a few hours.

Tabitha now lay naked in the shelter of his arms. He was asleep and yet he held her firmly tucked in beside him as if he were afraid of losing her.

That warmed her more than anything else ever had. She should have gotten up hours ago. It was already after four in the afternoon, but since she'd moved in with Valerius she'd become a certified night owl.

Her head lay against his biceps and his right arm was thrown over her waist. She ran her hand over his forearm as she studied that tawny masculine skin.

Valerius had beautiful hands. Long and tapered, they were strong and well-shaped. These last few weeks they had given her so much comfort and pleasure that she could barely breathe from the happiness that consumed her whenever she thought of him.

Her phone rang.

Tabitha scooted out from under him to answer it.

It was Amanda.

"Hey, sis," she said a little hesitantly. Over the last two weeks, there had been a major strain on their relationship.

"Hi, Tabby, I was wondering if I could come over for a little while and talk to you."

Tabitha rolled her eyes at the idea. "I don't need another lecture, Mandy."

"I swear it's not a lecture. It's one sister to another. Please."

"Okay," she said quietly after a brief internal debate, then gave Val's address.

"I'll see you in a few minutes."

Tabitha hung up the phone, then crept toward the bed. Valerius lay on his side with his hair fanned out around him. Stubble shadowed his face and yet he looked almost boyish as he lay there.

Even asleep the muscles of his body were evident and defined. Dark hairs lightly dusted every perfect dip and curve, making the terrain of his skin all the more masculine and alluring.

But it wasn't just his handsomeness that appealed to her. It was his heart. The way he could take care of her without taking over her. She knew he didn't like it when she fought beside him and yet he never said one word against it. He merely stood by and let her fight her own battles. The only time he interfered was whenever she was in over her head.

Then he would charge in and save her without making her feel incompetent or weak.

Tabitha smiled at the sleeping image of him.

How could someone come to mean so much to her in such a short period of time?

Shaking her head, she reached to dress and thought about the first time Valerius had seen the tattoo on the small of her back, a small Celtic triangle.

"Why would you mark yourself intentionally?" he'd asked as if aghast at the very idea.

"It's sexy."

He'd curled his lip at that and yet now he took a great deal of pleasure kissing and massaging the tattoo in the mornings when they returned from their patrols.

Impulsively, she picked up his black silk shirt from the floor and put it on. She loved the way his spicy male scent clung to the fabric. The way it clung to her skin.

She pulled on her pants, then went downstairs to wait for Amanda.

"Hey, Tab."

She turned to the left at the bottom of the stairs to spy Otto using the computer in Valerius's study. It was the only piece of technology she'd been able to find in Val's entire house except for the massive DVD collection that he kept hidden in a vault in his office, which explained his knowledge of pop culture.

"Hey, Otto, whatcha working on?"

"Trying to track the Daimon menace as always. I'm using Brax's program to see if there's a pattern we can follow to predict where they might be tonight."

She nodded. Otto had slowly warmed up to her, and since the Daimon attacks had started, he'd reverted to his basic black wardrobe.

Today he had on a black turtleneck, charcoal sweater, and black slacks. She had to admit he was a good-looking man when he wasn't trying to be a tasteless slob.

He'd even given up the IROC and now drove his Jag, claiming that it was no longer fun to antagonize Valerius since the Roman was so distracted by Tabitha that he never reacted to Otto's ribbings anymore. Nor was Gilbert there to react to him either.

She moved into the study to look over his shoulder. "Have you found anything?"

"No. There isn't a pattern, yet. I just don't understand what has caused this. If they want Kyrian, why haven't they moved on him?"

She sighed irritably. "They're playing with us. You weren't here for Round One with Desiderius. He gets off on making us afraid of him and on toying with our heads."

"Yeah, but I'm getting sick of the escalating body count. Ten people died last night and the Council is having a hard time hiding all this from the authorities. The public is freaking and they've only heard about a percentage of the actual total."

Tabitha cringed. "How many Daimons were killed last night?"

"Only a dozen. The four you and Val took out, Ash killed five, and then Janice, Jean-Luc, and Zoe killed one each. The rest of the bastards got away."

"Damn."

"Yeah, I don't like being on the losing side of anything. This really sucks."

Tabitha scowled as his list ran through her head. "You know, it's pretty sad when I'm human and I can take out more Daimons than a Dark-Hunter."

Otto gave her a droll stare. "You're not out there on your own."

She blew him a raspberry. "For the record, Valerius helps me, not the other way around."

"Riiiight."

Tabitha laughed at his playful scoffing until another thought occurred to her. "What about Ulric?"

"What about him?"

"How many did he kill?"

"None, why?"

None? That wasn't right. "He didn't kill any the night before, either, did he?"

"No."

A bad feeling went through her. No, surely she was wrong.

It wouldn't be possible, would it?

"Where did most of the kills occur last night?" she asked.

Otto punched a key and changed the monitor screen to a map of the French Quarter. She saw the areas highlighted in red wherever someone had died. There was a heavy concentration of red marks in the northeast quadrant.

"Who was assigned that area?"

Otto checked another screen. "Ulric."

She went cold. "And yet he didn't kill any Daimons?" she asked in disbelief.

Otto's gaze narrowed. "What are you saying?"

"Desiderius needs a body . . . Valerius said back when all this started that if a Daimon ever took over a Dark-Hunter—"

"That's bullshit, Tabitha. I saw Ulric last night myself and he was fine."

"But what if I'm right? What if Desiderius has taken him over?"

"You're wrong. Desiderius wouldn't be able to lay a hand on him. He was a medieval warlord. If there's one thing Ulric knows how to do, it's protect himself."

Maybe.

The buzzer sounded for the gate.

"It should be my sister."

Otto swung his chair around to the small video console that showed an image of the car's driver. It was Amanda.

He buzzed her in.

Tabitha went to meet her at the door, even though she couldn't shake the feeling that something wasn't right with Ulric. In spite of what Otto said, she wanted proof that she was wrong.

Tonight, she'd meet the Dark-Hunter herself and decide if her fear held any validity and if it did, he would be Daimon dust.

Swinging open the door, she saw Amanda getting out of her Toyota in the driveway. She was dressed in a pair of nice black slacks, a dark green silk top, and black sweater. It was really good to see her again.

Silently, Tabitha stood in the open doorway as she waited for Amanda to draw near.

Amanda gave her a tight hug as soon as she reached her. "I've missed you."

"I'm only a couple of blocks away."

"I know, but we haven't talked much lately."

Tabitha squeezed her back, then let her go. "I know. It's kind of hard to talk right now."

Amanda brushed the hair back from Tabitha's face in a very motherly fashion and smiled. "You look happy underneath that suspiciousness; are you?"

Tabitha frowned. "You are seriously scaring me." She looked past Amanda and scanned the street. "Has someone replaced my twin with a pod person?"

Amanda laughed. "No, goofball. It's me. I've just been worried about you."

"Well, as you can see, I'm fine. You're fine. Everything's fine. So what brings you here?"

"I want to meet Valerius."

Tabitha couldn't have been more stunned had her sister hit her. "Excuse me?"

"Ash said some things to me a couple of weeks ago that got me thinking. And with every day that passed without you racking this guy and moving in with me until this is over, I did more thinking. You've been with him night and day, haven't you?"

Tabitha shrugged with a nonchalance she didn't feel. "Yeah, so?"

"And yet I haven't had a single call from my homicidal twin telling me she's going to cut his head off and put it in a bowling bag if he says or does such-and-such one more time. Why, Tabby, I do believe that's a record for you."

Tabitha fidgeted guiltily. It was true. Not once in all their lives had she been with anyone that she wasn't threatening to kill the guy every other hour for some annoying habit.

But with Valerius . . .

Even when he annoyed her, it wasn't so bad. And the truth was, he very seldom annoyed her. They talked about all kinds of things and even when they didn't agree, he respected her opinions.

"You love him, don't you?"

Tabitha looked away.

"Oh God, Tabitha," Amanda breathed. "You've never done anything the easy way, have you?"

"Don't start on me, Amanda."

Amanda cupped her face and turned her head until their eyes met. "I love you, Tabby. I do. Of all the men—"

"I know!" she snapped angrily. "It's not like I woke up and said, Hmmm, who is the one man on the planet guaranteed to alienate me from my entire family for all eternity? Oh, I must go and find him immediately and fall hopelessly in love with him."

She took a deep breath before her anger overwhelmed her. "God knows, I didn't want to love someone like Valerius. I keep thinking that you are his perfect woman. You're elegant, sophisticated. Hell, you actually know which fork to eat with when you go out. I'm the idiot in college who went out with you and Dad and drank out of the finger bowl because I thought it was some kind of fucked-up clear soup."

Tabitha scoffed at her own words. "For that matter, listen to my language. I have to be horrifying to him and yet when he looks at me, I shiver."

Over and over, the arguments of why she didn't belong with Valerius ran through her mind. They should be completely incompatible and yet they weren't. It didn't make sense. It wasn't right.

Tabitha sighed. "The other night he took me to Commander's Palace and we sat down where they had this really elegant display sitting in the middle of the table. It was made up of all these exotic veggies and fruit and looked really tasty. So, stupid me, I grabbed my butter knife and started hacking at it to eat some of it. It wasn't until I looked up and saw the gape on the waiter's face that I realized I'd done something completely stupid. I asked him what his problem was and he said that he had just never seen anyone actually eat the centerpiece before. I was so embarrassed I wanted to die."

"Oh, Lord, Tabby."

"I know. Valerius, God bless him, didn't miss a beat. He reached over and started eating it too, then he gave one of those haughty, regal stares at the waiter, who quickly ran off. After he was gone, Val said for me not to worry about it. That he spent enough money in that place that I could eat the tablecloth next if I wanted to and if that didn't make me happy, then he'd buy the restaurant just so I could fire the waiter."

Amanda burst out laughing.

Tabitha had laughed too when he said it and the memory of his kindness still warmed her.

She gave her sister a sincere stare. "Don't you think I know that I don't belong with this man? I really, really don't. To me fine dining is slurping down oysters and drinking beer out of a bottle. To him it's a fifteen-course meal where people actually put the napkin in your lap for you and reset the silverware between every course."

"And yet you're still here."

"And I don't understand why."

Amanda smiled gently. "All I ever wanted was a nice, normal life with a nice, normal man. Instead, I end up with a husband who used to be immortal who has friends that are gods, demons, and animals that can take human form. And I don't even know how to begin to classify Nick. Let's face it, I'm married to a man who gave me a daughter who is able to talk to animals like Doctor Dolittle and who can use her thoughts to move just about anything in the house. And you know what?"

"What?"

"I wouldn't trade it for all the normality in the world. Love isn't easy. Anyone who says differently is lying to you. But it is worth fighting for. Believe me, I know, and that's why I'm here. I want to meet this man and see if there's any way I can soothe over Kyrian enough to where he can at least say Valerius's name without rupturing a vein."

Tears blurred her vision as Tabitha pulled her sister into another hug. "I love you, Amanda, I really do."

"I know. I'm the perfect twin."

Tabitha laughed at that. "And I'm the psychotic one." Stepping back, she took Amanda's hand and led her into the house.

Amanda gave a low whistle as she came inside and looked around the elegant interior. "Very nice place."

Otto stepped into the foyer to shake his head at them. "Kyrian will stroke if he ever finds out you were here."

"And you'll be limping if you enlighten him," Tabitha said.

"Don't worry. He won't hear it from me. I'm not that stupid." Otto headed for the door. "I'm off to meet up with Kyl
and Nick. We're going to get together tonight and do some
patrolling of our own and see if we can run some of these
bastards to ground."

Tabitha nodded. "You guys be careful."

"You, too." He inclined his head to them, then left.

"Why don't you wait in the library?" Tabitha said. "I'll
go see if he's up yet."

Amanda nodded.

Tabitha sprinted up the stairs and headed to Valerius's
room to find him still asleep in his bed.

She lifted the silk sheet up so that she could nip his hip
with her teeth.

He made a sound of pleasure before he rolled over onto
his back.

Tabitha's breath caught in her throat at the sight of his
nude body. She could stare at this man all day or night long.

She particularly loved the area of his body where short
crisp hairs ran from his navel to his groin. Unable to stand
the temptation, she bent over him and nibbled the little hairs
there.

His cock hardened. He placed his hand gently on her
head. "You certainly know how to wake a man up happily,
don't you?"

She laughed at that before she lightly nipped his skin,
then pulled away. "I need for you to get up."

"I am up," he said, glancing down to the part of his body
that was standing at full attention.

"Not that," she said, rolling her eyes. "My sister is downstairs and she wants to meet you."

"Which sister?"

She gave him a meaningful look.

His face went ashen. "I can't meet *her*."

Tabitha refused to listen to his argument. "Get dressed
and meet her. It'll only take a minute and then she'll leave."

"But—"

"No buts, General. I'll be waiting at the stairs and if you're
not there in five minutes, I'm going to bring her up here."

* * *

Amanda sat in a burgundy chair near a heavily draped window. She looked around the formal, elegant mansion. Unlike her home, there was nothing inviting about it. It spoke of a man who was stern and formidable, pretentious and condescending. Cold. Even a little evil and scary.

Everything she'd been told to expect from Valerius Magnus.

How had Tabitha ever hooked up with such a man? Her sister was none of those things.

Well, Tabitha could be evil, but in her twin's case that was an almost endearing quality.

It seemed to take forever before she heard Tabitha coming down the stairs.

"Tabitha!" The hushed tone was stern and commanding.

When Tabitha didn't lash back with a caustic retort, Amanda got up to investigate. She stayed in the shadows so that she could see Valerius with Tabitha on the stairs.

He was dressed in black pants and a black button-down shirt. From what she'd heard of him, she'd assumed his hair would have been cropped very short. To her surprise, it brushed down to his shoulders. His face was elegantly sculpted. Perfect.

Power and control bled from every part of him. This was definitely not the kind of man who attracted Tabitha.

Ever.

He glared at her sister as if he wanted to choke her. "You can't have her here. She has to leave immediately."

"Why?"

"Because Kyrian would die if he ever found out his wife was in my home. He'd lose his mind."

"Val—"

"Tabitha, I'm not kidding. This is cruel to him. You have to get her out of here before he finds out."

Amanda was shocked by his words. Why would he care how this affected Kyrian when Kyrian would gladly see him dead?

"Amanda wants to meet you, Valerius. Please? Just for a minute and then I'm sure she'll head home."

She scowled at Tabitha's calm, rational tone. Normally when her sister didn't get her way, she turned rather violent. Or at the very least, shouted.

His face softened instantly as he reached out and cupped Tabitha's scarred cheek in his hand. "I hate when you give me that look." He brushed his fingers over her eyebrow and smiled gently at her. "Okay." He dropped his hand to hers, then pulled it up and kissed the back of her hand.

Tabitha kissed his cheek before she stepped away and headed toward the library.

Her heart thumping at what she'd just seen, Amanda stepped back into the room so that they wouldn't know she'd been spying on them. But as she waited, images of their encounter played through her mind . . .

Valerius couldn't believe he was about to meet his enemy's wife.

Tabitha's twin sister.

He'd never been more nervous or unsure of himself.

But he refused to let that show. Stiffening his spine, he walked into the library, where Tabitha greeted her sister.

It was extremely odd to listen to them speak to each other. The only way he could tell their voices apart was their vocabulary. Tabitha had a unique way of speaking, whereas her twin sister was more eloquent and proper.

Amanda's eyes widened a bit as she scanned him from head to toe. Whatever she thought of him, she gave no clue.

"You must be Valerius," she said, stepping forward to offer him her hand.

"It's an honor," he said formally before he shook her hand very briefly, released it, and stepped back six paces.

She looked at Tabitha. "You two are the odd couple, aren't you?"

Tabitha shrugged before she tucked her hands in her pockets. "Thank God he's cuter than Tony Randall and I don't have Jack Klugman's nose."

Valerius became even more rigid.

Tabitha ran her hand affectionately down his arm. "Relax, hon. She doesn't bite. Only I do that." She winked at him.

The problem was, he didn't know how to relax. Especially not while her twin was staring at him as if he were something sinister.

Amanda watched her sister with the Roman general she had assumed she would hate on first meeting. To her surprise, she didn't.

He wasn't friendly, that was certainly true. He stood there with a crisp, arrogant look that seemed to defy her to insult him. But as she looked closer, she realized it was nothing more than a façade. He actually expected her to say something vicious to him and was just bracing himself to take it.

In fact, her psychic sense didn't pick up cruelty of any sort. Though he looked completely ill at ease, his gaze softened ever so subtly every time he glanced at Tabitha.

And there was no way to miss the way Tabitha reacted to him.

Oh, good grief, they really did love each other. What a nightmare!

"Well," Amanda said slowly, "I can stand here making everyone uncomfortable or I can go home. I should probably head back before it gets dark anyway. So—"

"My apologies, Mrs. Hunter," he said quickly. "I didn't mean to make you uneasy. If you wish to stay and talk to Tabitha, I'll be more than happy to withdraw."

She smiled at his kindness. "No, it's okay. I just wanted to meet you for myself. I've never been the kind of person to let someone else make up my mind for me and I wanted to know if you really were a three-toed, horned demon. But strangely enough, you look like an accountant."

"From her, that's a compliment," Tabitha said with a laugh.

He looked even more uncomfortable.

"It's okay," Amanda said. "Really. I just felt this insane need to know who was holding my sister hostage. It's not like her to not call me three dozen times a day."

"I'm not holding her hostage," he said quickly as if the accusation offended him. "She can leave anytime she chooses."

Amanda smiled. "I know." She looked at Tabitha and shook her head. "It's going to be hell at Thanksgiving, huh?

Never mind the terror of Christmas. And we thought Granny Flora was bad with Uncle Robert."

Tabitha's heart pounded at what her sister was saying. "You don't mind?"

"Oh, I mind, all right. I would sooner kill myself than ever hurt Kyrian, but I can't hurt you either and I'm not willing to lose you over something that happened two thousand years ago. Maybe we'll get lucky and one of the Daimons'll get Valerius before this is over."

"Amanda!" Tabitha snapped.

"I was joking, Tabby. Really." She took Valerius's hand and held it against Tabitha's. "One of these is not like the other, one of these does not belong," she sang under her breath.

Then she sobered. "Are you going to ask Ash for Valerius's soul back?"

Tabitha felt a bit awkward with that question. "We haven't gotten that far."

"I see."

Tabitha stiffened at the "Mom" tone Amanda used. "What's that supposed to mean?"

Amanda looked at her as if she had no clue. "It means nothing."

"Yeah, right," Tabitha said, her anger mounting. "I know that tone. You don't think I'm serious about him, do you?"

Amanda sputtered. "I didn't say that."

"You didn't have to say that, Amanda. You know, I'm really tired of being the brunt of the family jokes. I've never understood why I'm the weird, crazy one when Tia dances naked out in the bayous in voodoo ceremonies; Selena chains herself to fences; Karma is a bull inseminator; Aunt Jasmine is trying to splice a Venus flytrap with kudzu to make a man-killing plant to devour her ex—"

"She what?" Valerius asked.

Tabitha ignored him. "And you, precious Amanda, who is everyone's darling. First you unknowingly date a half-Apollite whose adopted father is out to kill you for your powers and then you end up married to a vampire that I have to tolerate even though I personally think he's a pompous, overbearing, humorless boor. Why am I the crazy one in all this?"

"Tabitha—"

"Don't *Tabitha* me when you know it seriously pisses me off!"

Amanda's eyes flared. "Fine, you want to know why you're the crazy one? Because you flit from one extreme to the other. Good grief, you had, what? Nine majors in college?"

"Thirteen."

"See? You are a flibbertigibbet. If not for us taking care of you, you'd be one of those homeless people you feed every night and you know it. It's why you feed them."

"I can take care of myself."

"Yeah, right. How many jobs did you have until Irena left you the store? She didn't want to retire, by the way. Dad paid her to because it was the only job you ever held on to for more than a few days."

"You bitch!" Tabitha lunged for her sister, only to have Valerius intercept her.

"Tabitha, calm down," he said, holding her back.

"No! I'm tired of being treated like the village idiot by those who claim they love me."

"We wouldn't treat you that way if you didn't act it. My God, Tabitha look at yourself. Look at why Eric left you. I love you, I really do, but you have done nothing but cause strife all your life."

"Don't you dare speak to her that way," Valerius snarled as he moved away from Tabitha to confront Amanda. "I don't give a damn who you are, I'll throw you out. No one talks to her like that. No one. There is nothing wrong with Tabitha. She's nothing but kindness to anyone. If you can't see all her good qualities, then there's something seriously wrong with *you*."

A smile instantly broke across Amanda's face. "And that really was what I needed to know."

"You were playing with me?" Tabitha snapped.

"No," Amanda said sternly. "This is no playing matter. But before I go make my husband absolutely miserable, I have to know that you two are serious and that Valerius isn't just another one of your 'let me make my family crazy' fixations."

Tabitha glared at her as her volatile emotions swirled. "There are times, Mandy, when I think I hate you."

"I know. Bring him by the house tonight and we'll try this again."

"I can't believe you're doing this for us," Valerius said.

Amanda took a deep breath. "No offense, I'm not. I'm doing this for Kyrian. Ash told me something and I'm here to make sure it happens."

And with that, she turned and headed for the door.

"Mandy?" Tabitha called, stopping her before she left. "Do we have a truce?"

"No. We have a volatile, homicidal family. But at least it won't be boring. I'll see you tonight."

Tabitha watched as her sister left. Deep in the pit of her stomach, a strong sense of foreboding settled. It was bleak and harsh. Frightening and cold.

It was almost as if she knew instinctively that tonight one of them would die . . .

Chapter 14

Dressed all in black lace, Apollymi sat looking to the uninitiated like a beautiful, ethereal blonde angel on her settee. She stared out of the open grand French doors onto her garden, where only black flowers grew in memory of her one true son who had been brutally taken from her.

Even after all these centuries, her mother's heart ached with the loss of him. With the feral, unending need she had to hold her child to her. To feel his warm touch.

What good was it to be a god when she couldn't have the only wish that had ever burned inside her?

This day was the most painful of all days. For this was the very day when she had given birth to her beautiful, perfect son.

And this had been the day they had taken him from her forever.

Tears glittered in her eyes as she lifted the small black pillow from her lap to her face and inhaled the spicy scent of it. Her son's scent. Closing her eyes, she summoned an image of his precious, most beloved face in her mind. Heard the sound of his commanding voice.

"I need you back, Apostolos." But her whisper went unheard and she knew it.

"He is here, Benevolent One."

Apollymi paused as she heard Sabine's voice from behind her. Sabine was her most trusted Charonte servant, since Xedrix had vanished on the night the Greek god Dionysus and the Celtic god Camulus had sought to free her from her prison in Kalosis.

Apollymi returned the pillow to her lap as she dismissed the orange-fleshed, winged demon.

"You summoned me, Mother?" Stryker asked as he came toward her.

She forced herself not to betray the fact that she knew he had turned on her. He thought himself clever.

It was enough to make her laugh.

No one could ever defeat the Destroyer. It was why she was imprisoned. She could be contained, but never annihilated. It was a lesson Stryker would learn one day all too soon.

But not today. Today, she still needed him.

"It is time, *m'gios*." The Atlantean term for "my son" was bitter as always on her tongue. He was a very poor substitute for the male child she had birthed. "Tonight will be the perfect time to strike. It is a full moon in New Orleans and the Dark-Hunters will be distracted."

And she wanted that human child! It was time to put an end to her captivity once and for all.

Marissa Hunter was a mild sacrifice she needed to return her son to his real, living state. And by all the power of Atlantis, she would restore her son.

No other life, not even her own, was worth one tiny part of his.

Stryker inclined his head. "Indeed, Mother. I've already set loose my Daimons to wreak carnage. Desiderius will return with the child at midnight and when they leave tonight, there won't be a single Dark-Hunter left breathing."

"Good. I don't care how many Spathi die or anyone else. I must have that child!"

She felt Stryker starting to leave.

"Strykerius?" she called.

"Yes, Mother?"

"Serve me well and you will be rewarded beyond measure. Betray me and there is nothing that can save you from my wrath."

Stryker narrowed his eyes on the goddess, who refused to even look at him. "I would never dream of betraying you, Mother," he said, masking the rancor of his tone.

No, he wasn't going to betray her tonight.

He was going to kill her.

After leaving her temple, Stryker summoned his Illuminati together before he opened the bolt-hole that would take his men to New Orleans. There they would do his will while he stayed safely tucked away from the Destroyer's notice. It was time he stopped the age-old conflict between human and Apollite.

A new era was dawning, and mankind . . .

It was time they learned their inferior place.

As for Acheron, now that he knew what the man really was, he knew how to neutralize him.

After all, not even the great Acheron could be in two places at once, nor could he stand against the assault that was about to begin.

Desiderius paused outside of a small voodoo shop. It was quaint and charming, and to most tourists, it looked like all the others.

The only thing that separated this store from all the rest that occupied designated areas of the French Quarter was the fact that here he sensed real power.

Closing his eyes, he inhaled the rich, musty scent of it. As a Daimon, he'd need her soul to live, but since he was in the body of a Dark-Hunter . . .

Killing humans was done for simple pleasure now, not for sustenance.

He smiled to himself as he stepped inside to find his target. It only took a second to locate her behind the counter, where she was waiting on a tourist who was buying a love potion.

"Hi, Ulric!" his victim said excitedly as the customer walked out of the store and left them alone.

Ah, good, she knew the Dark-Hunter. It would make killing her all the easier.

"Hi," he said, stepping up to the counter. "How are you tonight?"

"I was just about to close. I'm really glad you came by. After everything that's been happening around here, well . . . it's good to see a friendly face."

Desiderius's gaze went past her shoulder to a small snapshot hanging on a calendar that advertised scented candles. It was of nine women, two of whom he knew instantly.

His gaze darkened.

"How are Tabitha and Amanda?" he asked.

"They're doing okay. All things considered. Mandy's afraid to leave the house and Tabby . . . you've probably met her on the street."

Yes, Amanda was afraid to leave her house, which made their getting into it almost impossible.

But there was one way he knew to draw the sorceress out of her home.

He gave the woman behind the counter a tight-lipped smile. "Would you like for me to walk you home?"

"What a sweetie. Thanks, that'll be great. Just give me a sec to grab the money envelope and I'll do the paperwork at home."

Desiderius licked his lips. He could already taste her blood . . .

The night was eerily quiet as Ash walked alone through the St. Louis Cemetery No. 1 searching for Daimons who often came to claim the souls of the dead who had refused to move on.

The New Orleans natives called these impressive stone cemeteries the Cities of the Dead, a title that was wholly apropos. Because the town was below sea level, no one could bury the dead without the bodies making a most unwelcomed reappearance.

The full moon above cast distorted shadows of the statuary along the brick, stone, and marble crypts—some of which were taller than even he was. Although in places rather haphazard, most of the tombs were arranged into blocks that did in fact strangely mirror the layout and design of a city.

Each crypt was elegantly crafted as a monument to those

whose remains it contained. There were three classifications for the tombs: wall vaults; family vaults; and society vaults that were reserved for specific groups, like the round Italian Society tomb, which was the largest crypt there, and one that dominated the cemetery.

Most of the tombs showed signs of their age by having broken pieces of masonry either missing or askew, along with collapsed roofs, and blackened mold that grew all over them. Many held scrolled wrought-iron gates and fences.

It was beautiful here. Peaceful. Although the strategically placed holes in the exterior walls that allowed muggers to come and go at will were a constant reminder of how some of the occupants had come to reside here.

Ash reached out and touched the grave of Marie Laveaux, the famous voodoo maven of the city. Her grave was marked with Xs from those who would pay tribute to her.

She'd been a remarkable woman and in his long life, she had been the only human to know him for what he really was.

Sirens sounded off in the distance as police headed for a new crime scene.

As he turned away, Ash felt a ripple go through him like a debilitating blow. He hissed in pain as he felt a fragile, forbidden doorway opening and felt the evil pouring out of it.

The Illuminati were leaving Kalosis . . .

Suddenly, his vision became cloudy.

Ash no longer saw anything around him, overwhelmed with sounds and images of souls screaming in agony as they died. It was a sound unheard by mortals, but one that cut through him like shattering glass.

The order of the universe was being altered.

"Atropos!" he called, summoning the Greek goddess of fate who was responsible for cutting the life strands of mortals.

Tall and blonde with furious eyes, she appeared beside him instantly. "What?" she snapped.

The two of them had never gotten along; in truth, none of the Moirae could stand him. Not that he cared. He had far more reasons to hate them than they had to hate him.

Ash leaned back against one of the old crypts as he tried to staunch some of his pain.

"What are you doing?" he gasped.

"It's not me," she said indignantly. "It's something from *your* side, not ours. We have no control over it. If you want it to stop, stop it."

She vanished.

Wrapping his arms around his stomach, Ash slid to the ground. The pain . . . it was biting into him even more. He couldn't breathe. Couldn't think.

The screams rang throughout his head until it brought tears to his eyes.

Without his bidding, Simi came off his arm. "*Akri?*" she said, kneeling beside him. "What hurts you, *akri?*"

"Sim," he panted through the vicious stabs. "I c-can't . . ." His words trailed off into a groan.

She doubled in size and transformed from a young woman into her demon form. Her skin and horns were red, and her hair and lips were black, while her eyes glowed a dull yellow in the darkness.

She pulled him away from the crypt long enough to slide herself between him and the stone, then she wrapped her body around his. Her midnight wings folded around both of them as a protective cloak.

Ash's lips chattered from the agony as tears flowed from his eyes. He felt as if something were rupturing inside him. He had to block the screams or he would be useless.

Simi placed her cheek against his and hummed an ancient lullaby as she rocked him soothingly.

"The Simi has you, *akri*, and she'll make all the voices go away."

Ash leaned back in her arms and prayed she was right. Because if she didn't restore him soon, there would be no one to repair what was being torn apart.

Tabitha was filled with such a sudden sense of pain that it stopped her dead in her tracks.

Gasping, she reached out for Valerius, who was walking beside her.

"Tabitha? Is something wrong?"

"Tia," she gasped, her heart aching in a pain so profound

that she wasn't sure how she maintained her stance. "Something's happened to her. I know it."

"Tab—"

"I know it!" she shrieked, clutching his shirt. "Oh God, no!" She grabbed her phone and started dialing Tia's number as she ran toward her sister's store. They were only six blocks away.

No one answered.

She dialed Amanda, her heart thumping in her chest as she ran. This couldn't be happening. She had to be wrong.

She had to be!

"Tabitha?" She heard the tears in Amanda's voice.

"It's true, isn't it? You feel it, too?"

"Kyrian won't let me leave the house. He says it's too dangerous."

"Don't worry, I'm on the street and I'll call you as soon as I know something."

Tabitha clutched the phone in her hand as they neared the dark store.

Everything looked normal . . .

Valerius slowed down as he sensed death. There was an evil pall that hung over the store. He'd been a Dark-Hunter long enough to know even that much without any psychic abilities.

Tabitha tried the front door, which was locked.

"Tia!" she shouted, knocking on it. "You still here?"

No one answered.

She led him around back, into a small courtyard. The back door to the shop had been left ajar.

Valerius held his breath at the confirmation of his fears. Tabitha slowed down to a careful walk.

"Tia?" she called again.

Valerius pulled her away from the back door. "Stay behind me."

"She's my sister!"

"And I'm immortal. Stay behind me."

Luckily, she nodded.

Valerius opened the door carefully as he looked for anyone to move on them.

No one did.

The back room appeared completely normal. Nothing was out of place. It looked just as it had a few weeks ago when Tia had tended him here.

His hand on the dagger at his waist, he carefully approached the door to the shop, which was also slightly ajar. He pushed it open, then froze when he saw the pair of shoes sticking out from behind the counter.

His heart stopped.

"Stay here, Tabitha."

"But—"

"Dammit, Tabitha, stay!"

"I am not your bitch, General, and you don't talk to me that way!"

He knew it was her fear that made her so angry. She never knew how to cope with strong emotions. "Please, Tabitha. Stay here while I look."

She nodded.

Valerius pulled away and walked cautiously across the floor to where he saw the shoes. As he drew nearer, he saw the rest of the body.

Shit.

His chest tight and aching, he turned Tia over to see her glazed eyes staring out at nothing. Her neck was torn open as if a Daimon had attacked her, but her soul was still here. He could feel it.

Why would a Daimon not take her soul?

As he reached to close her eyes, he realized something else. Tabitha wasn't with him.

Panic threatened to consume him. It wasn't like her to really listen. Rising quickly, he dashed back to the storeroom, where he found her sitting before a video surveillance console that showed the flickering black-and-white images of Tia's death.

Tabitha sat there with tears pouring out of her eyes as she held her hands crossed over her lips. Her sobs were silent, yet they shook her entire body.

"I'm so sorry, Tabitha," he whispered before he shut off the monitor and pulled her into his arms.

"She can't be dead!" she wailed as she clutched him to her. "This isn't true. Not my sister. She's not dead. She's not!"

He didn't speak as he rocked her gently in his arms.

She screamed out in pain before she shoved him away from her and ran for the storefront.

"Tabitha, no!" he snapped, pulling her back before she saw Tia's body. "You don't need to see her like that."

She turned on him with a shriek and shoved him back. "Damn you! Damn all of you for this. Why didn't you just kill me? Why kill my sister? Why . . . ?"

Her eyes widened in horror. "Oh, God, they're going for my family." She pulled her phone out, no doubt to call Amanda again.

While she called her family, he pulled his Nextel out to notify the others what had happened. "Code Red to everyone," he said, his voice tight. "Tia Devereaux has been slain inside her store. Everyone needs to pull back and secure their families."

One by one, the Dark-Hunters and Squires checked in: Otto, Nick, Kyl, Rogue, Zoe, Jean-Luc, Ulric, Janice, Kassim—even Talon, Kyrian, and Julian. But there was no sign of Acheron.

Valerius tried to buzz him, then call him.

There was no answer.

His blood ran cold. Had the Daimons gotten to Acheron already and hurt him again?

"I love you, Mandy," Tabitha said as her lips quivered from her grief. "You be careful, okay? I'm going to find this bastard and I'm going to kill him tonight."

Valerius glanced to the now blank monitor screen. "Do you know who killed her?" he asked.

Tabitha nodded. "It was Ulric and now I'm going to kill him."

Nick was walking down Ursulines, headed for the house on Bourbon Street that he shared with his mother. After hearing Valerius's call about Tia, he'd gone immediately to check on his mother, who was working late at Sanctuary.

Since he'd planned on hanging around the outside of the bar to watch out for her until it was time for her to leave, he'd practically been there already when the call went out.

As soon as he'd reached the saloon-style doors that were monitored by Dev Peltier, one of the bears who owned Sanctuary, he'd been told that his mother had left work early because she wasn't feeling well. Nick had been absolutely furious with the bear until Dev had told him that Ulric had agreed to escort her home.

Given Nick's busted ribs, his mom was a lot safer with a Dark-Hunter than she would have been with him anyway. Still, he had a need inside him to check on her to make sure she was all right.

It'd been just the two of them his whole life. Impregnated by a career felon when she was only fifteen, his mother had been cast out the door to fend for herself. He wouldn't have blamed her had she given him up, but she hadn't.

"You're the only thing in my life I ever did right, Nicky, and I thank God every night for giving me you."

It was why he loved her so much.

Nick had never met his grandparents on either side. Hell, he'd only met his father a handful of times and only once that he really remembered. It'd been when Nick was ten and his father had needed a place to crash for the longest stretch of freedom the man had known as an adult—three whole months.

In a bad cliché, his father moved in, drank beer constantly, and knocked the two of them around before one of his felon friends had convinced him to take a stab at bank robbery, where his father had shot four people dead just for the hell of it. His father had been quickly convicted, then died a year later when some inmate had cut his throat during a prison riot.

Cherise Gautier left much to be desired when it came to her taste in men, but as a mother . . .

She was perfect.

And Nick would do anything in the world for her.

He heard static from his Nextel, which he expected to be Otto screwing with him again.

It wasn't.

Valerius's accented voice broke the stillness. "Nick, are you there?"

Just what he needed tonight. Grimacing, he jerked the phone off his belt. "What?" he snapped.

"I wanted to let you know that Ulric is Desiderius. He's already killed Tia. I don't know who's next, but I think you might want to check on your mother." Suddenly, Valerius's voice changed to one that made his blood run cold.

"Oh, wait . . ." Desiderius said tauntingly, "she's dead now." He made a sound of smacking his lips. "Hmmm, type O negative. My favorite. Of course, you'll be glad to know her last thoughts were of you."

Nick stopped moving for an instant before he dropped the phone and started running as fast as he could toward his house.

Over and over, he saw images of his mother in his mind. Of her gently teasing him while he grew up. The pride on her face the day he'd told her he was going to college.

His battered ribs ached and throbbed, but he didn't care if he ruptured both lungs.

He had to get to her.

By the time he reached the gate to his driveway, he was shaking so badly that he could barely punch in the code.

"Goddammit, open!" he snarled as the first code was rejected.

He reentered it.

The gates swung open slowly. Ominously.

Panting from fear and exertion, he raced up the drive to the back door.

It was unlocked. Nick entered, ready to do battle. He stopped in the kitchen to pull his Glock .31 out of the drawer by the stove. He checked the mag clip to make sure it was fully loaded with all seventeen rounds.

"Mom?" he called as he slid the mag in. "Mom, it's Nick, are you home?"

Only silence answered him.

His heart hammering, Nick crept through the house, room by room, expecting to be attacked.

He found absolutely nothing, until he reached the upstairs sitting room. At first, it looked like his mother was sitting in her chair like she'd done a million times before when
he'd come home to catch her waiting for him.

He'd bought this house just for this room alone. His
mother loved to read romance novels. All her life, she'd
dreamed of owning a home where she could have a perfect,
five-sided room to read her books in peace. The entire room
was lined with custom-made bookshelves. Every inch of
every shelf in here held a paperback that she had lovingly
chosen and cherished.

"Mom?" he said, his voice breaking off into a sob. His
hand shook as he held the gun out and stared through misty
eyes at the blond hair he could see over the top of the leather
recliner. "Please talk to me, Mom, please."

She didn't move.

He fought back his tears as he moved slowly forward until he could touch her.

Still, she was silent.

Nick cried out in grief as he buried his hand in her soft
hair and saw the paleness of her face. The vicious bite-wound
on her neck.

"No, Mommy, no!" he sobbed as he knelt beside her.
"Dammit, Mom, don't be dead!"

Only this time there was no comfort to be found in her
touch. No soft, loving voice to tell him that men didn't cry.
They didn't show pain.

But how could any man withstand this kind of brutal
agony?

This was his fault. All his fault. He'd been the idiot who
had befriended the Dark-Hunters.

Had he ever told her the truth . . .

She hadn't stood a chance.

"Mommy," he breathed against her cold face as he rocked
her in his arms. "I'm so sorry. I'm so sorry. I didn't mean to
hurt you. I didn't. Please wake up, please. Oh, please, Mom,
don't leave me."

Then his rage took hold. It steamed through his veins and
screamed out in shattering waves that tore him apart.

"Artemis!" he shouted. "I summon you to human form. Now!"

She appeared almost instantly with her hands on her hips and in a pique.

At least until she saw his mother's body.

"What is this?" she asked, curling her lip as if the sight of death disgusted her. "You're Acheron's friend Nick, aren't you?"

Nick laid his mother back in her chair, brushed the tears from his eyes with the back of his hand, and rose slowly to his feet. "I demand vengeance on the Daimon who did this and I demand it now."

She made a rude noise of dismissal. "You can demand all you want to, human, you're not going to get it."

"Why not? You give it to every other asshole who demands it. Make me a Dark-Hunter. You owe it to me."

She cocked her head and arched a brow at him. "I owe you nothing, human. And in case you haven't noticed, you imbecile, you have to be dead before you can become a Dark-Hunter." She let out a disgusted sigh. "Didn't you learn anything from Acheron?"

Artemis took a step back, intending to return home to Olympus, but before she could, the human knelt to the ground and picked up a gun.

"Make me a Dark-Hunter," he snarled an instant before he pulled the trigger.

Artemis froze at the loud, echoing sound of the gunshot. She couldn't breathe as she took in the sight of the man lying dead at her feet.

"Oh, no," she said breathlessly as her heart pounded. Acheron's human friend had just killed himself . . . right in front of her!

What was she going to do?

Her panicked thoughts raced. "He'll blame me for this." He'd never forgive her. Never. Even though it wasn't her fault, Acheron would find some way to blame it all on her, to say that she should have known and should have stopped him.

She stared in horror at the gore that spattered the front of her white dress. She'd never seen such before.

"Oh, think, Artemis, think . . ."

But she couldn't think straight. All she could hear was the sound of Acheron in her head as he told her why Nick and his mother meant so much to him.

"You'll never understand, Artie. They had nothing but each other and instead of blaming each other for ruining their lives, which many people would do, they bonded. Cherise's life has sucked and yet she's still kind and giving to everyone she meets. One day, Nick's going to marry and give her a houseful of grandchildren to love. Zeus knows, they both deserve it."

Only now Nick lay dead at her feet.

Dead by his own hand, and he was Catholic.

She could smell the sulphur already.

"Acheron!" she called, allowing her voice to travel through all dimensions. She had to tell him before it was too late. Only he could fix this.

He didn't answer.

"Acheron!" she tried again.

Again, he was silent.

"What do I do?" She was forbidden to make a Dark-Hunter from a suicide. But if she left Nick dead, his soul would be claimed by Lucifer and he would spend eternity in hell being tormented.

Either way, she would lose. Acheron would blame her for letting his friend suffer. He would think she'd done this on purpose just to hurt him.

And if she saved Nick . . .

The consequences didn't bear thinking on.

But as she stood there in indecision, one image came and stayed in her mind. The look on Acheron's face the day she had turned her back on his pain.

It was the only thing in her life that she truly regretted. The one thing she would change if she could.

There was no real choice here. She couldn't hurt Acheron like that again. Ever.

Kneeling down, she pulled Nick's body to her and restored him to what he'd been before the gunshot. She brushed his hair back from his face and spoke the forbidden words of a long-dead civilization.

The stone appeared in her hand. She felt its heat as his soul entered it.

Two seconds later, Nick's eyes opened. No longer blue, they were jet-black. He hissed as pain from the light pierced his now-sensitive eyes.

"Why didn't you call for Acheron instead of me?" she asked him quietly.

"He was mad at me," he said, lisping from the fangs that he had yet to grow accustomed to. "He told me I should kill myself and save him the trouble of it."

Artemis winced as she heard those words. Her poor Acheron. He would never forgive himself for this.

Nor would he forgive her.

Nick pushed himself up. "I want my vengeance."

"I'm sorry, Nick," she whispered. "I can't give it to you. You didn't adhere to the course of the bargain."

"What?"

Before he could say anything more, she raised her hand and sent him to a special room in her temple.

"Where are you, Acheron?" she whispered. The world was falling apart and he was nowhere to be heard.

It wasn't like him to be so careless.

Afraid something bad had befallen him, she closed her eyes and searched for him.

Desiderius walked down the street as if he owned it. And why not?

He did.

He held his arms out and leaned his head back as he heard the screams of the innocent in his head.

"You should be here, Stryker," he said with a laugh. Only Stryker could truly appreciate the beauty that was this night.

But time was running out.

He had to return with the Hunter child by midnight or the Destroyer would revoke his body.

"Father?"

He turned at the sound of his son's voice. "Yes?"

"Acheron is still missing, just as Stryker promised, and we've found our way in."

Desiderius laughed. At long last he would have his revenge on Amanda and Kyrian.

And as soon as he delivered up the child, he would finish off the main course with Tabitha for dessert.

Chapter 15

Valerius was torn between his loyalties and his duties. The Dark-Hunter in him wanted to find Acheron, but the man inside refused to leave Tabitha, who was keeping vigil in her sister's store until the coroner, Tate, arrived.

One by one, she'd contacted her family and assured herself that they were safe.

She hesitated on the last number to be called. "I can't call my mama and tell her," she said, her tears welling. "I can't."

The phone rang.

By the look on her face as she saw the caller ID, he had a good idea of who it was.

Valerius pried the cell phone from her hand and flipped it open. "Tabitha Devereaux," he said quietly.

"Who is this?" the woman sounded a bit frantic.

"I'm . . ." He hesitated at giving her his full name since she would no doubt register it as the name of an enemy and panic even more. "Val," he said firmly. "I'm a friend of Tabitha's."

"This is her mother. I need to know she's okay."

"Tabitha," he said, gentling his voice as he offered her the phone. "Your mother wants to know if you're okay."

She cleared her throat, but didn't take the phone from his hand. "I'm fine, Mama. Don't worry."

Valerius put the phone back up to his ear. "Mrs. Devereaux—"

"Don't say it," she said, her voice breaking. "I already

know and I need my baby girl home with me. I don't want her to be alone. Could you please bring Tabitha here?"

"Yes."

She hung up.

Valerius ended the call, then returned the phone to Tabitha, who slipped it into her pocket.

He felt completely helpless against her grief, and he hated that most of all. It seemed like there should be something that he could say at such a moment and yet he knew from personal experience that there wasn't.

All he could do was hold her.

"Hey, everyone?" Otto's voice called out over the Nextel intercom. "I'm at Nick's house. The front gate was open and something really bad went down here. I need a head count immediately."

Kyl came back right away, as did Talon and Janice. Julian answered in next, followed by Zoe and then Valerius.

They all waited for the next one to check in.

No one did.

"Nick?" Otto called. "You out there, Cajun? Come on, buddy, answer me with something smart-ass."

No answer.

Valerius went cold.

"Jean-Luc?" Otto asked.

Again, nothing.

"Acheron?"

A feeling of severe dread ran through Valerius as Tabitha gave him a panicked look.

They knew the next name before Otto spoke it.

"Kyrian? Kassim?"

Only static filled the line.

Valerius pulled the Nextel off his belt and pushed for Otto alone. "What happened at Nick's?"

"Cherise is dead and there's no sign of him. I found his gun lying in a pool of blood by his mother's body with one round missing, but it's not what killed Cherise."

Valerius ground his teeth as he understood Otto's meaning. "Daimon attack?"

"Yeah."

Tabitha cursed, then bolted off her stool. "I have to get to Amanda."

"Otto, meet us at Kyrian's." He opened the line back out to the group. "Janice? Talon? Zoe? Can you start searching for Jean-Luc?"

"Who left you in charge, Roman?" Zoe sneered.

Valerius wasn't in the mood for this bullshit as he went after Tabitha. "Stow it, Amazon. This isn't about my heritage. This is about your brothers-in-arms and their lives."

Julian came back at him. "I'll meet you at Kyrian's."

"No, please. Stay with your wife and children. Make sure they're safe."

"All right. Let me know what you find out."

Tabitha was already in the driver's seat of her Mini Cooper. Valerius got inside and slammed the door shut.

She threw it in reverse and didn't bother to open the wooden gate. She crashed through it as she squealed off into the street.

Valerius braced himself against the dashboard while she careened them through traffic at a deadly pace, toward her sister's house.

Once they reached it, she didn't stop at Amanda's tall iron gate, either. Valerius held his arm up to shield his face as she drove straight through it and tore the iron posts off their stone facings.

Tabitha skidded to a stop just in front of the door and launched herself from the car without even turning it off.

Valerius didn't hesitate to follow.

From the outside of the house, everything looked normal. The lights were on, and as Tabitha kicked open the front door, they could hear a television somewhere upstairs.

"Mandy?" Tabitha screamed out in a shrill tone.

Her sister didn't answer her.

"Hey, Dad?" someone called from upstairs. "Your dessert's here."

Artemis paused outside the cemetery where she sensed Acheron's presence. She shivered in revulsion. She'd always hated such places, while he seemed to prefer them.

"Acheron?" she called as she walked through the stone wall.

The dark ground was uneven, making it hard for her to walk. So she floated through the area.

"Acheron?"

A flash of fire shot near her head.

Artemis ducked and moved to return the blast until she caught sight of Acheron's pet. She curled her lip at the demon until she saw Acheron lying in its arms. He looked terrible as he writhed there as if in the throes of torture.

"What have you done to him?" Artemis demanded of the creature.

The demon hissed at her. "The Simi did nothing, you heifer-goddess. You the one who hurts my *akri*. Not me."

Any other time, Artemis might argue with it, but Acheron lay there as if he were in excruciating pain.

"What happened to him?"

"It's the souls them Daimons are eating. They scream when they die and there are too many of them tonight. The Simi can't make it go away."

"Acheron?" Artemis tried again as she knelt beside him. "Can you hear me?"

He recoiled from her.

She tried to reach for him only to have the demon lunge at her.

"Don't you touch my *akri*!"

Damn the Charontes! The only one who could control them was . . .

No, there were *two* people alive who could control them.

"Apollymi?" she spoke to the mist around her. "Can you hear me?"

Evil laughter echoed on the breeze. The Atlantean goddess couldn't come out of her prison in form, but her powers were so great that she could extend her will and voice even through her limitations. "So, you speak to me, bitch. Why should I listen?"

Artemis clamped her temper down before she answered insult with insult and drove the older goddess away. "I can't help Acheron. His demon won't let me. I need your help."

"And why should I care?"

"Because I . . ." Artemis ground her teeth together before she spoke the most difficult word of all for her. "Please. Please, help me."

"What will you give me for this service? Will you return my baby to me?"

Artemis curled her lip at the thought. There was no way she'd ever release him. "I can't do that and you know it."

She felt Apollymi pulling away.

"No!" she said hurriedly. "Do me this favor and I'll release Katra from my service. She'll be yours alone to command and will no longer have torn loyalties between me and you."

Once more she heard the ancient Atlantean goddess laughing at her.

The laughter ended on a short note. "I would have helped him anyway, you gullible chit. But I thank you for the gift."

A red, eerie haze fell over the area as the Destroyer withdrew her voice. It formed the shape of a hand that then cradled Acheron's body. Acheron cried out as if the pain were more than he could bear. His whole body turned rigid and strained.

"*Akri?*" the demon wailed, its face terrified.

Then suddenly, Acheron went completely limp as the mist evaporated.

Artemis let her breath out slowly as she watched him in fear that Apollymi might have actually worsened his condition just for spite. The demon cuddled him to its bosom while it stroked his long black hair away from his face.

His chest rose and fell normally.

"Sim?" he breathed as he looked up at the demon with a tender expression that made Artemis hate him.

"Sh, *akri*, you needs to rest for the Simi."

He raked his hand through his hair until he noticed Artemis standing in front of him. All the tenderness fled his expression. "What are you doing . . ."

His voice trailed off as if he suddenly became aware of something.

He vanished instantly, leaving her and the demon alone in the graveyard.

Folding her arms over her chest, Artemis huffed at his rudeness. "A thank-you would have been nice, Acheron!"

But she knew he didn't hear her. He had a remarkable ability to tune her out.

Her only consolation was the demon looked every bit as baffled until its eyes widened and it flashed to the form of a human female with horns.

"They gots baby Marissa!" the demon breathed before it too vanished.

Tabitha lunged at the Daimon, who laughed as he stepped to the side and brought his fist down across her back. Pain exploded down her spine.

Valerius roared with rage before he shot a bolt at the Daimon.

It missed.

The Daimon laughed again. "Let's see if the Roman general dies crying for his human love the same way the Greek did."

Tabitha couldn't breathe as she heard those words. Kyrian wasn't dead. He wasn't.

"You liar!" she snarled.

She turned to watch Valerius fight the Daimon as more of them came running from the stairs. They swarmed into the room like angry ants.

Two of them grabbed her. Tabitha slugged them, but her blows seemed to glance off them without fazing them at all.

Valerius broke free from his opponent to hand her one of his swords.

She took it from him before she turned to face three Daimons. She stabbed the one nearest her, but he didn't explode.

He smiled at her instead. "You don't kill the servants of the goddess, human. The Illuminati aren't typical Daimons."

She swallowed her panic before it defeated her. "Valerius? What goddess are they talking about?"

"There's only one goddess, you pathetic fool. And it's not Artemis," the Illuminati said an instant before sinking his teeth into her neck.

Tabitha cried out from pain.

Suddenly, she was thrown away from them. She looked to see Valerius engaging the Daimons.

"Don't you touch her."

The Daimon *tsked* at him. "Don't worry, Dark-Hunter, before she dies, we'll all sample her blood. Just as we did her sister."

Tabitha screamed as pain racked her. "Damn you!"

Another Daimon seized her from behind. "Of course we're damned. The Spathi wouldn't have it any other way." He backhanded her, knocking her off her feet.

Tabitha tasted the blood on her lips, but she wasn't daunted. She wasn't about to let them get away with this.

As she stumbled away from the Daimon toward her sword that had skidded to the foot of the stairs, she glanced upstairs and froze. Horror consumed her.

Kyrian lay at the top of staircase, his body on the landing while his head rested on a step, his right arm fully extended. A bloodied Greek sword had fallen halfway down the stairs. His sightless eyes were open and a small trail of blood ran from his lips. But it was the gaping wound in his chest that held her transfixed.

They had killed him.

A few feet away from his body, two bare, feminine legs peeked out from under the hem of a pink nightgown in the doorway of the nursery.

And then she saw Ulric stepping over Amanda's body with a crying Marissa in his arms as he started for the stairs.

"Daddy!" the toddler wailed as she fought against the tight hold the Daimon had on her to reach her father. Pictures flew from the wall into Ulric, who paid them no heed.

"Daddy, Mama, get up." Marissa pulled the Daimon's hair and bit at him. "Get up!"

"Amanda! Amanda! Amanda!" Tabitha didn't know who at first was calling her sister's name as terror filled her. It wasn't until she couldn't scream anymore that she realized the hysterical shrieks were hers.

Grabbing her sword, she ran up the stairs for the Daimon. He knocked her back. She slipped on Kyrian's blood and went tumbling back down.

Valerius caught her from behind before she fell the whole way.

"Run, Tabitha," he breathed in her ear.

"I can't. That's my niece and I'll be damned if he's going to get her without a fight."

She pushed herself away from Valerius as a phantom wind whipped through the room. It tore through the house with a vengeance, hurtling lamps, plants, and anything small around.

And as it touched the Daimons, they fell one by one with nothing more than a gasp.

Clutching Marissa to him, Desiderius, who was still in Ulric's body, ran past her and Valerius into the living room.

Tabitha followed, intending to reclaim her niece.

"Desi!" he cried as his son fell and then vanished into nothingness. "Desi!"

"It hurts, doesn't it?"

Tabitha turned to face the voice she knew so well.

It was Acheron.

He walked slowly through the shattered doorway as if nothing odd had happened.

Marissa stopped crying the instant she saw him. "*Akri, akri!*" she called, reaching out for him.

"What the hell are you?" Desiderius asked.

Ash held his hand out and Marissa was torn free from Desiderius's arms. She floated across the room to Ash, who cuddled her close to his chest.

"I'm her godfather, with a heavy emphasis on the *god* part." Ash placed a kiss on Marissa's head.

"Rissa want her mommy and daddy, *akri*," Marissa said as she locked her tiny arms around Ash's neck and squeezed him tight. "Make them get up."

"Don't worry, *ma komatia*," Ash said soothingly. "Everything's fine now."

Shrieking, Desiderius lunged at them and rebounded off what appeared to be an invisible wall.

Valerius stood beside Tabitha as Acheron approached them.

Ash held his hand out and Kyrian's sword flew into his grip. He handed it to Tabitha. "Have at it, Tabby. Desiderius is all yours."

"Stryker!" Desiderius called as he pulled out what appeared to be an ancient amulet. "Open the portal."

"There is no portal," Ash said with a sneer. "Not for you, asshole."

For the first time since the whole horrendous night had started, Tabitha smiled. "Eat steel, you sorry bastard!"

She ran at him.

Valerius went to help her. In her current mood, she wasn't thinking straight and he wasn't about to see her hurt. She'd been hurt enough.

While Tabitha attacked the Daimon, Acheron paused on the stairs beside Kyrian's body.

"Close your eyes, Marissa, and make a wish for your daddy to hold you."

She clenched her eyes shut. "Daddy, hold me."

Valerius paused as Kyrian took a deep breath and blinked his eyes. The Greek looked as dazed as Valerius felt while he helped Tabitha fight the Daimon.

Ash handed Kyrian his daughter, who squealed in happiness that her father was alive. Then the Atlantean continued up the stairs.

Valerius didn't have time to contemplate the total bizarreness of that as Desiderius lunged for Tabitha.

He pulled the Daimon back. "Forget it," he snarled.

Desiderius fought his hold.

Yelling in triumph, Tabitha plunged her sword through Desiderius's heart. Valerius jumped back an instant before the blade went through the body and would have stabbed him as well.

Tabitha pulled it out and smiled until the wound on Desiderius healed.

He laughed. "I'm a Dark-Hunter, bitch. You can't—"

His words were silenced as Valerius delivered the one blow that *would* kill a Dark-Hunter.

He severed the Daimon's head from his shoulders.

"No one calls her a bitch and lives," Valerius snarled as Desiderius collapsed.

Tabitha was frozen completely by the grisly sight. She should have felt avenged.

She didn't.

Nothing could ease the pain this night had wrought.

Valerius pulled her into his arms and turned her away

from the body as Otto came crashing through the door's remains.

He stood there, surveying the damage that had once been her sister's prized home.

"Do I want to know?" Otto whispered.

She shook her head.

"Amanda," she breathed in an agonized tone as her tears started again.

How could her twin be dead?

"Tabby?"

Tabitha's breath caught in her throat as she heard her sister's voice from the stairs. She turned her head slowly, almost afraid it would be another specter.

It wasn't.

Amanda stood there, her face pale, her hair disheveled, her gown coated in blood.

But she was alive!

Shrieking, Tabitha ran for her and pulled her into her arms, holding her tight as her tears flowed yet again, only this time in happiness.

Amanda was alive! The words echoed in her mind.

"I love you, I love you, I love you!" she breathed against her sister's neck. "And if you ever die on me again, I'll kill you so dead!"

The two of them stood there locked in an embrace.

Valerius smiled at the sight of them, grateful for Tabitha's sake that Amanda was whole.

His smile died when his gaze met Kyrian's as the Greek came down the stairs with Acheron behind him. There was nothing but open hatred in the Greek's eyes.

"Where's Kassim?" Otto asked.

"He's dead," Ash said wearily. "He's upstairs in the nursery."

Both Valerius and Otto winced.

Tabitha let go of Amanda as she caught sight of Kyrian.

"You were dead," she breathed. "I saw you."

"They both were dead," Ash said as he stepped past the twins and headed into the living room. He held his hand up and clenched it into a fist.

Desiderius's body vanished instantly.

"You're a god?" Valerius asked him as Ash's earlier declaration finally seeped into his mind.

Ash didn't respond. He didn't have to.

"Why didn't you ever tell us?" Kyrian asked.

Ash shrugged. "Why should I? By tomorrow none of you will even remember that you ever learned this about me."

Tabitha frowned. "I don't understand."

Ash took a deep breath. "The universe is an extremely complicated thing. All any of you need to know is that Amanda and Kyrian are now immortal. No one will ever be able to kill them again."

"What?" Amanda asked, stepping away from Tabitha.

Ash looked to Kyrian. "I promised I wouldn't let you die and I am bound by my oath."

"Wait!" Tabitha said. "You're a god. You can bring back Tia!"

Ash's face turned pale. "Tia is dead?"

"Didn't you know?"

"No," Ash said quietly. He got that faraway look as if he were listening for something very faint. "She wasn't supposed to die tonight."

"Then save her!"

He looked as sick as Tabitha felt. "I can't help Tia. Her soul has passed on. I can't force it back into her body against her will. Amanda and Kyrian's souls refused to leave their daughter and I got here in time to restore them."

"What about my unborn baby?" Amanda asked. "Was it hurt by this?"

Ash shook his head. "He's fine and would appreciate it greatly if you'd drink more apple juice." Ash lifted his hands and everything in the house went back to what it had been before the Daimons had come.

Nothing was out of place.

"Ash," Tabitha said, moving to stand beside him. "Please bring Tia back for me."

He cupped her face in his palm. "I wish I could, Tabby. I really do. But know that she's watching out for you and that she loves you."

She saw red at his words. "That's not good enough for me, Ash. I want her back."

"I know, but right now I have other people to check on."

"But my sister . . ."

Ash took Tabitha's hand and placed it into Valerius's. "I have to go, Tabitha." He turned to Otto. "Jean-Luc is alive, but seriously hurt. I need you and Nick to get him back to his boat."

"We don't know where Nick is," Otto said quietly. "I found his mother dead."

Ash vanished immediately.

"I really hate it when he does that," Kyrian said as he shifted a now-sleeping Marissa in his arms.

Tabitha didn't move while her sister sat down on the floor and started crying.

Tabitha sat beside her and pulled her close.

"What a day," Amanda sobbed. "I saw my husband killed. Kassim . . . Tia and now Cherise."

"I know," Tabitha said. "I'm not so sure we're the ones who won this time around."

"No," Kyrian said as he joined them on the floor. "We're still here and they're not. To me, that's winning." He pulled his wife against his chest and kissed her on the head.

Tabitha turned to see Valerius heading for the door with Otto.

By the time she caught up, he and Otto were outside the house.

"What are you doing?" she asked him.

"We didn't want to intrude on a family moment," he said quietly. "Your sister needs you."

"And I need you."

Valerius was stunned as she walked into his arms.

She wrapped her arms around him and held him close while Otto turned off her car.

"I'll leave the keys in it and see you guys later." He got into his Jag and drove off.

"Thank you," Tabitha whispered as she tucked her head in below his chin. "I wouldn't have made it through tonight without you."

"I'm sorry I wasn't of more help and I'm so sorry about Tia."

He felt her tears scalding his chest through his shirt.

"Your mother said she wanted you home."

Tabitha nodded. "Yeah, I need to go see her. She draws her strength from us." She pulled away as Amanda came out onto the front porch. "I'm going to see Mom."

Amanda nodded. "Tell her I'll be there tomorrow morning. I don't want her to see me like this."

Tabitha looked at Amanda's bloodied gown.

"Yeah, that's the last thing she needs."

Then Amanda did the most amazing thing of all: She reached out and pulled Valerius close for a hug. "Thank you for coming, Valerius, and for keeping Tabitha safe. I really appreciate it." She kissed his cheek before she pulled away.

Valerius had never been more stunned in his life. In that moment, he felt a strange sense of almost belonging somewhere. It was such a foreign, odd sensation that he wasn't sure how to cope with it.

"My pleasure, Amanda."

She patted his arm, then went back into her house.

Valerius helped Tabitha into her battered car and for once he took the driver's seat. He didn't say a word as she gave him directions to her mother's house in Metairie.

Neither of them spoke the entire way. His heart ached for her. Taking her hand, he held it quietly in the darkness while she stared out the passenger side window.

When they reached her mother's house, he got out and opened the door for her.

Tabitha drew a ragged breath as she contemplated facing her mother. For once her courage was gone.

Valerius handed her the keys.

She frowned at him as he stepped away from her. "What are you doing?"

"I was going to head back."

"Don't leave me, Val. Please."

He brushed a tender hand down her cold cheek and nodded. He kept his hands on her shoulders and in truth she needed to feel his touch as she knocked on the door.

Her father answered it, his face grim. His dour look lightened and tears filled his eyes as he saw her and pulled her up into a rib-crushing embrace. "Thank God at least you're all right. Your mother has been out of her mind with fear for you."

She hugged him back. "I'm okay, Daddy, so's Amanda and Kyrian."

Her father released her, then narrowed his eyes on Valerius. "Who are you?"

"He's my boyfriend, Daddy, please be nice to him."

Kindness was the last thing Valerius expected, so when her father held a hand out to him, he was stunned.

Valerius shook it and then was led into a house that was packed full of the Devereaux clan.

And as he stepped into the living room, Valerius felt something he'd never felt in all his life.

He felt like he'd come home.

Chapter 16

Ash entered Artemis's temple on Olympus without any preamble. In the middle of the large main room, which was surrounded by columns, she reclined on a white throne that looked more like a chaise longue.

Her *koris*, who had been singing and playing lutes, immediately rushed from the room and as one rather tall blond *kori* ran past him, he paused and turned to look after her.

"What are you doing here?" Artemis asked, and for once her tone was hesitant.

He turned back toward her and shifted the backpack on his shoulder. "I wanted to thank you for what you did tonight, but as I considered that, it dawned on me that you have never once in eleven thousand years done anything for me for free. The sheer fear factor of that realization alone has made me come seeking you. So what gives?"

Artemis wrapped her arms around herself as she sat on her white throne. "I was worried about you."

He laughed bitterly at that. "You never worry about me."

"I do, too. I called and you didn't answer me."

"I almost never answer you."

She looked away, reminding him of a cringing child who had been caught doing something wrong.

"Spill it, Artemis. I have a lot of crap to clean up tonight and don't want you on top of it."

She took a deep breath. "Very well, it's not like I can keep it from you."

"Keep what from me?"

"A new Dark-Hunter was born tonight."

His blood ran cold at that. Literally. "Damn you, Artemis! How could you do this?"

She came off her throne ready to battle. "I had no choice."

"Yeah, right."

"No, Acheron. I had no choice."

As she spoke, his mind connected with hers and the images of her and Nick went through him.

"Nick?" he breathed, his heart shattering.

What had he done?

"You cursed him," Artemis said quietly. "I'm so sorry."

Ash ground his teeth as guilt consumed him. He knew better than to speak in anger.

His will, even when not thought out, made reality. One wrong word . . .

He had damned his best friend.

"Where is he?"

"The bower room."

Ash started to leave, but Artemis stopped him. "I didn't know what else to do, Acheron. I didn't."

She held her hand out and a dark green amulet appeared. She handed it to him.

"How many lashes?" he asked bitterly, thinking it was Valerius's soul she offered him.

A single tear fled down her cheek. "None. It's Nick's soul, and I have no right to it." She pressed it into his hand.

Ash was so stunned he didn't know what to say.

He placed it into his backpack.

Artemis swallowed as she watched him tuck it carefully away. "Now you're going to learn."

"Learn what?"

"Just how heavy a burden a soul is."

He gave her a dry stare. "That I learned a long time ago, Artie."

And with that, he stepped back and willed himself to

Nick's prison. He opened the door slowly to find his friend in a fetal position on the floor.

"Nick?"

Nick looked up, his black eyes rimmed in red. The anger and pain Ash saw and felt from Nick tore through him. "They killed my mother, Ash."

A new wave of guilt slammed through him. In one fit of anger and with nothing more than a single sentence, he had altered their fates and had stolen from Nick and Tabitha the two people that neither of them should have lost.

It was all his fault.

"I know, Nick, and I'm sorry." He was sorrier than Nick would ever know. "Cherise was one of the few decent people in this world. I loved her, too."

He loved the New Orleans crew a lot more than he should. Love was a worthless emotion that had never served him anything but misery.

Even Simi . . .

Ash ran his hand over her tattoo as he fought back his emotions.

He made himself numb, then reached out to Nick. "C'mon."

"Where are we going?"

"I'm taking you home. You have a lot to learn."

"About what?"

"How to be a Dark-Hunter. Everything you think you know about fighting, surviving, it's nothing. I have to show you how to use your new powers and to see correctly with those eyes."

"And if I don't want to learn?"

"Then you'll die and there won't be any coming back from it this time."

Nick took his hand and allowed him to pull him to his feet.

Ash closed his eyes and took Nick home.

He'd never looked forward to training a new Dark-Hunter, but this one . . .

This one hurt most of all.

* * *

Valerius slipped out of the Devereaux house an hour before dawn. Tabitha had finally fallen asleep, and he had carried her upstairs to the room that she had shared with Amanda when they were children.

After placing her on the bed, he'd spent longer than he should have looking over the old photos on the wall of the two of them together.

Of them with their sisters.

His poor Tabitha. He didn't know if she'd ever heal.

He called a taxi and had it drop him at his house. The place was completely dark. There was no one there now, and he realized just how reliant he'd become on Tabitha.

These last couple of weeks . . .

They had been miraculous.

She was miraculous.

Now their time together was over.

Valerius opened the door to his house and listened to the silence. He shut and locked the door, then walked up the stairs to the solarium where Agrippina's statue waited.

He refilled the oil in her lamp habitually before he realized just how stupid he'd been, both as a man and as a Dark-Hunter.

He hadn't been able to protect Agrippina or Tabitha from the pain that was life.

Just as he couldn't protect himself.

But then, maybe life wasn't about protecting. Maybe it was about something else.

Something even more valuable.

It was about sharing.

He didn't need someone to protect him from the past. He needed the touch of a woman whose warmth chased away those demons. A woman whose very presence had made the unbearable bearable.

And in all these centuries he still hadn't learned the most valuable thing of all.

How to say "I love you" to someone.

But at least now he understood what feeling it meant.

His heart shattering, he touched Agrippina's cold cheek. It was time to let go of the past.

"Good night, Agrippina," he whispered.

Stepping down, he blew out her flame and walked out of the room that had been hers alone and into the one he had learned to share with Tabitha.

Tabitha came awake to find herself alone in her old bed. She closed her eyes and wished herself back to childhood. Back to the days when all of her sisters had shared this house with her. Back to the time when their worst fear was not having a date for the prom.

But time was ever fleeting.

And there was no way back.

Sighing, she rolled over and realized that Valerius wasn't with her. She felt the absence of him immediately.

She got up and pulled on a bathrobe her mother must have left in the room for her. As she walked past the dresser, she paused, then stepped back to see a ring on top of it.

Her heart pounded as she recognized Valerius's signet ring on top of a folded-up note.

Picking it up, she read the handful of words.

Thank you, my lady Tabitha. For everything.
Val

Tabitha frowned. Was it a kiss-off? Oh, yeah, that was just what she needed right now.

Why not?

She was almost angry until she read it again and realized that he hadn't signed it "Valerius."

He'd used her nickname for him.

A nickname he hated.

Her throat tight, she tucked the note into her pocket and kissed the ring he'd left her. She slid it onto her thumb and went to bathe.

Valerius was dreaming of Tabitha. She was laughing in his ear as she lay beneath him.

It seemed so real, he could almost swear he felt her hand on his back . . .

No, now it was buried in his hair.

And then she moved it away and ran it over his hip, down his thigh until she cupped him in her palm.

Growling in pleasure, Valerius opened his eyes to realize it wasn't a dream.

Tabitha lay on her side next to him. "Hi, baby," she whispered.

"What are you doing here?" he asked, unable to believe she was real.

She held her hand up to show him his ring. "How could I be anywhere else given the curtness of your note?"

"My note wasn't curt."

She scoffed at him. "I almost thought you were telling me to hit the road."

"Why would you think that? I left you my ring."

"Consolation gift?"

He rolled his eyes at her misbegotten reasoning. "No, that ring means that the wearer is worth his or her weight in gold. See?" He held it up so that she could see the regal crest.

A slow smile spread across her face. "I'm worth my weight in gold?"

Valerius moved her hand to his lips so that he could kiss it. "You're worth a lot more than that to me."

Her eyes misted as she looked up at him. "I love you, Valerius."

He'd never heard anything more precious to him. "I love you, too, Tabitha," he said, his voice thick.

Her smile widened as she pulled him into her arms and kissed him senseless.

She literally tore her shirt off before she wiggled herself up under him.

Valerius laughed at her eagerness before he kissed her gently on the lips.

She wasn't in the mood for that. They made love furiously, as if they wouldn't have another chance again.

Afterward, they lay in each other's arms. Valerius toyed with her hair as he contemplated their future. "So what do we do now, Tabitha?"

"What do you mean?"

"How do we make this relationship work? Kyrian still hates me and I'm still a Dark-Hunter."

"Well," she said raggedly. "Rome wasn't built in one day. We take it one step at a time."

Little did she know that those steps were going to be horrific.

The first one came the night of her sister's wake. Valerius had driven her to her parents' only to pull up short as they realized Kyrian, Amanda, and Julian and his wife Grace were there.

The animosity was tangible.

Tabitha had meant to stay with Valerius the entire time, but her Aunt Zelda pulled her away.

"I'll be right back."

Valerius nodded as he went to get something else to drink.

Julian and Kyrian cornered him in the kitchen.

He sighed wearily as he waited for them to start in on him. He set his cup down.

Kyrian grabbed his arm.

Valerius was about to lay him out cold when he realized that Kyrian wasn't hurting him. He pulled back Valerius's sleeve so that the scars of his execution were visible.

"Amanda told me how you died," Kyrian said quietly. "I didn't believe her."

Valerius jerked his arm away. Without a word, he started away from the two Greeks.

But Kyrian's voice stopped him. "Look, Valerius, I have to tell you that it literally kills me every time I see you. Can you imagine what it would be like if I had the face of the man who nailed you to the wood?"

Valerius gave a bitter laugh at the irony. "Actually, I know exactly how you feel, General. Every time I use a mirror, I too see the face of my executioner."

He may not have been twins with his brothers, but they looked enough alike that it was hard to see himself in a mirror without seeing them. It was why he was so damned grateful Dark-Hunters didn't cast reflections unless they wanted to.

Kyrian nodded. "Yeah, I guess you would. I don't suppose I could bribe or bully you away from Tabitha, can I?"

"No."

"Then we're going to have to be grown-ups here because I love my wife too much to hurt her. She's lost one sister, it would kill her to lose another one. She needs Tabitha." Kyrian grimaced as if in pain, then held his hand out to Valerius. "Truce?"

Valerius took his hand into his. "Truce."

Kyrian released him, then Julian offered his hand.

"For the record," Kyrian said before he left. "This only makes us friendly enemies."

Tabitha came into the kitchen as they left. "You okay?"

He nodded. "Kyrian decided to grow up."

She looked impressed. "I guess immortality agrees with him."

"Apparently so."

The two of them stayed at the wake until just after midnight when they decided to head home in Tabitha's beat-up Mini Cooper.

As they entered the foyer, they found Ash waiting for them.

"What are you doing here?" Valerius asked.

Ash came forward and handed a small box to Tabitha. "You know what to do. Just remember: Don't drop it."

Tabitha was aghast as she held the box that contained Valerius's soul in her hand. "We had decided that we weren't going to do this. I don't want to take Valerius's immortality from him."

Ash let out a long, tired breath. "Until you return his soul to him, Artemis owns him. Is that what you want?"

"No."

"Well, there you go." Ash headed for the door, then paused to look back at them. "By the way, Tabby, you're immortal now, too."

"What?"

He shrugged. "It wouldn't be fair to Amanda to lose you to old age."

"But how? How can I be immortal?"

Ash gave her a wry grin. "It's the will of the gods. Don't question it."

He slipped out the door and left them alone.

"Wow," Tabitha breathed as she opened up the box to see a royal blue medallion inside. It was vibrant with swirling colors that made it seem as if it were living.

She closed the box. "Well, what do you think?"

"I think you'd best not drop it."

She agreed.

Later that night when it came time to stake him so that she could return his soul to him, she learned something horrible.

She couldn't do it.

"C'mon, Tabitha," Valerius said as he sat up on the bed, shirtless. "You stabbed me the night we met without even blinking."

"Yeah, but you were a dirtbag then."

"I think I'm offended."

Weeks went by as Tabitha attempted to stab Valerius, only to meet with failure.

She even tried to pretend he was a Daimon.

It didn't work. Not to mention the small fact that they had yet to discover what would drain his Dark-Hunter powers and make him human long enough to die.

So they settled into a strange kind of peace. Tabitha moved out of her apartment over her store and left that for Marla to keep while she lived with Valerius.

They stayed together in the daytime and hunted together at night.

Still she couldn't stake him, but at least one afternoon, she'd learned his weakness: hurting her. It'd been an accident. He'd been reaching for his sword when he'd accidentally elbowed her. For two hours, his eyes had been blue.

Even so, she hadn't been able to stab him.

It was hopeless.

Until that summer. While Tabitha and Valerius were in the middle of training in the upstairs gym, the unthinkable happened.

One minute, she had been playing with Valerius; the next, Kyrian burst through the door, causing Valerius to strike her by accident. His eyes turned instantly blue. Before she realized what he was doing, Kyrian grabbed Valerius, threw him to the ground, and drove a stake through his heart and left it there.

"What are you doing?" Tabitha shrieked, rushing toward him.

Amanda caught her. "It's okay, Tabby," she said, forcing the box that held Valerius's soul into her hand. "Since you keep telling me that you can't do this, Kyrian volunteered."

"Yeah, and with any luck, you might actually drop it," Kyrian said evilly.

Tabitha scowled at him.

Grabbing the box from her sister, she knelt beside Val.

Valerius lay on the floor panting. His face was covered in sweat while he bled from his wound.

"Don't worry, baby. I won't drop it."

He offered her a trembling smile. "I trust you."

Tabitha's heart stopped as he died. Grabbing the medallion, she cried out as it burned her palm. Tabitha bit her lip and placed the medallion to the bow-and-arrow brand on Valerius's hip.

"Sh," Amanda said soothingly. "It'll stop burning in a second. Just think about Valerius."

She did, even though every sane part of her wanted to let go of the burning hunk of lava that seared her hand.

Finally, it started to cool.

Valerius didn't move.

Tabitha began to panic.

"It's okay," Amanda said. "It just takes a minute."

And after a few more, Valerius opened his eyes, which were now a permanent and vibrant shade of blue. His fangs were completely gone.

Tabitha smiled at the sight of him, grateful beyond measure that he was alive. "You don't look right."

Valerius cupped her face. "I think you look beautiful."

"I think I should stake him again just for good measure," Kyrian said.

"I think we need to be going," Amanda said as she got up from the floor, grabbed her husband, and made a quick exit.

"Oh, c'mon," Kyrian whined from the hallway. "Can't I please stake him one more time?"

"Hi, human," Tabitha said before she kissed him.

Then she pulled back with a cry as she realized something.

She was immortal. Now that Valerius was no longer a Dark-Hunter, he wasn't.

"Oh, my God," she breathed. "What have we done?"

But the answer was simple. They had just damned her to live out eternity without him.

Chapter 17

Four months later
Mount Olympus

"Your brother's getting married today, Zarek."

Zarek rolled over in bed to find his wife Astrid staring at him with that unnerving gimlet look that she seemed to reserve solely for him whenever he irritated her. "And I should care, why?"

"He's all the family you have left, and I would like for my baby to know both sides of his family."

Zarek turned back to his side as he pretended to ignore her. But that was impossible. For one thing, he loved her too much to ever discount her, and for another, she wouldn't be ignored.

He felt her hand in his hair as she toyed with it. "Zarek?"

He didn't answer. After Ash had returned to earth with Tabitha, he'd spent a lot of time in the *Peradomatio*, or Hall of the Past.

Astrid was wearing off on him after all. Being married to her had taught him much about justice.

No, that wasn't exactly true. Being with her was making the past somehow bearable, and now that she was pregnant . . .

He didn't want his son born into a world where forgiveness was an alien concept.

"It's not easy to let go of the past, Astrid," he said finally.

She kissed his shoulder, sending chills all over him. "I

know, Prince Charming." She rolled him over, onto his back, and leaned over him.

Zarek placed his hand against her distended stomach, where he felt his baby moving rambunctiously against his palm. His son was due in only two weeks.

"So, do I need to get dressed for a wedding?" Astrid asked quietly.

Zarek brushed her long, blonde hair back from her face so that he could cup her cheek. "I prefer you naked, in my bed."

"Is that your final answer?"

"What's wrong, Tabitha?"

Tabitha turned around to see Valerius behind her. He looked completely elegant in his black tie attire, but then he always looked that way. Unlike her, he never had a single hair out of place.

Her body warmed instantly at his approach. She wore a strapless wedding dress and was barefoot at the moment, having kicked off her high heels the minute they left the cathedral.

"Nothing's wrong," she lied, not wanting him to know just how sorry she was for all the strife she'd caused him.

And how she really would be the death of him one day.

Her heart ached.

"Are you ready to trade me in yet?" she asked playfully, even though her throat was really tight.

"Never, but there's a large crowd of people out in the backyard who are wondering where the bride is."

She wrinkled her nose at that. "Okay, I'm coming," she said, taking him by the arm.

He led her back outside into the thick of madness that was her family.

She'd opted at the church not to divide up the guests in the pews lest it become painfully obvious that there wasn't anyone on the groom's side.

Even four of the seven groomsmen had to be borrowed from her side. Only Ash, Gilbert, and Otto had been there for Valerius.

She was still angered that no other Dark-Hunter had come or sent good wishes.

Kyrian, Julian, Talon, and Tad had graciously volunteered to finish out the number of groomsmen so that her sisters wouldn't be without escorts. For that, she would love them always.

Her Aunt Sophie grabbed her and pulled her away from Valerius.

Tabitha promised her return before the women surrounded her.

Valerius smiled at the sight, then turned to go get them both a glass of champagne. Laughter echoed in the backyard, amidst the strains of the orchestra they'd hired. Tabitha had wanted a Goth band to play, but her mother had put her foot down and insisted Tabitha not make the ears of their guests bleed.

He looked around the crowd where people were laughing together and talking. Ash, Otto, and even Gilbert were standing off to the side with the other groomsmen. He longed to go over and join them, but knew from experience that though Kyrian and Julian tolerated his presence, they didn't like it.

How odd that he felt alienated even at his own wedding.

Taking a drink of champagne, he scanned the crowd until he found his wife with her sisters.

He smiled at the sight. Tabitha was absolutely lovely with her auburn hair down around her shoulders. Someone had placed little sprigs of flowers all through her hair and sprayed glitter in it. She looked like some ethereal fey out to seduce him.

The wedding director came up to inform him that dinner was ready to be served.

Inclining his head to her, Valerius went to tell Tabitha that they needed everyone to be seated.

He claimed his bride and led her to the bridal table.

Tabitha laughed under her breath as she sat in the chair and they actually got her scooted up without incident. She was finally learning how to do this properly. The first time Valerius had held a chair out for her had been a complete fiasco.

He took a seat on her right as Gilbert sat to her left.

The waiters started bringing out plates and filling the wineglasses.

Valerius took her hand into his, then kissed her knuckles. The sensation of his lips on her hand set fire to her. She'd never known a human being could be so happy and yet terrified at the same time.

Once everyone was served, Gilbert stood up to toast them. The band stopped playing.

Gilbert opened his mouth, but before he could speak, a deep, accented voice interrupted him.

"I know that it's typical for the best man to toast the couple, but I think Gilbert might forgive me for usurping his place for a minute."

Tabitha had to force herself not to gape as Zarek approached their table from out in the crowd.

Valerius's grip tightened on her hand.

Zarek paused directly in front of them and stared meaningfully at his brother.

"Weddings have always been a fascinating thing to me," he said, his voice ringing out. "A time when two people look into each other's eyes and promise each other that they will never allow anyone or anything to divide them.

"Out of two families, they come together to form a separate branch that links back to their roots. It's a time when two families are joined together because of the hearts of two people. A time when ill will and bad feelings should be put to rest along with the past."

Zarek's gaze went down the table, stopping at each of the current and former Dark-Hunters. "Weddings signify a new beginning. After all, no human alive has ever been able to choose his family . . . God knows, I would never have chosen mine." He quirked a smile at Valerius. "But as the Roman playwright Terence once wrote, 'From many a bad beginning great friendships have formed.'"

Zarek lifted a glass to them. "Here's to my brother, Valerius, and his wife Tabitha. May you both come to enjoy the happiness I have known with my own wife. And may you give one another all the love you both deserve."

Tabitha wasn't sure which of them was the most stunned

by Zarek's words. Her family, unaware of what an unexpected moment this was, cheered Zarek's toast.

Shocked beyond comprehension, neither of them took a drink.

Zarek walked over and gave them a wry, almost mocking grin. "You're supposed to take a drink now."

They did, but Valerius choked on his. He sniffed the glass suspiciously.

"Did you poison me?" he asked Zarek in a low tone.

Zarek rubbed his eyebrow with his middle finger. "No, Valerius. Even I'm not that cruel."

"It's nectar," a woman's voice said.

Tabitha turned to see a beautiful blonde pregnant woman behind her.

The woman placed a gentle hand on her shoulder, then kissed her on the cheek. "I'm Zarek's wife, Astrid," she said in a low tone that only the two of them could hear. She turned to Valerius and gave him a kiss as well. "We couldn't decide what to give the two of you for a wedding gift, so Zarek thought the best gift would be eternity together."

"Yeah," Zarek said in a surly tone. "That's the polite version of what I said."

Astrid gave him a playfully mean look before she looked back at them. "Congratulations to you both."

She handed Valerius a small bowl of something that reminded Tabitha of Jell-O. "It's ambrosia," she said to Valerius. "Eat it and you'll be able to hurl lightning bolts back at Zarek whenever he gets playful with you."

"Hey!" Zarek snapped. "I never agreed to that."

Astrid gave him an innocent stare. "This way, I figure you'll play nicer in the future with your brother."

Tabitha laughed. "You know, I think I like my new sister-in-law."

Astrid left them to join Zarek, who looked less than pleased. "Don't worry, hon, I'll make sure you have plenty of other things to occupy your time with than harassing Valerius."

Zarek's gaze softened the instant she touched him.

Valerius rose to his feet and walked around the table until he stood before Astrid and Zarek. "Thank you," he said.

He held his hand out to Zarek, who looked at it suspiciously. Tabitha half-expected him to turn away.

He didn't.

Taking Valerius's hand, he clapped him on the back, then released him. "Your woman loves you more than you know. She's a hell of a fire-cat. I probably should have given you something in Kevlar."

Valerius laughed at that. "I hope you two will stay for the reception."

"We'd love to," Astrid said before Zarek could answer.

The two of them took a seat at the table with Selena and Bill while Valerius came back to her.

"Bon appétit," Tabitha said as she held the ambrosia out to him.

He ate it, then kissed her.

"Mmm," Tabitha breathed, inhaling the scent of her husband. *"Pedicabo ego vos et irrumabo."*

I intend to have my way with you upstairs and down.

Valerius smiled. "And I intend to let you." His face turned serious as he stared at her and his love for her consumed him. *"Amo*, Tabitha. *Amo."*

Epilogue

One year later

"Look at the poor bastard," Kyrian said as he sat inside the Café Pontalba with Amanda, Grace, Julian, Bill, and Selena having dinner. "I should have been kind and killed him when I had the chance."

Through the doorway on their right, they could see Tabitha and Valerius walking toward the St. Louis Cathedral.

The women frowned as they watched them.

"What?" Amanda asked.

"He's so screwed," Bill said before taking a drink of his beer. "I wonder what he did wrong this time."

"What are you two talking about?" Selena asked.

"I know that Devereaux walk," Kyrian said, shaking his head. "It's the 'You're not going to get any tonight, pal, so don't even ask' walk."

"Oh, hell yeah," Bill agreed. "Be glad you married the only one of the sisters who won't rack you in a fit of anger, Kyrian. You seriously lucked out."

"I beg your pardon?" Selena glared at her husband.

Kyrian laughed.

"I wouldn't laugh if I were you," Amanda said, her voice tense as they saw Tabitha tell Valerius to "talk to the hand."

Then she continued to walk in front of him as Valerius followed and made placating gestures.

"I really hate that walk," Bill muttered.

"I think you're both going to see that walk up close and

personal tonight," Julian said before he pulled out his Nextel phone. He scrolled through the names before he clicked the talk button. "Hey, Otto? Where are you?"

"Café Du Monde. Why?"

"Can you see Valerius and Tabitha? They look like they're heading down the Pedestrian Mall toward you."

Otto made a sound of disgust. "Yeah, the two of them need to go get a room."

"Pardon?" Julian asked.

"They're lip-locked like two horny teenagers."

Amanda and Selena gave their husbands indignant glares.

"No way." Kyrian got up and dashed out the doorway with Bill one step behind him.

He walked the block over to see Tabitha and Valerius stopped in front of Selena's store.

Sure enough, the two of them were necking.

"Excuse me?" Bill said. "You know, there are public decency laws here?"

Tabitha scoffed at Bill. "Do you remember what happened to you the last time you tried to tell a Devereaux what the city laws were?"

Bill went pale.

Tabitha laughed, then returned to what she'd been doing before Bill so rudely interrupted her.

Read on for an excerpt from
Sherrilyn Kenyon's next book

SINS of the
Night

Sighing, Danger pulled into her driveway and did her
best to clear her thoughts. She saw Keller's SUV. Damn. She
really wasn't in the mood for his five thousand questions tonight. Not while she was trying to sort through all this.

After getting out of the car, she made her way into her
house. It was eerily quiet. How unlike Keller not to have a radio blasting or be in the middle of a boisterous phone conversation with a friend.

"Keller?" she called, heading for the living room.

She paused in the doorway to find her Squire sitting on
the couch across from an unknown man.

"Hey, Danger," Keller said in a nervous greeting. "We
have a guest. He's um . . . he's Ash's Squire."

The man stood up and Danger's gaze quickly fell to the
white garment draped on the arm of her chair.

It was a coat.

And it belonged to Ash's Squire—who was blond . . .

Danger's reaction to her "guest" was swift and automatic, and it happened without any premeditation on her
part. She pulled out her dagger and threw it straight into the
man's heart. He burst apart into a golden dust just like any
good Daimon would.

"*Mère d'un dieu,*" she breathed. Kyros had been right.
The man was . . .

Entering the room from the doorway on her right!

Her jaw dropped as he sauntered into the room with an

arrogant swagger and a less-than-amused smirk. He pinned her with a droll stare as he moved to stand in front of her. Her dagger shot from the floor where it had fallen after he'd exploded into dust, and into his hand. He held it out to her. "Could you please refrain from the theatrics? I really hate doing that. It seriously pisses me off and it ruins a perfectly good shirt."

Danger continued to gape as she stared at the hole in his black turtleneck where the dagger had gone in. There was no blood. No wound. Nothing. Not even a red mark.

"What are you?" she breathed.

"Well, had you listened before you stabbed me, you would have heard the 'I'm Acheron's Squire' part. Apparently that somehow escaped your hearing and you mistook me for a pin cushion."

He was certainly a snotty bastard.

"He has some really sweet talents, Danger," Keller said from the couch. "He made all the Daimons explode without touching them, but he won't tell me how he did it."

Danger took her dagger from Alexion's hand, then, without thought, touched the ragged tear in his shirt. He felt solid underneath. Real. There was warm skin beneath the silk and wool fabric and it was hard and masculine. Yet human beings didn't shatter like Daimons and no Daimon reappeared after death . . .

In that moment, she was terrified of him, and terror wasn't something Danger St. Richard felt.

Alexion ground his teeth at the sensation of her soft fingers on his flesh. His body roared to life as he watched her examine him like a scientist with a lab experiment that had gone tragically wrong. She was very short for a Dark-Hunter which meant Artemis must have taken an unusual liking to the woman. The goddess preferred to create Dark-Hunters who were equal in height to the Daimons they fought.

No more than five two or three, Dangereuse was petite and athletic. He'd seen her many times lately in the sfora as he kept watch on what the Mississippi Dark-Hunters were up to.

There had been something about her that had caught his interest. An innocence that still seemed to be inside her. Most

Dark-Hunters were jaded by their human lives and by their duties. But this one . . . She appeared to have avoided the cynicism that eternal life often brought.

Her dark, chestnut-colored hair was worn in a long braid down her back, but pieces of it had escaped to curl becomingly around her face. Her features were angelic and delicate. If not for her carriage and self-assuredness, she would have appeared fragile.

And yet there was nothing fragile about her. Dangereuse could more than take care of herself and he knew that well. As one of the newer Dark-Hunters, she was only a couple hundred years old and had died while trying to save the noble half of her family from the guillotine in France during their revolution. It had been a monumental task she had set for herself and she would have succeeded, if she hadn't been betrayed.

Not to mention the woman had the most kissable mouth he'd ever seen. Full and lush, her lips were the kind that a man dreamed of tasting at night. That mouth beckoned to him with temptation and the promise of pure unadulterated heaven.

She also smelled of sweet magnolias and woman. It had been over two hundred years since he'd last tasted a woman. And it was all he could do not to bend his head down and bury his face against her soft, tender neck and inhale the scent of her. Feel the softness of her skin against his hungry lips as he tasted the supple flesh there.

But then, given her first reaction to his presence, he didn't think she'd react much better to being mauled by him.

Pity.

Danger swallowed in sudden trepidation as she looked at the man before her. He was just as Stryker had foretold . . . right down to the white cashmere coat.

It's all true. All of it.

He was Acheron's personal destroyer who had come to kill them for questioning Acheron's authority. She felt the sudden need to cross herself, but caught herself just in time. The last thing she needed to do was to let him know she feared him.

Her extremely superstitious and Catholic mother had always told her that the devil wore the face of an angel. In this case, it was most certainly true. The man before her was without a doubt one of the choicest examples of his gender. His dark blond hair held golden highlights and brushed the top of his collar. He wore it in a casual style that swept back from a perfectly masculine face. His well-sculpted cheeks were covered with two days' growth of whiskers that added a savage, fierce look to him.

Like hers, his eyes were the midnight black of a Dark-Hunter and yet she sensed that he wasn't one of them. For one thing, he didn't drain her Dark-Hunter abilities.

There was an aura of extreme power and lethal danger from him. It rippled and sizzled in the air around them and made the hair on the back of her neck rise.

"What are you doing here?" she asked, forcing herself not to betray anything other than nonchalance. Although the earlier dagger throw had most likely tipped him that she wasn't exactly ambivalent to his presence.

His smile was wicked and disturbing. "You invited me."

Was that a play on her new suspicion that Ash might be a Daimon? No Daimon could enter someone's home without an invitation. Or was he just making an idle comment?

"I invited *Ash* here. Not you. I don't even know who you are."

"Alexion." His voice was deep and well-cultured. There was only the faintest trace of some foreign accent in it, but she didn't know what nationality it was from.

"Alexion . . . ?" she prompted, wondering what his surname was.

"Just Alexion."

Keller joined them. "Ash sent him here for a couple of weeks to check into what you were saying about a Rogue Dark-Hunter."

She arched a brow at Keller. "Is that what Alexion told you?"

"Well, yeah, but then I called Ash and he corroborated it."

Good boy that he didn't accept the man's word. "Did Ash say anything else?"

"Just to trust Alexion."

Yeah, right.

Danger sheathed her dagger before she addressed Alexion again. "Well, it appears I spoke too soon. I was checking into the Rogue thing myself tonight and everything's fine so you can feel free to return to Ash now."

Alexion narrowed his dark eyes on her. "Why are you lying to me?"

"I'm not lying."

He dipped his head down so that he could speak in a low tone just for her hearing. His nearness was disturbing and intense. It actually raised chills over her body as his hot breath fell against her skin. "For the record, Dangereuse, I can smell a lie from nine miles off."

She looked up to see the deep curiosity in those . . . She frowned. No longer black, his eyes had turned to a peculiar hazel green that practically glowed.

Just what the hell was he?

Alexion pinned her with a fierce stare he no doubt hoped would intimidate her. It wasn't working. Danger refused to be intimidated by anyone or anything. When he spoke, his voice was scarcely more than a primal growl. "My only real question is why would you protect your Rogue?"

She moved away without answering. "Keller? Can I have a word with you in private?"

Alexion gave a short laugh at that. "I will leave the two of you alone." He headed for the hallway that would take him to a guest room.

Danger ground her teeth. *Don't tell me Keller already set him up in my house!*

She waited until she was sure Alexion had left them and lowered her voice. "What the hell happened tonight? You look like someone beat you."

"They did. I ran into a group of Daimons and when I told them to back off, they said they were untouchable now. They said that they were working with the Dark-Hunters."

Anger whipped through her that they would dare to beat her Squire. "They attacked you?"

"No, I beat my own self up. What do you think?"

She ignored his sarcasm as she realized why the plasma TV hadn't been blaring when she came in. It was shattered. "What happened to the TV?"

Keller looked at it and shrugged. "I don't know. I was flipping channels after we got back and I paused on QVC to see this cool camcorder they were advertising and the next thing I knew, it blew up. I'm not sure if it was the TV or if Alexion has a thing against QVC."

Thank the Lord and his saints that her Squire hadn't blown up as well.

"And where did Alexion just head off to?"

"I put him in the guest suite that Ash uses whenever he visits."

She clenched her fist to keep from choking him. "I see."

"I didn't do anything wrong, did I?"

Yes, but she didn't want to get into it with him. If he stayed ignorant of all this, maybe Alexion would spare him. Either way, she refused to put Keller in any danger.

"You're fine, sweetie. Why don't you head on home before it gets any later?"

Luckily her Squire didn't argue and he was too dense to recognize the slight tremor of fear for him in her voice. Just in case Alexion intended to fight, she wanted Keller out of here and tucked safely at home.

"Okay, Danger. I'll see you tomorrow night."

"Ahh," Danger hedged at that. "Why don't you take a few days off? Go see your sister in Montana."

He frowned at her. "Why?"

She offered him a smile she didn't feel. "I have Acheron's Squire here. I'm sure he can—"

"I don't know," he said, wrinkling his nose. "He seems all right, but I think I'll hang close to home, just in case."

"Keller . . ."

"Don't mess with me, Danger. My number-one mandate is to protect you. I may be human, but I'm your Squire and that includes all the inherent risks that come with the position. Okay? I was raised in this world and I know all the freaky shit it sometimes entails."

She couldn't argue with that. "All right. Go home and I'll keep in touch."

He nodded, then gathered up his coat and left.

Danger took a deep breath as she headed for Alexion's

room. She really didn't want him here, but what else could she do? *Keep your friends close and your enemies closer.*

So long as he was in her house, she could monitor his activities and see what he was doing. Not to mention she still wasn't thoroughly convinced about Kyros and his agenda. She'd heard a lot of weird things lately, including that some of the local Dark-Hunters were drinking human blood. For all she knew, Kyros was setting her up.

Until she had more information, she would play this coolly and see for herself what was going on.

At the end of the hallway, she pushed open the door to find Alexion studying one of the Faberge eggs that she collected. He stood before the small baroque-style dressing table, holding it carefully in his large hand as if he understood how much she loved her collectibles. She was struck by the gentleness of his touch as he closed it and returned it to its stand.

He was incredibly handsome standing there and her body reacted to him with an intensity that stunned her.

Alexion felt her presence like a sizzling caress. It was as if she made contact with his soul every time she drew near him. Something that was completely impossible since he hadn't owned a soul in more than nine thousand years.

He didn't know what it was about her, but his body reacted wildly to her. Turning, he found her in the doorway, watching him with a wary expression. Danger was afraid of him. Terrified actually. But she was trying hard to disguise it.

Why? He had done nothing to scare her . . . not yet anyway.

"I mean you no harm, Dangereuse."

"The name's Danger," she corrected. "I haven't gone by Dangereuse in a long time."

"Forgive me."

She took a hesitant step into the room. "So what's your story? You say you're Ash's Squire. Are you a Blue Blood, Blood Rites, or what?"

Blue Bloods were Squires who came from long generations of Squires. Blood Rites were the Squires who were charged with maintaining that the rules of their world were followed. They protected the Dark-Hunters and were a police force for other Squires. Of course, Alexion had been serving Acheron since before the Squires' Council had existed. He wasn't a true Squire. He was Acheron's Alexion, an Atlantean term that had no real translation into English. Basically, he would do whatever was necessary to protect Acheron and Simi. And he truly meant whatever.

But he couldn't tell her the truth of his status. "I'm a barnacle chip," he answered in Squire slang, meaning that Acheron had recruited him to be his Squire. In a weird way, it was even true.

"How long have you served him?"

He gave a short laugh at that. "It seems like forever most days."

Her dark eyes flashed suspicion and intelligence at him. "And how is it that you did that little trick with the dagger?"

He quirked up one side of his mouth at her vague questions. "Ask me what's on your mind, Danger. I don't like to play games. We both know I'm not human so let's not do the polite song and dance while you tiptoe around me trying to figure me out."

Danger seemed to appreciate his frankness. "Are you here to spy for Acheron?"

He laughed at that. "No. Trust me, he doesn't need anyone to spy for him. If he wants to know something, he does."

"What do you mean?" she asked nervously.

"I meant what I said. Acheron is able to find things out on his own."

"Then why were you sent here?"

Alexion glanced away. Perhaps he should tell her the truth for once. Most likely, she wouldn't believe him, but what could it really hurt? "In short, I am here to protect you as much as I can."

Danger couldn't have been more surprised had he come right out and admitted to being Acheron's destroyer. "Protect me from what?"

"Those who would see you dead. You are in a precarious place, Danger. The one who has gone Rogue will kill you instantly if he learns you have betrayed him."

Funny, Kyros had been remarkably understanding about that. "What do you know of it?"

"More than I can share."

Then they were at an impasse. "In that case, you'll understand if I ask you to stay in a hotel room while you're here?"

He actually laughed again at that. "You've met with him and confronted him, haven't you?"

"I don't know what you're talking about."

He closed the distance between them. His presence was mammoth in the room. Overpowering and yet strangely comforting. It was as if his aura were putting off soothing vibes. He was also extremely compelling in a very sexual way. Acheron was the only other person she knew who had that strange "do me" factor that enticed everyone who came near him to strip his clothes off and throw him down for a wicked night of play.

What is wrong with me?

"You know," Alexion said in a deep tone, "for an actress you certainly can't lie worth a damn."

She stiffened at his words. "I beg your pardon?"

"You heard me. So what lie did Kyros tell you? I hope he was at least more creative than the 'old Acheron is a Daimon' standby."

She didn't know what surprised her more. The fact that he knew what they'd said about Acheron or the fact that he spoke of Kyros as if he knew the man personally. "How do you know about Kyros?"

"Believe me, I know everything about him."

Danger was even more confused now. Was he telling her the truth? Or was he using the truth to distract her? "So tell me, is Acheron a Daimon?"

Those eerie green hazel eyes narrowed on her. "What do you think?"

"I don't know." And that was the honest truth. "It makes sense. He is from Atlantis and we all know that the Daimons are from there as well."

Alexion scoffed at her. "Acheron was born in Greece and grew up in Atlantis. That hardly makes him a Daimon."

"He never eats food."

"Are you sure? Just because he doesn't eat in front of you, doesn't mean he doesn't eat at all."

He did have a point with that. "Then what about you? If Kyros is so wrong, how did he know that you were going to come here in your white coat, huh?"

Alexion froze at her question. "Pardon?"

"You have no answer for that one, do you?"

No, he didn't. "How could he know about me? No one knows I exist."

"Then he's right. You are lying to me about your purpose. You're here to kill us all."

Alexion couldn't breathe as her words went through him. How could anyone know about him? It wasn't possible. Acheron had taken great care to make sure no one knew he existed. "No, I'm not. I'm here to save as many of you as I can."

"And I'm supposed to believe you, why?"

"Because I'm telling you the truth."

"Then prove it."

That was easier said than done. "Prove it how? The only way to prove to you that I'm not out to kill you is to not kill you and last I checked you were the one throwing the dagger, not me."

Danger gave him a hostile glare. "What was I supposed to think? I come into my house to see my normally ebullient Squire cowed on my couch, looking beat-up, and my TV blown to kingdom come. Then this blond *man*, and I use that term loosely, whom I was told would come to kill me, stands up wearing the exact white coat that I was told he'd have on. What would you have done?"

"I would have said, 'Hello, can I help you?'"

She rolled her eyes at him. "Sure, you would."

Actually, he would, but then he had one distinct advantage over her. He couldn't die. At least, not from something born of this earth.

"Look, Danger, I know you have absolutely no reason to trust me. Before tonight you never even heard of me. But you know Acheron. Have you ever seen him hurt anyone? Think about it. If Ash really were a Daimon, why would he be helping the Dark-Hunters?"

"Because he uses us to fight his own kind so that his mother doesn't kill him."

Alexion went cold at that. Acheron would lose his mind if he heard those words. More to the point, there would be no salvation for any Dark-Hunter here. Acheron would destroy them all without blinking. When it came to the existence of his mother, Acheron didn't play or take chances.

"What do you know of his mother?"

"That she cast him out of the Daimon realm and now he uses us to get back at her and his people."

"Trust me, that is a complete lie."

She snorted at him. "The problem is, I don't trust you. At all."

"But do you trust Kyros?"

He saw her answer in her dark eyes. No, she didn't. But it spoke a lot for her that she hadn't turned on her Dark-Hunter brother. She was still protecting Kyros. He could admire her for that.

"Look, Danger. Open your heart and listen with your feelings. What does your gut tell you to do?"

"Run for the hills with my Squire and let you guys duke it out."